Praise for ~~*a novel*~~

I loved it! It's a fine story. Engaging plot, loveable characters, and the scenes when Kat opens herself to her gift of healing touch are powerful and moving.

—Elizabeth Cunningham,
author of *Return of the Goddess,*
The Wild Mother, and
How To Spin Gold, A Woman's Tale

I found this well-written novel of personal discovery very enjoyable to read.

The witch house is the sort of property many of us would dream of inheriting, the family history intriguingly mysterious, and the love interest—bless him—someone a modern self-respecting woman could fall for without feeling like a hormone-driven nitwit. The heroine is thoughtful and intelligent and the other characters well drawn and believable as well.

This felt like a sort of Wiccan version of the *Ya-Ya Sisterhood* at times, about Kat's discovery of her own identity through her discovery of her birth mother's. Very good rousing ending.

—Elizabeth Ann Scarborough,
Nebula award winner
and author of many novels of her own
and with Anne McCaffrey

About the Author

Dahti Blanchard is an author, musician, doula, mother, and partner who lives with her family and way too many animals in a nearly finished (it's only been worked on for ten years so far!) log house in a tiny enchanted forest in the Pacific Northwest. She grew up in the woods in upstate New York and holds a degree in what her children have fondly but inaccurately referred to as "the lucrative field of early music."

She is a member of the Re-Formed Congregation of the Goddess-International and a student of Cella, the academic branch of RCG-I.

She's had articles and reviews published in several magazines including *SageWoman*, *PanGaia*, *Blessed Bee*, *Home Education*, and the online magazine *Matrifocus*, work published in the anthology *Mama Stew*, and she's had two feminist plays produced.

About the Cover Art

Artist Jillian Pate had the difficult task of creating a book cover based on a painting in this novel. The author's descriptions of the painting were so intricate that creating a cover that lived up to the novel's depiction seemed impossible.

Instead of trying to show every detail in the painting, Jillian Pate was moved to focus on only one aspect: the moment Rose meets her destiny and glances over her shoulder at her beloved husband.

This cover art takes the point of view of Rose's husband in a poignant blend of love, desperation, and fate, guarded and celebrated in the ever-present circle of women— Maiden, Mother, and Crone—in the phases of every woman's life.

Dream of the Circle of Women

A Mystery
By Dahti Blanchard

Spilled Candy Books
Niceville, Florida USA

Dream of the Circle of Women
Copyright 2004

By Dahti Blanchard

Published by: Spilled Candy Books,
                Spilled Candy Publications
                Post Office Box 5202
                Niceville, FL 32578-5202
                Dream@spilledcandy.com
                http://www.spilledcandy.com

ISBN: 1-892718-49-9 (trade paperback)
First edition
First printing: May 2004
Printed in the United States of America

Library of Congress Card Catalog Number: 2004100237

Cover Art copyright 2004 by Jillian Pate
Find more cover art at
http://www.spilledcandy.com/Jillian_Pate.htm

Acknowledgements

Books are seldom written without the help and encouragement of many people and this one is no exception. If I thought carefully I could easily come up with a list almost as long as the story. Suffice it to say that I am grateful to many people (and even a creature or two), especially the following:

Jennifer Blomgren, Kate Snow, JoAnn Elliot, Libby Urner (and honorary member Marion Bartl) of the wonderful and wacky Wednesday writers group who came to know my characters almost as well as I did and let me know when I wasn't listening to those characters. They also made me laugh a whole lot and continue to do so.

Thanks go to my lovely Bellingham Cella sisters. A sweeter bunch of witches I've never known.

Thank you to Ruthy of the Port Townsend Candle Store whose beautiful candles and friendly assistance help fuel and light my creativity.

More thanks to Elizabeth Ann Scarborough and Elizabeth Cunningham, two of my favorite authors who were generous enough to read the work of an unknown writer.

To Anne, the beloved matriarch of our cat clan. The character of Minette is a niced-up version of her majesty.

To my son, Nick Blanchard-Wright, simply because he is my favorite son, and to my husband, Steve Wright who never fails to remind me to pursue my dreams.

And most of all to my daughter Mical Blanchard-Wright. Her help and feed-back on this project were invaluable. Plus she brews a mean cup of tea and knows just what Miss Manners would suggest in any situation.

Chapter 1

It always started with the circle of women.

Usually they were surrounding an ancient tree whose topmost branches were decorated with a necklace of stars while a full, pregnant moon looked on. It would have been a lovely scene except that a sense of terrible urgency hung in the air as the women sang a chant that was impossible to hear.

Suddenly, as men in long robes approached, the circle broke and became a snake, threading its way to the waves crashing on the nearby shore. Holding hands and still chanting, each woman followed the next, disappearing beneath the waves.

As the robed men began to run, a pounding heartbeat thundered from the opposite direction. It was a horseman, with cape and long hair whipping behind him. His mouth formed a silent scream, but the only sound that could be heard, that was felt, was the pounding of the hoof beats racing to the water's edge.

Just before the men from either direction could reach the unbroken chain of women, the last woman in line looked up at the horseman. With tears in her eyes, but still chanting, she raised her free hand in a gesture that somehow conveyed love, sorrow, and farewell all at once. Then she, too, disappeared beneath the sea.

Now there was sound, deafening sound. It came from the crashing of the waves and the rage of the robed men.

But above it all came the rhythmic thundering of the hoof beats and the anguished cry from the horsemen's lips, "Rose! NO...!"

I echoed that scream, "No...!" until I sat straight up in bed, my heart pounding. I forced myself to come awake. Not again! I'd had that same dream three times now and, as frightening as it was, it made no sense to me. I wasn't even in it!

Throwing back the covers, I swung my feet to the floor and then sat with my head in my hands as I waited for my heart and breath to return to normal. Deciding that a glass of water would help, I reached for the lamp switch—but there was no lamp there. That brought me fully awake. And then I remembered where I was.

I had only been in this house for two days. It had belonged to my mother, a woman I had never known. On the day of my birth, she had kissed me goodbye (or at least so I had imagined) and handed me over to some official who had seen to it that the proper forms were filled out and filed safely away before my new parents could claim me. Until the day of my fortieth birthday, I never knew who my birth mother was. When I was eighteen, my adopted mother tried to help me find her, but was told that my birth mother wanted no contact, and I didn't pursue it. Although she never admitted it, I thought Mom was actually relieved. My adopted father had died when I was sixteen, and I was their only child. Mom wanted to do what was best for me, but I thought she was secretly afraid of losing me if I found my birth mother. I understood after having my own daughter and divorcing her father. I had tried very hard not to make Rowan feel torn between her father and me, but it was not easy. Now that she was nineteen and no longer living with either of us, it still wasn't easy.

Mom died suddenly when I was thirty-nine. I had barely gotten over the shock and was still working on my grief and loneliness from losing her when I received yet another shock. On the afternoon of my birthday, which I was spending as quietly as possible with Rowan and her partner, Keisha, the mailman delivered a certified letter. It seemed that though my birth mother had wanted no contact with me, she had known all along who and where I was. She, too, had just died of heart failure and had left me all her possessions. These included a small sum of money, a 1986 Jeep Cherokee, and her house in upstate New York. I was now the owner of a two-hundred-year-old, five-bedroom house in a tiny town near the Canadian border.

My first thought was to sell it. No, that was my second thought. My first thought was: Why in hell did this woman who wanted nothing to do with me leave me a house that had been in her family for two hundred years? Then I thought to sell it.

It was Rowan who talked me out of it.

"Mom, at least go see it first! Aren't you curious? You might have relatives you don't know about. It might be a really beautiful house, and you could live there. You were the one who said now that I'm not here anymore; you'd like a change. Didn't you tell me that you needed a change of scene to get through your writer's block? You haven't written or illustrated a book for a while. This might be a new source of inspiration."

"It might be an old rundown heap of a house," I told her, "and need huge piles of money to repair it."

"It might," she agreed dryly. "Or it might be haunted, or it might be painted the wrong color. Or it just might be a place that you love. At least find out. After all, you probably spent time there in your mother's womb. Maybe it'll be familiar. Wouldn't that be weird?"

"I'll think about it," was all I would give her. The truth was I *was* afraid of it being familiar. This was a home of a family that hadn't wanted me. What if the house didn't want me either? It wasn't part of who I was. That wasn't true. It was part of me. I couldn't get past that fact. Then I had the first dream.

It happened that very night. It was so vivid and strong and seemed to come out of nowhere. It came again a week later, and though I didn't know why it was so, the dreams caused me to make the decision to go stay in the house for a time, and as I told Rowan, "We'll just see what happens."

So here I was. Two days in the house, with mixed emotions, confusion, only a slight relief from the writer's block, but no more dreams. Until now.

I walked carefully across the room and flipped the light switch on the wall by the door. Looking around the room, I spotted my faithful laptop and felt instantly better. Maybe I hadn't produced a whole lot of work on it lately, but it was a familiar old friend. The house had not seemed familiar to me at all, but I did take a surprising liking to it right away. Sort of like a new acquaintance you hope will become a good friend, but you don't yet know what to say to each other.

As soon as the lawyers had taken care of the details, I bought a plane ticket before I could chicken out. Before I knew it, I had sublet my apartment in Seattle and threw a small party to say goodbye to my friends (who all thought I was crazy, but that was okay because I thought I was crazy, too). I assured my agent that this temporary move would stimulate my creative juices, and then I was gone. I knew it was important for me to be by myself when I first saw the house, so I convinced Rowan, who was dying to check it out, to wait a month before she came to visit. That would give her and Keisha time to earn some more summer money and still have two weeks to come to New York before returning to college.

On the first Monday in August, I flew into Syracuse and drove the one hundred miles north to Newbridge. I had made arrangements to lease a car and was glad to have the time to get used to the new scenery before my first encounter with the house. New York State was definitely different from the Pacific Northwest. I felt as if I were in a different world.

I had little trouble finding the town. Though the population was only about 2,500 people, the area was peppered with even smaller towns, and they were clearly marked on the map I had bought when I picked up the car. There was certainly no feeling of coming home as I drove past the first houses of Newbridge, but neither was there the feeling of dread I now realized I had half been expecting. Parts of the village were very old. A few of the freshly whitewashed houses spoke of generations of loving care. Other parts were fairly new, with doublewide trailers predominating. Though in its early days it might have been, this was no longer a wealthy town.

I drove past an old three-story brick building with a sign in front proclaiming it to be the Newbridge Central School. Two blocks on was the library, which shared a building with the First Federal Savings and Loan. Somehow the name of the bank struck me as funny—could there actually be room for a Second Federal Savings and Loan in this little place? And if so, what might it be sharing space with?

I forced my thoughts back into place as I crossed a short bridge over a narrow, rushing body of water. A plain wooden sign informed me that it was the Oswegatchie River.

I'll have to look up the history of that name, I told myself and vowed that one of my first ventures out would be to the tiny library.

I had been used to doing my research at the Seattle Public Library. Looking for what I needed in a library the size this town had to offer would certainly be an adventure.

It suddenly struck me that I was here—in this place I knew nothing about but now owned a home in. No, I reminded myself, not a home—simply a house. I had the address, but not a clue to where the street might be. Right after the bridge, I arrived in the real business district: one curving street with a post office, a drug store, two restaurants, a hardware store, a small grocery, and a gas station. Assuming that gas station owners and attendants know everyone, I pulled the car in and up to the first gas pump. I was about to get out to pump my own gas, but before I could open the door, a young man with short, dark hair and stained coveralls stuck his head near my window.

"How much would you like, Ma'am?" He was wiping his greasy hands on an old handkerchief and gave me a detached but friendly smile.

"Oh, fill it up, please," I told him. Then I got out of the car and followed him to the pump. "I was expecting to get it myself." I laughed. "I'm really used to doing that where I come from."

"Oh, where is that?" he asked.

"Seattle. I've lived there most of my life, but I'm actually going to be staying in Newbridge for a while. I've inherited a house here, and I thought I'd come stay in it for a time."

I was shocked to find myself babbling. What in the world was wrong with me? *Just come right out and ask him if he knows where the house is,* I thought.

"Actually, I was hoping you might tell me how to find the house. I've never been here before, but I have the address."

Brian (I assumed that was his name since it was embroidered over his breast pocket) looked a bit interested at this. "Sure, what is it?"

I had it committed to memory and told him, "34 Maple Hill Road. Do you know it?"

Brian nearly dropped the pump handle. "The old Whitney house? You inherited that?"

"That's it," I assured him. "Is there something wrong?"

He merely shrugged and then gave me a lopsided grin. "No, sorry. I was just a bit surprised. Tess Whitney died a few months ago, and nobody's been there since. I just didn't know she had any relatives left. Except Toby, of course, but he hasn't stepped foot in there in all the years I've been alive, and I don't suspect he wants to now. But I guess you know all that. So you're related to Tess, huh?"

I was now feeling a bit uncomfortable but curious. I didn't want to talk to a stranger about Tess Whitney—my mother—at this point, but who was Toby? "I'm sort of a long lost relative," I fudged. "But I'd like to meet Toby. Does he live around here?"

"Off and on," Brian said. "He travels a lot. I don't think he's here right now. That'll be $15."

"Thanks. Brian, is it?"

He looked perplexed for a minute, and I thought I'd made a stupid mistake assuming that was his name. Who knew how many attendants shared Brian's coveralls?

"How did you know?" He seemed almost frightened, but when I pointed to his pocket, he laughed. "Oh, right. I forgot it was there. I'm actually wearing my own coveralls today. Here, let me get your change, and then I'll draw you a little map. You can't miss the house. It's the last one on the road, and there are only two others before it."

I drove away with a piece of paper that contained a small map and a large grease stain sitting on the seat beside me. It did the job, however. Within ten minutes' time, I found a badly weathered wooden mailbox with letters I could barely read—but they were just visible enough for me to know I had found the right address. The driveway was not long but was lined with tall maple trees that obscured the house from the road. As I came to the end of the drive, I had my first view of the house. I don't know what I had expected, but this wasn't it. The house itself was at least as weathered as the mailbox. No paint had been applied to its exterior for close to one hundred years was my guess, but there was something very appealing about it, nevertheless. It was a fairly large box-shaped building. Several huge paned windows gave me hope that there would be plenty of sunlight shining through. There was no trim or decoration except for the door. It had been painted a wonderful shade of red with interesting designs and symbols of many colors on top. It should have looked out of place, but it didn't. I found myself eagerly scrambling for the key a lawyer had sent me and, climbing out of the car, I gave a brief glance to the Jeep parked next to my rental as I headed to the door. The house was surrounded by a meadow, which in turn was surrounded by trees. All along the walkway and lining the front of the house grew a profusion of herbs. They were obviously planted with great care and fit perfectly with the house. Despite myself, I was charmed. As I pinched a leaf from a plant that gave a pungent lemony smell, I realized these plants had probably been tended by my birth mother. For the first time, I caught myself thinking of her as a real person and wondering what she had really been like.

I became aware of an unusual pair of eyes peering at me through the leaves of a tall plant. One eye was blue, one green, and as I squatted for a closer look, I saw that they belonged to a longhaired, tan-colored cat. It looked almost as weathered as the house.

"Who are you?" I asked it. It didn't come forward at the sound of my voice, but neither did it retreat. "Do you belong here? Have you been fending for yourself all this time? If you decide you want to share the place with me, we might be able to come to some arrangement." I looked expectantly at the animal, but it didn't seem inclined to acknowledge my generous offer, so I left it there.

The stairs up to the porch seemed sturdy enough. I quickly unlocked the door and gave it a push. I expected a spooky little creaking sound, but that didn't happen until I stepped over the threshold. The floorboard creaked again as the cat bounded past me and stopped in a doorway, looking back at me. It apparently had decided to take me up on my offer after all. Either that or it felt it owned the house and was trying to decide if it should share with me or not. I left it to ponder its own thoughts and began to explore.

There was a coating of dust and a few cobwebs here and there, but it was otherwise a tidy house. The door opened to a hallway with an oak stairway that led to the second floor and to a closed door on the left. To the right and past the stairs were more rooms. The doorway the cat had stood in led to a living room that held a sofa and three chairs, an old piano, and a huge bookcase. The wooden floor was partially covered with a threadbare Oriental carpet, and on the walls hung two framed copies of paintings by Maxfield Parrish. There were squares of darker wood where other paintings had obviously hung but were nowhere to be seen now. On the inside wall was a stone fireplace with a large mantle, which was empty except for two brass candleholders. A door from the living room and one from the hallway both led to a dining room with a large wooden table and eight chairs. A built-in china cabinet held dust-covered dishes.

At the end of the hallway, next to the dining room, was the kitchen. There was no doubt that this had been one of Tess' favorite rooms. It was large and old-fashioned but had an almost cheerful atmosphere, even after months of being left alone. Dried herbs and flowers hung from the rafters, and jars of herbs and spices still covered the wooden countertops.

"The woman liked her herbs," I muttered to myself as I ran a finger across the dust-covered chopping block.

The cat meowed agreement as it made its way across the floor to a spot by the refrigerator. It looked at the two empty bowls there, then at me, and meowed again. Well, that answered that question. This was undoubtedly Tess' cat.

"I'm sorry," I told it. "I wasn't expecting to have a housemate, so I don't have any food for you."

Though it was a pretty scruffy-looking cat, it definitely wasn't skin and bones. Either someone else was feeding it or it had fended well for itself in the months since Tess' death. I knew I would have to make a grocery run before too long and decided I'd pick up some cat food, too.

"We'll have to have a name for you if you're going to stay here with me," I said as I leaned over and tried to place my hand near enough to let the creature get used to my scent but not so close that it felt threatened. "I can't call you Cat— since that's my name, too. Spelled with a *K*, mind you, and it's short for Katrina, but it would be just too confusing to have two Kats, don't you think?" Apparently, it had no opinion on the subject, so I left it sitting silently by the empty bowls and continued to explore the house.

The closed door at the foot of the stairs opened to an artist's studio. I stood in the doorway without moving for some time, taking in the fact that Tess had obviously also been an artist. I had known—practically from my first memory of my adopted mother reading what became some of my favorite, beautifully illustrated children's books—that that was what I wanted to do when I grew up. My adopted mother, who professed not to have a single artistic bone in her body, nevertheless encouraged my prolific output of childhood art-work and made sure I had instruction as soon as I was old enough. To find that my birth mother was also an artist was somewhat of a shock.

I pulled myself back from my thoughts and looked once more at my surroundings. This room was not tidy, by any means, but it was wonderful. It was the largest room so far, with several windows to let in plenty of sunlight. There were canvases, brushes, jars, and rags strewn everywhere. A half-finished portrait of a young woman sat on an easel.

I didn't stay in the studio for long. I was afraid that this was where I would find what might be left of my birth mother's spirit, and I wasn't ready for that yet. I quietly closed the door behind me, but I knew that I'd be drawn back here before long.

The stairway produced fewer squeaks than I would have expected, and I stopped on the landing at the top to look out the window. There was a small barn and a fenced pasture. Neither looked as if it had been used in a very long time. The hallway was narrow with three bedrooms on one side and two on the other. Four of them were sparsely furnished, but the fifth was filled with colorful and comfortable-looking furni-ture. There was another stone fireplace here, and I realized I was directly above the living room. The bed was made, but the layer of dust everywhere made me hope there was a utility room with a washer and dryer that I just hadn't discovered yet. I would need to wash the bedclothes. Then this, I decided, would be my room while I stayed in the house.

At the other end of the hallway, I discovered one flight of stairs leading upward and a narrow set leading back down. At the bottom I found the hoped-for washer and dryer in a utility room that led back into the kitchen. Suddenly, I real-ized I was both hungry and tired and so would put off tackling the third floor—which was most likely an attic—until later.

I made a run back into Newbridge to buy groceries, and after feeding the cat and myself, I did wash the bedclothes and laid on the bed for a short nap. My body, however, ignored the concept of short. I woke early the next morning to find the cat curled against my back, my clothes and hair rumpled, but I was oddly relaxed for sleeping in a strange house.

As I started to get up from the bed, the cat casually hooked a claw into the back of my blouse. "You can let go right now...whatever your name is," I told it, struggling for something to call it.

It hung on for a moment more, obviously not wanting me to think it would follow any instructions I might give it. Then it let go and turned the other way, the better to ignore me. As it turned, I got a good enough glimpse to tell it was a female. Now that that was established, I decided it was time to come up with a name.

"I told you my name. Now, what's yours? Let's see, how about...." Suddenly, a name popped into my head. "Minette?" I had no idea where the name came from, but the cat turned back to look at me and meow once before turning her attention to the delicate art of washing her paw. "Minette, it is," I said and then got out of bed, the better to ignore her.

I started the second day in the house wide-awake and with even more curiosity. Who was this woman who had given me up at the beginning of my life and then had left me the remnants at the end of hers? I had a suspicion I'd find some of the answers in the studio but, since I still wasn't ready for that, I decided I would explore the attic right after breakfast.

As I sat drinking coffee in the kitchen, sunbeams flooded through the windows, enticing me out into the actual sunshine. I picked up the coffee cup and headed out the door to sit on the back step. Minette trotted along beside me but continued on down the step and went off to perform whatever catly duties were on her agenda. I sat, took a sip, and then looked around at the back yard. The grass was high, but even this was tidy. The fenced pasture covered a good deal of the area, but there was also open meadow leading to the line of trees. I became lost in thought enough that I didn't even notice the woman emerging from the trees until I heard her speak.

19

"Mother!" There was a bit of exasperation in her voice. "Mother, are you here?"

I was too surprised to say anything and just observed her instead. As she came closer, I could see she was somewhere around my age, probably a little bit older. Her slightly graying, black hair was tied back with a rubber band, and her jeans and blouse appeared clean but worn. Two thoughts struck me about her: she looked like someone who was used to hard work, and she seemed vaguely familiar in that way that some strangers do. Then she saw me. At first she seemed frightened, then astonished, and then…I'm not sure. She tangled one hand into her ponytail and the other she wiped along her jeans as if to clean it. Then she continued toward me.

"Hi. Excuse me. I'm…who are you?"

"I'm Katrina Benson. I'm…I'm the new owner of this place."

The woman looked at me for a minute. "For just a second, I thought you were Tess. I mean, you don't really look like her up close, but she used to sit here on the step when I was young and…." She did a double take. "You're the new owner? You've bought the place?"

"No." I hesitated. I wasn't sure how much to say. "I've inherited it. I never met Tess but she, um, left it to me. Are you my neighbor?"

"I'm sorry. I just never expected to see anyone here, other than my mother. Yes, I am your neighbor." She held out her hand and, as we shook, she said, "My name is Rita Lawrence. Our house is just through the woods, and my mother slips off sometimes. Since Tess' death, I usually find her over here. I don't know why—I don't think she and Tess ever got along. Maybe it's just because they were the same age and knew each other all their lives that Mom has a hard time knowing Tess is gone." Rita took a breath and then went on. "I didn't know Tess had any relatives left. Are you a long-lost cousin?"

I was surprised to find that I had formed an opinion of this person so soon, but I had. With little to base it on, I found that I liked her and hoped we could be friends. I also realized that here was a source of knowledge I might tap. Rita had known my mother probably all her life.

"Not exactly. Would you like a cup of coffee? "

"No, thanks," she said, but she did come sit on the bottom step. "I used to sit here with Tess sometimes when I was little. She had horses, and she'd let me help feed them and sometimes ride them, and then we'd sit here and talk about them. I was horse-crazy then."

I felt a twinge of jealousy and then told myself how ridiculous that was. I'd had a wonderful mother and father. No horses, though. "This is a bit awkward, I guess, but Tess Whitney was... she was my mother."

Rita's jaw dropped and then closed again. "What?"

"It was a surprise to me, too. She put me up for adoption right after I was born, and I never saw or heard from her again until a couple of months ago. I was notified that she'd died and left me this place. All my life, I knew I was adopted, but I didn't know who my birth parents were or that my mother knew where I was. I still don't know who my father was." I stopped speaking suddenly, amazed at myself for telling this stranger so much. Neither of us said anything until the cat appeared and pounced at something near Rita's feet.

"Minette!" Rita exclaimed. "You gave me a scare."

"What did you say?" My voice was barely a whisper.

Rita looked at me oddly. "I said the cat gave me a scare. Have you met her yet?"

"Her name...it's Minette?"

"Yep. Tess has had three Minettes that I know of. All from the same line of cats, too. She had other cats with other names, but I guess she really liked this name. Minette is the only cat she had for the last four or five years, though. Are you all right?"

I collected myself and smiled at her. "Sure. Minette is an interesting name. She seems in pretty good shape to have been by herself since Tess died. Did you or your mother take care of her?"

Rita laughed. "Not my mother. They hate the sight of each other. Well, maybe that's a little strong...no, it's not.

They really don't like each other. I've been feeding her. She sneaks over to our house once in a while, but mostly I've brought food and left it in the barn here for her. Have you gotten near her yet?"

"Gotten near her?"

"Yeah, she doesn't take to people much. She loved Tess, of course, and she tolerates me, but she's independent."

"I guess I should be honored then. She came right in the house with me yesterday and slept with me last night." I didn't want to sound like I was bragging, especially if this woman was attached to the cat, so I added, "I don't know how well my clothes are going to fare. She did grab my blouse this morning when I moved before she gave me permission."

Rita's laugh pealed across the yard. "You should be honored. Most people can't get that close to her. She obviously took a liking to you."

Minette must have been listening because she rubbed against my leg as if emphasizing Rita's words and then bounded back across the yard before I got cocky enough to think she liked me too much.

"This seems so strange." Rita's voice was quiet, but she looked directly at me. "Tess never said a word about... about having had a daughter. But if she put you up for adoption, I guess she wouldn't. My mother must not have known, or it would have been blabbed all over town." Then she seemed to have regretted her words. "I'm sorry, Katrina. I didn't mean that to sound rude. But I just never thought of Tess as someone else's mother."

"That's okay," I reassured her. "Most people call me Kat, by the way. I hope you'll do the same. It sounds like you were pretty close to Tess. I had a wonderful mom who died this last year. I miss her a lot. I still don't know exactly how I feel about this whole thing. Finding out that Tess apparently knew where I was all along and then leaving me this place. In some ways, it feels pretty bizarre, and I'm still not sure why I decided to come here. I hope this doesn't feel too awkward for you."

Rita looked at her hands. "Why should it feel awkward to me?"

"Well, it really does sound like you were close. You knew her well, and I didn't know her at all, and here I am. It feels pretty awkward to me." I smiled a bit to soften the words.

"Obviously I didn't know her as well as I thought I did, or I would have known about you, right?" Rita also smiled, but I sensed a tinge of sadness. "I did love Tess, and I miss her. My relationship with my mother has never been ex-actly…easy. Growing up, I escaped to this place a lot. My mother was never happy about that, but I was always glad Tess was here. I'm sorry you didn't know her."

"I'm not sure if I'm sorry about that or not. I don't know why she gave me up. And if she knew who and where I was, why didn't she ever contact me? I know it's irrational, but sometimes I find myself being angry with this woman I never met. And I don't even know what she looked like!" I fidgeted with my coffee cup and then laid it aside. "And now here I am babbling all this to you when I've just met you. I'm sorry."

Rita smiled again. "Don't be," she said. "This place just sort of does that to you. I babbled a lot to Tess all the years I came over here. And *I'm* sorry. I don't mean to make you feel bad about how well I knew…your mother."

"Maybe we should both stop apologizing. I'm really glad to meet you, Rita. I'm hoping you might be willing to help me get to know who Tess was. It's great to have a neighbor to talk to." I stood up and glanced into the house. "I spent a little time yesterday exploring the house but didn't get to the attic. Want to come look it over with me?

She looked back the way she had come and then shrugged. "I was looking for my mother, but obviously she's not here. She'll be okay. I guess I could come in for a little bit."

"Is your mother sick?" I wasn't sure how to politely ask if her mother was suffering either physically or mentally.

23

"No." Rita sighed. "Lately, it seems like her mind wanders a bit, and then she'll disappear. Sometimes I find her over here walking around, but most of the time she's just sort of hiding out at home. I shouldn't say this, but, even though I want to know she's okay, I think it's a relief for both of us to find some space from each other. I came back to live with her and take care of her a couple of years ago after I got divorced, and it looks like some things never change. Know what I mean?"

I wasn't sure that I did know, but I didn't tell her that as she followed me through the door. I knew that, no matter how well she might know it, I couldn't for the moment share Tess' studio with Rita. The rest of the house seemed fair game.

"I've been everywhere but the attic," I told her. "Have you been up there?"

"A few times when I was young. I love old attics—there's usually so much in them around here that goes way back. I don't remember Tess being much interested in showing me any of the old things from her family, though. From what I remember, her attic was fairly neat and organized. I was surprised at that the first time I saw it because ours is anything but. And my mother was always telling me about each little item we came across in ours—she was always proud of how long her and my dad's families had been here. I think it was the one interest she and I shared." Rita was quiet for a moment and then added, "Tess' family…your family… must have been here just as long. She just didn't talk about it like my mother did."

"Well, let's go see what's there."

When I went back to the studio, I had to be alone. I was afraid that was where I would really have to confront Tess. But in the attic, where there might be a barrage of memories stored up by this family that was mine and yet not mine, I didn't mind having company. We made our way up the first flight of stairs, down the hallway, and to the second flight which, I now saw, ended at another closed door. Going first, I struggled with the hard-to-open door, and when I finally managed, I saw that Rita was right. This was an un-commonly tidy attic. It was a good-sized room, but for some reason not as large as I had imagined it. There were several trunks and things that had been common in years gone by but would be considered treasures now; at least I knew they would be in Seattle. I noticed two large spinning wheels, but-ter churns, wooden buckets, and three sewing machines from different eras before I stopped trying to take it all in at once. There was a lot to explore here—but it was stacked so neatly. Tess and I definitely hadn't had this in common. I could relate much more to the one place in the house she seemed to be able to just let herself go—the studio. As I looked around, something struck me as more odd than how tidily the objects were placed. It took me a moment to figure out what it was.

"Rita, look at all this stuff, and yet, there's hardly any dust up here. Isn't that weird?"

Rita took her hand from a stack of books on an old table and looked around. "You're right," she replied. "Maybe it's just airtight and not much dust gets in. There are cobwebs on the ceiling, see?"

"Do you think Tess came up and dusted this stuff? It seems a bit odd. I don't think I'd...." We both froze as we heard the stairs creak. I laughed and said, "I'm going to have to get used to the sounds here. Minette makes a lot of noise for a cat."

I turned to the door to invite her highness in, but the words stopped at my lips. Standing in the doorway was a short, thin, older woman with bluish-gray hair, who was wear-ing a faded green, polyester dress and a black scowl. I was sure I knew who she was immediately and felt a decided twinge of sympathy for Rita.

"Mother, what are you doing here?" Rita walked to the door but moved back as her mother stepped in.

"Funny, I thought I'd ask you the same thing," her mother said pointedly.

For a moment, Rita reminded me of a guilty little girl as if this was something that had happened often in her life. Then she seemed to shake herself loose. "I came over here looking for you, but I found Kat instead. Mom, this is Kat Benson. Kat, this is my mother, Harriet Sloan."

"Pleased to meet you, Mrs. Sloan." I smiled at the woman and waited to see how she would reply. I didn't think she looked all that pleased to meet me.

"How do you do?" At least she seemed to be going for civil. "Are you a realtor or something? This place isn't for sale, you know."

"Yes, I know. I'm the new owner."

Harriet was silent while she took this information in. Then she asked, "How can you be the new owner?"

"Mom, she inherited it. Tess left the house to her." I noticed Rita had inserted herself between her mother and me, almost as if she were trying to protect one of us. But which one? Surely she couldn't be afraid I would hurt her mother. And that frail little woman couldn't possibly hurt me. I had a good seven inches and many pounds on her.

"So, are you one of her witch friends? If you are, you'll go to Hell—right where she is now—unless you repent."

Ah, the acid tongue. Perhaps Rita had been trying to protect me from that. Poor Rita looked very embarrassed. She needn't have worried. I found her mother a little entertaining. I thought it best not to let either of them know that.

"No, Mrs. Sloan. I'm not one of her witch friends. In fact, I never met Tess. I may have other things to repent, but right now that's not one of them." I suppose I shouldn't have been flippant, but it slipped out.

"Who are you then? Why else would she leave you this house?"

You could practically see the old woman's brain whirring as she tried to piece something together. It suddenly struck me odd that I thought of her as an old woman, and yet I thought of Tess, whom Rita had said had been the same age as her mother, as a stately, middle-aged, Miss Rumphius type. And I was obviously progressing in seeing Tess as a real person if I was acquainting her with a favorite children's book character. Rita snapped me out of my reverie.

"Mom, please. It's not our business. Let's leave Kat to what she was doing and go home. I'll make you some tea if you want." Rita was definitely trying to steer her mother out the door, but Mom wasn't buying it.

"You seemed to be real cozy with her for it not being our business." Harriet looked at her daughter and then at me. Her face went pale, and she pointed a finger at me. "Wait a minute. You can't be." Slowly, she walked around me. As she looked me over her eyes kept returning to my face. "You don't look much like...." She looked at Rita accusingly and then back at me. "Are you her daughter?" she whispered.

That certainly startled me, and I glimpsed a surprised look on Rita's face, too. "Yes, I am," I finally said. "But as I said, I never met her."

"Mom, you knew about Kat?" Rita's surprise deepened.

"I knew she had a baby," Harriet spat. "I didn't know what happened to it, though." The accusing look returned as she turned back to Rita. "How long have you known about it? I suppose Tess told you all about it."

"No, I just found out when I met Kat."

Suddenly, Mrs. Sloan seemed to become a whole different person. "I'm sorry," she said to me. "Tess and I were not friends as you can probably tell. As a good Christian woman, I certainly didn't like some of her ways. But that's no reason to take it out on you. Will you be staying here long?"

The switch in attitude took me so by surprise that it was a minute before I could reply. "I...I don't know yet. I'll be here for two or three months. I don't know after that."

The switch didn't seem to surprise Rita nearly as much, but she was now firm about getting her mother home. "Okay, Mom. I've taken enough of Kat's time. Let's go, and we can talk to her another day."

Rita escorted her mother back down both sets of stairs and then, as I stood on the back steps, Mrs. Sloan turned to me again. "Call me Harriet, dear. Why don't you have tea or coffee with me sometime? Rita can fix it for us, and we can have a nice little chat. Maybe you'd like to come to church with us Sunday?" Then she turned and walked slowly toward the place in the woods that I had seen Rita emerge from.

Rita looked at me just long enough to whisper, "There's more to tell you. I'll come by again, if that's all right?" Then, before I could answer, she turned and hastened after her mother.

Whew, I thought. *That was interesting.* I did want to find out more of what Rita had to say. Harriet had known Tess all their lives, but I didn't think I could trust whatever she might tell me about her. And what in the world had made Harriet dislike her so? Ah, yes, I remembered…she had implied that Tess was a witch.

I assumed that Harriet had somehow decided that Tess really was an evil, spell-casting, not-just-on-Halloween witch. Whether she used it as an excuse to explain something that had happened between them in the past, or because her "wandering mind" assigned that roll to my birth mother, I didn't know. That there were other kinds of witches, I knew, because—*A.*—I lived in Seattle and—*B.*—Rowan had been interested in all things Wiccan since the age of fourteen. Though I had to admit I didn't really know much about small, rural towns on the East Coast, it seemed unlikely to me that someone of Tess' generation who, as far as I knew, had lived all her life here, might be a Goddess-worshipping, card-carrying witch. I dismissed it all from my mind and made my way back up to the attic.

Eventually Minette found me there and sat on an old cushion as she watched me paw through piles of family artifacts. I spent most of the rest of the day discovering antiques that would fetch a dandy price in a Seattle store but had been, for the most part, simply the everyday tools of several generations of one family. I had known only one set of my grandparents. My adopted mother and I had both been only children, and Aunt Amelia was my father's only sibling. Family heirlooms had not been a major part of our lives. The history in this attic alone boggled my mind. Curious as I was, however, I suddenly felt like an outsider spying on someone else's family. The thought made me momentarily furious, but at who?

My birth mother? Myself? Or all the people who had used these things and just by the very fact of living had made my life possible?

The heat, the history in the room, and my thoughts were all beginning to make me feel claustrophobic. I decided I would finish exploring this part of the house another day. Without thinking, I picked up Minette and, leaving the attic, I closed the door behind us. The cat, I swear, looked surprised but made no protest, and I scratched her ears before setting her down to maneuver the stairs on her own.

After eating a light dinner and taking a walk part way into Newbridge and back, I tried to work on an outline for a story and then gave up and went to bed. I was tired and went to sleep easily, but my sleep was far from peaceful. That was when I awoke for the third time from the dream of the circle of women.

Chapter 2

Early the next morning, I crawled out of bed and pulled myself in and out of the shower. I didn't understand why this dream was haunting me or what it meant. I was used to treating my dreams in a rather Jungian way. I supposed each symbol and character represented some aspect of myself, but this dream was different than any I'd had before. This seemed so outside of myself—more like I was observing something happening to someone else. I told myself I would let it go for now and take my mind elsewhere. After breakfast, I tidied up and set out on foot into town. It was time to check out the library.

The Newbridge Public Library was one room, but like Tess' house, not what I had expected. Recognizing my prejudice about little towns, I realized I had thought I would be walking into a dusty room with a few books and a librarian who, if not old, would at least be wearing her hair in a tidy bun. The person who smiled at me from the circulation desk was wearing a ponytail instead of a bun. And he wasn't old. Rowan might quibble with me, but I definitely didn't feel that "somewhere in your forties" qualified as old age.

Looking around, I saw a small but well-equipped library with far more books than I would have expected. There were two public use computer stations, three long wooden tables surrounded by matching chairs, and a couple of inviting-looking, overstuffed chairs. The book stacks were neatly kept, and I was looking forward to seeing what was there, but my first interest was in the children's section. I was convinced I could tell what a library was really like by its children's space.

"Let me know if you need any help."

My attention was drawn back to the casually dressed man at the desk, and I stepped toward him.

"Thanks," I said. "I'm new here, and I wanted to look over the library. It seems very nice." I hadn't meant to sound patronizing, but I was afraid my surprise was showing. His next words made it obvious he knew what I had been thinking.

"You were expecting a dingy little room with one light bulb and not many more books, a dirty wooden floor, and maybe a spittoon?" He grinned as my face must have expressed my embarrassment, and I was on the verge of deciding I didn't like this person. That must have shown on my face, too, because his grin softened. "I'm sorry. It's just that you looked so surprised when you walked in, and I was sure you were expecting something different. I'd heard that someone from Seattle had moved into the Whitney house, and I assumed...I really am sorry. Maybe you're not that person."

I tried to sense if he was feeling any embarrassment, but if he was it didn't show. "How did you know? I am staying at the Whitney house, but I only got here two days ago. I've only met a couple of people so far, so...."

"It's one of the stereotypes of a small town that does turn out to be true," he said as his dark brown eyes twinkled in amusement. "Everybody knows what's going on with everybody else. Even when you're brand new in town. Maybe especially when you're brand new in town. Look, I should stop teasing you now. By the way, my name is Simon DeBerry."

"Hello, Simon," I said dryly. "I guess I don't have to tell you my name—you must know it already."

"Okay, so maybe we don't know everything right away. Nobody told me your name. You do look familiar, though. Have you been here before?" Then, I'll be darned if Simon DeBerry didn't look embarrassed! "I'm sorry. I didn't mean that to sound...you know," he stammered.

It was my turn to be amused, and I should have been sorry to say that I enjoyed his discomfort, but I wasn't sorry.

I simply said, "No, I haven't been here before. I'd like to look over the children's section." I knew I was being petty, but I did not tell him my name. It was also pointless—I'd have to give it to him if I wanted to get a card and check anything out, but I decided that for the moment Mr. DeBerry could stay in the dark about that much at least. He looked at me oddly, and then pointed toward one end of the room.

I walked toward the section and was immediately enchanted. The space was not large, but it was colorful and comfortable. There was one short table with several chairs just right for short legs, but what really took my attention was a wonderful loft with railings all around and pillows spread in a circle large enough to hold fifteen to twenty children and a few adults. Underneath the loft were shelves full of picture books with juvenile chapter books to the side of that. On the other side of juvenile non-fiction were several rows of young adult fiction. Though it had been my experience that most teens wanted books aimed at them to be located far from the children's section, I was willing to bet the teenagers who came to this library used the loft as much as any of the younger children.

I heard soft footsteps come toward me across the carpet. When I turned and saw that it was Simon, I said, "This is really a wonderful children's section..." at the same moment that he said, "Now I know why you looked so familiar...."

We both stopped, and I noticed that ready smile leap to Simon's face again. "Thank you," he said to me. "I've tried to make it a fun place for all the kids." He reached into a shelf under the loft and pulled out three picture books. "I do know your name after all, but not because somebody in town told me. One of your books has a picture of you on the back cover." He flipped over the books, and, finding what he was looking for, he held it up to me. "Your hair was long in this picture, and you were wearing glasses. Otherwise, I would have recognized right away that you were Katrina Benson— one of our favorite story time authors. I have to say, though, my favorites are some of the picture books you've done for older kids."

I have to admit, it was gratifying to find out he knew (and liked) my books. And he had tactfully not said he didn't recognize me because I was obviously a bit older than I was when that picture had been taken. Maybe he would turn out to be not such an annoying person after all.

"Thanks. I'm never sure what libraries might have my books." He started to protest, but I raised both hands in front of me as I added, "And that has nothing to do with the size of the town." I began to scan the titles of some of the other books and recognized many old favorites. "Are you the library director?" I asked as I pulled a book from the shelf.

Simon propped the books he was holding on the table and gave me a lopsided grin. "Director, reference librarian, children's librarian, cataloger, page, chief cook, and bottle washer, all in one. And shameless volunteer solicitor. I don't suppose you'd consider coming in for a story time or program or two and talk about writing and illustrating your books, would you?"

Okay, the guy had me. I had always loved talking to children about my books and helping them illustrate their own stories. And just maybe it could help push me back into getting some work done. Some of my best material had come out of working with Rowan and her friends when they were little.

"Sure," I found myself telling him. "Just give me a few days to settle in, and then let's talk about what you'd like me to do."

"Great." Simon was about to say more, but just then two people walked through the door and greeted him. He acknowledged them with his smile and then turned back to me. "I'll get a library card ready for you. Welcome to Newbridge." He headed back to the circulation desk.

33

After a minute, I turned my full attention to exploring what else the Newbridge Public Library had to offer.

I spent nearly two hours looking everything over. Hunger finally pushed me to make some selections and think about walking back to the house to get some lunch. I walked to the front desk with a small load of picture books, a history of the area, and the newest novel by Miriam Grace Monfredo. Another reminder not to think in stereotypes—I hadn't even seen this book on my most recent foray into the Seattle Public Library. It was my turn to smile as I filled out a registration and waited for Simon to ready my card and check out my books.

"This is a wonderful library. And I really mean that. Have you been the chief cook and bottle washer for a long time?"

Simon handed me my new card. "About five years. It's a nice town, too. I had to go away for many years and come back to realize that, but it is. I hope you enjoy your time here."

I thanked him, and then, as I left, I noticed the space had filled considerably while I was browsing. Apparently the library was a popular place in Newbridge.

On the way back I thought about Rowan and realized I hadn't called her since I'd gotten here. I needed to call the phone company and get a phone hooked up and find out about an Internet provider. I would have to come back into town later to use a pay phone to do all of those things.

Minette was sitting among the herbs again when I came up the path. She fell in behind me and followed me into the house. We both seemed to have the same idea as we headed into the kitchen. The cat went straight to her food bowl, and I opened the refrigerator. As I ate my sandwich, I looked through the picture books and began to get the old urge to just paint—almost anything would do. And it struck me that the best place to do that would be the studio. It was time to confront a ghost.

Minette sat in the doorway rather than following me in. Apparently even she thought I had to do this on my own. I wondered briefly who the young woman was whose portrait had not been finished. As I rummaged, I found several different types of work. There were a few other portraits, but there were also landscapes and some fantasy scenes that looked very real. Tess' paintings were not sentimental, but they each had a simple beauty to them. I doubted that this woman had been solely self-taught. Her work was very good. In a corner, I found two portraits that had obviously been done fairly recently. One was of a handsome older man with thick white hair and a mustache. The other was a woman—and I knew without a doubt that it was a self-portrait.

For the first time, I was looking at a likeness of my birth mother. I didn't know if she had purposely flattered herself or not, but Tess was beautiful. My own eyes looked back at me from the canvas, but otherwise I couldn't see myself in this face at all. Her long hair was black with streaks of silver shot through it. High cheekbones and a strong nose highlighted her oval face. A slight smile sat on her pink lips, but the eyes reflected a quiet sadness. I resisted seeing that sadness, but I couldn't help it. It was there. Tess had not spared herself the lines around her mouth and eyes, but rather than detract from her beauty, they added to it.

I took the unfinished portrait from the easel and set Tess' on it instead. That face seemed to watch me as I moved about the room.

I continued to sift through what was there and found watercolors and sketches, besides the oils. Some of the sketches caught me off guard—they reminded me a little of pictures I had seen in some of Rowan's books on witchcraft. But somehow these were more real and even ordinary-looking. There were women in robes with some of the symbols I'd seen on the front door woven into the robes. Some of the women were older, some young, but almost all of them were pictured among plants, trees, and rocks. If Harriet Sloan had seen these, I'm sure she wouldn't have approved. They weren't pictures of wicked old witches, but they had a decided pagan flavor to them that I found appealing, but I was certain Harriet would not.

I found a folder filled with gorgeous watercolors of woodland animals. I was so captivated by them that I cleared a space on a countertop and spread them out. I almost hated to admit how much I liked Tess' art, but I thought these would have been perfect for a children's book. The animals looking back at me were not the cute Bambi types found in many children's books. They conveyed a beauty, reality, and wildness that seemed ready to leap off the page. Though I was resisting it, I knew a story was forming in my head that wove and wound itself around these pictures.

Well, why not, I thought. *Nothing has to come from it, and at least I'll be writing again.*

It didn't take me long to retrieve my laptop from the bedroom and set it up on the counter next to the pictures.

I was so buried in what I was doing that I didn't look up until the last sentence was finished. I had felt inspired while writing before, but I didn't remember ever being so possessed of a story coming from someone else's artwork. And it was good—I was sure of it. I would look at it all again tomorrow and make any changes I needed. And then?

Then, I would decide what to do with it. If nothing else, I certainly felt as though I had cut through the writer's block. And that wasn't all. I still felt the urge to paint.

I picked my way through Tess' supplies until I had what I needed. Placing an empty canvas on a tabletop easel, I chewed absent-mindedly on a brush while I contemplated the acrylic paints before me. I didn't really have anything in mind until the first stroke of the brush, when it hit me that I was going to paint my dream.

At first, that frightened me. Then it excited me. Once again, I felt almost taken over and was unaware of most everything else around me as I made the outline of the circle of women just as the circle was breaking and the women were starting toward the sea. I don't know how long I had worked, but I gradually became aware of a knocking sound. It took me a moment to realize that someone was at the front door. I hurriedly covered the paints and wrapped the brushes in a wet cloth.

I closed the studio door behind me and noticed Minette tucked snugly next to the banister on the bottom step of the stairs. She opened one eye and let it follow my movement to the front door but didn't get up.

As I opened the door, Rita's hand paused as she was just about to knock again.

"Hi," I greeted her. "Sorry, I guess I didn't hear you at first."

"That's okay. I just thought I'd come by and see if you'd eaten dinner already. If not, I have a casserole I thought we could keep warm in your oven and get a chance to talk a little bit more."

Now I saw she had a covered dish tucked to her side.

"Is it really dinner time?" I hadn't been aware of how long I'd been in the studio. I pushed the door open further and gestured to Rita to come in. "That's really nice of you. Sounds great. I can make a quick salad, and we can eat in the kitchen."

As we headed down the hallway, I asked, "Has your mother eaten?" I trusted I didn't sound too hopeful that she wouldn't be joining us.

"She's at my brother's for the evening." Rita placed the casserole in the oven and twisted the knobs before turning back to me. "It seemed like a good chance to talk without... well...without her interrupting. She can be a little intense, can't she? I hope she didn't bother you too much yesterday."

"Not at all." I threw a smile Rita's way to reassure her. "She has some definite opinions, and she obviously didn't like Tess, but she was actually quite nice in the end." Perhaps I shouldn't have added that "in the end" part, but there it was.

"She's always been opinionated, but she seems to have gotten worse lately. I don't know. It seems like her mind has started to wander a little in the last few months. Nothing major, but she seems...different." Rita gave herself a little shake and changed the subject. "I thought maybe you might have more questions about Tess or the house, and I have to admit, I'm a bit curious about you. I'm afraid you'll find we're a nosy bunch in a small town like this."

I grinned as I handed her some plates and silver for the table. "I was told something like that when I went to the library this morning. I'll just have to get used to it I guess."

"What did you think of our library? Not what you're used to, I bet."

"Certainly not as big as I'm used to, but it's a great little library. The children's section was lovely, and there were even some of my books there."

Rita stopped what she was doing. "Your books? Are you a writer?"

"I am. I write and illustrate children's books mostly." Most of what we needed was on the table, and I quickly searched for a potholder to pull the casserole from the oven.

"So you're an artist, too?" As we sat at opposite sides of the table, Rita looked at me. "You know Tess was an artist?"

"I know. I've been looking through some of her work in the studio. It's very good."

"Yes, she was good. I know she sold some of her stuff to people in New York City, but she never said much about it. She must have done all right with it, because she always had money to do what she wanted. She lived rather simply here, but she did like to travel." Rita reached for the salad. "I have a few things she did for me. Portraits were sort of a specialty of hers, and she did some beautiful things of my kids for me when they were younger. I have them hanging in my room at home." She sighed. "My mother doesn't want them in the living room. I guess because Tess did them."

"Do you know why your mother disliked her so much?"

"Not really. Tess never said anything bad to me about my mother, but I know she didn't like her either. I asked them each why once, a long time ago, but Tess just said sometimes there weren't explanations for things, and she hinted that maybe it wasn't any of my business. My mother wasn't so polite about it." Rita kept her eyes on her plate as she said, "Mom would only say that God doesn't like witches and neither does she. You may have noticed she's a bit religious."

I stopped chewing. "Does she really think Tess was a witch?"

There was a silence.

Finally, Rita looked up. "Well, the thing is, Tess *was* a witch." Then, in a rush, as if I wouldn't hear her out if she didn't say it quickly, Rita went on. "Not a wicked witch like my mother thinks. Actually, my mother thinks lots of things are wicked. You'll probably think I'm crazy, but Tess was a witch—a good one—and when I was growing up, I wanted her to show me how to be one, too, but she said it wasn't that easy, and that I should just be who I was."

I was all ears now. "What do you mean? What made her a witch?"

"The kids always called her a witch when I was little, but they just did that because she was different. She lived out here all alone for a lot of years, and she never went to church. That was her first big sin in my mother's eyes. Sometimes she dressed differently than other grownups—there were times when she wore a cape, and we never saw anybody else do that except at Halloween. But none of them ever knew that she was a real witch. She told me she was mostly a green witch— she could grow almost any kind of herb, and she knew what to do with them. She did teach me a little about that, but my mother wouldn't let me grow any at home."

"So, she actually said she was a witch?"

Rita looked disappointed. "You don't believe me, do you? If you'd only known her. She did other things, too. Magic things. At least, they seemed magic to me. She kept telling me, though, that magic was just ordinary things that people didn't know how to explain. Oh, I don't mean she put spells on people and turned anybody into toads."

She gave an ironic little laugh.

"I asked her once to tell me how to do that so I could get rid of my brother, but she said she couldn't do anything like that and if she could, she wouldn't anyway because whatever you do comes back to you three times over. I told her it would be worth it if I could just get rid of Arthur. That was the one time I remember her getting angry with me. She said that cursing others was never worth it because you always paid for it worse than they did."

I pressed her for more. "What kind of magic things did she do?"

Rita's eyes pleaded with me to believe her. "Little things that other people might not notice. She really could make plants grow when no one else could. And I saw her heal animals with just her hands. I would bring little mice and birds to her that I thought sure were going to die, but she'd hold them for a long time and then whisper something and let them go. And I swear they always lived! I told my mother about that only once—and got spanked for lying. She really did do it, though, Kat. I'm not nuts."

"Rita, don't look so miserable. I've seen a lot of strange things happen. I do believe you. But did she actually say the words, 'I'm a witch'?"

Rita waved her fork in the air. "Yes," she said. "I asked her after I'd brought several of the animals to her. She said she was, but that the word meant different things to different people. She said some people chose to be witches and that some were born to it and had to choose to accept it. I knew she was telling me she was born to it and that it would be easier for her if I didn't tell anybody else. You're the first person I've told in all these years. But you're her daughter. I thought you had a right to know."

Well. I didn't know what to say after that, and we sat in an uncomfortable silence for a time.

Rita pushed food around on her plate and then looked at me unhappily. "You don't really believe me, do you?"

I grasped for the right words. "It's not that I don't believe you. It's just...a little hard to take in. Are there other people here who consider themselves witches?" I looked at her carefully. "Are you one?"

"No. There was a time I wanted to be, but I don't know that it always made Tess happy to be one. No matter how much fun I had with her, there was always something a little sad about her. I didn't know what it was, but maybe I understand a little better now." I let that pass although Tess' portrait flashed into my mind. "I'm sure there's no other witches here. Tess was a loner, and most everyone else thought she was strange. This isn't the kind of place where you'd find a lot of witches."

No kidding—it had never crossed my mind that I'd find one here. My attention snapped back at Rita's next words.

"I don't know why she stayed here really. The only other person she did much with, that I know of, is Toby and that was only in the last few years."

I jumped on that. "Who is Toby? A young man at the gas station the other day said something about a Toby—I got the impression he was another relative. I forgot about it until now. Why didn't he inherit the house?"

Rita's eyes looked a little less restless. "Did the young man have dark hair and a silly little grin?"

"I guess. His name was on his pocket...Brian." I was impatient to know about Toby.

"That's my son. One of them. I have two sons and a daughter. Brian is my baby. Jessica and John are just two years older. They're twins."

At another point in time, I would be interested in finding out about her children. But right now I didn't want to get sidetracked.

"Brian seemed like a very nice young man. When I told him I was looking for the Whitney house and that I'd inherited it, he said he was surprised because he didn't think Tess had any relatives except Toby. Who is he?"

Rita's brows furrowed, and she shrugged as she said, "I'm not sure why Brian called him a relative. Toby was Tess'...friend."

"They were close?"

"From what I'd always heard, they were sweethearts in the early days. I guess something happened, though. Tess was one of the only women to go off to college from here in those days, and they broke up then. Toby married someone else, but she died a couple of years ago. He and Tess sort of got back together again after that."

A prickle was starting at the back of my neck. "They got back together as a real couple?"

"Not exactly." Rita read the question in my eyes. "I know he never came here to this house. I got the impression that she wouldn't let him. I don't know why. I guess I just thought that was one of her oddities. But they traveled a lot together in those last two years. Tess always seemed the happiest I'd ever known her after each of those trips. In fact, they had just come back from a trip to France and England when she suddenly died. When I saw Toby after her death, he was really broken up. So, in that way, yeah, I think they were a real couple. But they didn't get married or live together." Then Rita saw the new look on my face. "What is it?" she asked.

"Rita, let me go get a portrait from the studio. I'll be right back." The chair scraped loudly as I pushed it back and got up. It took me very little time to fetch the painting of the white-haired man and practically shove it in Rita's direction. "Is this Toby?" She nodded her head in assent and looked from the painting to me.

"What?" she asked, and then I could sense the same thought I had just had cross her mind. "No. Do you think he could be?"

"Do you?" My hand felt a little unsteady as I propped the portrait against the window near the table. We both looked and wondered if the face looking back at us was that of my natural father.

"I don't know Kat. I never heard of Tess being involved with any other man, but who knows? I didn't know she had you either." Rita sighed. "I used to feel close to her, but now that I think of it, she didn't talk about herself much to me. And, once I got married and didn't live next door and with having kids and all, I didn't see very much of her for a long time. When I moved back in with my mother, I came to see her more often—whenever she wasn't traveling with Toby. You know what my mother's like, so it wasn't easy, but it was almost like I fell back into the old pattern of when I was a kid—I'd escape for a bit and come here."

This was all filling me with more questions than I could process at once. I was finding little bits and pieces of Tess, but I still didn't understand. Here was a woman who had given up her daughter—who knew why? And yet, it certainly sounded as if she had acted in a very motherly way toward the girl Rita had been. It wasn't exactly that I was jealous, but I wanted to know how she could have been so loving to another child and give up her own. And why did she leave me this place? And what about my natural father?

"Rita, your son said he didn't think Toby was here. Do you know where he is?" I had to go with one thing at a time.

"The last time I saw him, he wasn't too clear about where he was going. He's traveling somewhere. But I do know he said he'd be back by the first part of September. I wonder if he knows about you."

I wondered the same thing. "Then I guess I'll have to wait until he gets back to talk to him. Will you let me know if you hear that he's back?"

She agreed, and I continued to question her as we finished our meal. "What about the rest of Tess' family? Did she ever have any brothers and sisters? Did you know her parents?"

"She was an only child, and I know both her parents died in a car crash when she was in college. I don't know much else about them except…." Rita hesitated.

"Except what?" I prompted.

"Except that I heard her mother was…different, too."

"Different how?"

"Tess never told me this, but I always wondered if she was a witch, too. There are little stories I'd hear about Tess' mother being able to see things before they happened, that sort of thing. My mother said they were nonsense, but I wasn't so sure after knowing Tess."

We finished eating, and both started clearing up. I decided it was time to talk about something else. As we washed and dried the dishes, we gave each other brief histories of our own lives. I told Rita that James and I had been married and had Rowan while we were still in college. We thought we were madly in love, but by the time Rowan was two years old, we discovered we weren't any longer. The breakup had been sad but not horrible. We realized we wanted very different things in life except for our daughter. We divorced, and within a couple of years, James had remarried. I never had. He had two more children and now a second ex-wife. He had always been a good father to Rowan, and he and I were actually still friends.

Rita had been married right after high school and started her family, but it wasn't a particularly happy marriage. "Dan drank a lot. Still does for that matter," she told me. "He expected me to be happy just taking care of the house and him and the kids. And I guess I was for a while. But we never had much money, and I wanted things for the kids, so I wanted to work somewhere to help out, but every time I'd bring it up, he'd get really mad. I never did anything about it until after the twins left home and then Brian got his own place, and I realized I had to do something else or go crazy. So I got a job. It's not anything grand like writing or being an artist, but I love it. Without asking Dan, I started working three days a week at the post office. He blew up when he found out."

"Then what happened?" I turned out the kitchen light and pointed down the hallway to the living room. We settled ourselves into chairs before she continued. "He told me I had to quit, and I told him I wouldn't. He threatened to leave if I didn't give up the job. I really believe he thought I would give in at that, but I didn't."

"So he moved out?"

"Yep." A little smile played at the corner of her lips. "I know I was supposed to feel terrible about that, but it was such a relief. All of a sudden I couldn't believe I'd spent so many years living with a man I didn't even like very much. Don't feel sorry for him, though. He immediately moved in with a girlfriend I'd suspected he had. And you know what? She's always worked and still does! She's a waitress at the Road House restaurant."

"Don't worry," I said. "I wasn't feeling very sorry for him. How did your kids feel about it?"

"They were old enough that it didn't effect them too badly. They knew we hadn't been very happy together, and they were used to not seeing too much of their father when they were growing up. They were typical teenagers. They were thinking more about their own lives than what was happening with us. The twins had gotten scholarships and grants, so they were in college and having a good time. But they're good kids, too. Brian helped me a lot—he thought it was great that his old mom had gotten a job. I spent about a year and a half living on my own for the first time, and I was really getting to like it a lot. I was even starting to think about traveling a little bit. Tess told me about places she'd been, and I checked a lot of travel books out of the library." She got a far-off look on her face and was silent for a time.

I could guess what had stopped her from traveling. "How did you end up living with your mother again?"

"It started to become obvious that she shouldn't be living alone. I thought maybe Arthur would have her come live with him, but he and his wife weren't interested in that at all. And I was surprised that Mom didn't want it either. Arthur was always 'the good child' as far as she was concerned, but she didn't want to leave her house. So, even though she was angry at me for getting a divorce, everyone decided it would be best if I moved back in with her."

"Why in the world was she angry at you for the divorce?" My mother, who had adored my ex, was still really supportive when we'd divorced.

Rita shrugged her shoulders. "Oh, she told me it was all my fault. I should have stayed with Dan and done what he wanted. She's a little old-fashioned, shall we say? I wouldn't say she and my father were very happy together either, but she certainly wouldn't admit that. And she says she never would have dreamed of leaving him—or letting him leave."

"Your father's dead?" I asked gently.

"Um-hmm. He died several years ago. You know how people say you marry a man just like your father? It was sort of true with me. Dad was a heavy drinker, too.

When he wasn't drinking though, he and I had a good time together. But I'm afraid the drinking did him in."

I thought about my life with my parents. After listening to Rita, I realized I had nothing to complain about. I had nothing but good memories of my kind and gentle father. The pain was terrible for the teenager I had been when he died, and my mother had missed him greatly, but she and I had had a happy relationship, and we'd even gotten through my teenage rebellions with that relationship intact. I was hit with a strong pang of missing them both.

Neither of us spoke for some time, and I thought how I'd known Rita for such a short time, how our lives were so different, and how I supposed we didn't really have much in common, and yet we'd been able to talk to each other so freely.

We did have one very big connection, however: Tess.

Rita's chair was near the bookshelf, and she had put out her hand to idly trace circles in the dust layered on the tops of the books. I would have to do some dusting here. That would be a chore, but looking through the books would not. I loved books, which was certainly a plus in my profession, but I was convinced I would learn more about Tess by knowing what books she chose to own.

Rita's attention was caught by one of the books she had fingered, and she pulled it from the shelf. She wiped the dust with her sleeve and turned the book to its spine. "It's a library book." She handed it to me as she reached to pull two more from the shelf.

"Tess' death was really sudden, I take it. I guess…I guess I'll return these for her." What an odd feeling that was.

"It was sudden." Rita handed me the other two books—one was a mystery I had read some time ago and the other two were travel books. "She never complained about being sick, and I always thought of her as being remarkably healthy. But, if she were having problems, it would be like her not to say anything. I don't know if Toby knew she had heart problems, but I don't think so. He seemed shocked when she died."

"I'll have to look through and see if there are any other library books and take them back tomorrow. I suppose the librarian will be glad to get them back. He's—" I searched for an appropriate word. "He's interesting."

Rita chuckled. "Simon? He is interesting. And not bad to look at either. Living with my mother, I'm not supposed to notice those things, but I do. He's done great things with the library since he came back and took it over."

I was curious. "Came back? He mentioned something about having been gone a long time and coming back. Did he grow up here?"

"He was a couple of years ahead of me in school, so I didn't notice him too much. I had a big crush on one of his younger brothers when I was in fifth grade, though. He has two brothers and a sister. One of his brothers lives here, but the others left after going to college. Most people my age didn't escape—we stayed put. Simon is one of the few who went away and then came back."

"What made him come back?"

It was a fine little town, but I wasn't sure I could see what would lure someone back when they'd had a taste of the rest of the world. Unless Simon DeBerry was trying to escape from something out there.

"His wife died six or seven years ago. He has a little boy. I think he's about eight or nine. Maybe he wanted to be closer to his family again. I know his mother and father take care of Jacob when Simon's working."

"You know a bit about him, and you think he's nice-looking. You sure you don't have a crush on him now, instead of his brother?" I teased.

Rita laughed out loud. "Hardly. You'll find everybody knows a bit about everybody else here. Besides—" I was amazed to see her blush. "—if I were going to have a silly schoolgirl crush, it would be on someone else."

My eyes widened at her. "Anyone in particular?"

"No, not really...I mean...oh, for God's sake, I'm too old for this."

I wasn't sure whether to prod her any further, but I hoped there was someone out there who helped her get away from her mother from time to time.

"There is a guy who I hadn't ever thought about in...in that way, but he's been very nice to me lately. I keep getting the feeling he wants to ask me out, but I don't know that for sure. And besides, my mother would probably put a wrench into that really quick." Rita glanced at the watch on her wrist. "Oh, no," she said. "Speaking of my mother, my brother will be bringing her back any minute. I better get back."

Most women in their forties who had been married and had grown children didn't have to worry about their mothers putting wrenches into their possible love lives. I found myself wondering if Rita had ever dreamed of escaping completely from Newbridge.

I went to the kitchen to get Rita's casserole dish. After handing it to her, I followed her to the door to say goodnight. She held the doorknob in her hand and turned to me.

"Thanks, Kat. I hope it helps some to hear about Tess. It helps me to talk about her. And thanks for listening to all the other stuff, too. See you soon."

After she left, I returned to the living room and found Minette curled onto the still warm seat I had abandoned. "Social hour is over," I told her. "You missed it."

I gathered up the library books and set them on a spot on the shelf where I would see them in the morning. As I ran my hand absently over a row, my eyes scanned ahead and stopped suddenly as my brain registered what I was seeing. Dusty as they were, I would certainly know them anywhere. I had had thirteen books published so far, and as I pulled them out and counted in amazement, I saw that they were all here.

I didn't know what to think. I'd known nothing of her or her artwork, but Tess had obviously been keeping track of mine!

Chapter 3

The next day was Friday, and I woke to bright sunlight streaming through the bedroom window. I glanced at my little travel clock, and it digitally screamed at me that I had slept late. I was not used to sleeping until ten o'clock, but I'd had a restless night. No dreams, though. Part of my plans for the day had been to get up early and work on the painting I'd started, but now I would have to put that off. I wanted to get into town and see if I could catch Rowan home and then call the phone company.

When I went downstairs and into the kitchen, I found Minette sitting, staring at the back door as if she were trying to open it by sheer will. If I weren't in a minor hurry, I might have been tempted to wait it out and see if she could do it. But she meowed at me disgustedly, and I thought it best to let her out.

"Yeah, yeah, I slept late, so sue me," I said conversationally as I pulled the door open.

She declined to answer, and with her tail at full mast, she scooted out.

I drove the car this time since I had several errands to do. I would have to think about getting the Jeep checked out so I could take the rental back.

Once I was in town I tried calling Rowan first but got her answering machine. I left a message telling her I was fine, and I hoped to have a phone soon and would call and give her the number. Then I called the phone company, and when I finally was able to reach a human being instead of voice mail, I got him to agree to hook up a phone line for me early in the next week. Then I headed for the post office to let them know I was planning to receive mail at Tess' address. I should have known, in this town, that it was hardly necessary. The post office was a small, one-story, brick building and, as I stepped through the door, I heard my name called in greeting. This was one of Rita's workdays. A few people were checking their boxes and looked up as I returned Rita's greeting. She stood behind a wood-paneled counter sorting through a box of small packages. A stocky, balding man in his early sixties stood near her, and she introduced us.

"Ed, this is Kat Benson, my new neighbor. Kat, this is Ed Mason. He's the postmaster here. What can I do for you?" Ed nodded and moved away but not before I had noticed a look of curiosity in his eyes. No doubt he would quiz Rita after I left.

"I was wondering what I needed to do to have mail forwarded to me at the house. I still have my address in Seattle, so I don't exactly want a change of address."

"It's all taken care of," Rita informed me. "You now know people in high places. I already took care of it, and there's probably junk mail being placed in your mailbox as we speak."

I laughed and said, "Thanks. I think."

My next stop was the library, and then I would go to the little grocery before heading home. I would have to ask Rita where she went for groceries. People in Newbridge must have to travel to a bigger place for most of their shopping.

As I walked into the library, I was caught off guard. There at the circulation desk sat my stereotype: a gray-haired (in a bun, no less) woman with glasses perched on the end of her nose. She smiled at me curiously and then what looked like recognition lit her eyes.

Good grief, I thought *She probably does know who I am. I don't know if I can get used to this or not.*

I was about to set Tess' overdue books on the counter when the room was rocked by a peal of laughter from several occupants of the children's loft. I looked up and saw Simon with a book in his hand, surrounded by several munchkins. As he continued reading (very dramatically), the spontaneous howls of laughter kept erupting. And no wonder. It was one of the best readings of Roald Dahl's wonderfully disgusting *Revolting Rhymes* I'd ever heard. He obviously knew his audience. I was willing to bet there were no sweet-little-fuzzy-animal stories in the pile of books for this crowd. I smiled to myself and turned back to the woman at the desk.

I tried to modulate my voice so as not to disturb the reading, but the raucous laughter made it impossible to speak softly.

The woman chuckled and fairly shouted in my ear, "Unless you're in a big hurry, you might want to wait if you have a question. Story hour's almost over."

I nodded and headed for the periodical section. It was always interesting to find out what magazines a library carried.

In a short time, the laughter turned to shouts, and the not surprisingly loud sound of child-size feet pounded down the loft steps. The noise didn't stop for some time as the crowd gathered up books and then individuals pushed and shoved their way to be at the head of the line for checking them out. A few mothers attempted to hold them in check, but enthusiasm was high. Simon picked his way through the group, lifting a child here and there high into the air and setting them back down again, making all of the children squeal with glee as he did so. He finally found his way behind the desk and began helping the older woman with the checkout. As the last book was finding its way into a backpack, the crowd had thinned considerably. The noise factor had lessened by several decibels, and I thought, *There's one more stereotype dispelled.* I never once heard Simon or the gray-haired woman say, "Shh!"

51

"Well, that was a happy crowd." From where I was standing I could see the woman hand some books to Simon.

"I'll say," he replied. Then he saw me. "Hi. Nice to see you back. I hope that little bit of noise didn't scare you off from coming in and talking to us about your books."

I snickered inwardly at the idea that it had been a "little bit" of noise. "Not at all," I replied. "I like an enthusiastic audience." He laughed at that as I carried Tess' books to the counter. "I discovered these last night in Tess' bookcase. I thought I should bring them back. Can you tell if she had any others out, and I'll look for them if she did?"

The woman looked at me with interest as Simon brought Tess' record up on the computer screen. "Nope. There are three of them there? That looks like it. Thanks for bringing them back. I'm sure that would make Tess happy if she knew you brought them in. She used the library a lot but never had an overdue book." Well, there was another thing she and I didn't have in common.

A boy, who had stayed behind in the loft, started down the steps, and the creaking made us all look up. He looked to be about nine or ten with round, horned-rimmed glasses, cropped brown hair, and a happy, mischievous look that seemed permanently set on his face.

"Hey, Jake. C'mere, sport," Simon called to him. "I want you to meet someone." The boy obliged. "Remember all the books by Katrina Benson we've read?"

"Yep," he said profoundly.

"Well, this is Katrina Benson." Simon gestured to me, and Jake turned intelligent eyes my way.

"Cool," he said. I thought perhaps he could only speak in one-syllable sentences. But then he opened up. "We used to read lots of them when I was little. I used to make my dad read the one about the troll who wanted to be a knight over and over. And the last one you wrote about Japanese-American kids who had to go live in camps during World War II was sort of sad, but a good one. I like that you write for older kids, too. Where did you learn about the kids in the camps?"

That was considerably more than one syllable. "It happened to parents of a friend of mine where I grew up," I told him.

"Where's that?"

"Seattle, Washington. My friend's parents lived on a farm about fifty miles from there, and when the war broke out, they and their families had to leave until the war was over. The book is really about them, and the pictures of the children in the book are their grandchildren—my friend's children."

"Wow," Jake said, reverting back to single syllables.

Simon took over. "This is my son, Jacob. Jake to his friends."

"You can call me Jake."

I considered that generous for a nine or ten-year-old boy. "And you can call me Kat. Nice to meet you, Jake."

"And this is my mother, Ruth DeBerry. Remember, I told you I was shameless about recruiting volunteers?"

The woman's eyes crinkled as she tried to look sternly at Simon, but the stern just wasn't working. "It's true. He has a whole flock of volunteers to do his bidding, including his poor old mother."

"Oh, Grams, you love it." Jake rolled his eyes. "And besides, he doesn't make you work half as hard as he does me."

"Yes, but I pay you, remember? A fairly generous allowance, by my reckoning." Simon placed a hand on the top of his son's head and turned him in the direction of the back of the library. "Go unload that cart of books in the back room for me, please."

"I want a raise," Jake mumbled, but I saw the grin on his face deepen as he shuffled away.

"Yeah, well, good luck with that," his father shot after him.

This was not the atmosphere I'd encountered in any library I'd been in before.

Simon seemed to read my thoughts. "We all get a little rowdy after story hour, but it is quiet at times, honestly."

"I'll keep that in mind," I said. "If I'm into heavy duty research, I'll come another time, but if I want to have a good time, I'll come at story hour."

"Do that," he said, and his eyes held mine for a minute until I looked away.

Whoa, what was that? I wondered. Could he actually have been flirting with me, and in front of his mother, yet? *Come on, Kat, get a grip*, I told myself. *It's time to find your-self something meaningful to do if you actually think some-one's using library story time to flirt with you.*

After I left the library, I headed to the grocery. I passed a few people on the sidewalk, most of whom looked at me intently and then turned away when I caught their eyes. I didn't think much of it though until I entered the grocery and got the same treatment from the occupants of the store. I heard a few people whisper softly to each other and couldn't help but feel a tad paranoid, but I tried smiling tentatively at one or two. I got a quick smile back from one woman, but she hurried on, filling her little hand basket with items. I'd heard stories about people being unfriendly to outsiders in small towns, but so far, with the exception of Harriet Sloan, the few people I had met had been very nice to me. And even Harriet had changed her tune in that odd way after the first few minutes of talking to her. So this reaction now left me wondering if I was encountering the small town phenomenon or that the grapevine had worked very quickly and these people knew I had inherited the Whitney house.

Was Tess' reputation for being different part of my inheritance? I caught myself thinking that there could be worse traits to be passed on, but I wasn't all that certain these people would agree.

For the first time since I'd arrived, I was feeling un-comfortable around other people. I gathered the things I needed hastily and brought them to the single counter at the front of the store. The tall man in the apron who waited on me did smile briefly and that put me a little at ease. If I was going to stay here for any length of time, I didn't want to have to feel this way, and perhaps feeling a bit too reckless, I decided

I could at least give everyone something to talk about. No one was in line behind me so I caught the clerk's eye.

"Hi. My name's Kat Benson. I'm staying at the Whitney house for a while. This is a very nice town. I'd never been here before." I flashed my teeth at him.

I'd broken the ice. Now it was his turn. "Nice to meet you," he managed to say. "Are you renting the place?"

Okay, Tess, I thought. *You're not here to defend yourself, and maybe this isn't fair, but might as well stir things up a bit, I always say.*

"No, it belongs to me now. Tess left it to me. She was my mother." I wasn't sure if that would make me more or less of an outsider, but it certainly did make the already quiet store even quieter. I took my change from the clerk's hand, smiled brilliantly at everyone who was looking my way, and walked out.

I spent the afternoon back up in the attic going through more of the family treasures. I let my attention wander where it would, rather than being very systematic. This was the sort of thing that would capture Rowan's imagination, and I thought of how much fun this might be really getting into these things with her. How odd to think that this was part of her heritage, too. A part that had been denied to her, also, but rather than stew over it, she would be fascinated.

I found the usual trappings that families stored away, but the difference between these trappings and what I was used to was that these went back probably a couple of hundred years. My breath caught as I opened one old oak trunk that was full of clothes from different eras. I lifted some out very carefully and held a couple of dresses out to examine better. It was like looking at a wardrobe of theater costumes except that these weren't replicas—these were the real things. Some of the material seemed very fragile, but most of the articles were in remarkably good condition. I replaced the things

I had pulled out gently and closed the lid. This would definitely be a big hit with Rowan. When she flew out, and if Keisha came with her, I knew she would have all three of us trying on every item as soon as she saw this. I found two more trunks of clothes and wondered if some of these shouldn't be in a museum. Rita had said most attics in Newbridge were full of old things. I supposed it wasn't as big a deal to people who had lived their whole lives surrounded by the history their ancestors had left behind.

Late in the afternoon, I made my way back down the stairs with every intention of going into the studio. However, as I glanced out the window from the second floor landing, I caught a glimpse of Minette emerging from the ground near the corner of the house. That seemed so strange a picture in my mind that I decided to go investigate. When I got to the spot, Minette had walked away but now came bounding back to my side. A slanted wooden door covered a mound beside the house and I saw that rotted boards had created a hole just large enough for a cat to squeeze through. It occurred to me that this must lead to a cellar. I hadn't even thought of the likelihood of a cellar under the old house. The houses I had lived in had been built on foundations but had not had full cellars. I also hadn't seen a door inside this house leading to one. Thinking how odd that was, I lifted the door carefully and peered down the stone steps before me. I could see very little in the darkness beyond the steps so I hurried to the car to find the flashlight I had placed in the glove compartment.

The stone walls in the large room I found below the stairs were cool but dry. Partially lining the walls were several tall shelves, some filled with glass jars. I shone the light on them and read several labels telling me they were different kinds of preserves. I assumed Tess had canned these. Other than a few more food items you'd expect to find in cool storage, there was very little else to be found. I shone the flashlight over the walls several times but found neither a light switch nor another door.

I was startled out of my exploration by something brushing against my leg. I stifled an exclamation and then let it out when I saw it was Minette. "Way to go," I told her. "Scare me half to death. You enjoy doing that, don't you?" I played the light around the room one more time and then climbed back up the short flight of stairs to the welcome light outside.

As I walked to the back door of the house, it occurred to me that Tess had indeed been an unusually tidy person. The house had been exceedingly clean, other than dust and cobwebs that had obviously made their way into it after she had died. She seemed to have very few personal items except for her artwork and supplies and books. I mentally checked off each of the rooms I had seen and could remember very few knickknacks. There was no television or VCR and no computer other than the one I had brought with me. There were two bathrooms, one each on the first and second floors. There had been soap and towels and extra toilet paper but few items in the medicine cabinets above each of the sinks. In fact, I didn't remember seeing even a comb or brush.

And then the most odd thing of all struck me. Surely the room I was sleeping in had been Tess' room. But I had seen no clothes in the closet or dresser.

After entering the house, I hurried up the stairs to the second floor and looked in each bedroom to be sure I hadn't missed seeing the clothes in one of them.

Nothing.

Where could they have gone? The only person I could possibly think of who might know would be Rita. I would ask her the first chance I got.

That night I went to bed with a hundred thoughts swirling in my head. No wonder, then, that I awoke in a sweat, my heart again pounding and the images of the recurring dream refusing to leave my mind. I glanced at my clock glowing in the dark. Three o'clock. I knew it was useless to try to go back to sleep so, slipping my feet into a pair of shoes, I headed down to the studio. Might as well work on the painting while the images were fresh.

Though I was barely aware of her, Minette kept me company through the rest of the night as I worked feverishly, not stopping until well after dawn. I stepped back and yawned loudly as I pushed hair out of my eyes. The painting was completed.

Leaving it there, I left to crawl back into bed, barely able to get my shoes off and let my head touch the pillow before dropping soundly into sleep.

This time it was my stomach that woke me. Hunger helped push the grogginess away, and I dressed quickly and headed to the kitchen. I made myself eat before I set foot in the studio. The painting sat on the easel, and I stood for a long time just looking at it. Why was I having this dream? It had been easy to paint because it was more vivid than any other dream I ever remembered having.

But where was it coming from?

I could see no connection between it and this house or even Tess. Now that I'd seen a likeness of her, I knew that none of the faces of the women in the dream were hers. A connection was there. I could feel it, but I was no closer to knowing what that connection was than I had been the first time I'd dreamed it. I knew I was hoping the painting would help somehow.

I took it from the easel and carried it into the living room. I placed it on the mantel and then left it there. But for the rest of the day, I slipped in and out of the room to peek at it. I believed that there was always a meaning to our dreams. I would get to the bottom of this one somehow.

I spent the rest of the weekend in a slight fog. I did not go back into Newbridge, instead finding enough to occupy my time at the house. On Sunday, I spent most of the time out of doors. I walked in the meadow and pasture and snooped in the barn, with Minette as my almost constant companion. I was not surprised to find the barn in clean condition as far as barns go. There was not much there—a few items of horse tack and old straw bales that must have been left over from the days

Rita had described. There were bowls near the door where I supposed Rita had been feeding the cat.

Back outside, a short distance from the barn door, I noted a large metal barrel with a lid on it, and it dawned on me that I was looking at a burn barrel. I realized I would have to figure out what to do with the trash. In Seattle, I was so used to the trash and recycling being picked up that I barely thought about it. Another thing to ask Rita about.

Well, no time like the present, I thought and headed toward the path leading to the woods where I had seen Rita come out that day. If I hadn't been in the slight fog from my lack of sleep, I might have considered this a foolish undertaking. I had no idea what Rita's house looked like or whether it was just through the woods or several houses away. But I didn't think it was too far if Harriet walked to what was now my house. Worse case scenario...I'd have gotten a walk in.

The path through the trees was well-beaten and, as it turned out, led me straight to my destination. Rita was weeding in a good-sized garden filled with vegetables and a rainbow assortment of flowers. The path left the woods very near the garden, which was on the south side of a large house not very different from Tess' except that this house was painted white with green trim. It was a fine-looking house, but I actually preferred the weathered boards of my own. Was I developing a loyalty to the Whitney house already? How curious.

Rita saw me and raised a hand in greeting. Removing an old pair of gloves, she dusted the earth from her jeans and rose to meet me. "Hi. You found your way through okay I see."

"It was a nice day to go for a walk, so I thought I'd head this way and see if I could find your place." I searched for a sign of hesitancy on her face at having me show up at her home, but I found none.

"This is it. A bit isolated, but not any more than yours. There are ten acres here, same as yours. I loved it as a kid. The woods are actually half on our land and half on yours."

We stood chatting for a few minutes, and then Rita asked if I'd like to come in for some lemonade. When I accepted, she looked slightly sheepish and said, "The house isn't as clean as it could be. I'd much rather clean up the garden than the house."

"Don't worry about it," I told her. "I'm not used to a very clean house myself. The condition of Tess' house was a complete shock to me. Except for the studio, it was practically spotless. Did she really keep it that way?"

Rita had not moved toward the house. Perhaps Harriet was home, and she didn't want to talk about Tess within her hearing. Fair enough. Neither did I.

"Tess was a very neat housekeeper. I always thought she had just enough things to make her house interesting but not enough to make any clutter. I always liked that about her place, but I'm afraid it's not the way I am. Between my mother and me, this place is packed."

"That's the way I am, too." I was exaggerating slightly, but this seemed like a good time to get to the point. "But Rita, you said Tess' death was sudden. Was she at home when she died? I didn't even see a dish out of place when I arrived. Only the dust that would have accumulated after she was gone."

Rita's eyes looked momentarily haunted. "She was at home. Toby called me because he hadn't been able to get a hold of her on the phone so I went over." She was quiet for a brief time. "I found her in a chair in the living room. She was already gone."

"I'm sorry," I whispered. "I had no idea."

"I called the police and an ambulance right away. Of course, it was too late. Later the doctor told me it was heart failure."

"They did an autopsy?" I questioned.

"No. They saw no reason to. They must have found enough signs because they were certain." Rita looked at me. "The next day, I went over and straightened up the house— what little there was to do. She had some dishes and a kettle of soup I'd made for her out on the table. I know it sounds silly, but I kept thinking she'd be mortified that she'd died without cleaning up, so I did it for her. Then I locked up the house and didn't go back in again until the other day. Not even to feed Minette. I guess I should give you the key. I'd forgotten about it."

"No, go ahead and keep it—if I lose mine, I'll know there's another one I can get. But Rita, I was just wondering, did you do something with Tess' clothes? Give them to a charity or something?"

Rita appeared slightly defensive. "No, why? I wouldn't have touched her clothes."

"There aren't any there." When she looked perplexed, I went on. "I mean, nothing. I just realized yesterday that I hadn't seen any. Not in any of the closets or dressers in any of the rooms. It seemed odd, and I thought maybe they'd been given away."

"I don't understand," she said. "I really didn't touch them. And I can't think of anyone else who would have. You really didn't find anything?"

I shook my head. Her surprise seemed sincere. Besides, there was no reason for her to lie about it. She'd had no idea I existed, and I thought she must know me well enough at least to realize that I would have understood if she had given any of Tess' clothing to charity. "A little mystery." I tried to keep it light. "On top of all the rest of the mysteries of Tess' life. Never mind. It's not a big deal." Maybe it wasn't a big deal, but it would nag at me. I knew it would, just like the dream.

We did go into the house then for the lemonade and, though I was prepared for the worst, the house was not the mess I was expecting. True, there was very little empty space, but for the most part, it was pleasant, homey clutter. I wouldn't have necessarily expected this of Harriet, but it didn't surprise me about Rita.

As we sat at the kitchen table sipping the cold lemonade, Harriet came into the room. She showed no surprise at seeing me there, and I suspected that she had watched my arrival through a window. I also suspected that not much slipped past her. She smiled at me and pulled a chair out for herself at the end of the table.

61

"Rita, I'd like some lemonade, too, please." Rita got up to do her bidding, whether from force of habit or because it was just easier that way, I didn't know. Harriet turned back to me. "How are you? It's a beautiful Sunday, isn't it?"

"It is," I replied. "A good day to take a little walk."

"A good day for church, too." She kept on smiling, but I knew that had been aimed as a rebuke at me. "You weren't there." Rebuke confirmed. "Maybe you go to a different church. Which one do you belong to?"

"Mother...." Rita placed a glass in front of her, spilling a bit of lemonade on the table as she did.

"Actually, Harriet, I don't belong to a church. Spirituality is a personal thing for me, and I observe it in my own way." I hoped that would be enough to say, but, of course, it wasn't.

"Ah." A pause. "So what does that mean?"

"Mom, come on," Rita pleaded. "Kat just came over to visit for a minute. It means what she just said...it's personal."

Harriet didn't even look at her daughter. "Rita's so afraid of offending anyone. But I was just being friendly. Church certainly doesn't hurt anyone, even when they don't think they belong. Why don't you come with us next week? You might like it, dear."

"I'll think about it," I told her noncommittally.

I'd begun to believe that Harriet had a completely one-track mind, but she surprised me over the next hour that I was in her home by changing the subject and telling me about some of the history of the area. Her knowledge went back quite a ways and, of course, she knew which families had been here a fair amount of time and which ones were new-comers—only having lived here a generation or two. Rita and I had no chance to visit, but I actually found what Harriet had to say fascinating.

When she'd apparently felt she'd passed on enough history, Harriet abruptly shoved her chair back. "Well, thanks for coming to visit, dear. Come again some time. Why don't you meet us here at 9:30 next Sunday, and you can ride to church with us?" The woman just never gave up.

After she left the room, I stood up, preparing to leave. Rita looked slightly uncomfortable. "I'm sorry, Kat. That's just the way she is."

"Rita, stop apologizing for everything. I really enjoyed listening to your mother talk about Newbridge. And who knows, if it keeps her quiet about it, maybe I'll go to church with her one Sunday." I paused. "She wouldn't expect me to go every week, would she?"

Rita stifled a laugh. "No doubt. She can be relentless, you know."

I was sure she could be. "Well, I'll worry about that later. You were wrong about your house, by the way. It's a lovely home."

"Thanks." I could tell she was pleased that I had said that. I wondered if she was used to more criticism than compliments. Despite my own confused feelings about Tess, I was glad that she had been kind to this woman.

Rita followed me out the door, heading back to her garden. "Are you going to be home for a few minutes tonight?" she asked me.

"I'm not planning to go anywhere. I'm tired, so I thought I'd try to get to bed early. Why?"

"I didn't get to show you the pictures that Tess did for me. I just thought I could bring a couple by to show you. But if you're tired, I can wait for another time."

"No, that would be nice. Why don't you come by about 7:00?"

When Rita arrived that evening, I was in the living room, rummaging through Tess' books. I found some that I would have expected from what I had learned about her so far. There were many wonderfully illustrated books on herbs, and I found myself curiously interested in finding out more. I would at least like to identify some of the plants growing profusely around the outside of the house. I was surprised, but perhaps shouldn't have been, to find archeological books of all kinds, most interestingly, ones by Marija Gimbutas and Buffie Johnson on theories of Goddess cultures. There were several books on different periods in history, particularly seventeenth-century England. There were also several children's books besides the ones I had written, and many books of fiction of all kinds. There were titles I knew, and a great number that I didn't. I looked forward to reading my way through them.

I had pulled out one of the books on herbs when I heard the knock at the door. "Come in, Rita," I called. I looked up as she stood in the doorframe to the living room. "Hi. I was just looking through Tess' bookshelf. There are some real treasures here."

Rita looked at the book in my hand. "She read a lot. She had a wonderful voice for reading, too. I used to love it when she read to me."

I was speechless for a moment. It struck me once again how loving Tess had been to this other person—treating her almost as a daughter. Then a new thought hit me. I'd been thinking rather selfishly. I had assumed Tess had given up her own baby daughter because, for whatever reason, she didn't want her—me. But perhaps, just perhaps, she had found this other little girl who needed her because she missed the little girl she had given up.

All right, Tess, I vowed. *One way or another, I'm going to find out what happened.*

I pointed to the pictures I saw in Rita's arms. "Are these of your children?" I asked.

She laid them on one of the chairs and held up the top one to show me. "There's one here of all three of my kids when they were little and one when they were all teenagers. They didn't spend a lot of time here, but enough so I think Tess really captured what they were like." It was easy to see which one was the young man from the gas station in these pictures. Without knowing him, I still had to agree that Tess had captured something that was more than just the way Brian looked. There was a certain tilt to his head that conveyed the friendliness I'd encountered. And, as Rita had described it, there was that silly little grin. The twins looked more reserved, but that could have just been the age they had been at the time. All three bore a strong resemblance to Rita.

"This one is a watercolor Tess did for me when I was about twelve. It's of the two horses she had that I loved so much, but she put them in a wild setting. This has always been one of my favorites." I reached to take the painting from her hands, and as I gazed at it, she moved to put the two pictures of her children back on the chair. I could see why she counted this as one of her favorites. It was wonderful.

Suddenly, I heard a sharp intake of breath and looked to Rita to see what was wrong. She was staring at the fireplace. "Kat!" she exclaimed. "Where did you find it?"

I wondered what she was talking about. "Find what?"

"The painting. Tess' painting. I haven't seen it in a long time. I wondered what she did with it." I followed her eyes to the mantle. She was looking straight at the painting of my dream.

"I don't know what you mean, Rita. That's a painting I just finished yesterday."

"It can't be." She moved to the mantle to get a better look. Then she swung back around to me. "I don't believe this. I can see now, the difference, but it's only in style. It looks just like the picture Tess kept over the fireplace, see?" She lifted the painting and it fit perfectly over the darkened spot on the wall. "It's even the same size. And you've got all the women, and the same number of men, and the man on horseback. I always thought the sea was beautiful but scary in her picture, but the tree the women were around always caught my attention first. And yours looks just the same as Tess'. She wouldn't tell me much about the picture, but she had a title for it and I figured it must be from a book." She looked back at me in amazement. "You both read the same book. What was it? I'd love to read it."

My throat went dry. "It wasn't from a book," I said hoarsely. "Rita, tell me, what was the title she gave it?"

Rita turned her perplexed look back to the canvas on the mantle. "She called it *Dream of the Circle of Women*."

Chapter 4

Thank goodness the next few days were busy ones for me or I might have gone half mad thinking about the fact that Tess and I had each painted the same dream. For surely that's what her title had meant. She had had the same dream. But how was that possible? The first explanation that came to mind was not one I was ready to contemplate, so I buried myself, instead, in work. I didn't know if it was my mind's defense mechanism that had chiseled away at the writer's block or if the painting had unlocked something inside of me, but I suddenly became as prolific as I had been previously blocked. Ideas flew through my mind and by the end of the week, I had several sketches and outlines for stories completed. This would make my agent very happy.

The phone company was not nearly so quick as it had led me to believe it would be, and so it wasn't until the next Friday that a line was hooked up and a phone working again in Tess' house. In the meantime, I had gone to the library twice to use the Internet and check my e-mail. I was looking forward to hearing Rowan's voice on the phone, but sending e-mail back and forth helped to assure me all was well with her. Several friends had also sent messages demanding to know if I was surviving without some of the things they considered necessities. My responses were brief, but I let them know that I hadn't died yet of the lack of a Seattle latte, the symphony orchestra, or the sight of Mount Rainier on a clear day. Not only that, but I wasn't even in withdrawal from no television, phone, or Internet provider. I wasn't going to push my luck, though. Thankfully, the library was providing the means of communication for now, and the phone was coming soon.

The first day I had gone to the library that week, it had been a busy place, and it took me some time to get my turn at a computer. Never at a loss for things to do at a library, this was not a problem. I spent the time happily doing research for one of my story ideas. When I had finished with the computer, I headed for the desk to check out a few books. Simon was just giving instructions to a young woman who I assumed to be another volunteer before he turned to me. The corners of his mouth turned up when he saw me, and I thought, *I really like his smile.*

"How are things going at your new, old place?" He scanned the barcodes from the cover pages into the computer.

"Fine," I said. "I'm still getting used to the house, and I'm waiting to get the phone in so I came in to use the Internet here. I'm glad you have it."

"Installing computers and automating the system was my first big project when I came to this library. I'm happy we've got things you can use."

I glanced at him to see if he was teasing me. I supposed it was okay if he was. I wondered if I'd ever get over being the big city person here.

Simon handed my books over. "By the way, I hear you stirred things up a bit at Harvey's the other day."

"Harvey's?" I questioned.

"The grocery store." His grin deepened as it dawned on me what he was talking about, but he lowered his voice for the next words. "It was probably smart of you to just drop a bomb like that. There would have been a lot of conjecture, and the stories would have gotten more and more wild until somebody found out the truth. But Tess really was your mother?"

I looked straight into his eyes to see if there was a trace of mockery there, but I could find only kindness reflected back at me. "Yes. I didn't know anything about her until she died and I was notified that she'd left me the house. It's been very strange, and I have a lot of questions that I haven't gotten answers to. I'm not sure why I dropped the bomb—as you put it—but, I don't know, things were feeling a little unfriendly or I was feeling a wee bit paranoid and I just did it. I don't know why I did it, or why I'm telling you this." At the moment I was feeling just a wee bit confused.

"It sounds like a very Tess-like thing to do, actually. She would have given them something to talk about and then just walked away, too. At least that's the way I heard it happened." That last was almost a question, but I didn't answer it.

Instead, something he said had caught my attention. "You said it was a Tess-like thing to do. Did you know her very well?"

Simon placed his hands on the desk and took a second before he answered. "Not really well. I barely knew her at all when I was growing up. Just who she was, like everyone knows everyone else here. But she came into the library a lot after I moved back, and we talked quite a bit. I'd say we got to be friends. Not close friends. I don't think she got close to many people besides Toby and Rita, but I learned to appreciate her a whole lot more than I had as a kid." He laughed. "And vice versa. I think she considered me as a friend, too."

I wanted to ask him more, but other people came to the check out behind me. I could see that Simon wanted to say more also, but this just wasn't the time. "Thanks. I'd like to talk to you more about this some time," I said as I picked up the books from the counter.

"Any time," he told me.

I went to the library again on Thursday, and Simon greeted me as I walked through the door. I got the distinct impression that he had been waiting for me. I smiled but did not stop to talk first, instead heading straight for the vacant computer. There was something about the man that made me slightly uncomfortable, though I didn't understand what it was. That I found him attractive had nothing to do with it. I was sure of that. Really.

This trip was solely to check and send e-mail. I would have liked to ask Simon more about Tess, but this was just too public a place. It would have to be some time when there was no one else in the library—whenever that might be. I closed my e-mail and stood up to leave. I had not heard anyone walk near me, so I was startled when I nearly collided with Simon.

He put out a hand to steady me. "Sorry. I didn't mean to startle you."

"You did startle me. I mean…it's all right. I guess I was lost in what I'd been doing."

He looked at me thoughtfully. "I just wanted to say that I've been feeling our conversation the other day wasn't finished. About Tess, I mean. It's hard to talk here. If you'd like to continue it, we could meet somewhere. LaRoue's has good coffee. It's the little restaurant just across the bridge."

The expression on his face was sincere. He seemed only to be offering me a chance to talk about Tess with a bit more privacy. I was relieved. Or at least, I thought I was. I needed no complications at the moment.

"Thanks. I appreciate that. The only people I've talked to so far at all about Tess are Rita Lawrence and her mother. I'd like a chance to hear more from someone else who knew her."

"Rita probably knew her the best. She's a good person to talk to. You wouldn't get quite the same perspective from her mother." He said that seriously, but it made me laugh.

"Yes, I know. But maybe by hearing several people talk about her, I'll begin to get more of a whole picture of Tess. I really do appreciate that you're willing to talk to me about her. When's a good time to meet?"

"I close early at 4:00 on Fridays. I could be there by 4:15 if that works for you." He quirked his eyebrows to make it a question.

"I'll see you then." As I left, I briefly wondered if there would be people at the restaurant who would whisper when I entered there. The incident at the grocery had shaken me a little. But, if I was going to stay in Newbridge for any length of time, I would have to get used to the people and they'd have to get used to me. Let them whisper. I wouldn't hide. I'd never get the answers I was looking for if I did.

My telephone was in and working by three o'clock on Friday. Since it would be lunchtime back in the Pacific Northwest, meaning I had a good chance of catching Rowan at home, I gave the phone a test drive.

"Hello?" Rowan's cheerful voice answered the third ring.

"Hi, Sweetie, it's me."

"Hey, Mom! You got your phone in? Tell me all about the place. Your e-mails aren't long on detail. Not what I'd expect from a writer, you know."

"You get what you pay for," I joked. "All my details go into my books. I did get the phone in just now. You're my first call. Will that make up for the lack of detail?"

"As long as I get it now. What's it like there?"

I described the house to her in all the detail she'd asked for. When I told her about the attic and its contents, she was as exuberant as I knew she would be. She could hardly wait to get here to check it all out for herself.

"What have you found out about Grandmama? Have you discovered any other deep dark secrets of hers? What do people say she was like?" Rowan had never been lacking in the question department.

"I'm not sure I like being considered a deep, dark secret," I teased her but immediately became serious. Of course, it was accurate as far as Tess had been concerned. "I haven't found out too much. There's a woman named Rita who's a neighbor near my age who grew up spending a lot of time with Tess, so I've been talking to her. I get one picture from her, and then there's Rita's mother who has a whole different take on the woman. She didn't like her at all."

"Ooo…that sounds intriguing. Why not?"

"Well…." What to say over the phone? "I'll tell you more when you come, but Harriet, Rita's mother, is kind of an interesting old character. She's really religious, and apparently Tess didn't share her sense of religion. In fact, Rowan, both of them say Tess was—I know you'll love this—they say Tess was a witch. To Rita, that was a good thing. To her mother, that made Tess all bad."

"Whoa! Are you serious? You're kidding, right?" Though she was more than three thousand miles away, I could tell Rowan was sitting on the edge of her seat.

"No, I'm not kidding." I told her basically what Rita had told me. "But that's only two people. I'm meeting with someone else who knew her in a little bit."

"Who's that?"

"The local librarian." I offered no more than that about the librarian. "Apparently she was close to a man named Toby, too, but he's traveling somewhere right now. I heard he'll be back in September. I'll definitely be talking to him."

"Mom, what is it?" Rowan could usually tell when I was holding something back. "There was something more in your voice when you mentioned Toby."

"I don't know, Rowan. I just think he might have a lot more to tell me when I meet him. It sounds like maybe he knew her better than anybody." I didn't tell her of my suspicions about my paternity. There was really nothing to base those suspicions on yet.

"Well, I want to know more about the witch thing. Grandmama is beginning to sound like she was an interesting person. Have you come across anything witchy at the house?"

I knew what she meant by that. "There are some books here you'll find interesting. And she obviously loved herbs. They're growing all over around the outside of the house and there are dried bunches hanging in the kitchen."

"A green witch!" Rowan said happily. "I wish I'd met her."

"So do I," I said dryly, "but she made that impossible. I want to find out why. I'm beginning to feel she must have had a good reason for giving me up."

"Why do you say that?"

"I don't know. I just feel it. And there is something else, Rowan. Something really strange." I hesitated.

"What is it?" she prompted.

"I told you about the dream I had before coming here? The one about the circle of women?"

"Yeah, you had it twice. Have you had it again?"

"Two more times. But that's not all. I made a painting of it. And when Rita saw it, she thought it was one that Tess had done. She told me she hadn't seen it for a long time, but that it was the exact same scene." I waited for her response.

"Okay, Mom, that does it. I'm getting there as soon as I can. This is fascinating. Keisha can't get away until the second week in September, but if I can get off work any earlier, I'm coming first and she can come when she's done."

"I'll be glad whenever you can come," I told her. "I have to go now. It's almost time to meet the person I told you about. Say hi to Keisha for me. Talk to you soon."

After we hung up, I gathered up my wallet and keys and headed for the car. Minette was sitting on the porch rail as I swept down the steps, and she meowed at me as I passed her but she didn't move. "Goodbye to you, too," I called and got into the car.

I parked the car in the lot next to the restaurant and looked it over for a minute before getting out. It wasn't an impressive building—one story with a porch and old, faded shingles covering the outside walls. But it was in a good location, just above the river. I was a few minutes early, so I entered and headed straight for an empty table by a window. It was a good choice. The window looked out over the river, which was moving rapidly, and to the trees beyond its bank. The scene captured my imagination and, of course, my thoughts turned to painting it. I was caught up in the different shades of color that would go into such a deceptively simple view until I was brought back by a female voice.

"What can I get you?" The waitress wore a yellow uniform, the color of which was greatly overshadowed by her bright red hair. The scarlet lipstick she wore was the only thing that could possibly have overshadowed her hair.

"Just coffee, please. Although you might wait a minute. I'm meeting someone else here shortly."

She nodded and left without saying anything further. I looked around and saw that there were only a few other customers. A man and a woman sat on stools at a long wooden bar, and two other tables were occupied. The man and woman had been looking at me as the waitress walked away, but quickly turned back to the bar when they saw my eyes move their way.

Out of the corner of my eye, I noticed someone come through the door and I turned to see if it was Simon. A rare, familiar face shot a smile my way and, empty coffee mug in hand, the young man altered his course from the counter to my table. His mother was right: he did have a silly little grin, and I was happy to see it.

"Hi," he said, placing his empty hand on the back of the chair opposite me. "Remember me? I'm Brian, from the gas station. My mom told me about you. How's it going?"

"Fine, thanks, Brian." He had obviously walked over from work for a coffee break—he had greasy coveralls on—although not the same ones. The pocket on this one was embroidered with the name Tom. Today, most of his dark hair was covered with a cap with the brim turned backwards. "Rita's told me a little about you, too. It's really nice having her as a neighbor."

"It was weird for her to find out that you were Tess' daughter," he said with the bluntness of youth.

"Probably not any weirder than it was for me," I said and then could have bitten my tongue. "I was adopted and didn't know about Tess until after her death." I wondered how many times I was going to be repeating this. "I appreciate that your mom has been helping me to get to know a little bit about her."

Brian's grin faded only slightly. "Mom really liked Tess. And no matter how strange people say she was, Tess was a nice lady. I hear you met Grandma, too."

"I did." Fortunately, I was spared of having to think of what to add to that as Simon strode toward the table. He greeted us both and started to pull out a chair for himself. "I'm sorry," I said. "Brian, would you like to sit with us?"

I was relieved when he declined, saying that he had just stepped in to fill his coffee cup and had to get right back to work. I liked the friendly way he had about him, but right now I wanted to interview one person at a time about Tess. I turned to Simon and wondered how to start, but he did it for me.

"Haven't ordered yet? This isn't the coffee capital that Seattle is, but for a plain old cup of coffee, they do it really well here."

"That's good to know," I said. "Although it would be blasphemous to admit this in Seattle. I'm not actually a coffee aficionado. I can drink just about anybody's coffee."

As if on cue, the waitress returned, and this time the scarlet mouth formed the ghost of a smile. Was I a little more respectable now that I'd been seen with two long-time residents? Quit being so paranoid, I chided myself, and to make up for it I smiled brightly back at her. We ordered the coffee, and after unsuccessfully trying to talk us into dessert to go with it, the waitress walked away.

"Did you get your telephone in?" Simon asked.

"I did, just before I came. I had just enough time to call my daughter first, before coming here."

"Is she back in Seattle?"

"Um hmm." I picked up the spoon in my place setting and absently fingered it. "Her name is Rowan, and she's working at a bookstore for the summer, but she's about to go into her junior year as a music major at the University of Washington."

"Really?" He seemed genuinely interested. "What instrument?"

"Cello. And she's very good at it." I couldn't help bragging a little.

"I bet she is. I managed to get Jake interested in fiddle a year ago, so he and I have fun sounding bad together. Do you play an instrument?"

"I've played piano since I was six. If I hadn't known practically from the beginning of my memory that I wanted to be an artist and a writer, I might have been more serious about

74

music. I've gotten to accompany Rowan all these years—that's always fun. And I bet you and Jake don't sound all that bad."

His eyes twinkled as he said, "Oh, we do. Trust me. But we have a great time. Mostly laughing." Then he turned slightly more serious. "Is there still a piano at Tess' house?"

I looked at him in surprise. "There is an old piano. I've barely touched it, but I thought I'd get it tuned before Rowan and her friend, Keisha, come to visit so I could play some music with them. But how did you know? Have you been to the house?"

"No." Simon studied his hands for a second and then looked back at me. "I don't think very many people have been in the house for a long time. Tess wasn't big on inviting people over. But she did tell me that she had a piano, and she played the one at the library for me a few times for some kids' programs. She taught an art class for older kids for several weeks last summer, too. It took me a while to talk her into it, but I think both she and the kids were surprised at what a good time they had at it. A few of their works and a painting that Tess did are still hanging in the library. I'll have to show them to you."

"I'd like to see them." The waitress brought our coffee, and it gave me the time I needed to construct in my head what I wanted to say aloud. When she left, I stirred the dark liquid in my cup but didn't take a drink. "Simon, tell me truthfully how you saw Tess. I'm certainly picking up that she was...an unusual woman."

I read sympathy in his clear eyes as he thought how to answer me. "She *was* an unusual woman, in many ways. I won't lie to you: Tess wasn't exactly the most outgoing person in town. People thought of her as...." He struggled for the right word.

"Strange?" I supplied the word. "It's all right. You don't have to be careful with me. I didn't know her. It's not like you'd be hurting my feelings. I'm just trying to get an accurate picture of her, and trying to find out why she left me her house when she'd never met me."

"But she did meet you." I looked at him quizzically. "When you were born. And before." He looked slightly embarrassed. "I mean, as a father, I remember talking to the baby before he was born. I felt like I knew him, and certainly his mother felt it even more. From what I do know about Tess, if she left you her house, she never stopped thinking about you since the day she gave you up."

I stared at the man with my lips slightly apart until I realized what I was doing and abruptly closed my mouth. He was right. Even if I wasn't always thinking directly of Rowan, still she was always tucked somewhere in the back of my thoughts and had been since that time I'd felt the first movement deep within my own body that made me really understand there was another being there. That Simon understood that was a wonderful thing, but neither of us had given our children away. What had Tess felt?

"So," I said, "she left me her house after all these years. But I do want to hear what she was really like, or at least how people saw her, so I can make some attempt to understand why she did that and what happened."

Simon nodded. "All right. Here's what I know about her. She didn't mingle with people much. She talked politely to anyone who spoke to her, but she rarely started a conversation. When I was young, we were a bit afraid of her. But that's just because kids—*and* adults—will make up stories about anything they don't understand. And we made up stories about her. My mother didn't grow up here, but my father did. When Tess died, he told me she had always been different but not such a recluse when she was young. He did say she was always beautiful. It surprised me that he said that because I don't remember him having said much about her any other time."

"How did you get to be friends with her? Just because she used the library?"

He peered at me over the rim of his cup. "I sort of started off on the wrong foot with her when I moved back here. Just like I started to do with her daughter last week." I raised an eyebrow at him. "I know I annoyed you when I joked about your expectations of a small town library. I tend to do that."

"Is that an apology of sorts?"

"No. Call it an acknowledgment of sorts."

I laughed and set my own cup on the table. "Well, acknowledgment of sorts accepted. What did you do to Tess? It couldn't have been too bad if you ended up friends with her."

"I took a matter lightly that she considered serious," he said. "She got an overdue notice for a book, and when she came in to tell me it was my mistake, I made the further mistake of making a joke out of it. That's why I can remember that Tess never had an overdue book from that time on. And she was right: that one wasn't her mistake either. Technically, it was a computer error, but ultimately, in her eyes, it meant that it was my error."

"So you're telling me she had no sense of humor." I looked at him with mock horror. "And have I inherited that? Are you telling me I have none either?"

Simon's smile was infectious. "No, I'm telling you that neither of you understood my sense of humor at first. Eventually, Tess came to appreciate it. And I'm hoping you will, too." I said nothing as I made sure that he didn't notice the slight quickening of my traitorous pulse at that last little bit. "Actually, it was Jake who broke the ice for Tess and me."

"How so?"

"He was four when we moved here, and one day when I had him at the library with me in the early days, he threw a serious tantrum. He didn't have them often, but when he did, they were spectacular. Several people, including Tess, were there to witness the scene. I did my dad thing and sort of slung him over my shoulder to take him out of the room when all of a sudden, he just stopped. I looked over my shoulder and saw him looking upside down at Tess who had come close enough to show him something in her hands that she wasn't letting anyone else see."

"What was it?"

"I didn't see it then, but it was one of those little snow globes...the ones with a scene inside? She showed it to me later. It was a Halloween one with a witch on a broomstick with a cat and a toad. Which just goes to prove Tess did have a sense of humor after all, and it got Jake's attention enough to shut him right up."

I looked at Simon intently. "Why did it prove she had a sense of humor?"

He didn't avoid my eyes. "Because most of the stories that were made up about Tess had to do with her being a witch. You know how kids are. I think she had that globe in her bag to laugh at herself, or everyone else, or both. Anyway, she actually brought up the incident to me a little later, with real sympathy for Jake. His mother—my wife, Lynn—died when Jake was three, and Tess talked to me about how hard that must have been for him. Everyone else had been avoiding talking to me about it—but she understood what he was going through. Jake has long outgrown the tantrums, by the way, but Tess was always friendly to me after that."

We were both silent as I sorted through my thoughts. My inner portrait of Tess was becoming more colorful, but more confusing at the same time. She was serious but had had at least a slight streak of humor in her. She kept to herself, and yet she was sympathetic and understanding toward some- one she barely knew. And, though she'd given up a child, she'd been kind and caring to at least two other children. She was a fine artist and an attractive woman who had never mar- ried.

I still wasn't clear just what her relationship with Toby had been. I'd have to dig more for that information. She had half-jokingly been labeled a witch most of her life, but so far I knew of only three people who had taken that seriously. That Tess was one of those three left me wondering how I should take it. I contemplated telling Simon that Tess had told Rita she was a witch, but in the end, I took the coward's way out and didn't pursue it. I didn't know him well enough to know how he would react, and it was a little disconcerting to realize that I didn't want to appear foolish to him.

I drained the last of the coffee from my cup. "Thank you for telling me about Tess."

"You're welcome." He touched my hand lightly, briefly. "I'm not sure it helped much."

"Oh, but it did," I assured him. "As confusing and conflicting as it is, I'm starting to get a picture of a real woman instead of just my inadequate fantasies of who she might have been. And...." I hesitated and then went on, "I'm glad to know she understood what Jake was going through in having lost his mother. I know it must have been doubly hard for you, losing someone you love and hurting for Jake."

"It was," he said softly. "And that sounded like it was coming from someone who knows. If I'm not being too nosy, what happened to Rowan's father?"

"Not anything as terrible as what you went through." I waited as the waitress appeared to refill our cups. Then, "Though divorce is never fun, in some ways I've had it easier than a lot of women. Rowan was two when James and I split. He and I managed to remain something like friends through it all, but I couldn't help feeling badly for Rowan. He remarried and had two more children. He's always been a good father, but he and his second wife divorced, too, so all three kids have had to juggle their time with him. It's not an ideal situation for a child, but it could have been worse."

We talked for some time more about both Rowan and Jake, and then, though I had not touched my second cup at all, Simon finished his and set the cup back in its saucer. "I really do hate to end this," he said sincerely, "but I have to go. I have to pick up Jake. But I would like to talk to you more, Kat. About anything."

There was a niggling little voice in the back of my head saying, okay, now's the time to just cut this off nice and clean before you run into any complicated expectations. I'd heard that voice before and almost always heeded it. This time, I chose to ignore it. Simon had racked up points by being (so far) different than most men I had known and being a good father. Though he was not what I would have described as handsome, there was no denying I found him physically

79

attractive. I decided to test his ability to deal with a self-proclaimed feminist.

"I'd like that, too, Simon. How about going to dinner with me tomorrow night? You'd have to pick the place, but it would be my treat."

Surprise leaped to his face, and I thought with disappointment that he was going to lose points by being too much of an old-fashioned guy. But the surprise immediately curled into the smile I was coming to appreciate as he said, "There's a wonderful Italian restaurant in Watertown, about thirty miles from here. But there are two conditions—you have to let me drive, or at least buy the gas, and I pay for today's coffee."

"It's a deal," I said. "And Jake's welcome to come, too."

Simon's smile broadened, but "I think not," was all he said to that. "I'll pick you up at your house at 7:00?"

"You did what?"

There was no doubt Rita was an old-fashioned woman. She had walked over the next morning and found Minette and me both contentedly pawing through some of the herbs in the front of the house. I had decided it was high time I learned a bit about them, so I picked up one of the many books on the subject from the living room bookshelf and headed outside to try my hand at identifying some of the plants.

I greeted her happily with, "Look! I can already tell there are lemon balm, foxglove, mullein, and lady's mantle here. And I think this is sweet woodruff."

She began to point out others to me, and I turned the pages in the book to match them with what she was telling me. We chatted as we made our way slowly through the different names, and I gave her the cause for her inquiry when I told her about having had coffee with Simon and that I had asked him out to dinner.

"You actually asked him? For a date?"

"C'mon, Rita." I laughed at her. "It's not that big a deal, but yes, I suppose I did. It was really pleasant talking to him, and when he said he'd like to do it again, I suggested tonight."

Rita looked at me as if I had just arrived from Mars. "They just do things differently on the West Coast, don't they? It never would have occurred to me to ask a guy out. Who pays?"

I laughed out loud at her expression. "Well, I think that's something people work out, but in this case I do. I asked him and made it clear I was paying."

She shook her head and a smile spread across her face. "And he agreed?" She let out a peal of laughter of her own. "Maybe that's what he's been waiting for. I don't know that he's gone out with anyone else here. I assumed no one else measured up to his wife. But maybe he's just cheap."

I rolled my eyes at her. "Or maybe he's just not as old-fashioned as you are. Anyway, we're going to an Italian restaurant in Watertown that he thought was good. And it's not a big deal."

"If you say so," she said. She reached to a vine growing up the side of the house from which she snapped a purple blossom and tucked it into my hair behind my ear. "Here, you might want to wear this tonight."

"What is it?" I asked suspiciously.

"Look it up," was all she would say as she reached to pet Minette, who was in a rare mood and let her.

I was sure they were both smirking at me as I thumbed through several pages before I found a matching photo of what she had placed in my hair.

Rita erupted into laughter again as I snapped the book shut and pointed my finger at her. "You may come in for tea," I told her loftily, "but only if you can act your age."

The star-shaped blossom was called a passionflower. I was glad to see this playful side of Rita. However, I said nothing further about it, but neither did I remove the flower from my hair.

I was nearly ready when Simon arrived that night. I opened the door and invited him in and explained that I knew Tess' cat was in the house somewhere and I thought I'd better make sure she went out before we left. I was hoping she hadn't gone up to the attic. I'd had such a hard time with the attic door earlier that day that I decided to just leave it open.

I could tell he was curious about the house so I suggested he help me look for Minette. She was not in the living room, but I lingered for a moment as I saw Simon's eyes scan the bookshelf appreciatively. He looked around the rest of the room, and I thought he was about to comment on the piano but instead, he saw the painting on the mantle and went to get a closer look.

"I'm surprised there aren't more of Tess' paintings here." He looked back at me. "Is this the only one?"

"Actually, that's not Tess' either," I told him. "It's one I did recently. It looks like there were others hanging on the wall for a long time, but they weren't here when I arrived."

Simon studied my painting. "This is really unusual," he said. "It's so different from your work in your children's books. It's an amazing picture, but I just assumed it was Tess', not yours." He turned back to me. "Where did the idea come from?" he asked me with genuine curiosity.

"I…it's just something that came to me. I have to sit with it for a bit before I can talk about it." I was feeling very awkward. "I don't mean to sound like a temperamental artist. I hope you don't mind."

"Of course not." He let it go as easily as that.

"There's a lot of Tess' work in the studio," I said. "Want to see it? Minette might even be in there."

He followed me to the door and, sure enough, Minette was asleep on a small pile of rags in the middle of the room. I picked up the cat, which must have been very drowsy because she settled against my shoulder and purred.

Simon had come into the room and was standing in front of the easel that held Tess' portrait. "Did she do this?" he asked.

I nodded. "She must have. Is it a good likeness?"

"Definitely." He touched the side of the canvas. "She was somewhere in her sixties, but she was still a beautiful woman. Talented, also. Isn't it interesting that you became an artist, too?"

I said nothing as he looked around the room at some of Tess' other work. He lifted the portrait of Toby and turned to me. "This is a good one. I know she and Toby were together again and looking at this, I'd say she must have cared about him a great deal."

"What makes you say that?" I felt the same way about the portrait, but I wanted to know what Simon saw in it.

"I'm not sure. I guess, just that it's done with such detail. Like she lingered over the work. What little I saw of Tess' art, it seemed like she had a way of capturing the essence of something rather than just painting a nice picture. She's done that with Toby." He replaced the painting. "That wasn't a very good explanation. It's just the way the painting makes you feel."

On the contrary, I thought it was a wonderful explanation. In fact, I thought it added more points in Simon's favor, if one were counting points. "Ready to go?"

I took Minette to the porch and put her on the railing. She was obviously not happy about this, and to emphasize that fact, she jumped from where I had placed her and, with great dignity, she walked slowly down the steps and away from me without looking back.

"I'll let you back in as soon as I get home," I told her, but she made no sign of listening to me. I grabbed the sweater and shoulder bag I had left on the stairs and, after locking the front door, I followed Simon to his car and climbed in.

The evening went very well. The drive to Watertown was a relaxed one, and I realized I'd definitely lost that slightly uncomfortable feeling I'd had around Simon. One of the things I discovered I liked most about him was how easily he laughed and how much he made me laugh. Tortelli's was a quiet little restaurant, tucked away in an alley that I thought would be hard to find if you didn't know about the place. It must have enjoyed a good reputation, however, as the tables were all full and the food was excellent. There was no feeling that you needed to hurry in and out, and Simon and I lingered, talking long after we had finished our meal. At first we chatted more about our children, and eventually I learned about the death of Simon's wife. They had met in graduate school and married a couple of years later. They had waited a few years before having children. When Jacob was two, she had been diagnosed with cancer and died a year after that.

"We lived in Portland, Oregon, so Jake and I were West Coasters for a little while," Simon told me. "We stayed there for another year, but it was painful. I was working long hours and decided I wanted to spend more time with Jake. We flew back to visit my folks, and it was the best time Jake and I had had all year. My parents have a farm, and Jake loved being with the horses and cows. He'd wanted a dog in Portland, but it just wouldn't have worked. Then my mother wrote and told me the job at the Newbridge library was opening up and that the board was looking for someone who could modernize it, so I decided to apply for it. After I left for college, I never expected to come back here, but it's been a good move. We rented a little house in town with a big enough yard for a dog, and after some adjustments, we both settled in. Lynn's parents weren't too happy about it. They live in Oregon. But I make sure they get to see him at least once or twice a year. He flew out there for a week at the end of June. It was just the right amount of time for him to spend with them before he got too homesick for Jasper—the dog. I assume he missed me a bit, too, and I admit I was anxious for him to get back."

We talked around the edges of several topics that night. I laughed more than I remembered doing for a long time. No wonder Simon worked with books—he was a good storyteller. We shared stories of the places we'd both been in

Washington and Oregon as people who spend any time on the West Coast seem to do whenever they chance to meet. We talked more of Tess also, and at one point when Simon mentioned something about Toby, I was seized by what seemed like a tiny memory that I couldn't quite hold onto. I tried to fathom what it might be, but it wasn't until I let it go that a frustratingly small piece of the memory slipped into place. It had something to do with his last name. When Simon told me his full name was Toby Underwood, it rang a little bell in my head. But for the life of me, I couldn't place where I'd heard Underwood before. I probably had met someone else with that name, but I couldn't think where.

There was a gorgeous full moon that night, and after leaving the restaurant, we had walked to a park where there was a trail we could easily maneuver under the moon's brightness. We strolled and talked some more until I stifled a yawn, which made Simon look at his watch. "No wonder you're tired," he said ruefully. "I can't believe it, but it's nearly midnight."

On the ride home, I broached a subject I'd been curious about but certainly hadn't known Simon well enough to ask him without seeming rude. Perhaps I was tired enough now that I didn't care. "Simon, how do you get away with having such long hair here?"

He shot a quick glance my way. "You don't like it?" he asked.

"Oh, no, I like it a lot," and then realizing how enthusiastic that must have sounded, I hurried on, hoping he hadn't noticed. "I just meant that you're the only guy I've seen in Newbridge with a ponytail. Lots of men have long hair in Seattle, but Newbridge just doesn't seem like a long hair kind of town."

"You mean, it's a redneck sort of place?" He grinned at my discomfort. I'd put my foot in my mouth again. "Don't worry," he said, "it *is* a redneck sort of place. My hair's been long since I was in college. I've always liked it that way. Maybe it was my little way of rebelling when I came back— not cutting it off to fit in, I mean. I was willing to give the place a chance by moving back, but I wasn't willing to give up who I'd become. People give me a little hard time now and then, but it's always light-hearted. And I kid them back. One of the things I found out about Newbridge, and I suspect it's true about most little towns, is that the people can be intolerant of what they're not used to. But if you give them a chance, they can get used to almost anything. If you can have a sense of humor about it and give them time to think of you as one of them, you can even get away with long hair."

I smiled at his explanation, but it made me start thinking about Tess again. Though she'd lived here all her life and her family for generations before her, it didn't sound like she'd ever really been accepted as one of them. Was that because she was too different, or was it because she didn't want it?

When we got to the house, Simon walked to the porch with me, but I didn't invite him in. I'd had a wonderful time and I told him that, but I wasn't willing to take anything too fast. Fortunately, he seemed to be feeling the same way because he made no move to enter the house.

He waited for me to unlock the door, and then he touched my hair lightly and his smile was softened by the moonlight. "I had a great time, too. Can we do it again? Very soon?"

I stood on the porch for a while longer after he left, captivated by the way the moon shone on some of the herbs I'd learned to name just that morning. As I turned to go inside, I had to admit there were some things I definitely was starting to like about this place.

Minette greeted me from the stairway and I reached to scratch her head absently. I locked the door from the inside, left a soft hall light on, and headed straight for the bedroom. The cat followed me and then climbed quickly onto the bed ahead of me.

After heading to the bathroom, I hung up my clothes and pulled on my nightshirt. Then I moved Minette enough so that I could crawl under the covers. I don't know which of us fell asleep first, but it was a short race.

It wasn't until the next morning at breakfast that it suddenly hit me. I had most definitely put Minette outside and locked the door before I left with Simon.

How had she gotten back in before I came home?

Chapter 5

Over the next couple of weeks, I began to feel more comfortable in Tess' house and even found myself beginning to think of it as mine. I had been unnerved a bit the day I realized that Minette had gotten back into the house after I locked her out. I found Rita that day, told her what had happened, and asked her if she had come over to the house for any reason while I was gone since I knew she had a key. She assured me that she had not. I wondered if someone else had a key, but nothing had been moved or taken. A week or so later, it happened again that I knew the cat had gone outside when I did. I spent an enjoyable afternoon sitting on the grass in front of the house with a sketchpad that I filled with renderings of the herbs there. But when I went back inside to put something in the oven, I discovered Minette contentedly munching away at her food in the bowl beside the refrigerator. Obviously she had her own way in and out that I hadn't discovered yet. I tried to keep an eye on her whenever she did go out, but she proved elusive. If I didn't know better, I might have assumed that she was trying to keep it secret.

I took time to have Brian check out Tess' vehicle. He assured me it was in great condition, both because it had been driven only by the proverbial little old lady and because he had done all the work on it in the last couple of years. His mother assured me that he was one of the greatest mechanics living. I trusted them both and did the necessary paperwork to have the title put officially into my name and then gave up the rental car.

A few days after my dinner with Simon, he called to invite me to have dinner with him and Jake at their house. If I felt the slightest apprehension about accepting the invitation, I ignored it. I had most definitely enjoyed myself on our evening out and getting to know someone was not a commitment.

I easily followed the directions I had been given and parked the Jeep in front of a small, two-story house with weather-darkened wood shingles covering the outside. I rang the bell and, almost immediately after, the door flew open. I was enthusiastically greeted by Jake and a large golden-colored creature that appeared to be made up of several different flavors of dog. Simon soon followed but much more calmly. He greeted me with that easy smile of his, and as I returned it, I realized I had been looking forward to that particular smile all day.

I had brought dessert, and Simon took it from me and headed to the kitchen. Jake gave me a tour of the house with the dog, Jasper, shadowing his heels. The most important room in the house, in Jake's opinion, was his bedroom. So, while we fairly rushed through the few other rooms, I got a good look at his. It was obviously a well-loved space. Clothes, action figures, and books were strewn around, but there was enough open space to maneuver. He showed me several of his treasures with pride and kindly pointed out the books I had written that were in his bookcase. He was just introducing me to Hector and Ratcliff, his pet rats, when Simon poked his head in the door.

"Dinner's ready," he announced.

We ate the meal in the back yard, which was a large, fenced space with a huge maple tree shading the picnic table. A tall ladder against the tree led to a tree house which, Jake informed me, I would get to inspect after dinner.

Before the evening was finished, I had indeed inspected the tree house, helped feed the rats (and in the process thoroughly impressed Jake by not being squeamish about holding them), and went along as Jasper took the three of us for a walk. My success with his animals must have prompted Jake to invite me to accompany him and his father to his grandparents' very soon to ride horses.

"You'd have to promise not to laugh at me," I told him solemnly. "I've never ridden a horse before. I used to take my daughter to riding lessons but never got on one myself."

"You're kidding!"

I'm afraid I may have gone down a notch in Jake's estimation.

"Never? Well, we can teach you, can't we Dad? Grams and Grandpa have four horses, and they're almost always nice. They hardly ever throw you off."

I was given my first riding lesson three days later and was grateful to have it be one of the horses' nice days—I wasn't thrown off. Jake showed me how to tack up my horse and then told me he was sure I would learn how to do it by myself in no time. Lady, the gray mare they had given me to ride, lived up to her name. I was taken on a trail ride through the woods with Jake leading the way and Simon bringing up the rear. I felt fairly safe with this arrangement, and so I relaxed and enjoyed myself.

Simon's parents' farm was not large but had been in his father's family for a very long time. I could see why Jake liked it here. There were animals everywhere. Besides the confined horses, cows, and pigs, there were chickens, cats, and at least two dogs roaming freely about the place. Jasper had come along and seemed right at home.

The elder DeBerrys were a congenial couple who obviously adored their son and grandson. When the ride was finished, they ushered us into the house for lemonade and cookies and insisted I should call them Jack and Ruth.

For a city person who had always loved being a city person, I had to admit I found this family and their country life appealing. I wondered if Simon had felt that way about it growing up. He had said that he had left not planning to return permanently, but here he was, and Jake clearly thrived in the environment.

Simon drove me home, and when we arrived, Jake and Jasper quickly hopped out of the car. "Wait a minute, sport. Where do you think you're going?" Simon stopped him before he had let go of the door handle.

"Aren't we going in?" Jake directed his question at me.

"Sure," I answered him before Simon could override the decision. I could tell Jake was curious about the place. There were probably several people in Newbridge who were. "Come have a look. You might be a little disappointed, though. There's not a lot of stuff here. Not even a television."

Jake looked at me with something that appeared to be pity but said nothing further. He and Jasper headed to the porch before his father had opened the car door.

"Is it all right? Jake tends to be a little pushy." Simon stood beside the car.

"Of course, it is. Honestly, I was going to ask you in." I smiled at him. "I think it's time the house had some visitors."

Minette did not agree with me. At least, not about four-legged visitors. As I opened the door, Jasper nosed his way ahead and seemed to be delighted at the sight of Minette, who stood momentarily frozen with a look of what could only be interpreted as shock and horror. She had just started down the hallway to greet me, and now she backed her way into the kitchen, hissing and spitting the whole way. Jasper seemed to take this as an invitation to play, but before he could make a move, Simon gave a command that made the dog whine, but he immediately sat his bottom on the wood floor. He couldn't keep it still, but he stayed more or less in place.

"Jake, you better take Jasper to the car." It wasn't quite a command, but the boy unhappily took it as one and, holding Jasper's collar, he headed toward the door.

Minette would probably never forgive me for this. "He's fine." I told them. "He doesn't hurt cats, right?"

Jake shook his head vigorously. "He loves cats." Something compelled him to add, "They hardly ever like him, though."

91

I laughed. "I don't think Minette's going to be any exception. She'll probably go hide, but if she gets too close, you might want to hold onto him." It wasn't Minette's safety I thought I had to worry about.

I gave them a short tour of the house, but Jake's curiosity was fairly quickly satisfied. I could tell he agreed with me that there wasn't too much of interest there for him, although the studio held his attention the longest. He asked several questions about the sketches I was working on and was impressed by the paintings Tess had done of the wild animals. When we had concluded the tour, he asked if it would be all right to go throw sticks for Jasper in the field.

Simon watched him go and then turned to me. "Sometimes he has the attention span of a goldfish." He chuckled. "Thanks for letting him see the place. It's always had an air of mystery about it. I think Jake was just expecting more mystery. It is a great place."

"Thanks," I said. "It's beginning to grow on me. If someone had asked me if I wanted a very old house that needs paint and probably some other repairs, I would have said no. And I almost didn't come here when I learned it was mine, but Rowan convinced me I had to, and now I'm glad I did. Don't worry about Jake. If I were—what, ten years old...?"

"Almost ten."

"Almost ten then, I wouldn't find it very exciting either. I am thinking of getting a TV and VCR. They help me to come up with ideas for my books once in a while. Want some iced tea? It's all made up."

"Sounds good, thanks." Simon followed me to the kitchen. "Do you think you'll stay here, or sell the place, or...?"

"It's too early to know what I'll do. I'll stay through October and decide after that. I sublet my apartment until then anyway." We sat at the table where we could see Jake and Jasper through the window. "I'm not quite sure what I'm looking for here, other than to find out more about Tess. I always knew I was adopted, and my parents were wonderful. But sometimes I'd have these little fantasies about who my real parents were, and I have to say, none of them looked like what I know of Tess. And who knows about my birth father...." I stopped in the middle of that sentence for two reasons. First, the painting of Toby flashed into my mind, and second, I wasn't sure that Simon would be interested. Though I considered myself a friendly person who got along easily with other people, I had a few close friends who I confided in, and I certainly didn't discuss my life story and feelings with people I hardly knew. *Was there something about this house that affected that?* I wondered. I had already said more to Rita and Simon in the short time I'd known them than anyone I could remember.

Simon caught my hand and squeezed it gently. If the move was meant to make me snap out of my pondering and look at him, it did the trick. "It must have been hard not to know about your birth parents."

My first reaction to the sympathy in his eyes was discomfort, but that soon gave way to something else. There was something, some connection that made me loosen my tongue around both Simon and Rita, and I briefly, jokingly wondered if it was magic.

"Not as hard as you might think, at least, not until now. We really were a normal family, and I was happy with my parents. When I was a teenager, I started to think maybe I should know more about my background—you know, medical history—that sort of thing. Plus, I was certainly curious. But when my mom tried to help me find out and was told there was to be no contact, I dropped it without much problem. But now, I want to know why Tess left me this place when she hadn't wanted anything to do with me. And...." I looked at him and swallowed. "And since I know who my birth mother is now, I want to know who my birth father is, too."

"You know, I'd be happy to help you any way I can. Have you seen a birth certificate?"

"Yes, I have. The lawyers sent me a copy. It only lists Tess as my mother and no father." I was acutely aware that he was still holding my hand and didn't seem inclined to give it back. And I was in no hurry to take it. "Simon, how much do you know about Toby Underwood?"

He flashed me a look of understanding. "I know that Toby was married for many years, and after his wife died, he and Tess became close again. I say again because my parents have mentioned that they were high school sweethearts. Do you think he might be your father?"

"I don't know. I'm certainly looking forward to meeting him. Rita says he'll be back in September." I was about to say more, but I heard Jake explode through the front door, and I had just enough warning to remove my hand from Simon's. It seemed to amuse Simon, but he said nothing.

"Kat!" Jake's voice called down the hallway.

"Down here in the kitchen, Jake."

He burst into the kitchen with Jasper jumping in circles around him. He could barely contain his excitement. "Kat, you could have horses here! It's all fenced, and I saw a saddle and bridles in the barn...."

"Why were you in the barn?" his father asked pointedly.

"I just peeked in," Jake defended himself.

"It's okay. He was exploring," I told Simon. "I'm glad you found something interesting, Jake. I heard Tess used to have horses. I bet she knew how to ride them, though."

"You know how to ride now. Wouldn't you like to have a horse?"

"One ride doesn't mean I know how. I had a great time, though. I hope you'll ask me to go again." It was obvious Jake didn't understand my logic. "I don't know how long I'll be here either. It wouldn't do me much good to get a horse for only a couple of months and then leave."

"You're not staying here?" Jake looked puzzled.

"I came because I inherited this house, and I wanted to see it and stay in it for a little while, but I'm not sure what I'm going to do with it yet."

"Oh. Well, it's a nice house. I bet you'll decide to stay here. Down, Jasper." At Jake's command, the dog jumped up and licked his face.

"I had the impression maybe you thought this place was kind of boring," I teased him.

"No, I like it. You just need to get some things for it, like a TV and Nintendo." He grinned impishly. "And a horse. Then it would be a great place."

After they left, I pulled yet another herb book from the shelf in the living room and headed back outside. For someone who previously hadn't been able to tell one plant from another, I was starting to get good at recognizing several of the herbs and remembering some of their uses. The book I now had in my hands listed medicinal and magical uses and, though there wasn't any purpose in my knowing either, I had unexpectedly become fascinated with reading about them. Now, whenever I stepped outside and brushed against some comfrey or glanced at the beautiful lavender, a little thrill would shoot through me that I knew these plants.

Minette was most likely still in a snit as I didn't see her anywhere. Whenever I was poking through the herbs, she was usually there. After walking around several of the plants, I returned to the porch to sit on the steps and browse through the pages of the book. I was absorbed in reading about the healing and dream-producing properties of calendula when my attention was caught by the sound of a vehicle coming up the driveway.

At first I thought perhaps Simon and Jake had returned, but I soon saw that it was a fairly old pickup truck with a woman, who appeared to be in her thirties, behind the wheel. I had never seen her before, but she got out of the truck and strode to the porch purposefully. The first sign of hesitation was when she opened her mouth to speak. At first nothing came out. She hung her head and took a breath. I thought I'd better help her.

"Hi," I said in as friendly a voice as I could. "What can I do for you?"

She gave a nervous little laugh and found her voice. "Hi. I'm Donna Bartlett. You must be.... Are you the lady they say is Tess' daughter?"

"Yes." It was my turn to hesitate.

"I hope you don't mind my stopping by like this. Maybe I should have called first, but I didn't know your number, you see, and I never called Tess first before I came." She pushed the toe of one shoe into the dirt of the pathway.

"You used to come visit Tess?" I asked with some surprise.

"Well, not exactly visit. I mean, she was always friendly and all, but it's not like she invited me in or anything." Donna took a breath. "The fact is, I used to come to her to get some herb remedies she'd make up for me sometimes. Right now my son, Kyle, has a cut that's not healing very fast, and I thought...well, I thought maybe since you were her daughter...." She let the sentence trail.

At first, I didn't follow what she was asking of me. Suddenly the light bulb in my head turned on.

"You thought I'd be able to come up with a remedy for you?" I tried not to show her quite how shocked I was at the idea. "I'm really sorry, but maybe you didn't hear that I never met Tess. I am her daughter, but she gave me up for adoption. I don't know anything about herbs and remedies."

She looked somewhat embarrassed. "But I thought it might have passed to you anyway. You and she being of the same blood...."

"What might have passed to me? Knowing how to use herbs medicinally? Someone would have to study for a long time to know enough to do that, and I certainly haven't."

"Well, not just that. I swear, Tess had special ways to know what herbs to use. And she'd talk to the plants sometimes, like they were people. And she'd lay her hands to a hurt...." She dug her toe in the dirt again. "It was like...like she used magic." The last word came out a little breathlessly as if she were almost afraid to use it.

"Magic." I brushed a hand across my forehead and sighed. "Whatever it was that made her know what to do, I'm afraid I don't have it. I'm sorry, but you really should take your son to a doctor. I hope the cut isn't too bad."

"No, it's not deep, but it's taking a long time to heal." Her voice was heavy with disappointment, but she raised her

96

eyes to mine. "I'm sorry I bothered you. I hope you don't think I'm nuts. I just thought you would be like her. I guess that was silly of me."

"Did you come to get remedies from Tess often?" I was curious, but mostly I was attempting to put her at ease. It was quite an assumption to think that I automatically knew all about herbs just because Tess had. I suppose the real assumption was that Tess was a witch and so her daughter must have inherited that, too. Well, interesting. I wondered how many other people had quietly visited Tess to benefit from her "magic."

"There wasn't any answer at the back door so I thought you might be...." Rita stopped mid-sentence as she came around the corner of the house and saw the two of us. "Oh, hi, Donna."

"Hi, Rita. I was just...I just stopped by to see...." The poor woman was just not having an easy time of it.

"Donna stopped by hoping I could help her with some herb remedies, but I don't know enough about them." I tried (and failed) to make the woman smile. "I'm still trying to match up the plants with the pictures in Tess' herb books.

Rita perked up. "What sort of thing were you looking for?"

"Kyle cut his hand with his jack knife last week, and it still looks a little bad. Tess used to know just what to do for all the bumps and bruises he comes up with." Donna was looking hopeful again as she answered Rita.

"Do you still have any of the things Tess made up for you?" Rita asked.

"Yeah. I can never remember what they're for, though."

I caught myself wanting to tell her to write it down, but I stayed mum.

"If you have any calendula ointment, put that on it. It should help. If not, give me a call, and I'll make some up for you." Rita's solution startled me, both because she seemed so confident in prescribing something and because that something was the very herb I had just been reading about. I had just learned that it was good for cuts, but I never would have dared to tell anyone to use it for that.

Donna, however, was clearly relieved. "Thanks, Rita. I think I do have some left. I got it from Tess in February. It's still good?"

"Sure. Make certain the cut is cleaned out good and that Kyle keeps it clean, too."

"Okay. I'll see you later. I hope you don't mind that I stopped...." Donna looked at me at a loss for what to call me.

"Kat, short for Katrina. And not at all. I hope your son's cut heals quickly."

As she climbed into her truck and drove away, I turned to Rita and almost hissed at her, "Are you sure you know what you're doing? Shouldn't she take that boy to a doctor?"

"She should, but she won't." Rita sat beside me on the step. "She's a single mom with very little money and no in-surance. Her kids are always getting into something, espe-cially Kyle, and unless it's a major emergency, a trip to the doctor just isn't in the budget. Tess used to help her for free. Donna didn't mind talking about getting help from her. I know there were others who came to her, too, but they kept it quiet."

"Do you really know enough to help her? Do people come to you?"

"Yes and no. Yes, I know quite a bit. Tess taught me over the years, but she knew more than anybody I know about herbs. And no, people don't usually come to me because my mother would have a fit. I don't have enough herbs in my gar-den, just the ones I slip past her. I used to have them in my garden at my other house before I moved back in with my mother. I helped Tess make up ointments and tinctures and things here, though. If Donna needs more, I was sort of hop-ing you wouldn't mind if I did that here." Rita's eyebrows rose in question.

"Of course. And, I can't believe I'm saying this, but I'd be interested in learning about how to do that. I wouldn't be comfortable making things for other people, but I'm really fascinated by all these herbs. I've never even thought about them before—I mean I can kill a house plant faster than anybody I know, but there's something about identifying them and just looking at them that makes me happy." I winced at how simple minded that came out. "Sounds corny, doesn't it?"

Rita laughed and patted my hand. "No, they've just worked their magic on you, too. They grabbed me when I was a kid and never let go. I pestered Tess to tell me everything about them. When she really got into teaching me, she would tell me stories about each plant to help me remember their names and what their uses were. I tried to tell my mother one of the stories once. You can imagine how well that went over." She got up from the step and walked to a large bush filled with branches of soft, aromatic needles. She pinched the tip of a small branch off and brought it back to me. "Know what this is?"

"Rosemary," I said proudly. "Although I guess I can't feel too smug for knowing that. I do cook with it, and I'd know that smell anywhere. The only other things I know about it are that it's for remembrance and it tastes good."

Rita smiled. "It also helps with migraines, among other things. And there's an old saying that where rosemary grows, there a strong woman lives."

"Well, I guess Tess must have been a strong woman because that's a gorgeous bush. Do you think she planted it?" I pinched the needles and breathed in the scent.

"I don't think so. I think it's been here longer than that. I know she added a lot of the plants, but some of them have been here a long time. She said her mother planted some and so did her grandmother. She told me her mother's mother lived with them for a while when she was young. I suppose she learned a lot of what she knew about herbs from them." Rita picked a needle from the rosemary and began to chew it. "Kat, you know, Tess is here among the herbs."

Now that sounded a little corny to me, but I thought I knew what she meant. "Because she loved them you mean? 'Her spirit dwells here' sort of thing?"

"Well, yes, I think if it's anywhere, it's probably here, but that's not exactly what I meant." Rita made a sweeping motion with her hand to indicate all the herbs. "She's literally among them. Toby had her body cremated, and he gave me the ashes to bring back here. I spread them all around the herbs."

That stopped any speech on my part for a bit. It had crossed my mind that at some point I should ask Rita where Tess was buried and perhaps I'd go visit her grave. I wasn't sure what I would do once I got there, but that didn't matter now. She was right here, so to speak.

After a time, Rita broke the silence. "You okay?" she asked.

"Yeah. I'm fine," I answered. "It just hadn't occurred to me that…well that you'd brought her here. It caught me by surprise is all. But now that I've had a minute to think about it, it makes perfect sense. I bet she would have liked that."

"I hope so." She brushed invisible dirt from her jeans. "Toby thought about taking her ashes somewhere where they'd been together, but he thought she'd like it better if they were here. He didn't want to come to the house so he asked me to do it. I was glad he did. I…." She peered at me before she went on. "There wasn't a funeral. Toby said she would have hated that, and I agreed. So, I did a little ceremony on my own when I scattered the ashes. Well, not exactly alone. Minette sat right there by the rosemary bush the whole time."

I was touched by what she had just told me. I may not have ever met Tess while she was alive but, oddly enough, I was starting to feel that I was getting to know her a little. I pictured her smiling as Rita performed her ceremony.

"Thanks Rita." I gave her hand a squeeze. "I'm glad you and Tess were friends, and I'm glad we're friends. It's really making this whole thing easier for me."

After that, Rita made a point of spending time here and there on our "herb lessons" as she called them. Between writing, drawing and painting, reading, finding out all I could about herbs, and continually exploring the house, I was amazed at how quickly time passed. I did manage to squeeze in more time with Simon and Jake and loved every minute of it. I had gone to Watertown one afternoon with Rita to shop and had come home with something I was sure would please Jake. I invited Simon, Jake, and Jasper (where Jake went, Jasper followed) over for dinner one evening, and when the meal was over, I slyly instructed Jake to take a peek in the living room.

"All right!" I heard him whoop. "You got a television! Do you have cable?"

"No." I laughed at him as Simon and I came into the room. "But I did get a VCR, and I got a movie for us tonight. I thought I heard you talk about it, so I hope I got one you like." I reached for the video box and handed it to him.

"Hey, great choice," Jake said, and from the look in his eyes, I was certain he wasn't just being polite.

After the three of them left that night, I was rewinding the video and browsing through Tess' bookshelf yet again. I always seemed to come back to the herb books more than any others and, as I leafed through an illustrated encyclopedia of herbs, Minette hopped to the shelf beside me. She had evidently forgiven me more quickly than usual this time for letting Jasper into her territory. Glancing at her, I remembered Rita telling me about the cat standing by the rosemary bush as Rita said goodbye to Tess. I'm not sure why that prompted me to do what I did next, but I found myself going out into the warm night air. The stars blinked, and the moon shone brightly though it wasn't full. I thought I should look it up somewhere to find out what phase it was in. *Look out*, I told myself, *you're beginning to sound very witchy*. I stayed out just enough longer to take a little cutting of the rosemary and a calendula flower. I locked up for the night, and before Minette and I climbed into bed, I placed the herbs under my pillow.

I don't know that I expected anything to really happen. It just seemed like a nice thing to do. And who knows if the plants really had anything to do with the dream I had that night. But dream I did. Not the sweet flower-filled vision I might have hoped for. This was the fifth time I dreamt the same dream, but this night it did not stop where it always had before.

The voice cried again in anguish, "Rose!"

The horseman flew from his horse at the water's edge and flung himself into the waves as if he could bring her back. But it was no use. That unbroken chain of women had disappeared so completely it was as if it had never been. The man's anguish turned to fury as the robed ones shook their fists in their own anger at losing their victims.

Stumbling from the water, he drew a sword from the scabbard at his side and lashed out at the first man he could reach. He injured several of them, but he was too greatly outnumbered, and many of them carried staffs. Before he remembered the other responsibility that was his and sought to remount his horse, he was himself bleeding from several wounds, and one arm dangled uselessly at his side. He managed to half throw himself into the saddle, and the lashing of the frightened horse's hooves kept the others at bay. Then, seemingly with no need of a command from its master, the beast turned and sped away.

The scene abruptly changed.

A young girl dressed in coarse homespun sat rocking her body by a fireplace. She was dressed for travel—sturdy shoes, a wool shawl gathered around her shoulders, and a bonnet for warmth rather than decoration.

She chanted a quiet song to herself over and over and fingered the items that lay in her lap. A crimson cape was carefully folded there, and in the middle of its folds glinted a locket. At her feet sat a tabby cat, which seemed to be guarding the pack that the girl had recently prepared.

She looked up quickly as the door burst open. Her eyes shone with fear, but she did not stop her singing. The horseman reached for her as he stumbled across the threshold, and her eyes widened even more as she took in the extent of his wounds.

"Come, Kate. We must hurry." His voice was hoarse with desperation.

Though the fear in the child's eyes never diminished, she otherwise displayed an almost eerie calmness. "Don't worry, Papa," she told him. "I've packed what we will need and am ready. And you needn't worry about those terrible men any longer."

"What do you mean?" he croaked as he grabbed her arm.

"Though Mama told me not to, I did it anyway. She said whatever happened, we must learn to forgive or the hatred would never stop."

She looked into her father's eyes with something stronger than fear now. Stronger and more terrible. "

But how can we not hate them? They will pay for what they have done to Mama and the others. I laid a curse upon them. Them and their families."

Perhaps her father did not take her seriously for he gathered her up to hurry away. But she did not care.

She was satisfied with what she had done.

Chapter 6

Upon rising the next morning, I reached out to scratch Minette's head. I needed something to ground me, and the cat was up to the task. My fingers edged too close to the spot on her back that I had discovered she didn't like to have touched, and she swiftly reached out to swipe me with her open claws. She drew no blood. It was just a warning. I snatched my hand away, but we looked at each other.

"Okay, Minette. Something weird is definitely going on here."

She may have agreed with me, but she didn't appear to be all that interested. She butted my hand with her head to get me to go back to the area she did like scratched. I obliged while I attempted to tackle my thoughts. I could no longer ignore this recurring dream. I had thought it odd, even painted the scene of it, and to find out that Tess had done the same thing was incredible. But I'd managed to keep busy enough to avoid really looking too closely at what it might mean.

For the dream to continue with the father and daughter added a new element. The detail and clarity with which my mind had pictured it all was unbelievable. I guessed the style of the clothing to be somewhere from the seventeenth century, though I wasn't very familiar with the period. I would have to do some research. The faces of the woman named Rose who had drowned with the others, and the man and his daughter were also very clear to me, though they were not faces I had seen before. It might have made some sense if they had been people I knew and my mind had just reassigned dream roles for them, but that wasn't the case. I could recall no movie that remotely resembled my dream either. Just what was going on here?

I threw back the covers and practically jumped from the bed. I showered and dressed quickly and hurried downstairs. I ate only part of the breakfast I made myself before I was too restless for more. Leaving the dishes in the sink, I grabbed up a sketchbook and headed outside. I picked a bundle of lavender, which I secured with a rubber band I found in my jeans pocket, and inhaled deeply. Lavender was supposed to calm you, and I could use a bit of calming. It worked enough to let me fill several pages with drawings before a drop fell on the page and then another. I looked up to see the clouds gathering, closed the cover on the book, and tramped back into the house. Just as I opened the door, I heard the phone ringing in the kitchen, and I hurried to answer it. Diversion was good.

It was Simon. Within the first few seconds of our conversation, he could tell that something was wrong. "Kat, is everything okay?"

"It's fine. I just had a strange dream." I tried to keep it light, but suddenly it was too much. If I hadn't been in the state I was in from the dream, I might have thought things through before blurting, "Actually, Simon, it's not fine. I've been having a recurring dream since I found out I inherited the house. Remember that painting I did that you asked me about?"

"The one with the women in the circle?"

"That's the one. It's from this dream. I had it again last night, only there's more to it now. It's kind of hard to talk about it over the phone, though."

"Is that an I-don't-want-to-talk-about-it or do you actually want to talk about it in person?" he asked.

105

Might as well test his tolerance for the strange, I decided. "If you're up for it, I wouldn't mind having someone to talk to. What time do you close the library tonight? Want to come have dinner with me here? Only...." I wondered how to say this. "I...I don't think I want to talk about it around Jake."

"That's part of why I was calling. Jake's gone to Canada with my parents today, and they won't be back until late tonight. I was going to see if you'd go on a real date again...just the two of us. I close up at 7:00."

"Would you mind coming here?" I was grateful he wasn't offended about Jake. "I'd love to go on a real date another time, if that means going out somewhere."

"Of course, I don't mind. Can I bring a bottle of wine?" His calm voice was already starting to put me at ease.

"That would be very nice," I said. "And, Simon...this dream thing...I hope you don't think I'm crazy when I tell you about it."

"Quit worrying. I'm a good listener, and I won't think you're crazy."

Huh, I thought, *you haven't heard it yet,* but I said nothing.

"I'll be there between 7:15 and 7:30, all right?"

"All right. Thanks, Simon. I'll see you then." Suddenly, I remembered something. "Simon, wait. When you come, could you do me a favor?"

"Sure. What is it?"

"Will you see what you have at the library for books about clothing from anywhere between the sixteenth and eighteenth centuries and bring them with you?"

"No problem. Research for one of your books?" he asked.

"Not exactly. I'll tell you when you get here."

I spent most of the rest of the day flitting from one thing to another. I thought of what to make for dinner and determined that I had all the ingredients without having to go out to shop. That was almost too bad. I found I needed to keep moving. I attempted to write, and when that didn't work, I made a feeble attempt to start a painting of some of my herb sketches. By the time I heard a knock at the front door, around 4:30, I had started and stopped any number of projects. I was standing in the living room staring into the dream painting, and before I could stir enough to answer the door, it opened and I heard Rita call a greeting.

"In here," I called back but didn't move until she stood, slightly dripping, in the doorway.

"Just thought I'd stop in for a minute on my way home from work. Have you been out in this rain?"

"No." I made an attempt to joke with her. "Isn't it wet?"

"Well, most rain is. But I love a summer rain when it's nice and warm. When I was a kid, I used to put on my bathing suit and stay out in it as long as it would last, or at least as long as I could get away with it." She stopped talking and looked at me. "Hey, what's up? Are you not feeling well?"

I forced myself to move away from the painting. "I used to think that I wasn't so transparent, that only Rowan could tell sometimes what was going on with me. But since I've been here, you and Simon both...." I laughed weakly. "I'm fine. I'm not sick or anything. I've been having this strange thing happen, and when Simon called me this morning, I told him a little about it. He's coming over for dinner tonight, and now I don't know that I should have said anything to him. I can't *not* tell him the rest of it once he gets here, but I don't know how he'll react. Hell, I don't know how to react to it."

"What?" Rita stepped the rest of the way into the room. "You certainly have me curious now. You can't not tell me either."

"Have a seat," I said as I dropped into a chair.

She sat quietly the whole time I told her about the dreams and the painting.

"So, does that make me certifiable?" I concluded.

"Of course not." She finally breathed. "But Kat, you know what this means, don't you?"

"No. I wish someone could tell me."

"Have you ever heard of hereditary witchcraft?"

"Rita, these are dreams," I snapped. "They must mean something, but I don't think they make me a witch!" Hurt and surprise at my curtness colored her face. I was immediately contrite. "I'm sorry. I didn't mean to snarl at you, but this has really put me on edge."

"Okay," she said carefully. "But just look at the facts. There's some connection here. You've had this dream that obviously Tess must have had, too. And the dream is about witches."

"How do you know that?" I kept my voice controlled in an effort not to offend her again.

"What else could it be? Tess called her painting the *Dream of the Circle of Women*, the robed men wanted to hurt those women, and the girl put a curse on them." She paused, but I could think of nothing to say. "Something's triggered whatever this is, and I'd say it has to do with finding out about Tess. You've inherited from her all right, and I don't think it's just the house."

I looked at her unhappily. "I wish I knew what to do with this," I said.

We talked for a bit more, enough so that I felt confident she was over the moment of hurt feelings I'd caused. Before she left, she picked some fresh lemon balm leaves and dragged me to the kitchen while she boiled water to steep them. "Drink a cup when it's cool enough," Rita ordered. "It's a nice-tasting tea, and it helps sooth your nerves."

"Thanks," I said simply.

"You're welcome. Have a good time with Simon tonight. Is this another date where you asked him?"

"This was half-and-half. He called me to ask me out, and I asked him to come here."

"Ah," was all she said, but she laughed softly as she let herself out the back door.

I was slightly nervous as I opened the door for Simon that night. I'd already offended one friend today. What damage might I do tonight? Simon was carrying a full load in his arms with books in one and flowers and a bottle of wine in the other. I took the wine and flowers from him and breathed in the fragrance of the blossoms as he made his way to the living room to place the books on the shelf there. Between the flowers and the lemon balm tea, I was beginning to feel somewhat better.

"Dinner's just about ready," I told him, leading the way to the kitchen. "Are you hungry?"

"Starved," he said. "But—" He stopped me by taking hold of the hand I had the wine in and transferred the bottle to his other hand. "First, I want to know how you're doing. You sounded stressed on the phone."

"I'm okay, really. It probably seems ridiculous to get so wound up about a dream. I'm a little embarrassed about it. I'm not the flighty type who needs rescuing from her nightmares."

Simon entwined my fingers with his. "I know you're not flighty. And I'm not here to rescue you." He stood looking at our clasped hands for a moment without saying anything, and then his gaze slid to my face. "I care about you, you know. I'd like to help any way I can, even if it's just listening."

He had said just the right thing, and I could feel more of the tension slip away. "I appreciate that," I told him truthfully. "Let's eat first, and then I'll tell you all about it."

I had prepared a fairly simple meal, but in my need to keep busy, I had taken the time to find a tablecloth and candles and arrange the dining room as nicely as possible. I had placed some of the blossoming herbs into bowls that I had set on the table, and now I circled them round the bouquet Simon had brought. It was the first time since coming here that I had used the dining room, and now I was glad that I had. By the time we finished the meal, I had laughed enough at Simon's descriptions of encounters he'd had at the library that day that I was no longer nervous about telling him about the dreams.

He insisted on helping clear the table and drying the dishes before we made our way to the living room and settled on the sofa there.

We'd each had a glass of wine with dinner, and before I turned the light switch off in the kitchen, Simon poured another glass for each and handed me mine as I pulled my feet under me on one end of the sofa.

"Are you ready to tell me about it?" he asked gently. And so I did.

Simon was a good listener. He didn't interrupt me or try to distract me as I related the dream as it had first come to me, and then the new scene I had dreamt last night. Surprisingly, there was no hesitation in my telling. Having spent the day wondering where the dream was coming from and worrying about Simon's reaction, it was now a relief just to spill it out.

"And as if the dream itself isn't bizarre enough," I told him, "it appears that Tess might have had at least part of the same dream."

"How did you find that out?" I didn't seem to have scared Simon off yet.

"When Rita saw the painting on the mantle just after I finished it, she thought it was one that Tess used to have there. She said it was the exact scene and that Tess had given it a title. When I told her I had done it, she thought we'd taken it from a book we both must have read."

"And you're sure you didn't? What was the title?"

I took a breath. Here it comes, I thought. If he's a sensible person, he'll probably get up and leave right after this. "I'm sure. I would know if I'd read anything like this. I can't say about Tess. Rita says she called her painting the *Dream of the Circle of Women*. And...." His eyes did not leave my face. "Rita also says Tess told her in so many words that she was a witch."

I would have placed money on my assumption that Simon was a sensible person. But, instead of leaving at this point, he merely said, "I'm not all that surprised."

"You're not?" was all I could manage.

"No." He drank the last of his wine and set the glass on the floor. "I doubt that she meant she was the stereotype of a wicked old witch. But, if she meant that she thought differently and knew a lot about herbs and healing, among other things, then it wouldn't surprise me at all. And—" it was his turn for hesitation "—I normally wouldn't tell anyone this, but there were certain books I ordered for her interlibrary loan. They fit right in with this. But Kat, what's bothering you the most? Is it the dream itself that scares you or Tess' connection to it?"

"I don't know," I answered honestly. "It's not like I haven't had odd things happen in my life before, but this is about the oddest of them all. I'm used to being able to work with my dreams trying to tell me something."

"You don't think this one's trying to tell you anything? "

"Maybe, but I don't know if I'm ready to hear it. It's not like any dream I've had before, Simon." That was an understatement. "This seems much more literal. It doesn't seem symbolic, at least not in the usual sense. It's more like it's someone else's story, but I'm stuck with it. It doesn't show any signs of going away."

"You had the first one before coming here?"

I nodded. "Right after finding out about Tess and the house. After I dreamed it the second time, I decided Rowan was right that I needed to come. But I don't know quite what to do with this now. It's out of my realm of experience. I told poor Rita about it today, and she asked me if I'd ever heard of hereditary witchcraft. I just about snapped her head off."

"Maybe she just meant that there's a—pardon the expression—psychic connection of some kind going on here."

"What do you mean?" I asked warily.

"Can you be open for just a minute without biting my head off?" He softened his words with that smile that was beginning to cause specific symptoms in my nervous system. Not unpleasant symptoms.

"I've always prided myself on being an open person," I told him ruefully. "This is being a little more difficult."

"You know the rumors and stories about Tess. The thing is, they don't stop at just Tess. I've heard the same kinds of things about her mother and grandmother, although I've also heard that they didn't keep to themselves like Tess did. Maybe there is some kind of family connection that you're part of."

"So, you're saying I'm a witch, too?" This was the opposite of what I was expecting from him.

"Not if that's not what you want to call it." He looked around the room and then brought his gaze back to mine. "There are things that defy logic that happen to all of us. Some of them are simple, and we probably overlook them. Sometimes I can tell when Jake is in trouble or what he's thinking when he hasn't said a word. We all do that and think nothing of it. There are lots of things we can't explain logically so we try to dismiss them."

I thought about all the times when Rowan was a baby that I woke up every night just seconds before she did, knowing she was about to cry. James and I had only half-jokingly referred to it as my psychic connection to the baby. Somehow, that made much more sense and was easier to accept than what was happening to me presently.

"Even if I could accept that this dream has something to do with a connection to Tess, I still don't get it. It seems set in a specific time period from long ago."

"Is that what the costume books are for?" He reached for one of them and passed it to me.

"Um-hmm. You asked me if it was research for a book. Maybe I should make it one," I quipped as I turned the pages slowly.

"Maybe you should." He was serious. "Are you writing it down? This is stating the obvious here, but you are a writer. Maybe it would help you deal with it."

I looked up from the page. "I can't believe I didn't think of that. Maybe that's all it is, after all." I started to get excited. "It could be just a story I'm trying to write."

Simon burst the little bubble I'd started. "And the fact that Tess painted it long before you had the dream?"

"I don't know. Maybe it's...." I forgot what I was about to say as I stared at the page I'd just flipped to. There were in front of me, if not the exact clothes I'd seen in the dream, unmistakably the same style. "This is it, Simon. This is what the people were wearing."

He moved closer to peer over my shoulder and read the caption under the pictures I was pointing to. "Men's, women's, and children's clothing of the British countryside, 1610 to 1630."

"So now I know when I'm dreaming, just not what." I let out a sigh.

"I know this is easy for me to say, but maybe if you could just let go of it a little, it'll work itself out. Try to stop worrying about where it's coming from. Write it down and if more comes to you, well, write that down, too. Look at it as a gift." I looked at him doubtfully. "At the very least, it might be material for a new book."

"And at the most?" I questioned.

"Wait and see. This may be all you get. Or, you might eventually get more answers to what this is all about."

I studied him for a minute. "This is not what I expected from you, you know."

"Oh?" His eyebrows lifted. "What did you expect? A nice, small-town boy who's very down to earth and certainly wouldn't entertain the possibility that there are things out there that don't fit into our neat little slots?"

I laughed at his description. "Well, yes," I admitted. "Mind you, you already break any stereotype mold I could put you in by being a *male*, small-town librarian. And one with long hair at that." My hand started to touch his ponytail for emphasis, but at the last minute I thought better of it and pulled it away.

There was that smile again, and I had time to think that perhaps it should only be given out by medical prescription before he asked, "Are you disappointed?"

"Hardly," was my only answer as his hand touched *my* hair without hesitation. The book in my lap slid to the floor, but neither of us moved to retrieve it. The absurd thought flitted through my head that it was fortunate I could blame any damage to library property on the librarian in this case. Then I thought no more of the book at all as Simon's fingers gently traced my cheek on their way to lifting my chin. The only hesitation now was the soft question in his eyes. I answered it by moving closer, the easier for our lips to meet.

I won't say that fireworks went off, music sounded, or any of the other silly clichés people use for these moments. That would be an embarrassing use of the English language, not to mention that it would also be a lie. Suffice it to say, I enjoyed the moment. Thoroughly. And, from the expression on Simon's face as our lips parted, I would say it would be safe to assume that he felt the same.

As he rested his forehead against mine, I shut my eyes again and relaxed against him. "Thanks, Simon."

"For what?"

"For making me feel more comfortable about this."

He lifted his head and held my gaze with his. "Comfortable wasn't necessarily what I was going for here."

I couldn't help the laughter that bubbled up. "I only meant you made me feel more comfortable about the dream. That's not how I'd describe...this other."

He laughed now but very softly. "How would you describe it?"

"I don't know. I think I'd need to test it more before I'd know what—" My words were cut off in a very satisfactory way. I never did worry about describing it after that.

When Simon left that night, I was torn between being grateful and disappointed that he had to be home for Jake's return.

You're only here temporarily, I reminded myself. *Too much entanglement won't be good for anybody.*

Having duly acknowledged my sensible side, I proceeded to turn it off along with the lights as I made my way to bed.

Chapter 7

I took Simon's advice—both about writing the dream down and letting go of where it was coming from—to heart. The following week was a whirlwind but mostly a happy one. When I wasn't writing and Simon wasn't working, I spent a great deal of time with him and Jake. I believe it was obvious to Jake that something new had happened in his dad's and my relationship, but it neither seemed to worry him nor excite him. Simon and I had very little time alone, but that was all right. I was happy just to be with him without examining too closely why it made me happy.

We made arrangements for me to finally get around to presenting the program Simon had asked me to do at the library for the following Tuesday. Right after I agreed to it, Rowan called to tell me that she would be flying in on Monday. At first, I thought about changing the program time but decided against it. Rowan had helped with programs I'd given before. I would simply make her do it again.

Rita brought Brian to the house for a potluck dinner one night with Simon, Jake, and me. It was another of Harriet's nights to go to Arthur's, and Rita seemed particularly relaxed without her mother and happy to be with her son. This was probably more people than had gathered at one time in this house in many years. I didn't know how Tess would have felt about that, but it pleased me very much. Though Brian did not strike me as very sophisticated, he was intelligent and funny. All of them, including Jake, entertained me with stories of happenings in Newbridge and asked questions about my life in Seattle. Mostly, the house echoed with laughter, and it felt good. Even Minette spent time in the same room as Jasper without injuring him—although she did not stay long.

After Simon asked me a question about Rowan, I told them that she would be arriving in a few days. Jake wanted to know how old she was and, when I told him that she was nineteen, I noticed Brian perk up in interest.

"How long is she staying?" he asked casually.

"For three weeks," I answered and wondered if I should add more. I decided I should. "Her partner, Keisha is coming for the last two weeks. Then they both have to get back before classes start."

Brian was about to say something, but Jake got there first. "Dad says Rowan is a musician. Does she play fiddle?"

"No, she plays cello. But Keisha plays violin. I bet they'll play some fiddle music with you if you're interested."

"That would be cool. Is that what they're partners in, music?" You could trust Jake to get to the heart of things.

"They do play a lot of music together. But they're partners in other ways, too." This was never an issue with other people I knew, but I had a notion that it could be in Newbridge. I hoped it wasn't an issue with these people I had come to care about so quickly. I learned that it wasn't with Jake's next statement.

"Oh, you mean they're gay," he said matter-of-factly as he handed Jasper a leftover crust of bread from the table. Simon and Rita both hid smiles and only Brian coughed to cover the fact that he'd been startled into a laugh.

"Yes," I said and let it go at that.

The following day, I discovered that Rita had left a dish behind. After I knew she would be home from work, I walked to her house to give it back. It was there that Harriet cornered me and half invited, half commanded me to go to church with her. I had never responded well to commands, either as a child or as an adult. My first reaction was to bristle inwardly. I was about to refuse, but a friendly eagerness came over Harriet's face and I calmed down. What harm could it do to go just this once, and it would make her happy. Whether it would make her drop the pressure after that I doubted, but we could both deal with that later. With Rita as an uneasy witness, I agreed to meet Harriet at her home 9:30 on Sunday morning.

Sunday proved to be a gloriously sunny day, and as I stretched and peered out the bedroom window, I told myself I was truly meant to be a nature-worshipping pagan. I'd much rather be out among the herbs and the woods than be cooped up in a building listening to a sermon. Even in the city, I realized I'd spent most weekends with Rowan in the parks or, in the summer, taken her out of the city altogether to go camping. But a promise was a promise, I supposed. With a sigh, I drew back the covers and headed for the shower.

Minette was nowhere to be seen. I guessed that the beautiful day had already prompted her to rise and head out into it. Lucky her. I still had not found her secret way in and out of the house, and I reminded myself to keep as close an eye on her as I could. I was determined to find it.

After dressing in comfortable but—I presumed— acceptable clothes, I ate a hasty breakfast and headed for the path through the woods. I had given myself a little extra time, and it was a good thing because I was caught up in noticing some of the wild herbs that had just seemed like weeds to me previously. Between some of my now favorite herb books from Tess' shelves and Rita's instructions, I was gaining a new respect for even the much-reviled dandelion. I spent enough time trying to name as many of the plants as I could remember that I was not late, but neither was I terribly early. Harriet was dressed as nicely as I'd seen her so far and more than ready to go. I was happy to see Rita emerge from her room dressed in neatly pressed black slacks and a silky white blouse, obviously planning to go with us. I hadn't really wanted to face this alone with Harriet.

Until we arrived, I didn't even know what church Harriet belonged to. In all honesty, I wouldn't have been surprised if it were some exotic, rural group of snake handlers, but it turned out to be much more mundane than that. The Newbridge Methodist Church was on Maple Street, only two blocks behind the library, overlooking the river. It was an old wooden building but freshly painted white with red trim and had a small steeple containing a single bell that was ringing as we approached. Harriet hustled Rita and me inside and directed us to a pew near the front. No hiding in the back for her, especially when she was in charge of someone who so obviously needed saving.

My father had been an agnostic, and my mother had firmly believed that spirituality was something people found within themselves. Needless to say, I didn't spend much time inside any church during my growing years. In my teens and early twenties, however, I had earned some money as a fairly competent pianist, playing music now and then for small churches of different denominations. Because of this, the Methodist service was familiar to me, and even two of the hymns sung this day were ones I remembered having played several times. I entertained myself by singing the second line of the music rather than the melody. I always thought it was good to add a little harmony wherever I could. Rita smiled when she heard me, but poor Harriet frowned slightly, not sure if what I was doing was a good thing or a bad thing. But she let it go when the service reached her favorite part—the sermon.

It turned out that Harriet and I had something in common. We both listened to every word of the sermon. For different reasons and with very different reactions, but I don't think she realized that at the time. My father had been a history professor, and I had learned from him to listen carefully to people making speeches and then analyze what they said. At times, while I was being the musician for one church or another, it would annoy me that I couldn't just zone out the way I noticed several of the parishioners do. Young as I was, I often found myself wanting to ask questions or debate what was being said. Knowing that I wouldn't continue to get paid to play for any church I questioned almost always kept my mouth shut. The debates usually just played out in my head. But I always listened, and I found myself doing the same thing this day.

The minister was a tall, balding man, probably in his middle fifties. I considered it fortunate that he was not a fire-and-brimstone sort, but neither was he terribly inspiring. I'd had a little spark of interest when we'd driven up to the church and the sign in front had proclaimed the topic of the sermon: Love and Tolerance For All Our Brethren. Of course, I'd immediately wanted to add to the sentence the words *and sisters* (or would it have to be *sistren* for consistency?) but I'd had some hope for what was to come. It turned out that the aforementioned brethren were all of the Christian persuasion, though of any denomination or sect. Well, I guessed you had to start somewhere. I gave a surreptitious glance Harriet's way to see how she was taking this talk of tolerance for other (slightly different) beliefs. The irony of her intolerance toward Tess' alleged beliefs was obviously not on her mind as she smiled happily and bobbed her head often, in agreement with the minister's words.

Near the end of the service, there was a moment of discomfort on my part as the congregation was asked to introduce any visitors. It was obvious who the only visitor was. This was not a large congregation, and I was certain they all knew each other well. Nevertheless, Harriet made a great show of presenting "Katrina Benson, my new neighbor and I hope a regular visitor to our church during her time in New-bridge." As if that weren't bad enough, she went on to embarrass Rita by reintroducing her and adding, "Just in case you've forgotten who she is since her face is so seldom seen in our fine church." Rita's face turned slightly red, but otherwise she looked straight ahead without changing her expression. I heard titters from a very few people, but the minister beamed at Harriet, welcomed me profusely, and told Rita that he was glad to see her again. Soon after, an interesting attempt at a piano rendition of a Bach recessional signaled our chance to escape, but not as far as I might have hoped. There was still a line to wait in as the reverend stood at the open door to shake hands and have a word with each person who passed through. During the wait, a few members of the congregation came to give me a brief, friendly hello. I had been in Newbridge long enough now that I recognized several faces.

At a touch at my elbow, I turned in surprise to see Donna Bartlett with three well-scrubbed children in tow. She introduced me to all three, and I especially looked with interest at Kyle. He looked to be somewhere around Jake's age, and I had a feeling he wouldn't stay well scrubbed for long after leaving the church. He seemed to have, shall we say, a lot of energy. I could see no sign of an injury on either hand, so I presumed his mother had followed Rita's advice and it had worked.

When it was my turn at the door, the Reverend Foxworth introduced me to the woman beside him as "my wife, Mrs. Foxworth." She smiled pleasantly but said nothing. I murmured something I hoped was appropriate and moved toward the steps, but Reverend Foxworth was not finished. "I understand you are Tess Whitney's daughter." That stopped my forward momentum. I looked back at his still smiling face and wondered what he was going to make of that. Mrs. Foxworth's smile drooped slightly, but she continued to say nothing.

"Yes, I'm staying in her house for a while." I corrected myself. "*My* house now."

"It's too bad for both of you that you never got to meet her." He seemed very well informed, but I had to learn to get over being surprised about that.

"Did you know her?" I asked. From what I knew, I couldn't imagine that she had spent any time attending his church.

His smile deepened. "We had some…interesting conversations. We didn't often agree on things, but I think we both enjoyed our little debates." I looked him full in the face.

He actually meant it! Harriet and Mrs. Foxworth regarded him with little frowns but, for the first time, I gave him a genuine smile. Perhaps there was more to him than I'd first given him credit for.

"It was nice to meet you, Reverend Foxworth," I said as I turned him over to Harriet behind me.

"I hope to see you here often," were his parting words. I let that slip by without an answer.

I looked to where Rita had parked her car as she had gone on ahead of me. She was in what appeared to be a slightly heated conversation with a dark-haired, middle-aged man who loomed over her. I wondered if this was the ex-husband. As I approached, I caught her eye and she motioned to me in relief.

"We'll talk about it some other time, Arthur," I heard her tell the man before her. She turned to me. "This is my friend, Kat. Kat, this is Arthur."

I could see the resemblance in their faces as Arthur turned to me, making no attempt at covering his irritation with his sister. "How do you do?" he said in a way that didn't make me think he really cared to know. Though I always tried hard not to make snap judgments upon first meeting people, I was afraid I was going to have a hard time getting over this one. As much as I'd warmed to Rita at our first meeting, the opposite was true with Arthur. Plainly and simply, I didn't like him. I knew that wasn't fair. Brothers and sisters clashed all the time, and who knew what this was about. Perhaps he had many fine, redeeming qualities, but they weren't shining through in our first seconds of meeting. The scowl he'd kept on Rita never left his face until their mother approached with a woman, almost as tall and thin as Arthur, beside her. Then he pasted half a smile on that face that, if I had taken a liking to him, I might have called handsome, and bent to place a per-functory kiss on Harriet's cheek. She didn't seem to notice how half-hearted the kiss was.

She smiled up at her son and said in a sweeter voice than I'd heard her use before, "Arthur, why didn't you and Alice come sit with us? I see you've met Katrina. Katrina, this is Alice, Arthur's wife." This was a new side of Harriet—the doting mother.

"There wasn't much room, Mother. Alice and I were just fine in the back. I was surprised to see Rita here this morning. Weren't you, Alice?" I marveled at the talent this man had for being unlikable.

Alice had no time to squeeze in a reply before Harriet said, "I know, dear. She hasn't been to church in quite some time. It's made me so sad all the times that she just drops me off here but won't come herself."

I was beginning to get very annoyed with both of them for talking about Rita as if she weren't there. And I was even annoyed at Rita for letting them get away with it. It went on for a few minutes more with Rita standing in quiet misery while I thought of a tiny way to work some revenge.

"It was so nice to meet both of you," I broke in as sincerely as I could make it sound, "but Rita and I have to get going. She promised to help me get the house ready because my daughter's coming tomorrow. We may have to go to Watertown this afternoon to get some things—you know how it is. You won't mind taking your mother home, will you? Of course, you won't. It will give you some time to chat some more."

They all stared at me in stunned silence, so that I had time to propel Rita toward the car before I heard Arthur start to sputter behind us. But it was too late. Before he could get any real words out, we were in the car with the doors closed and Rita had conveniently snapped out of her family-induced stupor. She was at the stop sign at the end of Maple before she asked, "Where are we really going?"

"Anywhere you want," was my reply.

"We could go do whatever you need to do to your house to get ready."

"I don't really need anything. Let's go some place nice and have lunch."

Rita pulled the car onto the main street in the opposite direction of our houses. "I know a place about ten miles away I bet you'd like."

"Okay, let's go." It struck me a little late that I might have gotten Rita into more trouble than escaping was worth, but before I could voice my concern, she smiled a little sadly in my direction.

"Thanks for what you did back there, Kat. I know I should stick up for myself more, but it's easier to just do what I did as a kid and try to ignore them. That's not very mature of me, is it?"

I noticed a lone tear trickle down her cheek, and I couldn't help but feel sorry for her. I couldn't imagine letting myself be treated that way, but my guess was she'd had a lifetime of accepting it.

"So, does Arthur have *any* redeeming qualities?" I got the response I was hoping for as she laughed.

"He and Alice take Mom to their house for dinner once a week. I'm sure there are others, but it might take me thirty or forty years to think of them."

"What do he and Alice do to earn their living?" I morbidly wondered what someone as unpleasant as I found Arthur did for work. Animal control perhaps—specializing in euthanizing puppies and kittens?

"They're both teachers. Alice teaches second grade. Arthur teaches math at the high school."

"Ouch." I hadn't meant to say it aloud.

"I know." Rita made a face. "Brian hated math in high school. He had to take it from Arthur. Brian wasn't one of his favorite students. I don't think Alice is so bad at it."

"Do they have any children?" I asked.

"No," was Rita's terse response.

A thought struck me. "I know it's none of my business, but what were you and he arguing about when I interrupted?"

"You didn't interrupt. You saved Arthur from a strangling. It's what we always argue about—Brian."

I was puzzled. "What about Brian? He's such a nice kid."

Rita gave a little snort. "Not according to Arthur. He takes every opportunity he gets to tell me what a waste he thinks Brian is making of his life. He's sure he'll marry some uneducated girl and turn into an alcoholic, just like his father."

I was shocked into total silence until, finally, something struck me very funny and I let out what must have seemed totally inappropriate laughter.

"What?" Rita looked for the humor and couldn't find it. "What's so funny?"

I got myself under control. "Remember when you told me you'd asked Tess to teach you a spell to use on Arthur when you were kids?"

"Yes," she said carefully, humoring the lunatic sitting in the passenger's seat.

"Are you sure you didn't get one from her? One that worked very well because he sure seems like a toad to me."

We both laughed uproariously at that and then went on to have a fine lunch.

When Rita brought me home in the afternoon, I invited her to stay for a while. There was no need for her to go home and face the repercussions of the mini-rebellion I'd led her into quite yet. She helped me choose which bedroom would be the best for Rowan and Keisha. We supplied it with clean bedding and then had a grand time sprucing it up. We went through Tess' paintings and chose ones to hang on the bedroom walls that I thought Rowan would find the most appealing. Then we went out to the herb beds to pick flowers that would be both esthetically pleasing and would fill the room with a wonderful scent. It was a perfect opportunity for Rita to continue our lessons in herb lore and recognition.

As I was circling the house while filling a basket with late-blooming lavender, yarrow, passionflower, hyssop, fennel, sage, rosemary, and calendula (those were the ones I recognized), I was aware of a shrub-like plant that I had noticed before but hadn't been attracted to. It was almost isolated from the other herbs, occupying a tiny patch of ground near the back of the house.

As Rita made her way around the corner, I pointed it out to her. "What is that?"

She wrinkled her nose slightly. "That's belladonna." Seeing my blank look, she went on, "Also known as deadly nightshade. You probably don't even want to touch it without gloves on."

"What an odd name for it. Is it really deadly?"

"Actually, it is. You don't ever want to swallow it, and it's not good to get it on your skin either."

I was slightly horrified. "Why in the world would Tess have planted it here?"

"She didn't plant it. She told me her grandmother did. Tess kept the patch small, but she kept it because there are uses for it. She told me never to use it, that you really had to know what you were doing. When I was little and started coming over here, she kept a small fence around it so I wouldn't go near it. I know she used it a long time ago when one of the Jones brothers poisoned himself with some wild mushrooms."

Rita turned away from the nightshade. "There are other good uses for it, but she managed to scare me enough way back then that I've never been interested in them. I remember reading somewhere that it was used by Italian women a long time ago as drops they put in their eyes to make the pupils dilate so they'd look more beautiful. I thought that was one of the dumbest things I'd ever heard."

"Ugh," I said. "Maybe we should just get rid of it. Is there anything else here poisonous?"

"There are a few things you don't want to eat, like the foxglove, but nothing else like the nightshade. Most of the things here you can eat, you know."

"I'll watch you eat them first. Then if you're still standing, maybe I'll try them," I joked. "I suppose we could pull the nightshade up and burn it. There's a burn barrel out by the barn."

"Do you want to do that now? Got some extra gloves?"

"I'm not sure if there are any here or not," I said. I looked at the basket of flowers I was holding. "Let's just keep doing the fun stuff. The nightshade's been here for a long time without doing any harm. But since you or I will never use it, I'll pull it out when I get a chance."

"Okay. Do we have enough flowers or do you want more?" Rita took the basket from me and looked over what we had chosen.

"I think that's plenty. Thanks for the ongoing lessons."

"You're welcome." She flashed a smile at me. "It's really fun being around someone who's interested in herbs again."

She headed back to the front of the house, and I followed. Once inside, we put the finishing touches on making Rowan's room welcoming for her. Then Rita decided it was time to go home and face the music. She said that almost cheerfully, and it made me believe getting away had been good for her.

"Your mother won't make you live on bread and water for the night?" I teased.

"Heck, no." She laughed. "She'll be waiting for me to make dinner, so at least I'll eat well. Have fun with Rowan tomorrow."

"We'll be back from the airport in the afternoon. Stop by after work to meet her if you feel like it," I invited.

"Maybe I will. See you then."

After Rita left, I managed to get some writing done, fix a quick meal, and then a little before seven o'clock, I headed to Simon's house. We had made arrangements to go for a walk and then watch a video that Jake had insisted I would love. It had horses in it.

We made our way along a path by the river and, as Jake and Jasper chased each other ahead of us, I told Simon of my morning at the church and the encounter with Rita's family.

As I was being a bit irreverent about the sermon I'd listened to, it occurred to me that religion was one of the things that had not come up in any of our conversations so far. From the way he had handled my dreams and the idea that Tess called herself a witch, I knew Simon was open-minded, but I didn't know if he had a religious affiliation. Once again I had spoken before clearly thinking through what I was saying. Now, I glanced at him a little sheepishly.

"Am I in the process of offending you? Here I am being flippant about this, and I don't even know if you belong to a church or...." I didn't even know how to finish the sentence. As close as Simon and I had become in such a short time, I realized that there was still a great deal I didn't know about him or he about me. "I have this terrible tendency to assume people I like just naturally think the way I do, and I say things without thinking. It's not a requirement for my friendship, mind you. I really do have friends who think way differently than I do...." I trailed off and looked at him. "I'm botching this up pretty badly. Say something before I make it any worse."

Thank goodness, he flashed his trademark smile and reached for my hand as he continued walking, pulling me along with him. "You worry too much about some things. In case you haven't realized it, we seem to have a lot in common." He pulled a branch of a bush aside and held it until I stepped past it. "My parents are Catholic, so that's how I grew up. They're liberal, though, and the last time I went to church with them was before I went off to college. I spent some time trying out, adding, and subtracting things to my belief system, including Buddhism. But by and large, I'm not a churchgoer. When Lynn was pregnant with Jake, she started worrying about some sort of spiritual background for him, so I agreed to go to a Unitarian church with her in Portland because they're rather open. But there isn't one here, and I haven't felt a need to plug Jake into anything. He and I talk about pretty much everything. I figure he's getting enough to make choices in what he believes. How did you handle it with Rowan?"

This guy was too good to be believed. I knew there had to be a flaw in the design somewhere—there always was. But so far, except for the little misunderstanding we'd had when we first met, I liked everything I knew about him. There would probably be something we strongly disagreed on before long, but until then....

"She was exposed to all kinds of things," I answered him. "My parents were definitely not churchgoers, but I played music for different churches when she was young and often dragged her with me. James is Jewish, and when Rowan was in her early teens, she found Wicca. How's that for a religious background?"

"Sounds to me like she should have met Tess. Jake and I are looking forward to meeting Rowan, by the way. We won't bother you tomorrow, but how about having dinner with us Tuesday night?"

"Absolutely." I gave him a quick kiss and went ahead to catch up with Jake and Jasper. I knew Rowan would like both of them (all three, really—she would love Jasper, too) when she met them. What I hadn't told Simon was that she didn't know about them yet. I hadn't said anything further after telling her that I was going to meet with the librarian that day on the phone. I wasn't sure why. Maybe I didn't want to jinx things or make more of it than it was. Somehow, it had just been easier to say nothing.

Chapter 8

Rowan's plane came into Syracuse midmorning. As I watched her maneuver around other disembarking passengers once she saw me, I marveled at how much I had missed her. She hadn't lived at home with me since she was seventeen as she had moved out when she went to college a year early. We had always been close, however, despite the occasional mother/daughter flare-ups. It helped that she had chosen to stay in Seattle to attend the university, so I had seen her often in the two years since she had moved out.

In typical Rowan fashion, she dropped her carry-on bags on the floor, set her cello down more gently, and then threw her arms around me with a squeal. I hugged her in return and then drew back to look at that wonderful face. She had what I had always considered a lovely elf face. Her dark eyes were crinkled from that familiar grin she often wore. I was startled to notice that her high cheekbones reminded me of the picture of Tess. Her auburn hair floated in curls around her face as she leaned in to kiss my cheek. I was tall, but Rowan was a little taller still. Certainly I was biased, but I knew that she was a lovely young woman and I was very glad to see her.

"How was your flight?" I picked up a bag as she lifted her backpack and cello.

"Cramped and horrible food, but the people on either side of me were pretty interesting, once I got them talking."

I laughed at that. If those poor people had wanted quiet on their flight, they never had a chance. Rowan had always been friendly and very curious. And she was not shy.

"Let's get down to the baggage claim, and you can tell me about them." As I steered her in that direction, we began a discussion that covered many things and didn't stop until we had gotten into the Jeep and driven the hundred miles north to Newbridge.

I told Rowan most of the things that had happened since I arrived, and as we drove through town, I pointed out little, familiar things to her. Brian was at the pumps of the gas station and waved as we went by.

"Who was that?" Rowan asked when she saw me wave back.

"Rita's son, Brian." I told her. "I think he's a year or two older than you are, and he's very nice. I'm sure you'll meet him, and I want you to be nice to him when you do."

Rowan's eyes widened in pretend shock. "I'm always nice to people. But what makes him so special?"

"I really like him, his mother adores him, and his uncle thinks he's a bum."

"This would be Uncle Arthur, the one *you* think is a bum?"

"Something like that," I answered.

"I can tell I'll like Brian already then." She put her hand out the window to catch the wind as she had done as a child. "It would be interesting to meet both of them."

And she meant it. People had always fascinated Rowan.

"Well, you can meet Brian, but I'm not going out of my way to introduce his uncle. One meeting with him was enough for me."

As we pulled into the driveway, Rowan craned her neck eagerly to get the first view of the house. I tried to see it through her eyes, startled to realize how familiar it had already become to me. "Wow, Mom. What a great, spooky, old place." Rowan jumped out of the car before I had the engine turned off.

"Spooky?" I frowned. It hadn't struck me that way.

"Not bad spooky." She put an arm around my shoulders and gave them a squeeze. "Just, you know, really *old*. Like a lot's happened here. Don't worry. I like what I see so far."

We grabbed her luggage and instrument from the vehicle, and she followed me to the porch. As I was turning the key in the lock, Minette jumped to the porch railing. She spied Rowan and froze in place.

"Hello...oh, is this Minette?" I'd told Rowan about her. "Look at those eyes! What a beautiful cat you are."

Beautiful is not how I would have described her, but Minette seemed to take it to heart because, as Rowan started slowly toward her, the cat did not move. For her, that was an extremely friendly gesture. Rowan extended her hand gently toward her, and Minette sniffed it. Then, she swiftly swatted the hand, but she did not extend her claws or run away. Rowan left her hand in place, and when Minette sniffed it again and rubbed her head against it briefly, I knew they would be friends. Or as close as Minette would come to being friends.

Rowan wanted to see everything. We hadn't eaten lunch, but I knew she would rather satisfy her curiosity before her hunger. I showed her the downstairs rooms and saw her look greedily at the bookshelf in the living room. But as she started toward it, the painting on the mantel caught her attention.

"This is the dream?" she asked as she reached out to barely touch it. I nodded, and she peered more closely. "What about the rest of the dream? Are you going to paint that?"

"Probably. The faces of the man and the girl are so clear to me. It would be easy to reproduce them. Come see what else I've been doing." I coaxed her gently away and led the way to the studio. "I've been working on several things, and you can see some of Tess' work, including a self-portrait."

Rowan's reaction to the room was just as I suspected it would be. She was captivated by all of Tess' work, but when I showed her the self-portrait, she sat on a stool and held it in front of her. "So, this is Grandmama." She exhaled. After several minutes of silence, she looked up from the painting. "She was a nice-looking old witch, wasn't she?"

I burst into laughter and took the portrait away from her and set it on the easel. "Yes, she was. And I see a little bit of her in you. Now *that* is spooky."

"Want to get spookier? You and she have the same eyes." Rowan looked from the painting to my face. "Do you feel like you're getting any closer to knowing her?"

I frowned slightly in thought. "Oddly enough, I do. I still don't have a lot of answers, but the more I hear about her, the more real she becomes." I took her hand and pulled her from the stool. "Come and see the rest of the house. Then we'll get some lunch, and I'll show you what there is to see outside."

Just as I had predicted, Rowan was also captivated by what was in the attic. She insisted on pulling the trunks of clothes to a spot where they were easily accessible for trying on the contents in the near future. She found an old violin that I had overlooked and kept it aside to take downstairs with her. A box of old postcards, letters, and receipts also caught her fancy. Some of them dated back to the early nineteenth century. I knew there wouldn't be a lack of things to do while she was here.

After a quick sandwich, we went out the back door to do the "grounds tour" as Rowan dubbed it. She was suitably impressed with both the great number of herbs there and my growing ability to name them. I showed her the cellar, and she agreed with me on the oddness of there being no light source or door leading from there into the house.

"You looked it over really well for both?" she inquired.

"Yes, but it wasn't easy—it's very dark. I'll have to get a better light to look with one of these days." I also told her about Minette having a way into the house that I hadn't been able to pinpoint yet. "Maybe it's through the cellar somewhere. I've seen her go through the hole in the cellar door."

Rowan was delighted with the barn even though there was very little to be seen there. She spied the saddle and bridles and sat on one of the straw bales to look them over. "These are pretty nice. I think they could be oiled back into shape. Tess had horses?"

"So I've heard. A long time ago."

"Well, that proves right there she wasn't all bad." She grinned at me. Though I had never sat on a horse before coming to Newbridge, I had taken Rowan to many a riding lesson on a farm outside of Seattle when she was in her horse craze pre-teen years. She had loved it, but she hadn't been able to convince me to move to a farm so she could raise horses in her spare time, and she gave up trying when music took over her life. "Remember how much I wanted horses of my own? Here's your chance to buy my love—you've got the place for them now."

"I think I've paid enough for your love already, thank you." This was one of our ongoing jokes. "And you're not the first person to tell me I should get a horse here."

"Oh? Who else has brilliant ideas besides me?"

"A little boy named Jake. His grandparents have horses, and he's really into them. He thought I should get one." The opportunity had presented itself to tell Rowan about Simon and Jake, but before I got anything else out, we heard my name called.

"Kat, are you here?" It came from the front of the house.

Rowan looked at me questioningly. "It's Rita," I told her. "Come on so you can meet her." Rowan hung the bridle she was holding back on the wall and followed me to the front yard. Rita was standing just off the porch and smiled a little shyly as we approached. "Hi," I greeted her. "How was work?"

"Busy," she replied. "Just thought I'd stop to say hi and meet Rowan."

"Hi, Rita." Rowan didn't wait for introductions. She came closer and extended her hand. "I've heard a lot about you. Mom says you've been really nice to her, and you've taught her a lot about the herbs here."

Rita shook the offered hand and forgot about being shy in Rowan's easy friendliness. "I've heard a lot about you, too. Did you bring your cello with you? I hope we get to hear some of your music while you're here."

As we sat on the porch and chatted, I watched Rita fall under Rowan's spell. This daughter of mine genuinely liked people and usually made friends easily. I'd marveled at that when she was a child and was glad she hadn't lost those traits as she became an adult. Before long, they sounded like old chums. Rowan told her that we had been out in the barn looking at the horse tack and that she had suggested I should get a horse. Rita was amused.

"Did your mother tell you about her trail ride? I hear Jake told her she should get horses here, too."

Rowan looked at me with interest. "No, she didn't tell me. And who's Jake? This is the second time I've heard of him. A new boyfriend?"

"No, that would be his father, Simon," Rita said, and then she and Rowan both looked at me in amazement. "You haven't told her about them?"

To my annoyance, I colored slightly. "No. I just haven't gotten to it yet."

"Ohhh, do tell." Rowan enjoyed my discomfort. "There really is a new boyfriend here?"

"I wouldn't call him that, exactly," I began.

Rita snorted. "I don't know what else she'd call him. And he's obviously smitten with your mother, even though she's the one who asked him out first."

"Really?" Rowan turned to Rita. "Is he cute?"

"Oh, definitely. He's the cutest librarian you've ever seen."

A light snapped on in Rowan's head. "Ah, ha! The librarian you were going to meet. I pictured a woman at least Tess' age—and you let me go right on thinking that."

I tried to retrieve some of my dignity. "All right, both of you. I have been spending time with him and his son, Jake. You and I are going to have dinner with them tomorrow night, Rowan. But don't get all excited. He is really nice, but I'm not going to be here forever, you know. And I'm not sixteen years old. We're friends."

"Good friends," Rita offered. I frowned at her.

"Well, tell me this." Rowan's eyes twinkled. "Do *you* think he's cute?"

I gave her a serious look. "Oh, definitely."

That night Rowan and I sat in the living room and talked more. It had only been slightly less than a month since we'd seen each other, and I couldn't believe how much we had to say to one another. But then, I felt as if I was in a whole other world than I'd been in a month ago. At one point, I made my way to the kitchen to get us some tea, and when I returned, Rowan was engrossed in looking through Tess' books. She glanced up as I entered the room.

"There are some pretty interesting books here." She held up a couple of them, and I came closer to see which they were. "She was definitely into herbs, wasn't she?"

I gave her a nod. "And I've been going through most of her herb books. For some reason, since coming here, I've been into them, too."

"You think Tess passed that down to you? Maybe you're a green witch, too." She was only half joking.

"All right, Rowan. Tell me about this witch thing. You know a lot more about it than I do. Rita said something about hereditary witchcraft. Is there really such a thing?"

She set the books back on the shelf. "Yes, but the definition I've always heard of it is when someone learns about things like herb lore directly from a family member who is a witch. It's the tradition that's passed down, not necessarily anything supernatural. I'd like to know what kind of witch Tess actually thought of herself as. It seems most likely she was a solitary."

"Meaning?"

"Meaning that she didn't belong to a coven or a group. This doesn't seem like the type of place that would harbor a great number of witches."

"I wouldn't think so." I chewed my lip. "Maybe it's just this house. I've heard that her mother and grandmother were 'different,' too. Rita says Tess used to heal hurt animals she'd bring to her. I don't know how much I believe, though."

"What about your dreams, Mom?"

"What about them?"

She held my gaze. "What do you believe about them?"

"I really don't know." I sighed. "They seem tied to this house, but I don't know how. I tried to dismiss them as just parts of a story I could write, but Simon reminded me that Tess had seen the same thing."

"Ah, so Simon knows about all this, and you're still 'friends.'" She used her fingers to frame quotation marks around the word.

"Don't make fun of me or I'll quit talking to you." I tried to sound stern, but it didn't work.

Rowan grinned. "Okay, but what did he think of it?"

"He thought I should just be sort of gentle with my-self, let it go, and see what happens. He also suggested there are things that aren't logical that happen to all of us."

"I think I'm looking forward to meeting him." Her grin broadened, and then she became a bit more serious. "Have you thought of the possibility that the dreams could be real? I mean that they're about something that really hap-pened?"

She hit the very thing I had been avoiding. "How could that be, Rowan? Have you ever known something like that to happen to someone?"

"I've certainly heard stories about that sort of thing. But to be honest, no. I haven't known anyone it's happened to. I've known some really interesting things to happen to people, though."

Minette walked into the room and made a show of making herself comfortable on the back of a chair. I regarded her thoughtfully and remembered. "There's another strange thing I haven't told you about. I decided I needed a name for the cat after I realized she belonged here."

"So you're the one who named her Minette? Where did that come from? I don't remember you suggesting it for the cat we had when I was growing up."

"You named Fred, remember?" I gave her a playful poke. "But I don't know where it came from. It just popped into my head and stuck. The thing is, later, when I met Rita, she told me that that was what Tess had named her."

Rowan didn't say anything for several minutes. Finally, she said, "Mom, I know you must be having a hard time with this, but I hope you don't mind my saying that I think it is so cool. You were obviously meant to be here." A thought hit her. "I wonder if I'll get anything. It's my line of women, too. I'll have to pay attention to my dreams while I'm here."

I hadn't thought of that. "It'll be interesting to see," I granted her. "One of the things I'm having a hard time with in all of this, even though I know it's not true, is this feeling that I'm somehow being disloyal to your grandmother. Grandma Helen." I hadn't realized how much I felt that until I said it.

"No, it's not true," Rowan comforted me. "We both loved Grandma. There's nothing disloyal about what you're doing. But this place is part of you. Tess was your flesh and blood, and you are connected to her. With everything happening, you can't deny that."

"You're right. And I wasn't expecting to feel any kind of attachment to Tess, but that's starting to happen. I don't know if that's healthy or not."

"Mom—"

"Okay." I cut off her protest. "I don't know if I'm just making this up or not because I want it to be so, but I'm beginning to believe that she didn't give me up lightly. And I mean to find out what really happened."

I changed the subject abruptly. "I really am glad you're here."

Rowan's smile reflected her understanding at my need to let go of the topic for a while. "Me, too. Keisha and I have been having a great summer, but I've missed you, too. And she's hoping you'll make her some of your yummy tacos when she comes. She misses those taco feasts you've fixed for us."

I laughed at her. "It might be hard to find the ingredients here, but I'll see what we can do. I'll put you both to work to pay for it, though." I suddenly remembered what was happening tomorrow. "Speaking of putting you to work, I'm giving a little program at the library tomorrow afternoon about my books. You can help."

"Glad to," she replied. "Just like the good old days. What do you want me to do? Anything with music?"

"Definitely. Maybe we could focus on the two books where the stories are based on music."

"Like we did for the Bellingham library?"

"Exactly." We both got into the excitement of the planning, and by the time I realized how exhausted she must be from jetlag, Rowan and I had a terrific program worked out.

We climbed the stairs together, and I gave her a hug outside her room. As I headed to mine, I noticed Minette follow quietly into Rowan's. Absurdly, I was both pleased that the cat had taken to Rowan and miffed that she had given up on me so easily. However, before I completely drifted off, I felt the weight of a cat-size body hop onto my bed and curl into the curve of my back.

Then I was lost in a peaceful, dreamless sleep.

Chapter 9

The crowd waiting at the library for us the next day surprised me. Simon had placed flyers, advertising the program, around town and handed them out with the books people checked out. I suppose I shouldn't have been surprised. I was now a double celebrity: the strange lady staying at the witch house and someone who had published books you could actually find at the library. It was hard to tell which of those two things people found the more interesting. The number of adults equaled the number of children. We spent an hour on the program and another half hour or so answering questions. Rowan's cello was a hit.

After the program was finished, three children actually presented me with their own private copies of some of my books and asked me to sign them. Simon had pulled all the copies the library owned from the shelves and asked me to do the same to them. All in all, it was a successful and fun affair. Donna Bartlett was there with her three children. I had noticed Kyle and Jake sitting together at the beginning of our presentation and was only briefly aware of Simon sliding in between them at some point when one or the other of them made a few antsy movements.

There had been time only for very brief introductions when we. arrived, but as people finally drifted away, it was time to introduce Rowan properly to Simon and Jake. Simon

139

turned the checkout over to his mother and another volunteer and then came back to the children's corner to help me gather things up.

Jake and Rowan had already formed a bond. I over-heard them talking about fiddle music and horses.

"Your mom didn't do too bad riding Lady," I was gratified to hear Jake say. "'Course, Lady's the oldest, easiest horse my grandparents have. Do you play violin, besides cello?"

"I do play it a bit, but I spend a lot more time with my cello. My friend who's coming next week plays violin way better than I do. I hear you play, too. Shall we form a trio and play some fiddle tunes when she comes? And, by the way, I used to take horse riding lessons."

Rowan had really caught his attention.

"I know. Kat told me. I'm riding in a barrel race for 4-H this weekend. Want to come watch? Maybe you could go riding with me, too."

"Sure." She had won another firm friend.

"Oh, ho," I teased him. "Now that you have someone who knows how to ride, does that mean I'm out as a trail rid-ing partner?"

Jake turned my way. "Oh, no. You know how to ride now. I showed you. We could all go, and you and Dad can take the slow horses."

"How considerate." Simon laughed at Jake and then turned to me. "Thanks, Kat. It was a great program. And Rowan, thanks for the music. The crowd loved it all."

Rowan placed her cello in its case. "Thanks. I hear we're coming to your house for dinner tonight. I'm looking forward to it. I've heard a lot about both of you."

I shot a warning glance in her direction, but she smiled innocently back at me and didn't let on that most of what she had heard came from Rita.

Before we left the library, Rowan met Simon's mother, who heartily endorsed Jake's invitation to come ride the horses at her farm. Then we piled our belongings into the car and drove back to the house.

I had some time to do a bit of work in the studio while Rowan practiced her cello. I hadn't noticed what time it was until she poked her head in the doorway.

"I think it might be getting close to time to leave," she informed me.

"Okay." I began to clean up the area I was using, and I noticed she had the old violin tucked under one arm. "Is that still playable?"

She ran a finger lightly over the finish. "It needs some work and new strings, but it seems in pretty good shape. We'll have to ask Keisha, but I think it might be a pretty nice violin."

"Is it something you would use?"

"Not really. The one I have is just fine for what little I play. Now, if we'd found a nice antique cello, I'd really be excited."

"If we find one, it's yours."

She laughed and left to return the violin to its case.

Dinner was just being started when we arrived, which was just fine for all concerned. My offer to help was gratefully accepted, and Simon and I worked companionably in the kitchen while Rowan was perfectly happy spending the time with Jake, Jasper, and the rats. When we were finally ready to sit around the table, I had a moment of mild confusion. It hit me that here were representatives of two different parts of my life—before knowing about Tess and after—sitting before me. I shook myself inwardly to dispel the feeling.

Not surprisingly, the talk over dinner tended toward horses and music with a few other topics thrown in randomly. At one of those random junctures, Rowan turned to Simon. "Mom says you're the entire library staff. It's a great library. How do you manage by yourself?"

"I don't, really," Simon replied. "There are several volunteers who help. A lot. That wouldn't go over in a bigger library, having volunteers do as much as mine do, but this is a small place. We're lucky to have a library and a board that lets me do as much as I do."

"What happens if you get sick? Or take a vacation? Does the library close down?" she wanted to know.

"Neither Jake or I have been sick very often in the five years I've been there, but I have a couple of volunteers who know what to do when I'm not there for a day or two. I go to training and conferences once in a while, too. For vacations, the board made an arrangement with the Watertown library to send a librarian to fill in. The library's open four and a half days with nice hours so—all in all—it's a good job." He looked at his son. "Plus, Jake can be there any time, too."

"Lucky you," Rowan told Jake.

"Sometimes," he said. "Sometimes it's boring, and sometimes he makes me work too hard." Simon snickered. "And most of the time, Jasper can't be there. But sometimes it can be fun. Dad tells good stories, and not just for the little kids. He has a chess club and other neat stuff there, too. I guess I like it."

"My mom made me spend a lot of time in libraries, too," Rowan confided to him. "She does a lot of her writing work there. Sometimes, I thought they were boring, but I love books, so I could usually find something interesting to do."

Jake agreed and then launched us back into another discussion of horses. By the time the evening was over, plans had been made for two trail rides and for Rowan and me to accompany Simon and Jake (and Bob the Wonder Horse) to the fairgrounds in Watertown for the barrel races.

When the week was up, Jake informed us sadly, school would be starting again.

"In case you wanted to know," Rowan began as I drove away, "I like both Simon and Jake a lot."

"And Jasper," I added. "You can't just like Jake and not Jasper. They both would be upset."

"And Jasper," she agreed. "Why didn't you tell me about Simon before I got here?"

"I don't know," I hedged. "It's not a big deal. I wasn't trying to hide anything from you. It's not like it's serious or anything."

"Methinks thou doth protest too much." Rowan laughed at me. "I saw the way Simon looked at you a couple of times. And, at the risk of a denial from you, I have to tell you, you looked the same way back."

"I do like him a lot, I'll grant you that. But I'm not going to get too serious. For a lot of reasons." I hoped she would let it drop there, but of course, I should have known better.

"You haven't really been serious about anybody that I know of since you and Dad split. Why is that? I never had the feeling you were pining away over him."

"No, I never pined over him," I said and glanced her way. "Your father is a good person, but I wasn't terribly hurt when he left. We both agreed it was over and, except for sometimes feeling badly for you, I've never regretted it."

"You didn't have to feel bad for me." She looked at me in surprise. "I made out very well. You and Dad didn't fight over me, and I know I got double the presents and attention I would have gotten if you'd stayed together. Besides, Dad was always so afraid I'd think he was giving more time and attention to Laura and Jamie that I got even more out of him. Is that why you never went out with anyone for very long? You were afraid I wouldn't get enough attention?"

"Maybe. That and I didn't meet anyone I was that interested in."

"Well, guess what, Mom. I'm a big girl now—I don't need as much attention. Not that I don't appreciate it. But you *look interested* in Simon to me."

I pulled into the driveway with a sigh of relief. "Thank you for your approval, my dear, if that's what you're trying to convey. But let's just drop it for now."

"Oh, come on, Mom." Rowan reached for her door handle. "You gave me the little approval pep talk after I brought Keisha home the first time. Now it's my turn." She grinned at me and hopped out of the car.

143

I sighed again. I loved the girl dearly, but she could never be accused of being an easy child. And apparently she didn't want me to think of her as an easy adult either.

In the week before Keisha was to arrive, except for the trip to the fairgrounds, we spent most of our time in New-bridge. Rowan and I agreed that we would save our sightseeing trips for the two weeks while Keisha was here. We spent a little time planning where we might go for a few day trips. Simon, Jake, Rita, and Brian supplied us with descriptions of some of their favorite places so that we were looking forward to seeing the Thousand Islands and St. Lawrence Seaway, visiting Montreal, and hiking one of the Adirondack trails. Jake convinced us we should definitely go see Upper Canada Village, which was a living history museum, and take him with us.

After Rowan's trail ride on Wednesday, Rita brought Brian by the house. He seemed slightly uneasy at first, but Rowan worked her usual magic on him, and they were soon trading friendly insults and having a great time. When Rowan discovered that Brian played "a little bit of guitar," she insisted he go get his instrument so they could play some tunes together. She overrode his protest that he couldn't read music and asked to borrow the Jeep to give him a lift to pick it up. The poor boy looked slightly dazed as she led him out the door, but he went without any further protest.

Rita watched in amazement as they left. "That girl doesn't have a shy bone in her body, does she? I wasn't sure she'd like Brian, but they seemed to become friends easy enough."

"Why didn't you think she'd like Brian?" I asked in surprise.

I watched the struggle on her face and knew she wished she hadn't said anything, but it was too late. As she thought of the words to say, I led her to the kitchen.

"Well, she's from the city and she's in college, just the opposite of Brian. I guess I see her as a lot more sophisticated. Do you know what I mean?"

"Yes," I said slowly, "but she's not a snob, and Brian is an intelligent and very likeable person. You've been letting Arthur influence you too much."

She sat at the table and stared out the window as I pulled a pitcher of lemonade from the refrigerator. "I hope not." She shuddered. "I wanted to go to college and couldn't, and I worry about Brian sometimes. Arthur's rants don't help."

"Why couldn't you go?" I wondered. It hadn't occurred to me that she had wanted to.

"There was only money for Arthur to go, according to my mother anyway. She kept telling me there wasn't any need for me to go to college—I would just get married and have kids anyway. And then Dan asked me to marry him, so I did."

It was a wonder this woman had any self-confidence at all. "What about your father? Did he ever encourage you?"

"My father went along with whatever my mother said when he was home. He worked in the talc mines, and when he wasn't working, he spent a lot of time at the taverns." She had been tracing lines in the frost of her glass, and now she looked up. "But I didn't mean to get off on this track. I just meant, Rowan and Brian don't have much in common, but they seemed to hit it off."

"That's not so unusual, Rita," I said gently. "You and I became friends right away and which of us went to college had nothing to do with it. And, if you think about it, we have a student-teacher thing going here, and it's not me that's the teacher."

The thought startled her. "You mean the herbs? But that's just because I learned a lot about them from Tess."

"It doesn't matter where you learned it, you know a lot more about it than I do, and you're a great teacher." I hesitated before I added, "And you can always go to college whenever you want to. If you want to. You or Brian."

145

"I'm too old...." She started to protest and stopped herself. "I'll have to think about that. Brian doesn't want to. But sometimes I think he'd like to get out of Newbridge and experience something else. I don't think he knows what, though."

"At least Rowan and Keisha will be new experiences for him right here," I offered.

"What's Keisha like? Is she as friendly as Rowan?"

"You mean, is she as pushy?" I laughed.

"No, I meant friendly." Rita laughed back. "I really like Rowan, you know."

"Funny, so do I. Keisha is very nice, and she can be just as rowdy as Rowan, especially when they're together. But sometimes she's a little quiet when she first meets people. She doesn't pounce right away like Rowan does."

"How did...how did they get together?" I could see that she was curious but unsure of how much she could politely ask.

"They met at a music camp when Rowan was sixteen. They were good friends for some time, and then by the time they were both ready to go to college, they knew they wanted to be together. They both were accepted at the University of Washington, so they got an apartment together. It was nice for me to have Rowan in the same city. She went to college a year early, and I wasn't ready to completely let go yet. Since I could see how happy she was with Keisha, it was easier to come here."

"I know what you mean. It was hard enough when the twins went off to college and with everything else going on, I wasn't ready to let go of Brian either. But I want him to be happy, too. I want him to know that it's all right if he decides to leave Newbridge." She was silent for a time. "Did either you or Rowan have a hard time when she realized she was...I mean...?"

"A lesbian?" I supplied the word she was hesitant to say. "Neither her father nor I had a hard time with it other than the usual worry parents have for their children's happiness and safety. I'm glad that she loves someone who so obviously loves her back. And Rowan was always an amazingly secure child. Notice I didn't say an easy child, but a secure one. She knows who she is, and she seems happy to be that person. I think she and Keisha have been given a little bit of a hard time by a few people. Not much, though. We come from a pretty open kind of place, and Rowan and Keisha both are pretty friendly." Suddenly, I wondered why she had asked the question. "Rita, do you have a hard time with it?"

"Of course not," she answered immediately. "But Kat, you know that there are some people here who would have a hard time with it. Including my mother and idiotic brother."

"Does everyone else here feel that way?"

"You know that neither Simon nor I do. Or Brian. There are other open-minded people here, too, but there are also people who are afraid of all kinds of things. They're usually the ones you want to watch out for."

I thought about what she had just said. "How did you get to be one of the open-minded ones? I mean, if your family feels just the opposite…."

"Despite what you must think, I don't always knuckle under to what my family says or thinks."

"Rita, I'm sorry. I didn't mean to imply…."

She waved a hand in front of me. "It's all right. I did learn to think for myself early on." She looked momentarily surprised. "And I suppose one of the biggest influences I had was Tess."

"In helping you to learn to think for yourself?"

"That, and being open-minded." A tiny smile played at her lips. "She considered herself different, and she certainly thought everyone should be allowed their differences."

"She said that?" The idea pleased me.

"Yes. And you know what?" She held her bottom lip between her teeth before telling me. "The more I get to know you, the more you're beginning to remind me of Tess."

I decided to take that as a compliment.

Before we could say any more, I heard Rowan and Brian return. Before long, they had their instruments out in the living room and were tuned together. Rowan loved to play all kinds of music on her cello, up to and including rock. One of her favorite groups was a quartet of cellists called "Apocolyptica," and they were best known for their renditions of some heavy metal "classics." I was used to the incredible sounds Rowan could coax out of her instrument, but it was a complete surprise to Rita. What was a surprise to me was how good Brian was on guitar. He couldn't read music, but his "little bit of guitar" was far more than his modesty had let on. I think he had been afraid that he wouldn't have a clue on what to do with the classical music he assumed was all that could be played on cello. Rowan managed to get him loosened up enough to even try some variations on a bit of Mozart. Rita and I played the appreciative audience, which wasn't hard to do. Though they cracked jokes about the sound of Mozart on electric guitar, it actually sounded rather good.

"Hey, you're a lot better than you led me to believe," Rowan told Brian when they finally stopped to put their instruments away.

"Thanks. You're not too bad yourself," Brian teased her. "I've never heard anybody play cello like that before. You didn't learn those Metallica pieces at college did you?"

"No, I have some great CD's I listen to and other musicians to play with. Do you play in a band?"

"Not a real one. Just some people who like to get together sometimes. I'd love to play in a real band, though." I thought he sounded a little wistful.

"You should. Get one together." Rowan's philosophy was if you want something to happen, just do it. It didn't always make her life easy, but it usually made it interesting. "Let's play some more music when Keisha gets here. She loves jamming, too."

"Sounds good." Brian unplugged his amp and closed his case.

I had what I thought was a brilliant idea. "How about one night of totally silly music after she comes? We can all have dinner here and invite Simon and Jake to bring their violins, and I'll play piano. Rita can be our percussionist." I turned to Brian. "Would you mind?"

"Nope. Especially if I get a free dinner out of it."

His mother playfully grabbed his collar. "He means to say he would love to. But Rita will be happy being the audience."

The week passed very quickly. Rowan and I had a wonderful time together, and I was pleased that she and the friends I had made here had taken so well to each other. By the end of the week, though, I could tell she was missing Keisha and looking forward to her arrival. I was glad that we had had the week together, but I found myself looking forward to Keisha's visit also. They obviously adored each other, and I loved spending time with both of them. I had my own take on that grand old cliché when they had gotten together. I hadn't lost a daughter. I had gained a second one.

Keisha's plane was due into Syracuse at 9:30 Tuesday morning. It fell to me to set the alarm and get Rowan out of bed. I hated the job and always had. Rowan could be a bear first thing in the morning until she had her breakfast. Other people needed their coffee. She needed her food. When she was living at home with me, I made it a rule to stay out of her way as much as possible if she didn't have time to eat before having to be somewhere. This morning, I made sure our stomachs were comfortably full before we were ready to head out the door. However, before we even made it out of the kitchen, I had my cranky housemate to contend with. Minette's food dish was empty, and as I passed her and the offending bowl, she reached out and swatted my pant leg. I yelped in surprise and turned to admonish her. Seeing what the problem was, I decided it was quicker and easier just to fill the bowl. Rowan laughed at the two of us, and I scowled in her direction.

"Don't laugh," I said. "She reminds me a lot of you."

"Just keep us both fed then, and you won't have any problems." She smiled sweetly, picked up her backpack, and started down the hallway.

The plane was half an hour late, but Keisha, one of the first passengers off, was smiling broadly. "I got bumped up to first class," she told Rowan gleefully as they hugged each other.

"No way! How did you manage that?" Rowan pulled back just enough to peer into her face.

"I'm sure they mistook me for a movie star," she joked, and Rowan rolled her eyes.

Keisha disentangled herself and threw her arms around me. "Hey, Kat! It's so good to see you. Has the princess been pining away quietly until I got here?"

I snorted at her affectionately. "Neither of you knows how to pine—or do anything else—quietly. She is happy to see you, though, and so am I."

Her beautiful face grinned back at me. She was the youngest child of parents who were of Jamaican and Japanese descent, and there was no getting around it: she was drop-dead gorgeous. For the most part, however, she was oblivious to that fact.

I gave her another hug before Rowan picked up her bag and pulled her toward the direction of the baggage claim area. I was looking forward to the next two weeks, but keeping up with the combined energy of these two was going to be a challenge.

Keisha's reaction on first seeing the house wasn't all that different from Rowan's. "What a great old place," she said, looking around as she stepped from the car. "It looks like a fine witch house to me."

"Don't you start in, too." I wagged my finger at her. "I was counting on you being the sane one here."

"Bad choice, Mom." Rowan's eyes crinkled. "Come on Keish…Minette's on the porch. You have to meet her."

The temperamental cat watched them make their way to where she sat on the railing, and then, at the last minute, rudely hopped down and sprinted away.

"Oh, well," Rowan said. "I guess she only hangs out with women from witch families. You're just not witch material, Keisha."

"What do you mean?" Keisha demanded. "For all you know, I could be descended from Tituba, the black witch they *didn't* hang in Salem."

"Right," Rowan replied. "Your dad's parents came here from Jamaica, and your mom's family is from Japan."

"There are witches all over the world, you know."

"All right, ladies." I came up the steps, pulling the key to the front door from my pocket. "It's an odd thing to be in competition over. That cat is just plain finicky."

We got Keisha's things settled into their room, which delighted her. I had taken to drying lavender and putting it in all the rooms. I was coming to associate the smell with the house, and Keisha noticed it right away.

"It smells great in here, Kat. Can I see the rest of the house now? Rowan's e-mail this week was tantalizing. I can't wait to see the attic."

So, once again, I gave the grand tour.

I had left the front door open, and eventually, Minette quietly appeared and followed us. I discovered that I was beginning to feel a pride in this place as I showed it to Keisha. I still thought of it as Tess' house, but there was a definite feeling of ownership starting to overtake me. I noticed Rowan, too, displaying a tendency toward showing things off as if she were very familiar with it. And, just as I had predicted, she insisted the three of us try on some of the old clothes in the trunks. Many were too small for all of us, but some came very close to fitting and we spent a great deal of time laughing and admiring ourselves and each other. We had dragged an old, wooden framed mirror to the center of the room, and Rowan and Keisha were in the middle of studying their reflections with great amusement when I heard Rita's voice call up the stairs.

"In the attic, Rita. Come on up."

"The door was open, so we barged right in." She came through the doorway, followed by Brian, and they both stopped short when they saw us in our old finery.

"Wow!" was all Rita said. Brian said nothing, but stood with his mouth half open and looked first at Rowan and then to Keisha. Keisha was definitely an exotic-looking fairy-tale sort of young woman in the white gown she had found.

"Hey, Brian, put your eyeballs back in place, bud, and I'll introduce you," Rowan teased him. "I can tell you right now, though, she's not your type."

I felt a strong urge to smack her on the head for embarrassing him but refrained. Besides, she and Brian had become good friends in the short time they'd known each other. He took it in stride, and even shot back at her, "Worried I might be too appealing?"

Rita's mouth was now agape at this exchange.

"Excuse me. If this little juvenile moment is over," said the object of their mock contention as she stepped forward, "I'll introduce myself. I'm Keisha, and you must be Brian, the hotshot guitarist."

She reached her hand toward his. As he shook it, he said with none of the modesty he'd displayed when he met Rowan, "I am."

I decided it was time to step in. "Keisha, this is Rita, the hotshot's mother and my good friend." I waited while they exchanged friendly hellos and a bit of small talk. Then, picking up the hem of the long skirt I was wearing, I said, "I'm headed for the kitchen to see what we've got cold to drink. How about if Rita and I meet you all down there?"

"Are you going to play the nineteenth-century hostess in that dress?" Rowan asked.

I looked down at my attire, then reached for the clothes I had discarded earlier. "I'd probably spill something all over it. I'll change in my room on the way down."

When I met Rita in the kitchen a few minutes later, she was just placing some lavender sprigs in a pitcher of lemonade.

"That looks nice," I said appreciatively.

She looked at me a little nervously. "Brian wanted to meet Keisha, and so did I for that matter. But I actually stopped to talk to you for a minute if you have time."

"Sure. What's up?" I looked more closely at her. "Anything wrong?"

"I don't think so." She twirled some lavender between her hands and then let out a little laugh. "I've taken a chapter from your book, so to speak, and now I can't believe I did it."

"Rita, what on earth are you talking about?"

"Remember a while ago, you asked me if there was anyone I was attracted to?" She hesitated.

"Yes," I prompted her gently.

"His name is Sam Taylor. He's a teacher at the high school. Arthur doesn't like him at all...."

"There's a point in his favor," I said dryly.

"He comes into the post office sometimes, just to talk. I...he's really nice. He was one of Brian's teachers, and he was a good one. I just never thought of him as someone I might be attracted to until recently and then...oh, hell!" I looked at her in semi-shock. It was the first profanity I'd heard her utter. "I might as well just spit it out. I asked him out."

"You did?" I was in real shock now and couldn't help laughing at the expression on her face. "What a bad influence I must be. Where and when?"

"You're assuming he said yes."

"Of course, he did. Give me details."

"Well, we were talking, and I thought of you and Simon, and it just popped out. I asked him if he'd like to go to lunch sometime." She looked at me.

"And?"

"And I guess that was all it took to loosen him up. He asked me to go to dinner and a movie with him on Saturday."

"You said yes, of course."

She frowned. "I did, but I wasn't even thinking by that point. I was in shock over what I'd done. But what will I do about my mother?"

I couldn't believe I was having this conversation with a woman over forty. "What do you mean, what will you do about her? You're a big girl. She can't stop you."

"You've met my mother. How can you say that?" she asked, half in humor and half in panic. "I could deal with that, though. I think. It's just that I can't leave her alone for the evening. She wouldn't have it, and neither would Arthur."

"Well, that settles it then. Arthur can have her over. Or he and Alice can visit her at your house. Come on, Rita. Don't let them stop you." Something dawned on me. "Or is it more than that? Do I detect a slight hesitation here?"

"Not hesitation. More like panic." She plopped herself into a chair at the table. "I haven't gone on a date since I was eighteen. It's been twenty-two years! I won't know what to do."

"You'll manage," I assured her. "Don't let your mother or Arthur spoil it for you. Go and have a good time! In fact, have him pick you up here if Arthur goes to your house. I'd like to meet him. Do you think he can handle meeting me, and Rowan and Keisha? Are we too overwhelming?"

Rita laughed as she reached for a glass. "If he can't handle it, I'll just tell him the date is off."

Our conversation was cut short as the others piled into the kitchen. I knew Rita didn't want to talk about it in front of them, and they spent the next hour dominating the conversation anyway. Laughter rang through the kitchen, and I saw Rita let go and relax. I barely heard the phone ring over the noise, but I managed to shush everyone so I could answer it. It turned out to be Jake.

"Hi, Kat," said his sweet and rough young voice. "Did Keisha come? Rowan said they would play some fiddle tunes with me, and I wanted to know if they would do that tonight if I can talk my dad into it."

I smiled at his eagerness. "Keisha might be too tired, Jake, but let me ask them if they're up for it." I placed my hand over the mouthpiece. "Jake can't wait any longer to play with you both. Can he come over for a little while tonight?"

"Sure," they both answered.

"Jake? They said yes. Are you at the library? No? I'll tell you what. I'll call your father and ask if the two of you could come over. Isn't this a school night for you?"

"Yeah. Don't remind me. And thanks, Kat. It'll be a lot better if you ask him. He'll say yes then."

Soon after he hung up, Rita and Brian decided it was time to leave. After saying goodbye to them, the three of us put together an easy soup for dinner, and not long after we cleaned up the remnants, Simon and Jake arrived. Jake was in heaven with Rowan and Keisha both treating him like the little prince. Though he wasn't very advanced on his instrument, they took him seriously and wove all kinds of wonderful notes and sounds into and around the simple melodies he could play. It even gave Simon and me time alone to sit on the porch and just be together. When they were done, Jake informed his father that he was getting old enough now, he wanted a full-sized violin instead of the 3/4-sized kid's one he'd been playing.

After they left, Keisha let out a big yawn and stretched. "I thought this was going to be a quiet old house, but it's kind of like Grand Central Station here, isn't it?"

"Yeah, isn't it great?" Rowan answered as she gathered up music paraphernalia.

"It was quiet for a long time," I commented, "but I think it's about time that people are having a good time here again. This has been a particularly whirlwind kind of day, though."

And for the next week, the whirlwind continued. We took some of the trips we had planned before Keisha's arrival, but we also spent some of the time in Newbridge. We had taken care of one bit of business by taking the violin Rowan had found in the attic to a stringed instrument maker in Watertown. Keisha told us that, with a little bit of work, it would be a rather fine violin. The instrument maker agreed, and so we left it with him to repair. He had quoted me a reasonable price for the repair and stringing and told me that it might be ready within two weeks. I would decide what to do with it after that.

By the time Saturday was here, both Rowan and Keisha were as interested in meeting Rita's date as I was. Rita had made arrangements for Arthur and Alice to spend the evening with Harriet. All three had given her a bit of a hard time about it, but amazingly, she refused to give in to their pressure. She was not prepared to have Sam deal with the

155

disapproving family as if they were teenagers, however. It delighted all three of us at the witch house (as both Rowan and Keisha had taken to calling it) when she really did decide to have him meet her here.

Keisha and Rowan talked her into letting them experiment with her hair, which was—to my way of thinking—a very brave thing for her to do. She arrived at 4:00, and we spent the next two hours joking and trying to put her at ease while the experimenting took place. Finally, it was done to everyone's satisfaction. Rita headed to my bedroom to change from her old jeans and faded shirt to whatever had been in the plastic covering she had brought with her.

Rowan, Keisha, and I sat in the living room engaged in a lively conversation until Rita walked tentatively back through the doorway. As we looked her way, all conversation stopped. The hairstyle that had finally been agreed upon was a French braid that started at her temples and gave a simple elegant frame to her face. She had applied just a little makeup, and the maroon shift and sandals were also simple. But the combination had caused a transformation.

As Rowan somewhat rudely but succinctly put it, "Whoa, Rita, you clean up into a stunner!"

"Rowan!" I started to scold, but Rita's happy laughter stopped me.

"Is it really okay? I don't look too silly?"

"Silly?" I asked incredulously. "Rita, you look gorgeous."

Keisha smiled at her. "That color is perfect for you. You look like a Goddess. Does she remind you of any particular one, Rowan? Aphrodite, maybe?"

"Oh, classier than that, I think." Rowan walked once around poor Rita. "Aphrodite's too out there. I think Rita has that hidden wildness that comes out at certain times. More like Pandora?"

"Stop it, you two!" Rita grinned at them and then looked to me. "Kat? I really look okay?"

"More than okay, my dear. And you're going to have a great time."

The much anticipated Mr. Taylor knocked at the door promptly at the agreed upon time. Rita momentarily gave the impression of a deer caught in the headlights of a car. Both Rowan and Keisha scrambled to open the door for him. Fortunately, they behaved themselves nicely once the door was open. I'm now ashamed to say that my first impression of Sam Taylor was one of slight disappointment—based on looks only. He was one of those people that you would not notice in a crowd. He was just about Rita's height, shorter than the other three of us looking him over. The top of his head was quite bald, but a profusion of graying, curly brown hair growing below the level of his temples hung almost to the top of his collar. His brown eyes looked out from behind wire-rimmed glasses. His clothes, though not highly stylish, were quite presentable. But when his eyes lit at the sight of Rita, the smile on his face transformed everything.

By the time they were ready to leave, my perception of Sam had also been transformed. The shy, nondescript, middle-aged man I had pegged him at first sight, turned out to be funny, outgoing, and easily able to hold his own when surrounded by Rita's protective friends. His obvious feelings for Rita added to my reevaluation. He was upgraded in my mind to rather nice-looking.

Rowan, Keisha, and I spent the evening at the first square dance any of the three of us had ever attended. It was sponsored by the Newbridge fire department and held at the fire hall. Simon, Jake, and even Brian had arranged to meet us there. I hoped fervently that there would be no fires in Newbridge while we were dancing away, but Simon assured me that the volunteers could easily jump into the truck parked outside if the need arose.

Whole families were there, dancing together. The more serious dancers wore the traditional square dance clothing—petticoats and wide-skirted gingham dresses for the women and jeans, boots, and fancy shirts for the men. Most people, however, were wearing whatever was comfortable. The live band was made up of several fiddlers and two guitarists. The fiddlers were mostly men who were at least in their seventies, but one middle-aged woman held her own. During a break in the dancing, Rowan and Keisha couldn't help themselves—they had to talk to the musicians. The result was that, once they laughed and joked with the old-timers enough, two of the men shared their fiddles with the strange young women, and they got to sit in on a set. Even Jake was roped into a song, and by the time it was over, he was ready to practice any amount necessary to become part of the band.

I impressed Simon with my willingness to try the dances, if not my skill at the results. A few waltzes were also played, and my ability to follow his steps while being held in his arms seemed to come more naturally. I was having a wonderful time on the one hand, but a little corner of my consciousness was reserved for making sure no one gave Rowan and Keisha a hard time. I was slightly amazed at turning into a protective mother hen over these two adult women who could certainly take care of themselves. But the talk I'd had with Rita about the people who would be upset over their partnership made me wary. I would do anything in my power to make certain that no one ever hurt them.

They did not go out of their way to announce that they were a couple. They did dance with each other, but they also took turns dancing with Simon, Jake, Brian, and me. I'm sure it dawned on some of the people there, and I saw surreptitious looks sent their way more than once. Part of that was probably the fact that there were very few people of color living in Newbridge, and Keisha was an exotic figure to many of the townspeople. And, I should admit, there were looks sent my way, too. A witch's daughter, a person of color, and lesbians all from one household were probably more than the residents of Newbridge had had among their ranks in a long time. But as no one actually said anything negative to us and several people had gone out of their way to be friendly, I decided to let my guard down.

The rest of the evening was a happy one, both at the dance and after we got home. Brian came by the house, officially to hang out with Rowan and Keisha. But I think he was just as curious as the rest of us to see how his mother had fared. We needn't have had any worries. The fact that she and Sam had enjoyed themselves immensely kept us all in high spirits. I went to bed thinking how much I was beginning to really enjoy this place. It was surprisingly starting to feel like home. No disturbing dreams appeared that night, and I awoke next morning looking forward to the day.

It's lucky for us, at times, that we can't see the future. I had no idea on waking that the day would end far differently than I was anticipating.

Chapter 10

That Sunday started pleasantly enough. The sun was shining as Minette and I made our way to the herbs to pick some flowers for a salad I was making for the afternoon. I picked; she supervised.

A few days earlier, Harriet had asked if the three of us wouldn't like to accompany her to church. I told her how delightful that would be, but we already had other plans for the day. She let it go more graciously than I had expected. We really did have other plans. We had been invited to a corn roast at the DeBerry farm.

Jake was very excited as he described how huge tubs of fresh corn were left to soak the night before and would be steamed in their husks on an open fire in the yard. In his view, the whole point of a corn roast was to see who could eat the most ears of corn. "I bet I can eat way more than any of you," he challenged.

I had no doubt he could, but Rowan and Keisha made a show of accepting his challenge. I was looking forward to the party, but I also approached it with a bit of trepidation. Simon's brother and his family were going to be there, and I had not met them yet. I forced myself not to think that meeting more of the family might make our relationship seem more serious. I was simply going to have a good time.

Simon's brother, Bill, was tall like his sibling, but there the similarities seemed to stop. Red suspenders over an old tee shirt held up his weathered jeans. His face, too, was weathered and tan, and he looked older than Simon, though I knew he wasn't. His hair was cropped close to his head, which was much more the fashion in Newbridge than Simon's long locks. He smiled readily and was boisterous and outgoing. He was certainly likeable, though I preferred Simon's quiet but deep sense of humor. Bill was a farmer like his father. His wife, Sharon, looked familiar to me, and I realized I had seen her around town. She was not as outgoing as her husband, but she was friendly enough. Their four children were a wild crew who obviously knew their way around their grandparents' farm. Two girls and two boys, they ranged in age from four to twelve. They hijacked their cousin as soon as Jake stepped out of his father's car ahead of us. We watched as they and Jasper disappeared around the corner of an outbuilding.

The corn, along with the mounds of other foods, was delicious. The amount of corn the children packed away astonished me. Jake did indeed declare himself the winner with a dozen empty cobs to prove it. The country setting felt old-fashioned and idyllic. I could tell that, new as this experience was for both Rowan and Keisha, they were enjoying themselves.

In the very early evening, when everyone was too stuffed to take another bite, Bill and Sharon took their brood home. We stayed on as Jake had easily talked Rowan and Keisha into a short trail ride before he had to go home and think about school the next day. I offered to help Ruth with the dishes, but she shooed me out of the kitchen to go check on the "children." Simon was helping his father in the yard, and when I stopped to tell him where I was headed, he smiled and told me he would meet me there shortly.

When I reached the hitching post in back of the barn, the three horses were nearly ready to go. None of them were actually tied. They munched grass contentedly as their would-be riders checked cinches and bridles. From that moment, things happened so quickly that it was a long time later before I remembered details of what had really happened. Jake's helmet was sitting on the ground beside him as he was testing the girth on the horse intended for Keisha. He placed his foot in the stirrup to see if the saddle would stay in place when I heard a *ping* and the horse reared and screamed. As it came back to all fours, it took off at a gallop, and I was horrified to see that Jake's foot had slipped through the stirrup and was caught. I screamed and ran after them but watched helplessly as Jake tried desperately to disentangle himself. Suddenly, the horse stopped short just as Jake's foot came loose, and he was propelled some distance before I heard the sickening thud of his body hitting the earth. I ran as fast as my legs could carry me to reach him. The first thing I noticed was one of his legs bent at an unnatural angle beneath him. But far worse, when my eyes traveled up his body, I cried out when I saw the bloody gash on his forehead. He lay completely still with his head next to a rock that was red with his blood and his glasses lay smashed on the other side. I threw myself down beside him and saw that he was breathing but very shallowly and his eyes were open but unseeing in his ashen face. I was barely aware of Rowan running toward us some distance away, and I could hear shouting that must have been Keisha and Simon.

I never stopped to think about what I did next, nor do I know to this day what compelled me to do it. It was obvious that a small part of his skull was crushed and at any other time it would never have occurred to me to touch it. I can only say that there was no thought to what I did—my hands moved of their own accord. Oblivious to the blood, I placed one hand gently over the terrible wound, and the other I slipped beneath his head. My eyes were closed, and all my concentration began to pour into those hands. I briefly knew that Simon and Rowan had reached us, and I took time only to command them not to move him. In a voice I scarcely recognized as my own, I said, "Carefully touch some part of his body so he knows you're here, but don't do anything else yet!" Then I lost all track of time or sense of anything else except that wonderful little boy so gravely wounded beneath us. My eyes had been closed as I felt energy flow from my hands to his head.

At first, I didn't hear the voice calling me, but as it gradually entered my consciousness, I opened my eyes. Rowan, Simon, and the horse were nowhere to be seen. Even Jake's broken body had disappeared. Instead, there was a woman standing before me, calling my name. I only had time to notice that she was large, with a flowing, red dress, her hair cascaded in long black curls, and she seemed very beautiful to me. Before I had time to wonder about her, I saw Jake peek out from behind her.

"I think this is who you are looking for," she said as if everything was normal and Jake had just been playing hide and seek.

I understood that she was there to help me, and I spared her a grateful smile as I held my hand out to the frightened boy. "Come here, Jake. I've come to help you. Do you trust me to do that?"

"Of course, I do, Kat," he said as he made his way slowly to my side but did not take my hand. "But how are you going to do that?"

"I'm going to take you back with me, all right?"

"Isn't it going to hurt a lot if I go back?"

I studied him closely and knew I couldn't lie to him. "Probably. For a while, anyway. But I'm working on fixing the worst of it right now, and I promise you, you'll get over it if you come back with me. Your dad would miss you too much if you didn't."

He looked stricken at the thought. "I'd miss him, too. You promise it will be okay?"

"I promise I'll do everything in my power to make it okay. Will you come?" This time he placed his hand in my outstretched one. We both looked at the woman, who smiled and nodded at us before stepping back.

My eyes flew open again, and I looked down to see Jake's body still lying on the ground with my hands in the same positions above and below his head. However, as I slowly lifted my hand from his temple, I couldn't believe my

163

own eyes. There was no blood on either my hand or his head. I shot a glance toward the rock. It was still blood-stained! Instead of a dent that had told me of the crushed skull, there was only a slight bump and the beginning of discoloration on his forehead.

Jake's eyes fluttered, and he managed to say, "My leg hurts, and I think I have to throw up," before I helped him to turn his head to be sick upon the ground.

Tears now began to stream down my face as Simon's hands traveled up his son's body. "It's okay, sport." I could hear the tears choking back the words he wanted to say. He looked quickly at me, and I couldn't read what was in his eyes.

Keisha arrived, out of breath, and threw herself down beside us. "There's an ambulance on the way." She panted. "How is he?"

"He has a broken leg and probably a concussion, but I think he's going to be okay," I managed to tell her.

"He will be." Rowan looked at me strangely. "You promised."

"I can't see," Jake suddenly complained. "Where are my glasses?"

Simon let out a half sigh, half sob in relief. "They won't do you much good, sport. They're right beside you in a million pieces. We'll get your extra pair as soon as we can."

I slipped my hand from beneath Jake's head and moved slightly so that his father could hold him. I absolutely knew that he was going to be all right, and that it would not hurt to move him now. When the shock wore off, I would have to deal with all that had taken place, but right now I kept everything but the present moment at bay.

"Simon," Keisha murmured hesitantly. "Your parents called the ambulance, but I told them to call the police, too."

Simon and I both looked up at that, and out of the corner of my eye, I could see Ruth and Jack hurrying toward us. "Why?" Simon asked quietly.

Keisha exchanged glances with Rowan who nodded at her. "I don't think it was just an accident. I saw two boys running into the woods right after it happened. I ran after them, but I couldn't catch them right away, and I thought it was more important to get help."

"You did just right, Keisha, thanks. Why would anybody want to hurt Jake?" Simon was puzzled. "Maybe they just saw it happen."

"Maybe," Keisha said, "but why did they run away?"

Maybe, I thought, it wasn't Jake they had intended to hurt. I had no time to pursue that thought as Jasper flew to Jake's side and Rowan caught him by the collar before he could hurt the object of his affection. Ironically, he had been kept in the house so he wouldn't spook the horses.

"Jasper," came Jake's weak voice, and he reached a hand out to touch the dog.

Ruth and Jack reached us soon after, and we all spent the time reassuring Jake and each other as we waited impatiently for the ambulance. We decided not to move him until the paramedics arrived with a stretcher. When they did, Jake cried out in pain as they first worked with his leg and then got ready to transport him. He never shed tears until he realized Jasper couldn't come with him.

"Please?" he pleaded with his father.

"Grandpa and I will take good care of him, Sweetheart," Ruth said as she touched her grandson's cheek lightly.

"You bet, Jake. We'll let him sleep on our bed, and he can help me gather the cows in the morning. You know how much he likes that." Jack also touched his grandson briefly as his eyes showed his concern.

One paramedic climbed into the back of the aid car while the other turned to Simon. "I assume you want to come with us, Simon?"

"Of course," was his reply. He had not let go of his son from the moment he had come upon him on the ground. It didn't register with me at the time that neither had I. He indicated me with a lift of his head. "I want Kat to go with us, too."

"She can't, Simon. It's policy. Only family members."

"I don't give a damn about policy, Jeff. I want her to keep her hands on him, and I say she goes." Simon was adamant.

Jeff was clearly hesitant until Jake got to him with, "I can't have Jasper. Please let Kat go with my dad and me."

"All right. Let's get moving, though."

"Ruth, will you and Jack get Rowan and Keisha to my house?" Ruth nodded, and after I climbed in behind the rest, I called down to Rowan. "After you talk to the police, get my car and come to the hospital. Ruth and Jack can give you directions."

We sped the thirty miles to the hospital in Watertown. The first concern was to keep Jake comfortable but awake and conscious. Simon and I talked very little to each other, but we had our hands on Jake and kept him engaged in simple conversation. Once we got there and he was wheeled to the emergency room, it didn't take the doctors long to confirm that he did have a concussion, but "thankfully, nothing worse as far as a head injury."

I stayed with them while Jake was settled into a room and finally able to sleep, though we were told he'd have to be woken every hour and watched for the next twenty-four hours. Simon sat in a chair next to the bed, and I stood next to him with my hand on his shoulder. He was slumped in exhaustion, but I knew he wouldn't be able to sleep for some time. I squeezed Simon's shoulder and would have gone to pull over a chair for myself, but he took my hand, turned it palm up and, after studying it for a minute, he placed a kiss in it.

"Thank you," he said softly. "Whatever happened back there, thank you."

I felt moisture gather in my eyes and, without saying a word, I turned away to pull a chair by his side. Sitting down, I felt my own exhaustion fall over me in waves, and I laid my head against him. I felt the comfort of his arm go round me and then, in what seemed only seconds later, I opened my eyes to see Rowan, Keisha, and Ruth standing on the other side of the bed looking down at the sleeping boy.

"I brought your car, Simon," I heard his mother say. "I'll stay the night with you, and we can figure out what's happening in the morning."

Simon saw that my eyes were opened and kissed the top of my head. "Take your mother home," he said to Rowan. "She needs to get some real rest."

"No," I started to protest. "I want to stay...."

"Kat," he said gently, "you've helped more than anybody will ever know. But he's going to be fine now, and I really do want you to get some sleep."

"What about you?" I asked.

"I'll get what little rest I can, but I'm not sleepy yet. You are. Come back in the morning, please?"

I hated to leave them, but he was right. I did need to sleep. And I found myself suddenly wanting to be back in my bed at the house. *My* house.

"All right, but I will be back first thing. What do you need me to bring when I come?"

"I can't think of anything, except yourself. Jake will want to see you when he wakes up."

"Oh, that reminds me." Rowan reached into her pocket. "We went by your house, and Ruth found Jake's other glasses." She handed them over to Simon.

Once we were in the car, I thought sleep would overtake me again, but instead, it eluded me. Keisha drove, and Rowan sat in the front passenger seat but turned so that she could talk to me in the back.

I yawned and then remembered. "What did the police have to say?"

"Nothing," Keisha said disgustedly. "I don't know if they didn't believe me or what, but they decided if there really were some boys there, they weren't responsible. They told me horses spook easily, and it was just an unfortunate accident. I was expecting one of them to pat the poor, inexperienced city girl on the head, they were so condescending."

"But you're sure you saw two boys, Keisha?" I asked.

"Yes, and I heard something hit the horse just as it reared. I swear."

That's when I remembered I had heard the pinging sound also. "I guess there's not much we can do about it then. It could have been even worse. Jake could have died!"

Rowan rested her chin on the back of the seat and didn't take her eyes off me. "I think he did, Mom. Or came as close as you can get and still come back." When I said nothing, she went on, "I got there in time to see more than anyone else except Simon. I know how badly hurt he was before you got to him."

"What did you see?" I whispered. Now was the time I dreaded. I was going to have to face what had really happened. What little I had had time to think about it at all, I had been half able to convince myself that it was mostly in my imagination. Jake hadn't really been hurt as badly as I'd first thought.

Rowan took a breath. "I saw the blood and the horrible wound. And then when you told Simon and me to touch him, I could feel something coming from you."

"And that was all?"

"No. I closed my eyes, and when I opened them, I saw a woman in red, and then I heard you promise Jake that everything would be all right. When I looked down at Jake, the wound was gone, and there was just a bump there instead. I know Simon saw the condition Jake was in at first, too."

I laid my head in my hands. "Rowan, so many things have been different here. I can't explain half of them. You... you saw the woman in red?" She nodded, and even though it was fairly dark, I could see her curls shake. "I don't know why I did what I did, Rowan. I don't know what's going on."

"I think you do, Mom," she said gently and placed her hand over both of mine.

I dragged myself up the stairs when we arrived home and barely had the strength to shed my clothes and pull on my nightshirt. I expected a return of my dreams that night. I was half right. My dream was populated by two of the people I'd dreamed of previously, but it was not either scene I'd visited before.

Rose sat upon the stool near the hearth, fingering the locket about her neck as she spoke to the child seated next to her. "Never forget, Kate, ours is a way of peace. No matter how difficult it may seem at times, we must be mindful to hurt no one."

"No one, Mama?" The girl held a cornhusk doll in both hands. "Granny Byer says she'll place a curse upon anyone who tries to harm her. Shouldn't we do the same thing?"

"Granny Byer's tongue is too loose at times. You know very well that you should curse no one lest the curse come back to you three-fold." Rose lifted pieces of three different herbs from a basket at her feet. "Now, child, let's see what you remember. Tell me what these are that I have in my hand."

"Betony, heartsease, and feverfew," Kate recited dutifully. "Can I look at the locket now, Mama?"

Rose smiled at her daughter fondly as she reached for the clasp at the back of her neck. "All right, love. But first, you must repeat the Rede with me."

Kate mouthed the words with her mother without taking her eyes from the locket.

"We must abide the Witches' Rede,
Apply with love and trust this crede,
To heal with joy this charge fulfill:
As ye harm none, do as ye will.
Abide always the rule of three:
What ye cast out returns to thee.
Welcome Her work with open heart,
Merry meet and merry part."

The girl dropped her doll and reached her hand toward her mother's eagerly. "Now, Mama?"

Rose laughed indulgently and placed her hand over Kate's. "You must always remember who you are. The women in our family are a line of healers. Just as I received this locket from my mother and will one day pass it on to you, so do we receive our healing gifts. From mother to daughter will they always be given." Only then did she release the chain and locket into Kate's waiting hand.

The scene faded into a night sky studded with thousands of stars. I stood beneath it foolishly attempting to count the stars until I heard a familiar voice in the distance.

"Sleep is healing, too."

Then a beautifully shaped hand snuffed out the stars as if they were candles, and I had only time to glimpse dark hair and a red dress before oblivion overtook me.

The smell of coffee woke me before I was aware of the phone ringing in the kitchen. I threw the blankets over a disgruntled Minette in my haste to get to the phone. It stopped ringing, and I heard someone speaking as I neared the kitchen.

Rowan held the receiver to her ear and looked up as I entered. "Let me see if Mom's up, Rita," she said and then placed her hand over the mouthpiece. "Do you feel like talking this morning?"

"Since it's Rita, yes," I answered and reached to take the phone from her. "Hi, Rita."

"Kat, I heard Jake got hurt! How is he, and what happened?"

I told her about the incident minus certain details. I knew that if anyone would understand, Rita would. But I wasn't ready to talk about it over the phone and not before I'd seen Jake again. I promised I would keep her informed of anything I found out and would call her later after I came back from the hospital.

Keisha handed me a cup of very black coffee, and I settled heavily into the nearest chair to drink it. "What time is it? Simon hasn't called, has he?"

"It's 8:30, and Rita's the only one who's called. No news is good news, you know. Simon would have called if there were anything wrong. But you know he's all right." Rowan placed a piece of toast in front of me. "Eat that. More will be up in a minute."

"Thanks, Mom," I said and took a bite of the toast. "I hope you two don't mind, but I'm heading back to the hospital as soon as I get dressed. You don't have to go with me. If you wanted, you could drop me off there and take the car to go do something fun."

"Right, Mom. Like we want to go anywhere else. We're all ready to go with you. Right, Keisha?"

"Absolutely," was her answer.

I smiled at them gratefully and took a few more bites to satisfy Rowan's role-reversing motherly side. Then I dressed quickly, and we were on our way.

Jake was awake but groggy when we walked into his room. "They have him drugged with painkillers," Simon told us as he yawned and rubbed his bloodshot eyes. "But the doctor's been in and said he's doing well. His head will probably hurt for a couple of days, but there doesn't seem to be any permanent damage. His leg's going to be in a cast for several weeks, though."

Relief washed over me at his words. It had begun to hit me this morning that my touching and moving his head right after he was thrown could have been a very bad thing to do. I had even known that at the time, but something overrode everything that I knew with my head.

Until I was at peace with what had happened, I didn't want to talk about it. I knew that at some point very soon, Rowan and I would have to, and perhaps I would tell Rita. But I certainly didn't want anyone who didn't know already that something very strange had taken place to hear about it.

"Hey, Kiddo," I heard Rowan say. "You'll do anything to get out of school, huh?"

Jake smiled wanly but answered quickly enough, "Yeah, but I wish I'd thought of a more fun way." He turned his head and saw me standing by his father. "Hi, Kat. Did you ride in the ambulance with us? I sort of remember that."

"I did, Jake. You scared us a bit."

"I did? You didn't seem scared. Where's Grams? Wasn't she here?"

"She went to get something to eat," Simon told him. "She'll be back for a little bit, and then she'll go home and take care of Grandpa and Jasper."

"Will you call Grandpa to see if Jasper's okay? And what about Hector and Ratcliff?" Even through the drugs, his first thoughts were of his pets. "And are all the horses okay?"

"I already talked to Grandpa, and everybody's fine. We'll get someone to go feed the rats."

"Not Grams. She doesn't like them." Jake looked at me. "Will you feed them, Kat? Or Rowan or Keisha could do it, too. But it has to be somebody who'll pet them while I'm not there."

"Don't worry," I said. "All three of us will do it, and that way they'll get lots of attention."

We stayed with them well into the afternoon as Jake drifted in and out of sleep. Simon managed to get an hour of rest on a pullout chair while I sat next to Jake's bed. From what he had told his father and the doctor, it appeared that Jake had no memory of the accident. He remembered helping Keisha with her horse and then nothing further until the ride in the aid car. I was relieved that he had no memory of how badly he had been hurt, for more than one reason. I didn't want him to be frightened, and selfishly, I was relieved that he wouldn't tell anyone else about my part in helping him.

Simon had tried to ask me more details about it soon after we'd gotten there in the morning, but I put him off. He seemed slightly hurt, but thankfully, he let it go. Maybe some-one else could have been happy if this were happening to them and thought of it as a miracle.

Too many strange things were happening to me, too fast, and I wasn't prepared to be happy about it. I really needed space to deal with it on my own.

There was another visit from the doctor late in the afternoon. She told Simon she wanted to keep Jake there for three or four days and that would give them time to set up what would be needed for him to recuperate at home. The library wasn't open on Mondays, so there had been no problem there, but Simon called to make arrangements for someone from the Watertown library system to take over for the rest of the week.

Jake was on the edge of sleep again when the three of us were preparing to leave. Simon held me close for a moment, but I pulled away more quickly than I had intended in my fear that he would once again ask me for more details than I was ready to give. I bent over to place a kiss on Jake's cheek, and he opened his eyes to look into mine.

"Kat, did your friend find you?" he asked drowsily.

"What friend is that, Sweetie?" I smiled down at him.

"I don't know who she was. And I can't remember when either." He shut his eyes again. "I just remember she told me to wait with her because she was a friend of yours and she was looking for you."

His voice drifted off.

"She had on a red dress...."

Chapter 11

Jake became visibly better each day. He never mentioned the lady in red again, and I doubt that he remembered having said anything to me. In the short time that Rowan and Keisha had known him, they had become very attached to him. We did very little sightseeing in the last week they were in Newbridge. Instead, they chose to spend a good deal of time entertaining Jake both at the hospital and when Simon was able to bring him home. I was happy to be there to see his face light up when he found both Jasper and the rats in good health. He'd worried about how they were getting along without him. He was getting healthier himself, but he was very pale, and I couldn't help thinking that he was one very slow-moving little boy compared to the dynamo he was used to being. This was definitely better than what could have been. I made myself turn away from that line of thought.

We didn't spend all of our time with Jake and Simon. Jake had many visitors and well-wishers, but I knew he needed spaces to rest, too. For that matter, so did Simon. Rowan and Keisha also spent some time with Brian. Two days before they were to leave, they decided that all three of them would spend the evening playing music at Jake's house.

Just after they had made the arrangements, the phone rang and I answered it. It was the instrument maker who was calling to say that the violin was ready earlier than we'd expected and we could pick it up any time. Inspiration struck me, and I called Rowan and Keisha into the kitchen for a conference.

"Am I right that neither of you wants this violin?" I asked them.

They looked at each other and shook their heads. "It really is a nice one, Kat, but I don't need another violin," Keisha said.

"Me either, Mom. You look like you have a plan."

"What would you think about my giving it to Jake? Would it be a good one for him?" I queried.

"That's a great idea!" Rowan said enthusiastically.

"It would be one he could use all his life and I think he'll grow into being good at it. He'll love it." Keisha beamed at me.

"Well, let's go get it then, and we can give it to him to play tonight."

The timing couldn't have been better. Jake was just starting to get well enough to realize how restricted he was and even wished he could go back to school already. The stream of visitors had been nice, but he wished he could get up and go play with them. His father confided to me that he was "beginning the cranky phase" and that he was bored. He had his violin out and waiting when we arrived.

"Too bad you have to play a kid's violin," Rowan told him casually. "Music sounds so much better on grownup instruments."

Jake's face fell as he looked at her. "I know. But this is all I've got. I wish I could have a full size."

"Do you really wish that? Like on-a-star kind of wish?"

"Rowan, stop teasing him!" I scolded.

She and Keisha laughed. "Mom has a little something for you," Rowan told him.

"What?" His face brightened.

"Maybe you just better look and see," Rowan said as I produced the case.

He opened it quickly and stared at what was inside. "You're going to let me borrow this?" he asked me excitedly.

"No, I'm giving it to you. It was in my attic, and I want you to have it. Keisha says it will be a good violin for you." I looked belatedly to Simon. "I didn't think to ask you first. Do you mind?"

"Of course not. It's very nice of you. Are you sure I can't pay you for it?"

For some reason, the offer stung me slightly. "No! I really wanted to give it to him as a gift. It looks like it's been in Tess'…in the family for a long time, and who knows how long it's been sitting in the attic. It would make me feel much better to know that it's loved and being played."

"What do you say, sport?"

Jake took his eyes off the violin long enough to raise them to me. "Thanks, Kat! Can I play it now?"

The rest of the evening was a delight. Jake tired much more quickly than he normally would have, but the time he got to spend playing with the others made him happier than he'd been since the accident. Keisha and Rowan taught him some new songs, and they laughed and played their music until they noticed Jake begin to fade. As they put their instruments away, Keisha told Jake she would miss their music sessions when they had to leave. His face fell again, and I was afraid he might cry.

"When do you leave?" he asked sadly.

"Day after tomorrow, kiddo, but we'll e-mail you a whole bunch," Rowan told him. You have to keep us informed about how Jasper and the rats are doing." She hesitated only slightly before adding, "And the horses. And Brian can come play with you after we go."

Jake looked at Brian with wide eyes. "You will?"

Brian was somewhat surprised but said agreeably, "Sure. We've got to be ready with some more songs when these two come back to visit us, don't we?"

Before leaving, everyone was required to sign Jake's cast. Several autographs had already been applied, but for some reason, we hadn't gotten around to it yet. I went last and couldn't help drawing a quick picture of Jake and his animals before I signed it with a flourish. It cheered him up immensely. After the two young women promised for the third time that they would see him before they went back to Seattle, we managed to make our way out the door.

After returning home, Rowan insisted we sit in the kitchen where she would brew us some mint and lemon balm tea. "It's time we had a real talk, Mom," she said ominously.

Keisha arched her brows at us and asked, "Should I go to my room now?"

Rowan shrugged her shoulders, but I answered with a sigh, "No. I know what this is about and you know as much as Rowan does, Keisha. Stay, but whatever we talk about is between the three of us."

Very little more was said until Rowan had put the water on to boil and retrieved the herbs to steep. Then, as the fragrance of the lemon balm and mint filled the kitchen, she sat at the table across from me, propped her elbows on the table's surface, and placed her chin in her palms. "You know you need to talk about it, don't you?"

I sighed again, feeling a bit dramatic. "I suppose so. But at the moment, I don't know what to say."

"You must be thinking about this a lot, Mom. Look how much has happened! I'm a little worried about you. I don't want to leave you here alone until I can get you to talk about it. I've always seen you as the strongest woman I know. Don't get mad at me for saying this, but you don't seem to be having an easy time of handling all this."

I thought of myself as a very strong woman, too. Of course, my first reaction to her words was to want to get angry, or at least defensive. But when I read the real concern in her face and Keisha's, too, I felt my anger deflate like a pinpricked balloon. "It's just all a bit much. First these dreams and strange coincidences, and now what happened to Jake."

"It's not just what happened to Jake." Rowan took one of my hands and massaged the fingers. "It's what's happened to you, too. It's like something woke up in you, Mom. You haven't said it in so many words, and Keisha and I have been tiptoeing around it, but you know that you pulled Jake back from death. You healed him of a terrible wound that only Simon and I saw. Granted, it's a bit out of the ordinary, but why are you having such a hard time coming to grips with it?"

"Why?" I released a laugh with no humor in it. "If I told almost anybody else what's been happening, they would think I was crazy. And if I'd had it happen say three or four hundred years ago, I'd be roasting on a nice little barbecue pit right now."

"Actually it would depend on where you were."

I looked at Rowan blankly. "What?"

"They would have burned you in most places, but in England and Salem, they hung their witches instead of burning them." Rowan let go of my hand. "Sorry. Just one of those useless facts that pop out of my mouth at the wrong time. Go on."

I bit my lip before continuing. "Up to this point, I've been half convincing myself that this is just a funny little cosmic game of coincidence. And all I've inherited from Tess, besides the house, is an overactive imagination. But what happened with Jake...." I turned haunted eyes toward her. "Don't you see? That changes everything. I could have, with a lot of work, forced myself to think that was just my imagination, too, if you and Simon hadn't seen it. You really did see it?"

"You know I did! And I know Simon saw, too. Did he see anything else besides how badly Jake was hurt before you touched him?"

"I don't know," I admitted. "I haven't talked to him about it."

"Mom! Why not? Doesn't he want to talk about it?"

"He tried to a couple of times right after it happened, but I didn't want to. I will when I'm ready." Now I was defensive. "I don't want other people to know about this. Am I supposed to be all bright and cheery about it? The mother I didn't know about before I was forty thought of herself as a witch and didn't seem to have a very happy life and, oh, gosh, isn't it nice, but here I am in her place and well, just maybe I'm a witch, too. I'm sure the people of this town would be thrilled if I could just fly around on my broomstick and tell them all."

Rowan's obstinate look settled on her face, and I braced myself. "Number one, how do you know she had an unhappy life? There are a number of things here that suggest to me she wasn't all that unhappy. Different, yes. But what's wrong with that? Number two, an ability to heal doesn't strike me at all as a bad thing. Unnerving when you discover it in yourself in such a dramatic way but still wonderful. And number three—" here she relented and smiled "—you haven't learned to ride a broom yet, so I think it's okay not to announce it to all the citizens of Newbridge. Break them in slowly."

What she had attempted with her humor worked. I felt the tension let go of my shoulders as I looked from her to Keisha. I gave them a tentative smile. "Well, that's a relief. Here I thought I was going to have to gather them all in the village square and ask them if they'd like to burn me now or later."

"Lucky for you, there's no village square," Rowan said as she poured the tea.

"Kat, what about the lady in red you and Rowan talked about. Who—or what—is she?"

I held the mug Rowan had handed me tightly in my hands as if to ward off a chill. "I don't know Keisha. When I had my hands on Jake and closed my eyes, everything went away except this woman, and then Jake was behind her."

"Was it like a dream or a vision?"

I thought before I answered. "It wasn't like the dreams I've been having. It was more real. I mean, I was there. I wasn't aware of Rowan or Simon or where I was with my hands on Jake. Is that a vision? I don't know. I haven't ever had one before."

"And Rowan, the same thing happened to you?"

"Not exactly. I was aware of everything happening, but for a minute, I saw this woman in red standing beside Mom, and a few minutes later, I heard Mom tell Jake she promised she'd help make everything all right if he'd come back with her. Only, I realized she hadn't said it out loud."

"So two of you saw the vision of the woman."

"Actually three." I had their undivided attention. "Jake saw her, too. I don't think he remembers it now, but at the hospital, just as we were leaving and he was about to fall asleep that next day, he asked me if my friend had found me. I asked him who he meant, and he said the lady in red who told him to wait with her, that she was a friend of mine."

"So who is she?" Keisha asked again.

"If I were the one who had to accept these things happening to me," Rowan said to her mug of tea, "I might be inclined to think of her as the Goddess."

"But since it's me, I'm inclined to think of her as some part of myself," I told her.

"Close enough," was her response.

By the next day, I was beginning to feel better. The talk had helped. I was definitely going to miss these two when they went back to Seattle, but I found that I was beginning to take strength from the house somehow. I could only think of it in these terms: there was a new part of me—or perhaps an old part I hadn't been aware of—and it was connected to the house. And it shocked me to admit to myself that I had grown to love the place.

Rowan and Keisha did see Jake again before they left, and Rita and Brian spent part of the last evening with us. Rita had offered to go to the airport with me so that I would have company on the way back, but I declined. I decided it might be good for me to have time alone and asked her instead to come to the house later.

Keisha gave me a hug before boarding the plane. "Thanks, Kat. You certainly know how to make sure there's excitement when a girl comes to visit," she said. "Except for the obvious, I had a really wonderful time. I hope things get easier for you. Keep an eye on Jake and Brian for us."

Rowan looked at me for a long time before giving me her stranglehold. She lifted her head back to look into my eyes. "If you need me, call and I'll hop right back on a plane. I mean it. I love the place, Mom. If it feels right, please keep it."

I was too surprised to say much other than, "I love you." And "Okay" in response to her calling to me to keep in constant touch online as she headed toward the gate.

The trip home was uneventful, but I surprisingly enjoyed the solitude. I'd made this trip enough now that the scenery had become familiar. For the first time, however, I noticed the beginning of a change in color in the maple trees along the way. I realized with a start that the fall equinox was not far away. I'd heard of the beautiful colors on the East Coast in the fall but hadn't experienced them myself. Now I was going to get that chance.

I let my imagination run wild enough to fancy that the house greeted me silently when I returned. I stood looking up at it from the path for a few minutes until I felt Minette rub against me. I leaned down to scratch her ears and gazed at the land around me. The weather was still warm, but there was a faint bite in the air. I saw that here, too, the color had started on the trees without my noticing. A feeling struck me that I'd never felt before. It was the most deliciously melancholy and yet hopeful emotion I'd ever experienced. The color meant the leaves were dying, yet they would go out in a blaze of glory. A yearning welled up in me that I didn't understand. I wanted to be out among the leaves as they danced their last steps of life and dance with them. I knew my herbs, too, would seem to die, and we would all have to hole up quietly while the beautiful white starkness of winter would blanket what might seem like a grave. But secretly, the color would be hiding in tiny protected corners, waiting to spring back to life. That was the melancholy and the joy of this moment. And this place was inviting me to become part of that cycle.

If anyone else had been there to see me, I would have felt foolish as a single tear spilled from my eye. But since there was no one else, I merely wiped the tear away and smiled. I wasn't making any commitments, but maybe, just maybe, I would heed Rowan's request. I just might have to keep this place.

When Rita came by late in the afternoon, she found me sitting in the kitchen amid books and herb cuttings. I looked up as she walked in and indicated a chair across from me. "This is it," I told her. "I've decided I really want to learn as much as possible about herbs and healing. Not just how to identify them, but how to use them to help people. Will you teach me?"

"That's a change, isn't it?" She looked at me for a long moment. "I'll teach you everything I know. What's made you change your mind?"

So I told her. I told her what had taken place when Jake was hurt, and of the dream about Rose and her daughter coming from a line of healers. Then I swore her to secrecy.

"But Kat," she protested, "being able to heal is a real gift. It's a wonderful thing!"

"Rita," I said seriously, "can you honestly tell me that everyone in Newbridge would see it that way? Did Tess want you to tell anyone about the animals she healed for you?"

"No," she admitted slowly. "But people knew Tess could do it. They came to her for help. Look at Donna."

"You said Donna's the only one who'll admit she came to Tess. I don't see that Tess got a lot of respect for what she could do. Except for just a few of you, no one seems to have a lot of good things to say about her."

A sad looked passed across Rita's face. "I think there are more people than you might think who would have a lot of good to say about her if they weren't such cowards. But it was partly Tess' fault. It pains me to say this, because I really loved her. But she shut most people out. She didn't give many people a chance to know and respect her."

"All right. But my guess is she had a lifetime to deal with her 'gifts,' and yet she didn't advertise them. I've lived forty years of a good life with very little mystery in it until now. I want your word that you won't say anything about this."

"Of course, I won't say anything. But if you're going to learn how to use the herbs, aren't you going to actually want to use them? And what about the healing in your hands? Aren't you ever going to use that again?"

"I don't know what I'm going to do about any of it yet." I opened one of the books in front of me. "I just know that I want to learn all I can. And I don't want you to say anything."

"No problem. Where do you want to start?"

Rita worked with me until it was time for her to go home and make dinner for her mother and herself. We pored through the books as she helped me begin to pick out the most practical information to start with. We spent some time out among my herbs, as I now thought of them, talking about what would need to be done to prepare them for winter. As I stood there looking around me, it hit me again. That feeling of melancholy and hope all rolled into one. I wondered if Rita could feel it, too.

We talked of other things for a few moments before she left. I asked her if she had heard from Sam. A lovely smile flitted across her face as she told me that he had come to see her at work several times and had asked her out again. He was taking her to dinner on Wednesday when her mother was scheduled for her weekly outing at Arthur's. She just hadn't told Harriet yet.

I went back to the work we had been doing in the kitchen and became so engrossed that it didn't register in my brain for some time that the phone was ringing. It was Simon wondering how I was doing with the silence that must have descended with Rowan and Keisha gone. "I do miss them already, but the silence is much nicer than I thought it would be," I told him. He asked if I'd like to come over after dinner, but I decided that I would stay home this night. "Rita and I were working on our herbal lessons this afternoon, and I have some more to do and then there's quite a lot to clean up. I'm going to try to get to bed early, I think. How's Jake doing? Can I come by tomorrow?"

"He's okay. We've been playing a lot of chess, checkers, and any other board game I can find. I'm going back to work tomorrow, so my mother's coming to stay with him. But if you wanted to drop by, they'll be happy to see you, or you can come tomorrow night." There was a silence. "Kat, are you trying to avoid talking to me?"

"No," I lied. "There's just been a lot happening for both of us, in case you hadn't noticed. But I'll come over tomorrow night if that's all right and stay after Jake goes to sleep. I promise we'll talk then Simon."

"All right, Kat. Good night."

"Good night," I answered back, but he'd already hung up.

The first thing next morning, I checked my e-mail. The cheery message I was hoping for from Rowan was the first thing I read. Their flight had been uneventful, and they missed me and the friends they had made here, but a fine Seattle drizzle was falling when they landed and they were not unhappy to be home. I laughed to myself. Only a child born and raised in the Pacific Northwest could understand that a drizzle could be a fine thing. Whatever the percentage of water is that a normal human body is made up of, a true Seattleite has at least one more percent. I sent a return message telling her I missed them both.

There was e-mail from my agent that I needed to answer and a few from friends that I would send greetings to later, but there was one more piece of mail that caused me to stare thoughtfully into my computer screen. I had sublet my apartment to my friend Gail through the month of October. She had lived in San Francisco for the past five years but had taken a consulting job for three months in Seattle. The timing had been convenient for both of us, and she had moved into my apartment the day after I left. Now she was telling me, she had an offer of another good job that would last through January. She needed to find another place to stay unless there was a chance I might not be coming back right away. Was it possible that she might be able to keep subletting my place? Minette padded into the kitchen where I sat at the table staring at the laptop. She meowed loudly as she passed me on the way to her food dish.

"E-mail from a friend that I really have to think about," I told her. "Thanks for asking." She ignored my humor and began to eat. I let my gaze move from the screen to the cat. What would I do about her when I left? She had been fine in the few months between Tess' death and my arrival, but I had to admit, I had grown attached to her. I briefly thought I could take her with me, but I knew that would make her miserable. She was used to roaming freely about a large house and acres of land. Being confined to a small, two-bedroom apartment in the middle of a city would not suit her.

I gave a great deal of thought to it the rest of the day. I sent a second e-mail to Rowan telling her of Gail's request and jokingly asked how she'd feel about spending Christmas in cold, snowy Newbridge. By the time I checked my e-mail late in the afternoon, she had sent an answer. It contained only these words, "Go for it, Mom!" A strong desire to see the place through fall and winter, two seasons I'd never really experienced before, seized me. Before I could change my mind, I sent a response to Gail: *Go ahead and stay in my apartment. I still have lots to do here.*

"At least that will give me more time to figure out what to do about you," I told Minette. She didn't seem worried as she groomed herself and then curled into a comfortable sleeping position on the chair beside me.

Jasper was the first to greet me at Simon's door in the evening. He rushed through as it opened and barked happily as he circled me. He stopped as soon as I petted him, and then I smiled up at Simon.

I was feeling sad that it was only Jasper of the inseparable duo who was well enough to greet me so enthusiastically but lost the sadness at the sight of Jake standing beside his father. Of course, his weight was all on his good leg and crutches propped him up, but what a wonderful sight I thought it was! He grinned at me as if he had accomplished some amazing feat, but then I suppose he had.

"Look at you!" I exclaimed.

"Watch what I can do, Kat." He hobbled about and made a few tricky maneuvers around the furniture faster than I would have thought possible. "I've been practicing all day. Grams said I drove her nuts, but she smiled when she said it."

"That's great! So can you go back to school tomorrow?" I was teasing, but he took me seriously.

"No. Dad says I can't go back until next week. I thought it would be fun to be out of school, but I still have to do all this homework! I guess it won't be so bad going back."

My laughter at his words stopped as I noticed the serious expression on Simon's face. "Is something wrong, Simon?"

He had ushered us into the living room, and as we sat, he patted Jasper absentmindedly. "I don't know," he said. "I got this phone call, just before you got here."

"What about?" I prompted, torn between curiosity and not wanting to pry.

"It was Donna Bartlett. Kyle's mother. She said she was going to call you, too, but when I said you were probably on your way over here, she said good, she needed to talk to us both." He looked at me oddly. "She didn't say what about, but she was crying. She asked if she could meet us here right away."

I was mystified. "What do you suppose that's all about?"

He shook his head. "I have no idea."

186

"Maybe something happened to Kyle," said Jake. "I hope not. He's my friend. But things happen to him a lot." He looked down at his leg. "Nothing like this, though." I noted that he seemed more smug than upset. I supposed, competition-wise, a broken leg was high on the scale of possible injuries.

We didn't have to wait long. Very soon, the doorbell rang and Jasper barked happily at the prospect of more visitors. He immediately stopped barking and sat at Simon's command, however, as we viewed the somber faces standing in the doorway.

Donna, grim but determined, held her son's hand in a tight grip. Kyle's head hung to his chest, but I could see just enough to know that his face was streaked with tears.

"Kyle has something to say to all of you," she said when we were once again sitting in the living room. "I want you to know that I didn't know about it until today or we would have been here much sooner."

Kyle's eyes brimmed over with more tears, but with his mother's eyes boring into him, he held his head up and looked straight at Jake. "I'm so sorry," he whispered. "It was my bee-bee gun that spooked your horse. It wasn't me that shot it," he tried to excuse himself. But as his mother's hand went to his shoulder, he added, "But I was there. It was Bobby Peterson who said it would be funny, and I went along with him, but I never thought he'd really do it!"

I felt a strong urge to take the little thug by the shoulders and shake him. Hard. Fortunately, I knew the difference between appropriate and inappropriate behavior, even if he apparently didn't. I sat with my hands in my lap and said nothing as Simon and Jake looked at him in disbelief.

Jake was the first to speak. "Kyle! Why did you think that was funny? I wouldn't let somebody do that to you. It hurt! A lot."

"I know, Jake. I am sorry. We didn't think anybody would get hurt." He looked to his mother with misery in his eyes, but she looked coldly back at him. "Besides, it wasn't meant to happen to you."

I felt my chest tighten painfully. "What do you mean?" I heard Simon ask sharply as I gripped the chair.

"I really didn't think Bobby would do it, or I wouldn't have let him carry my gun." Kyle looked at Simon desperately. "He said we should give those other two a little scare. Let them know we didn't like their kind here."

"What other two?" I hissed at the child.

But, of course, I already knew. He looked at me with fear, and I caught myself thinking that I couldn't really be a witch. If I were, he would turn into a toad right on the spot.

"Those two girls that are staying with you."

"And what kind are they that they aren't welcomed here?" I asked in a tone that didn't alleviate his fear. "One of them is my daughter."

"You know." He hung his head again. "They're gay."

I was sure that wasn't the word he and his friend Bobby had used when they discussed how funny it would be to scare them.

Jake had been hurt by his friend's actions, but now he was angry. "You tried to hurt Rowan and Keisha? You're an idiot, Kyle Bartlett!"

"No, Jake! We weren't going to hurt them. We just thought the horse would take off and the worst that would happen would be one of them would fall."

"Somebody did fall, Kyle. And you'll never know how badly Jake was hurt. Fortunately, he's going to get better." Simon studied him closely. "And why did you think it was okay to scare someone because they're gay?"

Kyle stuck out his chin. "Because being gay is a bad thing." His bravado quickly deflated. "But Mom says they might not be gay."

I could no longer sit still. I stood up, and it probably seemed to the boy that I was towering over him.

"They are gay, Kyle. And they are very nice people. They would never do anything so terrible to you, even if they knew what you tried to do to them. They went home yesterday, and I'm glad they're not here because they would be very hurt that somebody would do something so mean. They would be most angry that you hurt their friend Jake."

"I really am sorry," he said again. "Are you going to tell the police? Will I have to go to jail?"

Part of my anger left me when I let myself realize that it was just a terrified little boy standing before us. One who had come closer than he'd ever know to causing a friend's death, but a little boy nonetheless.

A profound sadness shook me, and tears spilled out of my own eyes.

Donna finally spoke. "I know it doesn't make up for any of it, but he told me tonight because he felt so bad he couldn't keep it in anymore. He's lost his BB gun forever. I took it to the dump on our way here. And he can't play with anyone for a very long time."

"Not even me?" Jake asked with the logic of a close-to-ten-year-old.

"You'd still play with me?" Kyle sniffled.

"Well, maybe not for a while. And you'd have to tell Rowan and Keisha you're sorry. But if you know what a bad thing you did, I would after a while. You are my friend."

Jake's capacity for forgiveness was astounding. And quicker than mine.

As I regarded the two little boys in front of me, another thought occurred to Simon. "Why isn't Bobby here with you?"

"Mom wanted him to come, too, but his parents said no," Kyle answered him.

I turned to Donna, who squirmed uncomfortably in her chair.

"It's true. When I went to talk to them, they wouldn't have anything to do with me. They said nobody could prove Bobby had anything to do with it. That it was just Kyle lying to get him in trouble. And besides...."

"Besides?"

Her eyes were troubled, but she didn't flinch from me. "They said besides, queers and their friends deserved whatever they got. Then they shut the door in my face."

"Ah. So I see where Bobby gets his attitude, but where did Kyle get his ideas of why it's okay to hurt someone who's gay?" I asked her. "Surely not just from Bobby."

"I've never said it was all right to hurt anybody!" she declared. "I truly am sorry about all this, Kat, Simon. When he asked me, I did tell him that gay people are sinners, but they *are* people. It's not okay to hurt them or scare them."

I sighed. "Donna, you met my daughter and her partner. Weren't they very nice to you when you were introduced?"

"Yes," was all she said.

"Have you met anyone else you've known was gay?"

"No. People don't do that here."

"Oh, Donna, please. You probably know more gay people than you'd ever believe, but they'd be too afraid to let you know. They love each other, and you think that's a sin, and this Bobby's parents think it's all right to hurt them and friends of theirs just because they love each other. That seems pretty messed up to me."

"Kat, please. I don't think it's all right to hurt anyone. And I've been told all my life what a bad thing it is for someone to be a homosexual. I've just never met anybody...." She glanced at me and then quickly at her hands. "Nobody's ever said it like that before."

I said nothing more to her but turned to Kyle. Jake's quickness to forgive had influenced me, but I wasn't ready to let him completely off the hook. "What you did was a pretty cowardly thing and could have gotten Jake or my daughter and her friend killed. But coming to tell us was a brave thing for both you and your mother to do. Keisha did see the two of you, so we suspected it wasn't an accident. You didn't know that, and she didn't see who you were, so there's no way we would have ever known. I can agree not to tell the police, but I'm leaving it totally up to Jake's father."

I saw a flicker of relief in his anguished eyes, but he looked at Simon for confirmation.

"Do you understand what a serious thing this is?" Simon asked Kyle.

"Yes, sir," he answered.

"I am really disappointed in you. I thought you were someone with more sense. But I agree with Kat. It was brave of you to come to tell us, especially after you knew you'd have to take the blame alone when Bobby's parents aren't punishing him. I want to see proof that something like this will never happen again before you can play with Jake again. But I'm not going to tell the police either. You have a chance of coming over to play with Jake in the future. I'm going to tell Bobby's parents that he's not allowed to."

"It won't ever happen again. I promise!"

And I was sure it wouldn't. I believed he really had learned his lesson, but at what a price!

After they left, I felt numb. Jake had a real need to talk about what had just happened, so I pulled myself together so I could give him the energy he needed from me. Finally, he exhausted himself, and I helped Simon get him to bed.

Then, tired as I was, it was time for Simon and me to talk.

Just as I had done with Rita, I told him what had occurred and then asked him not to talk to anyone about it.

I thought I heard pain in his voice when he asked, "Why would you think I would do that? It's obvious you don't want anyone to know."

"People would think I was crazy!" I said with exasperation. "Doesn't it seem far-fetched to you?"

"No," he said in a voice much calmer than my own. "I was there. Remember? I know what you did for Jake. I don't know how you did it, and I don't care. I'm just grateful to you, and to whoever the lady in red is, that you did. And if you'd stop shutting me out for a minute, I'd like to help you deal with it. You don't have to handle everything alone, you know. Sometimes it helps to share the burden. I could see you struggling with this, but you wouldn't tell me about it."

Several responses warred with each other in my head. I wanted to be angry with him and tell him that I've been handling things on my own for a very long time. I wanted to tell him not to push me. I wanted to tell him that I hadn't been shutting him out, but I knew that one was a lie. I also wanted to throw my arms around him and simply cry.

I compromised. I said, "I am used to dealing with things on my own. And you have to let me if I need to. But thank you for wanting to help." Then I put my arms around him.

He pulled me close and said in a quiet voice, "I do want to help. And I hated having you shut me out. But Kat, I'm not trying to take your strength away from you. I only wanted to add to it."

Then he kissed me, and I let go of the other responses.

Chapter 12

The next two weeks were strange ones for me. Anger would well up in me at odd times even though I tried to keep it at bay. I told myself that ignorance and bigotry were everywhere but so were compassion and decency. The problem was, I started looking at people differently, wondering which of them were the bigots. When I went to the store or library, there were some people who were decidedly less friendly than they had been. But there were others who made a point of speaking to me. However, no one spoke directly of Kyle and Bobby's hand in Jake's injuries or the reasons for the incident, though I knew gossip had spread through the town.

I had thought to keep the fact that they had been the actual targets of the boys' ignorance from Rowan and Keisha, but I realized Jake would probably tell them by e-mail. I called to talk to them after I had sorted out my own feelings about it as best I could. Their reactions were less angry than mine, though they were predictably upset that Jake had been the one to suffer from the bigotry. Sadly, they were used to the knowledge that there were people who hated them just for being who they were.

"I still love the place, Mom," Rowan told me. "Not everyone there is stupid. You have some wonderful friends, there and so do we. It sounds like Kyle, at least, is really sorry for what he did. That's a start. And maybe his mother's mind is swayed, just a little, to start thinking more openly."

"You won't be afraid to come back here?" I asked.

"Of course not. It was two little boys pulling a stupid prank that caused a lot more harm than they were expecting. Stupid things happen everywhere."

My anger dissipated after that phone call. I began a period of going inward more than usual even for a writer, but I wasn't unhappy about it. A combination of my love for the house and the daily change in the air as autumn became more pronounced, seemed to work a change in me, and I strayed less and less from home. I did take walks through the woods around my place fairly often. I had to be out among those trees as they dressed in their brightest colors and then slowly shed it all to the ground. Both Simon and Rita had warned me that hunting season was starting. Heeding their warnings, I dressed in a bright red jacket whenever I went out.

My work didn't suffer—I painted often, inspired by the riot of colors swirling and changing around me daily. Words also flowed from my head to my hands as I spun stories into my computer as fast as I could type. Overlaying it all was my growing love and knowledge of the herbs and what they could do. I spent contented hours gathering and drying plants either to be used later or simply for decoration.

What did suffer was the time I had to spend with Simon. When we were together, it was almost always in the company of Jake, which I loved. But twice, when he asked me to go somewhere where it would be just the two of us, I had to tell Simon that I couldn't go. Both times, I'd had something important to do, but I was afraid he was starting to get impatient with me.

All right, I thought with annoyance, *here come the expectations and complications.*

Had I been willing to be truthful with myself I would have also had to admit I was more than a little afraid to let our relationship develop beyond where it was at that point. But I had enough to deal with for the moment. Neither Simon nor I talked of the strain I know we were both beginning to feel between us. Who knows how long we could have continued to pretend that neither of us noticed anything wrong if it hadn't been brought to a head one late afternoon in October.

The season had definitely changed to full-blown autumn. It was as if the Earth had been drifting through the warmth of summer and failed to notice the first few signs of change in the air, just as I had. And it seemed that something was waiting for us to take that notice. When we did, the change was rapid. The air became crisp and cooler, though not yet cold. The trees were still half-dressed in their vivid colors, but the ground was now awash in the dying, fallen leaves, and the swishing sound they made beneath my feet wherever I walked both thrilled and saddened me. My herbs were no longer flowering, but neither were they dying yet. Most seemed determined to cling to their green lives as long as possible.

It was a Monday afternoon after I'd spent much of the morning going through the attic one more time. I had thought to organize some of the contents into what was valuable either monetarily or historically. My mind kept drifting, however, and I didn't get very far. I kept wondering why there were so few of Tess' personal possessions and remembering that Rita had said Toby would be back in September. Here it was the second week of October, and Rita did not know of anyone who had heard from him. What if he decided not to come back at all? I realized I had been counting on him to answer a great deal of my questions.

I gave up trying to sort any more for the day and made my way to the kitchen to grab a snack before beginning another painting. I had decided it was about time to paint more of my dreams. Minette sat by her empty food bowl and stared accusingly at me as I entered the room. I clicked my tongue at her.

"Don't worry. I'll feed you first. You'd never leave me alone if I didn't." I reached into a shelf to bring out the cat food bag which, I discovered, was nearly empty. "Oops." I stared back at her. "There's a little here. You can have that, and I'll run to the store. I need bread, anyway."

As I emptied what was left into her dish, she looked on disdainfully and then proceeded to make it vanish.

"Be right back." I grabbed the car keys and my wallet and then headed to the front door.

The truth was, I was feeling restless and welcomed the chance to be moving.

The tiny market was surprisingly crowded for a Monday afternoon as I maneuvered my way down the narrow aisles to locate the items I needed. I had the bag of cat food and was looking over the bread choices when voices in the next aisle broke into my thoughts. They were women's voices, though I didn't recognize them. A few of their words made my ears prick as I realized what the subject of their conversation was.

"Her mother was odd enough," said one. "And isn't it something that they both turned out to be artists? But did you hear about that daughter of hers? I thought there was something strange about those two girls when they first showed up here."

"What do you expect?" asked another voice. "That whole family has always been strange. Doesn't matter if she was adopted out. Blood always tells, I say. And now, it sounds like she's trying to be just like Tess. Get this: Edna says she heard that Simon told someone that she thinks she healed Jacob when he got thrown from that horse."

The words stunned me, and I was unable to walk away.

A third voice came from someone trying to be kinder. "Well, maybe she can heal some. You know Tess had a way about her. As strange as she was, she did help my Tim's arthritis. And when his eye got infected and the doctor wasn't around, she cleared that right up."

"Oh, come on, Sara," the first voice chided. "So she put some herbs on it. It would have gotten better anyway. I always told you, you should be careful about going to that woman for help. Some of those plants could be dangerous. And now this one seems to think she should act just as strangely as her mother did."

"Well, she can't be very good." The second person laughed. "Jacob had a concussion and a broken leg. I'd be embarrassed to claim myself as a healer if my patients ended up in that bad a shape."

The first old biddy began to cackle along with her now, and my growing fury finally pushed me from the spot. I rounded the corner and paused long enough to be sure that they would guess that I had overheard. I had met two of the women very briefly, but the third did not look familiar to me at all.

"Maybe you should take more care to see that the person you're gossiping about isn't standing so close by," I said much more calmly than I was feeling. "From what I hear, my mother was very knowledgeable about herbs, so I doubt that she put anyone in danger. And I don't recall ever having claimed to be a healer myself, so I don't think I have anything to be embarrassed about. If I were standing around gossiping meanly about someone...well, then I might be embarrassed."

The two who had been laughing now stood with their mouths open in shock. The third woman blushed hotly and put a hand toward me. "I'm sorry," she started to say, but one of the others grabbed her arm and, if she said anything more, I didn't hear it as I held my head high and took my items to the checkout.

I managed to get out of the store before tears of anger boiled up. But not just anger at the pettiness of at least two of the women. Mixed with the anger was a sense of betrayal by someone I'd trusted. I was hardly aware of shoving the bag I held into the back seat of the Jeep and then climbing behind the wheel. I left the parking lot quickly, but I didn't turn toward home."

The library was closed on Mondays, and I thought it likely I would find Simon at his house. I knocked loudly at the door and heard a response from Jasper. "Sit," Simon was saying to him as the door opened. When he saw me, a smile started to his lips but quickly faded. "Kat, what's wrong?"

"May I come in for just a moment?" I asked through clenched teeth.

"Of course." He opened the door further and then closed it behind him as he followed me to the living room. He gestured to a chair, but I shook my head.

"I won't be staying long." I looked at him with hurt and the anger still in my eyes. "I trusted you. I told you things that you promised not to repeat. How could you break a promise so quickly?"

A flicker of anger flashed in his own eyes. "I have no idea what you're talking about. Are you going to tell me?"

"I just came from the grocery store where some old women were having a field day laughing over what a strange family Tess, Rowan, and I come from. And they thought it was hilarious that you've been saying that I thought I healed Jake when he was hurt! How could you talk about that behind my back?"

"I haven't said a word to anyone. You asked me not to." His words were clipped but controlled. "I can't believe that you think I would. I thought you knew me better than that."

"Then where did they hear it? The only other people who know what happened are Rowan, Keisha, and Rita. And they wouldn't have told anyone."

"And you assume I would." The hurt I saw in his face made me falter for a second.

"One of the women said you told someone. What else would I assume?"

"Obviously that I'm guilty." He regarded me angrily. "I promised that I wouldn't say a word to anyone and I haven't. Apparently my word doesn't mean that much to you."

Simon's reaction left me feeling lost and confused. The women had specifically said that Simon had told someone, and my anger had seemed so righteous. How could they have heard it if it hadn't come from him? Surely Rita wouldn't have told anyone.

Simon broke through my confusion. "Have you been looking for an excuse to be angry with me?"

"What?" I asked him incredulously. "That's ridiculous."

"Is it? You've been pushing me away since Jake got hurt."

"I have not!" I said indignantly, but deep inside I felt a flicker of truth to his words. It had nothing to do with Jake, however.

"I really cared about you, Kat, and I thought you felt something, too. But you're so afraid of letting someone get too close that you're willing to jump at the first chance to believe I would hurt you. Why don't you just be honest with both of us and tell me to get lost instead of looking for excuses?"

This was not turning out the way I had expected. I didn't want to fight with him about how I felt about our relationship. I searched for the words to bring us back to what I thought should really be the subject here. But his next words stopped all thought and only served to make me furious.

"I'll make it easy for you. I won't bother you anymore. Let me just go get the violin you lent to Jake."

"Don't you dare!" I hissed at him as he turned toward Jake's room. "I gave that to Jake, and it's his. You have no right to take it away from him."

He regarded me coldly. "He is my son." A struggle played across his face as he slowly relented. "You're right, though. That's between you and Jake. It was very nice of you to give it to him. Thank you." The last words were given grudgingly, but they didn't stop my anger.

"You're welcome," I said stiffly, "but I did it for Jake, not you." My words stung him, and he said nothing more as we stood there awkwardly. I hadn't meant to end it like this, but I saw no way out now and turned to go. "Goodbye," I managed to say hoarsely.

I could feel him follow me to the door and, as I put my hand to the knob, he said softly, "Kat...."

I stopped but didn't turn, not wanting him to see the tears gathering in my eyes.

Finally, he said, "Nothing. Goodbye."

Back in the car, I took a moment to get myself under control. It would do no good to attempt to drive through a blur of tears. I pushed all my thoughts as far away as I could. I wanted to get to my house, my refuge, before the floods let loose.

Once at the house, I made it as far as the porch before I dropped into the first chair and simply stared ahead of me. The small bag of groceries lay at my feet when Minette suddenly appeared out of the bushes to sniff her promised food. She could just wait. I wasn't moving. I was prepared to ignore her completely until she did the one thing she hadn't done since I arrived. She jumped into my lap and curled herself into a ball with her head under the palm of my hand. It was so unexpected that it loosened the hold I had on my emotions. I buried my face in my other hand and cried.

"Now what?" I asked her when the tears showed signs of letting up. "Things have gone to hell here awfully quickly, haven't they?"

It was just as well, I told myself, that Simon and I weren't going to see each other anymore. He probably wanted much more from me than I was willing to give. I was not going to be here forever. And then I remembered I was going to be here until February. I had already told Gail she could have my apartment until then. I realized as well that not seeing Simon meant that I wouldn't be able to spend time with Jake. I'd grown very fond of him. It was a very small town. Certainly I would see him from time to time. Simon, too, even though we would probably avoid each other as much as possible. What a mess! Three and a half months in a place where there were so many people who hadn't liked my birth mother, and now they could turn their venom on my daughter and me. And two of the people I'd loved…well, cared about…I would no longer be able to share anything with. I was feeling very sorry for myself.

Rita found us still on the porch an hour later. I was so lost in my misery that I hadn't noticed her until she was on the porch steps. I looked up and tried to paste a normal look on my face. It didn't fool her.

"What's wrong, Kat?" She lowered herself to the chair beside me. "Have you had another of your dreams?"

I was annoyed to find my lip trembling slightly. "No. Much worse than that. I overheard some women at the store discussing Simon telling someone I thought I'd healed Jake when he was hurt. They had not very nice things to say about Rowan and Tess, too. I made a little scene, I'm afraid. Afterward, I went to confront Simon about it, and we…decided not to see each other again."

"Oh, no!" She looked at me with sympathy. "You don't think Simon really told anyone do you?"

"Well, Rita, what could I think? They actually said that he told someone. But when I did confront him with it, he got angry back. He said he didn't tell anyone, and he was upset that I thought he did." I turned my eyes to her, not wanting to voice the question that I had to ask. "Rita, you didn't tell anyone, did you?"

"Oh, no, Kat! I would never do that when you asked me not to. And I don't think Simon did either."

"Then who did? No one else knew."

"I don't know. But Kat, don't lose Simon because of this."

I avoided her eyes now. "It's too late. And it's not just this."

"Then what?"

"I really don't want to talk about it. Please? I shouldn't have started seeing him in the first place."

"I don't believe that for a minute," she said. "And I think you should talk about it. If Rowan were here, I bet she would make you."

"And I'd get angry at her." I hoped she took the not-so-subtle hint.

She smiled briefly and said, "Point taken. But if you want to talk at all, I'm here, you know."

I knew I was fortunate to have made such a good friend. "Thanks, Rita. I'm all talked out right now. But you are the first person I'll call on." I purposely chose to ignore the ache in my heart and so changed the subject. "What's happening with you? Is your mother getting used to the idea that you and Sam have a thing going?"

I watched her weigh whether to let me get away with the subject change or not and saw the precise moment she decided to let it go. She had one of those easily readable faces. "A thing?" she asked with a laugh. "I don't know about that, but my mother is behaving herself for the most part. It would be almost scary except that she manages to get some sort of remark in here and there about mature women making fools of themselves as if they were teenagers. That's kinder than some of Arthur's comments have been, but hey, I don't have to see him every day."

"He really is a piece of work, isn't he? What's his problem?"

She thought before she answered. "I don't know. A superiority complex, maybe? He's always thought of himself as someone capable of great things, and I've always been an embarrassment to him. Even when we were kids. He used to tell people I wasn't really part of the family, that our parents had adopted me out of pity and it didn't work out."

"Jerk," I muttered, but Rita seemed only amused.

"I don't care. Between my kids and now you and Sam, I don't see myself through his or my mother's—or Dan's—eyes anymore. Or at least, not as much," she added truthfully. "This might sound silly, but I'm just trying to figure out who I am, and it turns out I might not be such a bad person after all. There were times I'd wonder why Tess was so nice to me when she ignored most everyone else. When things were really bad, I thought she must just feel sorry for me." She made a face. "This really does sound silly for a grown woman. But I'm just starting to think about what it might be like to be happy. And I want you to be happy, too, Kat."

"It doesn't sound silly at all. It's about time you thought about yourself. Don't worry about me. I'll be fine." She looked at me skeptically. "Really. Simon and I just weren't meant to be. It's not a big deal." She didn't believe that any more than I did.

She did force me to follow her into the house where she could ply me with her cure-all lemon balm tea. The warm tea and friendly face did help, but only while she was there.

Once she left, I sat looking at the empty teacup and felt the tears begin to prickle once more. "Damn it!" I slammed my hand on the table, startling Minette from her perch on a wooden stool. "I am not going to let a man do this to me. I don't know if he's the one who said anything or not, but it's better that we ended things now instead of later. I'll miss Jake, but it's not the end of the world."

The cat flicked her tail and then went on to more important things, specifically, her food dish. I decided to follow her example although food didn't appeal to me at the moment.

I washed up the tea things and then made my way to the studio. Surrounded by Tess' and my artwork I could lose myself in my writing and not be intruded upon by regrets I refused to acknowledge. It worked until I was too tired to keep going and finally made my way to drop, exhausted, into bed.

My body cried for sleep, but my brain refused to shut down. I spent a restless, miserable night until my brain finally relented in the early hours of the morning and I drifted off into an unsatisfying, dream filled sleep.

I didn't know if it was good or bad once I awoke. I couldn't remember any of the dreams, only the residual feelings. They weren't happy ones.

For the next week, I managed—for the most part—to ignore the ache that was my constant companion by keeping every moment filled. Rita insisted on having me come to dinner twice, and I found an unexpected source of distraction in Harriet's entertaining ramblings. She made no mention of Rowan and Keisha, and when Rita and I talked of them, she smiled politely but refrained from adding the derogatory comments I would have expected from her. For whatever reason, perhaps because I had gone to church with her or because she now had something that made her feel sorry for me, she began treating me with more warmth than I'd received from her since my arrival. I found myself enjoying her stories of the Newbridge of her childhood.

The rest of the time, I kept as busy as possible. The days were starting to get chillier and, hoping to make myself a little more cheerful with blazes in the living room fireplace, I asked Rita where I could get firewood. By the end of the day, I had a truckload delivered and welcomed the mindless task of stacking the wood into a neat pile. It wasn't really necessary—the house was actually heated with an oil furnace, and I had already had that filled. But I needed whatever diversion I could find.

When writing and painting were no help, I would go outside and rake leaves. There was no real purpose to the raking. I started a pile that grew each day until a wind would gust and, just for fun, scatter most of my hard work. Then I would start again.

At one point, I had made a huge pile and found myself looking at it as if I were still a child. Think of all the things that could be done with that huge mound! I could picture Jake with no broken bones, jumping and somersaulting through it, but I pushed that image from my mind. As so often happens for me, a thin story line began to thread its way into my head, and I saw children make giant nests to burrow happily into. I thought I might as well conduct a piece of research and, looking around to be sure no one could possibly see how foolish I was capable of being, I waded into the thick of the pile and flattened a circle just big enough to hold my seated body. Cocooned within the leaves, I felt some of the hurt and anger I'd been holding onto begin to drift away. The sadness lingered, but that I could deal with. I lay back with my head on the crinkly cushion of the dead leaves and let my mind wander.

Surprisingly, for the first time since our confrontation, my thoughts didn't leap to Simon. Instead, the dreams I'd had and what they might mean pushed their way past the defenses I had built up to keep them out. It was time to face it. Tess had called herself a witch and, though I could only guess at what that meant to her, it appeared to me to have to do with being a healer. She healed animals for Rita and aided others with her herbs. I had a sudden vision of her going farther afield than just where the domesticated herbs surrounded the house. Rita had said that she was sometimes seen wearing a cape. I could easily picture her with a basket on her arm, gathering wild herbs in a meadow. It was a vision of a witch that could fit into practically any time period.

Whether the dreams I'd been having were mere pictures of my imagination or fantastically, something more historical buried in my psyche, I realized it didn't matter. I was Tess' daughter. I had inherited more than I'd bargained for from her, but there was no denying it. The power that I'd felt in my hands and the sureness of what to do the day of Jake's accident was very real. Where it came from, who could say? But Tess had had it, there were rumors that her mother and grandmother had it, and now it had fallen to me. I thought with a start, I wonder if it will pass to Rowan. She was of the same line, and she had seen the woman in red. I wished that she were here right now, so we could talk about it. But it came to me as a thought out of the chill autumn air that I was meant to be here alone for a time. This was something for me to explore for myself first. It was time to move forward and accept what I'd been given: both the house and the healing gifts were passed down to me from a woman I'd never met while she was alive, but I was just beginning to feel I might get to know her these months after her death.

I picked myself back up out of the leafy nest, feeling more at peace than I had in days. I'd been more than annoyed to find that I'd lost my appetite the day I had argued with Simon and had had to force myself to eat for the sustenance I needed. For the first time since then, I felt a grumble in my stomach and knew that I was hungry.

My steps felt lighter as I traversed the hallway and entered the kitchen, looking around in anticipation. I picked a large juicy apple from a bowl on the counter and took several bites before I noticed the light blinking on the phone answering machine. My heart did a little flip before I made myself walk to the phone calmly. It could be Rita or Rowan, I told myself. But it was neither them nor Simon who had called. As

I pushed the play back button, a voice that I'd never heard before but had been anticipating, filled the room.

"Katrina, hello. My name is Toby Underwood. I...I knew your mother and just got back to town after having been away for some time. I'd like to talk to you. Could you give me a call?"

I stared at the little red light on the machine as he carefully recited the phone number. At the click at the end of the message, the light flickered off, but I continued staring for some time. Finally, I gave myself a little shake and reached a tentative hand toward the phone. I took a breath and began to dial.

Chapter 13

Toby Underwood and I made arrangements to meet that evening after dinner. The phone conversation had been brief—I think we were both rather nervous. He had just gotten back to town the previous day, and when he had gone to the post office, he had seen Rita who told him I was here and gave him my phone number. He hoped I didn't mind.

"Of course not," I said politely with no hint of the turmoil my stomach was going through. "I've been looking forward to meeting you and hoping you can answer some of my questions." Such as, are you my father? But there was no polite way to ask that one right off the bat. "I'd rather not do this over the phone. Would you like to come here?"

I heard him draw a quick breath and then there was a brief silence. Finally, he said in an odd voice, "All right. I could do that. I actually haven't been in Tess' house in over forty years, and she asked me not to go into it until...well, we can talk about all that later. It's your house now, and she would be happy about that. I'm afraid it will be a little difficult for me, but I think it's time. When would you like to meet?" After those cryptic words, we set the time and hung up.

If I was hoping for a quiet, peaceful rest of the day to spend contemplating what I would ask Toby that evening, I was disappointed. I walked into town as much to settle my jittery nerves as to pick up a few items that I needed. I had two library books that were due and thought briefly of taking them to drop off, but I just couldn't do it. At that point I wasn't sure which would be worse, to see Simon however briefly or not see him at all. Well, here was an instance where it was definitely not going to be like mother, like daughter. I had no problem with my books being overdue for a day or so. I would put them in the book drop after the library was closed and there was no chance of running into Simon. Cowardly, I know, but I didn't think it was always wrong to take the easy way out.

Sometimes, however, fate refuses to let you take the easy way out. I got my few errands out of the way quickly and decided to drop in at the post office to see Rita on my way home. I'd just stepped through the door when my eyes went straight to the two people at the counter with their backs to me. My heart did a flip at the sight of the familiar ponytail and Jake's crutches. I was immobilized, trying to decide which would be more awkward, to slip quickly back out the door and hope they wouldn't notice or to stay and...what? The decision was taken from me as both Rita and Jake saw me at the same time. Rita smiled sympathetically my way, but Jake let out a whoop.

"Kat!" He hobbled quickly to where I stood.

"Hi, Jake. How's your leg doing?" It was an inane thing to ask but, with his father's inscrutable eyes turned on me, I wasn't feeling at my most eloquent. Jake didn't seem to notice.

"Okay. I wish I could get this stupid cast off, but you'd be surprised what you can do with crutches, even when you're sitting down." He grinned at me impishly and then turned suddenly serious. "I haven't seen you in a while," he said accusingly. "Jasper and I miss you. Dad says you're busy, but you were busy before and still had time to do stuff with us."

"Jake!" Simon stepped in quickly and put his hand on his son's shoulder. Before he could say anything more, I spoke directly to Jake.

"I miss you and Jasper, too." And your father, I thought, but wouldn't say it aloud. "Sometimes things just change, and it's not always easy." Oh, God, I was sounding even more inane than before. "I... I hope your dad will let me see you sometimes."

"I could come over to your house. Dad could drop me off. Right, Dad?" I sensed an attempt at a little manipulation in those words.

"We'll see," Simon told him noncommittally. He looked at me with hooded eyes, and I didn't trust myself to speak directly to him.

"That would be nice," I told Jake. "You're welcome any time it's all right with your father."

"I just sent some pictures I made off to my grandparents in Oregon and to Rowan and Keisha. I made a picture of Jasper playing my violin for them. And I made a tape for them to hear that I'm practicing. Rowan told me yesterday she'd send me one of them, too."

"You talked to her?"

"By e-mail. We e-mail lots."

Of course, they did. I hadn't said anything to Rowan about not seeing Simon. I wondered what Jake had told her.

"We have to go now, Jake." Simon pressed his son's shoulder. He hesitated before saying, "Goodbye, Kat. It's... it's nice to see you."

Good. He was feeling as awkward as I was. "You, too, Simon." Not trusting myself to say more, I turned quickly and walked to the counter where Rita had watched the whole exchange with interest. I hadn't meant it to be a dismissal, but I'm sure it seemed that way. I didn't turn around, but I could tell when they had left the building just by watching Rita's face.

She looked at me. "Two of the most stubborn people in Newbridge were just in here," she commented dryly.

I was confused. "I don't understand. What's so stubborn about Jake?"

She laughed in surprise. "I wasn't talking about Jake."

"Oh." Point taken and ignored.

She decided to let me off the hook for the moment. "Toby's back. Did he call you yet?"

I looked around and was glad to note we were alone. "Yes. I'm meeting him tonight."

"Where?" Rita asked curiously.

"At my house."

"Really?" Her surprise was evident.

"We only talked briefly, but he told me he hadn't been in the house in forty years. He agreed to come, though. It will be…interesting. I walked into town to do errands and just stopped by to tell you."

"Thanks. I told you, we're all nosy here. I'll be dying to hear what he says." The concern in her voice belied the idea that it was just nosiness.

"Don't worry. I may need to talk after. Come over when you get a chance tomorrow." I turned to go.

"Kat," Rita said softly. "He's a nice man. I hope…I hope it goes well."

"Me, too," I said nervously.

Thoughts swirled through my head as I walked briskly toward home. Just as I got to my driveway, one silly thought stuck out. I was going to have overdue library books for nothing!

I spent the rest of the afternoon working on the beginnings of a painting of the child, Kate, from my dreams. I could see her so clearly dropping her cornhusk doll to take the locket from her mother's hand. The eagerness and innocence on her face were at odds with the later scene where I had glimpsed fear and the loss of innocence after the death of her mother. I couldn't choose which face to replicate until I decided to do both, side by side. I began to wonder how the rest of the story of my dreams played out. What had happened to the child and her father? Did they make it safely away and, if so, what kind of woman had Kate become? I worked and reworked a story line, trying to give her a happy ending, but nothing I came up with seemed right.

I glanced at my watch and realized it was time to put this away for the day. I would make myself an early dinner and have everything cleaned up before Toby arrived. I was actually looking forward to a little feline companionship while I ate, but Minette—the traitor—did not show. I did not linger over the meal. By the time the dishes were washed up, I still had a half an hour to spare.

I found myself in the living room rummaging through Tess' books. I had thought to lay a fire but decided against it. It would have given my hands something to do for a few minutes, but it seemed a bit too cozy. This was not just a social call. I wasn't quite sure what you would call it. I had just selected a book on ancient works of art depicting Goddesses of all sizes and shapes and had begun thumbing through it when I heard the crunch of tires on the loose stones of the driveway. He's very early, I thought, wondering whether to be irritated or happy to get the initial meeting over. I placed the book on the shelf where I could retrieve it later, and walked slowly to the front door. I was expecting to see a single older gentleman, so I was confused at first to see a gray-haired woman step out of the driver's side of the car and make her way around to the passenger's door to help an elderly man climb slowly and painfully out. I was puzzled. This couldn't be Toby unless he had aged considerably and lost the vitality that had come across so strongly in Tess' painting of him.

The woman glanced up and saw me standing in the doorway. A little gasp escaped me when I got a good look at her face. It was one of the women who had been talking about Tess, Rowan, and me at the grocery store! Now what? Then I remembered she was the one who had tried to be kind and apologize.

"I'm sorry, Miss...Mrs. Benson. I hope you're not so angry with me that you won't try to help Tim." Her eyes pleaded with me to do something, though what I didn't know yet.

"What is it that you want me to help with, Mrs...?"

"Watson. Sara Watson. And this is Tim."

"How do you do?" Tim winced in obvious pain but was unwilling to dispense with politeness.

I was reluctant to leave the comfort of the door guarding my space into the house, but I couldn't just stand there. I crossed the porch and went down the steps to take the old man's other arm and helped the woman guide him up onto the porch and into the nearest chair.

"How can I help you?" I asked warily, afraid I already knew what they wanted from me.

"My husband has terrible arthritis Mrs. Benson, and Tess used to help him sometimes with it. The doctor's been giving him medicine for it, but tonight it hurt him something fierce and we thought...."

When she hesitated, her husband took over for her. "We thought, what with some of the things we've been hearing about you, that you've developed some of your mama's talents, and it was worth a shot to see if you would help me."

I looked at their expectant faces with dread, but shockingly, there was a little thrill hiding underneath. I didn't want this, did I? What if I could do more than just help Jake? What if I couldn't?

"Mr. Watson, I don't know that I can do anything for you. I seem to have been able to help someone once, but I don't really know if that can happen again. What did Tess used to do for you?"

"Sometimes, she'd make herbs up for me to take, and sometimes she'd just put her hands to the pain. I wouldn't ask you, but it got so bad tonight that Sara and I agreed to come ask. I wouldn't hold it against you none if you just tried and it didn't work. You couldn't make it any worse." He grimaced as a spasm of pain shook him.

"Please, Mrs. Benson?" Sara pleaded again.

"My name is Kat," I said almost irritably. "Where does it hurt the most, Mr. Watson?"

"My knees," he said, "and my name is Tim."

A little smile escaped me as I knelt in front of him. Any other time, I was sure I would have felt foolish, but amazingly, I didn't at this moment. I looked into his face. "I can't promise anything. But I'm going to try just putting my hands on them. You tell me immediately if it's too painful, and I'll stop."

He nodded, and I rubbed my hands together and then blew on them. I had no idea why I did that, I hadn't thought about it. I placed my hands over his knees and then gently lowered them until they barely touched. Involuntarily, I closed my eyes as I felt a surge of heat go through my hands and pass into his pain. He jumped slightly, startling me. I was afraid that I had hurt him.

"No, no, it didn't hurt," he said as I started to take my hands away. "I just felt something strong. I think... I think it's helping already."

I closed my eyes again and continued concentrating on my hands and his pain. I could feel the pain although it didn't hurt me. It was more of a strong force that emanated out from him and tried to push past my hands. But the energy in my hands enveloped it and gently worked on lifting it out and away. I wasn't aware of how much time passed as I let the energy work, but when I finally looked up and knew it was time to stop, I was surprised to see Toby walking from a car parked next to the Watsons. I hadn't heard a sound.

There was no question that this was Toby. He could have stepped right out of Tess' painting. Well, I would deal with him next. First I had to finish with Mr. Watson...Tim. "Did that help at all?"

Tim eyed me with relief and humor. "Yes, Ma'am. I might not be able to dance my way back to the car, but I can definitely get there on my own." Then he said earnestly, "Young woman, you have your mother's hands. She was a strange one, for sure. But she knew how to lift the pain out when it got bad, and you just did the same thing. I thank you. What can we pay you for your help?"

I was taken by surprise. "Pay me? Did Tess charge you for her help?"

"She would never take money, but she let us bring her some of Sara's pies sometimes." He looked at his wife.

Sara smiled tentatively before she spoke. "I make some fine pies, if I do say so myself. I'd be awful pleased if you'd let me bring you a couple."

I smiled back. "That would be lovely. But don't feel that you have to. I'm...this is all new to me. How often did Tess help you? I don't know if this lasts for a while or just a short time."

"When Tess did it, it always helped for a few weeks. And she'd give Tim something to put on it, too."

"I'll see if I can make something up for you."

I couldn't believe the words came out of my mouth. I would ask Rita to help me tomorrow, but I was astounded to find myself thinking that we could make a salve with oil from yarrow, lavender, and rosemary that I was sure would help. At least, I knew it couldn't do any harm.

By this time, Toby was standing quietly at the foot of the porch steps.

Suddenly all eyes turned to him.

"Toby, we heard you were back," Tim said. "Didn't expect to see you *here*." He waved his thumb at me. "This little lady has some of the same talents her mother had. We're sure grateful she was here."

Toby looked at me with interest. I thought I read pain in his face, but he smiled quickly and turned to the old couple. "How are you, Tim, Sara? It's good to see you. I just got back yesterday."

"Must've been quite a surprise for you to find out Tess had a daughter, eh?"

"Tim, you old fool, hush now." Sara clipped him lightly on the shoulder, where I assumed the arthritis wouldn't hurt him.

I watched Toby intently. Had he known about me for a long time or had he just found out when he arrived home?

I was suddenly anxious for the Watsons to leave. Heaven only knew how much gossip would fly tomorrow both from the fact that I had been able to help Tim and whatever speculation there would be about Toby coming to meet Tess' daughter.

"The world is full of surprises," Toby said without answering Tim's question. "So your arthritis is better?"

"Thanks to Kat here, it's the best I've felt since before Tess died."

"It's time to get you home before you say anything else you shouldn't," Sara said, grasping her husband's arm firmly.

"What are you talking about, woman? I never say anything I shouldn't. And I can get myself down the stairs now, thank you. Watch this." He didn't exactly dance a jig, but it was obvious that he was not in the pain he had been in coming up the steps. He turned back and held his hand out for Sara to join him. "Thank you, Kat. I really do appreciate it."

"It was really nice of you, after, well...you know," Sara said.

I did know, but neither of us needed to speak about the incident at the store.

"He's a good man, if a mite thick-headed, and I hate to see him in pain. Thank you so much." Sara turned and followed her husband to the car. As she would have opened the door for him, he waved her away and made a show of doing it himself. They both smiled and waved before driving off.

I stood for a moment staring after them. "That was... that was quite something." There was a tense moment before I looked at Toby, and then we both started laughing. The ice was broken.

"Tim is quite a character. Despite what many people think about Tess, she was quite fond of him. I know she'd be happy that you were able to help him." Toby smiled a little sadly. "Thank you for seeing me, Katrina. I'm sure you've heard all kinds of rumors since you've been here. I'm sorry I wasn't here when you arrived, but I needed to get away. I was...I was close to Tess, and losing her was hard."

"It's Kat, please. I do seem to have developed a little of her abilities. Just one of the many surprises I've encountered over the last few months." I shivered slightly and realized I had no coat on. The early evening air was growing decidedly chilly. "Why don't we go inside?"

Toby hesitated and then gestured for me to go first. "I haven't gone further than this porch in all these years."

"Why not? If you were close to Tess, that seems a little odd." Curiosity overcame politeness.

"I'm sure there's a lot that seems odd to you, Kat. I hope I can help you understand about your mother a little better." He followed me to the living room and paused in the doorway. There was no mistaking the pain on his face now. "I thought the next time I saw this room again, it would be with Tess," he said quietly.

"Come have a seat." I was feeling slightly awkward again. Minette was in the rocking chair, and I scooped her up and held her as I sat in her place. Amazingly, she didn't fight me and barely glanced Toby's way as he seated himself on the sofa. "Can I get you anything?" I belatedly offered to play hostess.

"No, thank you." Toby looked around the room and then turned to me. "I know this is difficult for both of us. I should have stayed in town until you got here after Tess died, but I couldn't. Her death was such a shock, you see." He gave a little humorless laugh. "I'm sure it all must have been a shock to you."

"So you did know about me before Tess' death!"

"Yes," he admitted. "I've known about you for many years. And in the last couple of years, Tess told me more."

"Toby," I said in a somewhat exasperated voice, "there's a lot I don't understand."

"I know," he said, with real sympathy. "Let me tell you what I can. First, let me explain about Tess and me. I'd known her all my life, and when we were in high school, we were...sweethearts."

"Rita told me that."

"I thought we would be married after we both finished college, but...something happened and we didn't marry. I eventually married someone else, but Tess never did. About three years ago, my wife became very ill. The doctors told us she would never recover. My wife, Marie, asked me if I thought Tess' healing powers were real, and when I told her I

216

knew they were, she asked me to have her come see her. Tess and I had barely spoken in all those years, but when I called her, she came right away. She told Marie she couldn't take away the illness, but she could make it less painful and possibly give her more time than she otherwise would have. She spent a good deal of time with Marie after that and, amazingly, they became friends. She was with us when Marie died, peacefully and without pain. After that, I went away for a while. I traveled to Europe and sent postcards to Tess often." Toby paused. "I loved my wife, but I began to realize that I'd also never stopped loving Tess. After all those years and all the things that were said about her and the solitary life she'd chosen...." He seemed to pull himself back from a distance. "Well, when I came home, I got her to talk to me, although not here. Never here. She wouldn't let me come into this house, and it wasn't until a long time later that I understood why. We spent time together, and eventually I got her to admit that she still cared for me. We started traveling together—that was when we were both the happiest. We had two wonderful years, and when she finally started telling me things that she hadn't told anyone...I convinced her we could be happy and should be together permanently. When we were in England a couple of months before her death, she agreed to marry me—as soon as she worked some things out."

I hadn't wanted to interrupt him even though what he was saying had answered very few of my own questions yet. Now I couldn't help myself. "What things?"

"She wanted to contact you and tell you everything. She was hoping you would forgive her and establish a relationship."

"Whoa, wait a minute. What everything? And how did she know about me? She has all of my books I've written... how did she know who I was? When I was a teenager, I tried to find her, but my mother—my *adopted* mother—was told that there was to be no contact."

"I don't know everything, Kat. And some of what I do know will be painful. But she's known all about you from the time she gave you up. Your mother...Helen was her name?...

kept her informed. She told me that Helen sent her letters and pictures every year."

I was unable to say anything as I sat in total shock. My mother had known about Tess? How could she? When I'd asked, she had told me she could get no information. She had made me believe that she had really tried. This didn't make any sense. I looked at Toby blankly.

"Tess told me that you didn't know. She had asked your mother not to say anything to you. I think she was trying to protect you from something, but I don't know what. That's one of the things she hadn't told me yet."

"How did my mother know about Tess?" I could barely get the words out.

Is this what happens to everyone when they turn forty? I wondered. *Just when you think you can't be any more surprised, some new shock comes along?*

"I don't know the details, Kat." The compassion in Toby's voice made me look up. "But she met your parents when she first went to college in New York City. Your adoptive father was one of her professors, I believe. She said they were wonderful to her, and they wanted children but couldn't have any." He stopped talking for a few moments. He looked as if he were examining his hands very carefully, though I doubt he even saw them. Finally, he spoke again. "Did you know Tess' parents were killed in a car crash?"

I nodded.

"She came home from college for a short time right after her parents were killed, and when I tried to see her, she wouldn't let me come into the house. We talked on the porch, and that's when I found out she was pregnant."

Silence again. This didn't appear to be any easier for him than it was for me. I broke the silence this time with the question I had wanted to ask since seeing the portrait of this man. "Toby, are you my father?"

He smiled sadly. "No, Kat. I wish I were. I wanted to be. I tried to talk Tess into marrying me then, but she wouldn't do it. Something terrible had happened to her, and she had changed. She wouldn't marry me. She wouldn't even let me come into the house I'd been in so often with her. I was so young and self-centered that I couldn't see something painful had happened to her even before losing her parents. I was jealous of whoever your father was and stormed off. She went back to the city for several months and then, instead of finishing college, she came back to live alone in this house. I didn't know anything more about you until she started telling me after we were together again."

Disappointment struck me. It had seemed so likely that this man was my father. After seeing the loving way Tess had portrayed him and in the short time I'd been talking to him, I realized I had really hoped it was so.

"Do you know who my father is?" I asked him, point-blank.

He looked at me. "I don't. I'm sorry. While we were in England, Tess said she would tell me, but not until she'd tried to contact you and told you first. She said no one else needed to know. It no longer mattered to me, and I told her so."

I got up from my chair and absentmindedly placed Minette on the floor. She sniffed at Toby, who didn't seem to notice, and then she left the room. I stood looking into the fireplace.

"Why wouldn't she let you come into the house? You said you found out later."

"Some of this may be hard for you to accept. Although what I just saw you do for Tim...well, you might be able to understand. You must have heard rumors about Tess since you've been here, and I know Rita has told you things. Tess was different from other people here. From the time we were kids, she was different, but that's part of what fascinated me about her. You know she could heal. She and her mother and grandmother grew herbs and knew more about plants than anyone else I've ever known. It's part of what the women in this family always did. Tess told me it went way back. This house has belonged to the oldest daughter in the family since it was built in the 1700's. She said things were passed down from mother to daughter and...not just the house."

I turned to stand with my back to the fireplace. "Rita told me Tess called herself a witch. Is that what you're getting at?"

Toby looked startled and then recovered himself. "Well, to put it bluntly, I suppose it is." A small twinkle lit his eyes. "You know, at first I didn't think you looked much like her. But she had a certain way of standing, and her chin would jut out when she was facing something difficult. Exactly the way you're doing now."

"I've been told I can be quite stubborn. I don't suppose I inherited that from her, too?"

"Quite possibly."

"But you still haven't told me why she wouldn't let you into the house. From what I can tell, she let very few people in other than Rita."

"That's true. And I'm not sure why she felt Rita was safe."

"Safe?" I pounced on the word. "What do you mean?"

The twinkle left his eyes. "Tess once told me it was both a joy and a terrible burden to be part of this family. I wasn't quite sure what she meant, but she said there were things that other people didn't have to think about that she had to be very careful of. She told me that she had committed the ultimate taboo in her family. In anger and pain, she placed a curse on someone, and the payment for that was more than she could bear. She became convinced that was why she lost her parents, and she was afraid that anyone close to her who came into this house would pay for her mistake, too. I know this may sound bizarre to you, but she firmly believed it. I would have tried to talk her out of it if she had told me that when we were young. But when we were older, I think just to have a second chance with her, I was more accepting of her...beliefs."

"But you're here now," I pointed out.

"She asked me not to come in until you had been here. I had worked on convincing her that whatever the curse and its consequences were, she had paid for it in full. I think she was finally ready to let go of things and trust in the world a little again. She and I were finally happy, and you see...she had talked to you briefly."

"What do you mean? I never talked to...." And then the puzzle piece fell into place. Now I remembered why the name Underwood had sounded familiar. "It was her, wasn't it? When my mother died. So many people called who had known my mother over the years. And there was a woman who said her name was...Rose...Underwood."

"Yes," he said softly. "She had been so afraid to make that call, but she felt so badly about your mother, and I know she wanted to hear your voice."

"Why did she lie? Why didn't she tell me who she really was?" I asked angrily.

"Kat, think about it and try to understand. Your mother had just died. It would have been too much all at once. She wanted to give you time and then see if you would be open to letting her explain why she had given you up and not let you know about her. I don't know what the whole explanation is, but I do know she thought she was protecting you. And you may not believe this right now, but she loved you. I never saw them, but she told me about the pictures of you and your daughter."

"My mother...Helen...sent pictures of Rowan, too?"

"Yes. She sent the last just before she died. She told Tess how sick she was, that she didn't have much time left."

I barely heard him. I was thinking of that phone call. I had been puzzled because I hadn't heard my mother ever mention that name. But the woman had told me she hadn't seen my mother in a long time, that they had been close many years ago, and that Mom had been very kind to her. We had chatted for some time and, though I had forgotten her name, I hadn't forgotten her voice. It was full of such warmth, and the things she had to say had comforted me. I had told her I hoped I would get to meet her in person sometime, and she had told me that she hoped for that very much, too. Then, in the press of things, I had pushed it all to the back of my mind. But now, I could recall almost every detail of the conversation. I felt a small lump in my throat. I had really wanted to meet that woman. She had impressed me as someone I would have liked very much.

I sat in the chair again as I pulled myself back to the present. I stared at Toby as another puzzle occurred to me. "Toby, where are the pictures and letters? I haven't seen any here. And Tess' clothes—there are none of those here at all."

He looked as puzzled as I must have. "I don't know. There are a few of her clothes at my house. In the last few months, she stayed with me there sometimes. But there's nothing here? Have you asked Rita?"

"Yes, about the clothes. She doesn't know anything about them."

"I don't know what to tell you. She kept only a few things at my house. And she loved this place. I think she hoped that once you and she could really talk, everything would somehow be all right and we would move in here. I know she worried that her cat wouldn't be happy anywhere else. I just can't imagine what happened to her clothes. Is anything else missing? Could someone have stolen them?"

I had had the same thought, but why would anyone take just her clothes? "I guess I wouldn't know if everything else is still here," I said. "But nothing looked out of place. Oh…there were pictures hanging in here—you can see where they were hung—but they were gone when I got here. Rita didn't know about those either."

Toby was perplexed. "Maybe you should call the police," he suggested.

"Maybe. But I don't have much to tell them." I would think about it later.

We spoke for a long time after that. Toby obviously needed to talk about Tess, and I was his perfect audience. I needed to hear about her. The Tess he described was very similar to Rita's version—they had both loved her. I knew that he would make himself available for me to ask any questions I wanted, now that he was back. The problem was, there were new questions that it seemed no one had the answers to. How was I going to find out what terrible thing had happened to Tess to make her want to curse someone? And because of the repercussions of that curse, or Tess' beliefs in those repercussions, she had given up both Toby and me. Rowan had thought that perhaps Tess' life wasn't all that unhappy. It sounded rather sad and lonely to me. Except for her friendship with Rita, she had kept herself separate from everyone until she and Toby reunited. And just when things were looking bright for her, she died. I told Toby my thoughts.

"I hope she went peacefully," he said. "But I believe she was happy at the last. At least, she had that." He turned away suddenly. "I was happy, too. It's still hard to believe she's gone."

"Had she been ill?" I asked.

"No. That's why it was such a shock. But the doctor said heart problems aren't uncommon in women her age."

We didn't end the evening in that somber mood. He told me of their travels together and about Tess' younger years. He related stories of her parents—my grandparents!—and how much he admired the things Tess could do—both her healing and her art. I began to realize that, in his own way, Toby was as different from the other inhabitants of Newbridge as Tess had been. The difference was that he had not alienated them.

As I saw him to the door, we both agreed to talk again soon. He looked back as he opened his car door, and I felt a wave of sadness for his loss.

What a waste, I thought. *All those years they could have been together.* A picture of Simon popped into my head, but I pushed it firmly away and closed the door.

That night, the first part of my dreams came back to me, but I no longer woke in a sweat or screamed. It wasn't until I awoke next morning that I realized this time that Rose and the man on horseback had changed. At some point in the dream, they had acquired Tess and Toby's faces. I got no insights from that fact, though. If anything, it only pointed up to me that there was still so much that I didn't know. Somehow, I would get my answers and know what had driven Tess to choose the life she had. I would get to know her fully, one way or the other.

Chapter 14

For the remainder of October, I strayed from the witch house and its grounds as little as possible. I went out to shop and take care of necessities, but the house kept calling me back, and a little thrill of possession would overtake me when I'd catch the first glimpse of it through the now almost bare branches of the maples lining the drive. I would have thought that the old house would be drafty and cold as the season changes brought more wind and rain. But it was evidently well-built, and I had had the furnace checked and cleaned when the oil was delivered. The house was warm and snug, and if I needed cheering, I could build a fire in the fireplace.

Unlike Tess, I had no aversion to having people visit with me there. Rita came often and a few times brought Sam with her. My fondness for him grew and influenced my perception of his looks until I began to wonder that I had ever thought he was unattractive. He was intelligent and funny, and it was becoming obvious that he adored Rita. The fact that he considered her intelligent and beautiful was apparent even to her, and she was blossoming under this new treatment.

Brian stopped in from time to time, I think just to check on me. He insisted on keeping the Jeep in good condition and wouldn't let me pay for it. He even helped me fix the door to the attic so that I could shut it again. He would tell me about the e-mail he'd received from Rowan or Keisha and asked me many questions about Seattle.

Surprisingly, Harriet made her way through the woods a few times to visit me. She usually came to the back door and knocked, and we would sit in the kitchen and talk over mugs of hot cider. Our conversations were mostly about what was happening in the town, and she never mentioned Tess, but I was growing a wary fondness for this odd little woman. I didn't like her treatment of Rita or understand her devoted adoration of Arthur, a person that I would have thought it would be hard even for a mother to love. But, of course, that was just my opinion. Further encounters with him had not changed my initial opinion of him.

Harriet and Minette did not hesitate to show their mutual dislike. After the first couple of visits, Minette would slink quickly out of the kitchen when she saw Harriet at the door.

Harriet continued to pressure me to attend church with her again. I didn't want to hurt her feelings, so I managed to put her off without actually saying no.

Toby and I slipped easily into being friends. He reminded me a little of my adoptive father and I had to remind him of Tess, if for no other reason than the fact that I was her daughter. After the first difficult evening of being in her house without her, he seemed to be able to accept things and move on. I invited him for dinner several times, and we both enjoyed his stories of Tess. Though I still didn't know what had driven her to give me up, I was also developing a decided affection for the woman. She *had* been strange, I decided, and there were things about her I would probably never understand. But between the picture Rita had painted of her in words and now the new information from Toby and the loving way he spoke of her, I finally began to feel that I knew my birth mother a little. And I also began to believe Toby that she had known and loved me.

I talked to Rowan of all this several times both on the phone and online. She expressed amazement at Toby's revelations and looked forward to meeting him at Christmas-time. Surprisingly, she talked very little of the one gaping hole in my life. I had finally told her, downplaying it as much as possible, that Simon and I were no longer seeing each other. I braced myself for shock, a lecture, anything but what I actually got from her.

"That's too bad, Mom. I really liked Simon. Make sure you stay in good contact with Jake."

And then she changed the subject! I think I was re-lieved. I hadn't wanted a big discussion delving into my feel-ings, but I certainly hadn't expected to be let off so easily. That was very unRowan like.

And I did manage to spend some time with Jake. He decided he wanted art lessons and managed to talk his father into letting him ask me to teach him. I agreed and picked him (and Jasper) up at the library for his first lesson. Simon was polite, but made it very clear that he would be paying for these lessons. It broke my heart all over again, but I agreed to that, too, and decided that somehow the money would get spent on Jake. We enjoyed the time we were together, and if we both felt the loss of Simon's easy smile and jokes that used to bind us all together, we didn't speak of it. In fact, he was as quiet on the subject as Rowan.

As October drew to a close, I braced myself for Hal-loween. I had always loved the celebration before. Rowan and I had spent happy hours planning and making costumes when she was young enough to trick-or-treat. When she was old enough to find her interest in Wicca, we still celebrated but now referred to the day as Samhain. We would decorate the apartment with harvest colors and foods and bury an apple in the little terrace garden at the top of the apartment building as food for any spirits visiting loved ones that night. We always spoke of it in fun, but I never failed to whisper a silent wel-come to my father who I still missed after all these years. And this Samhain I would also bury the apple for Tess and Helen—both of my mothers.

But I wondered if I would have any trouble on that night. Jake was planning to trick-or-treat, and Rita told me that there was always a costume party for families at the fire hall. She also told me that there was a little enclave of devoted anti-Halloween activists who objected to the holiday on religious grounds. Seattle had its share of them, too—there had been small protests around the theme by various groups in the last few years.

But I'd never thought to worry about them before. With the bits of hostility I was now encountering both as Tess' daughter and because of the gossip around what I'd been able to do for Jake and Tim, I did wonder. Besides, the house had the reputation of belonging to a witch, even if it was only in jest. Should I expect Halloween pranks that I would have to clean up?

Rita apparently had the same concerns, though she didn't voice them to me. Instead, she invited herself and Sam to spend the evening with me. Harriet was again spending the evening with her son, who, not surprisingly, counted himself among the numbers of Halloween disapprovers. I did not expect trick-or-treaters this far from the middle of town but, just in case, I bought a few bags of candy. The really good kinds—the ones I remembered Rowan eating first from her Halloween haul. I decided that if anyone was brave enough to make it to the witch house on a friendly visit that night, they deserved the best.

Toby, too, "found himself in the neighborhood" and dropped in. It was practically a party.

And at precisely 7:00, I had my first trick-or-treater. A short, gauze-wrapped mummy, unhampered by his crutches, made his way swiftly up the porch steps just as I was letting Minette out. I refrained from horrifying the mummy by telling him how cute he was.

Minette's reaction must have been more satisfying for him. She obviously thought him scary enough to take off like a shot at the sight of him.

I peered into the darkness to see if his father had driven him. Maddeningly, my pulse quickened slightly just at the little flicker of a flashlight that I knew Simon must have been carrying.

"Trick-or-treat!" the mummy yelled happily as he drew forth his optimistically large pillowcase.

"I wondered if I would get anyone tonight," I told him. "I should have known you can't keep down mummies with broken legs."

"You know who it is, don't you?" Jake's voice said disgustedly.

"Well, the cast and crutches were a clue. I'll make it up to you. Come on in, and I think I can find something to add to your little bag there." I turned to Simon, who had stepped out of the darkness. "Would you like to come in?"

"No, thanks, Kat."

I was annoyed at myself for being disappointed.

"I just thought...that is, Jake wanted to come show you his costume."

"Can he come in and show Rita and Sam and Toby while I get his candy?"

"Sure. I'll just wait here." The stubborn man leaned against a railing and, as I could think of nothing else to say, I left him there.

The mummy was satisfied with how suitably impressed and scared everyone was at the sight of him and was more than satisfied with the candy I dropped into his bag. "The really good stuff!" he exclaimed appreciatively. "That makes up for the box of raisins Mrs. Sullivan always gives out. Thanks, Kat! Bye, everybody!"

And with that, the mummy slipped unquietly into the night. After I put the candy bowl down, I followed him to the door, but he and Simon were already climbing into the car. I let out a sigh and turned back to my guests.

The rest of the evening was fairly quiet. I actually had two more families of costumed candy seekers. One family caught me off guard. It was Donna Bartlett and her children.

"I hope it's okay," Donna said timidly after the two younger children had shrieked the requisite "trick-or-treat."

Kyle, who was obvious as the tallest of the three pirates, hung back by his mother. I guessed that he was worrying what my reaction might be.

"Of course, it's okay," I said to two relieved faces and dropped the candy into three plastic bags. I was aware that coming here had been difficult for them and that, in an odd sense, this was their way of trying to make things all right again. I wouldn't deny them that comfort. "Happy Halloween." I smiled at the four of them, and even Kyle attempted to smile back.

At one point, when it was too late for any more trick-or-treaters, we heard a sound of something crashing outside, then silence. Rita, Sam, and Toby all followed me to the door.

My would-be protectors, I thought with amusement and gratitude.

There was a sound of running feet and one escaped giggle. I stood on the porch and looked out but could see nothing.

"I'd rather not have to turn anyone into toads," I called out, "so please don't hurt anything. And I'll make you a deal. I'll leave a ton of candy out you can pretend to steal, and if nothing else is stolen or broken, I'll refrain from casting any bad spells. Is it a deal?"

There was silence, then a laugh. "Deal," called a young man's voice out of the darkness.

I carefully placed the bowl on the bottom step and then went back into the house and shut off the porch light. The next day the bowl was empty, and there had been a half-hearted attempt at toilet-papering the trees along the driveway. But nothing was stolen or broken. I considered myself lucky.

After Samhain, the weather changed yet again. The second week of November ushered in the first snow. I had been anticipating this with a little fear, and yet I'd also been looking forward to it. Seattle got so little snow each year that when it did fall, it practically crippled the area. I'd gotten the sense that here, for the most part, the children were happy about the snow and all the things you could do in it while the adults viewed it with quiet acceptance and simply went on with their lives, though with a bit more work and preparedness involved. But on that first day of waking to the fresh blanket of untouched whiteness surrounding the house and frosting the trees, I could only think of how beautiful it was. I heated a pan of cocoa and stood at the kitchen window, warming my hands on the mug. As I gazed across the pasture toward the barn, I saw the first footprints breaking up the previously untouched scene. Minette was making her way from the barn to the house. I watched as she picked each foot up carefully, but swiftly. For some time now, she had waited to be let in, instead of coming in her secret entrance. I had no idea why. This morning, it was obvious that she could no longer get in that way, or surely she wouldn't have stayed out all night in the snow.

I opened the door for her and shut it quickly after her. The snow might be beautiful, but the air was cold. The cat shook herself off just to remind me that it was my fault she had been left out in the cold and wet. "You old fraud," I told her fondly. "You must have stayed snug and dry in the barn, because you're not a bit wet, except for your feet. Come on and eat, and I'll give you some milk." I knew she'd forgive me practically anything for a little bowl of milk.

That first snow melted and left everything looking barren for a few days, but I didn't mind. When I wasn't working in the studio now, I kept a fire burning in the living room and read my way through as many of Tess' books as possible. Studying the books on herbs, I felt as if I were back in college cramming for an exam. By the time spring returned and the herbs were preparing to blossom again, I would be much more prepared to know how to preserve them and use them. I stopped in the middle of the thought. Would I really be here when spring returned? I wouldn't have thought so when I arrived in August, but now I wasn't sure. I was used to the opportunities in the city that couldn't be found here. And the break with Simon had hit me harder than I expected, not to mention the hostility from some of the townspeople.

But I also hadn't expected to grow to love this place or feel that I'd found something I was meant to do as much as my writing and art. Healing was that something. Slowly and quietly, other people began coming to me who I gathered had also come to Tess. This time, instead of turning anyone away, I did what I could. I guaranteed nothing, made them promise to go to their doctors as well, and refused to take any money for laying my hands on their aches and pains or giving them an herbal remedy that Rita and I worked together to make. They were mostly small things, and I was glad. I did not want to have to test my abilities again on anything as frightening as what Jake had gone through.

And, just as had happened with Tess, with the exception of the Watsons and Donna Bartlett, no one who came to me talked of it to their friends and neighbors. That was fine with me as it probably had been with Tess. The pies, eggs, and handmade crafts that turned up at my door were always accepted if not always used.

By Thanksgiving, the snow had returned with a vengeance. I began to understand the hardship it could mean for many of the people living here and admired the hardiness with which most of those people, including ones who were less than friendly to me, conducted their lives around the cold and snow. I wondered a few times what life was like on the De-Berry farm this time of year, but unless I asked Jake, I would never know.

I knew that I was one of the lucky people who could still work even while snowed into my own little world. I was also lucky to have friends who helped with things that this city woman hadn't ever thought about. Brian kept my driveway plowed with the pickup and attachable snowplow he used to earn extra money. He had taken the Jeep into the station to mount studded tires on it the day after he had done the same to his mother's car. All in all, he made it possible for me to have the contact I needed with the outside world and comfortably hole myself up in the witch house and continue to work.

The day before Thanksgiving, I put the final touches on a package I was sending to my agent and took it to the post office. I had worked on, put away, reworked, and then reworked again, a story to go with Tess' watercolors of the wild animals. I had taken the paintings to Watertown several weeks before to get color copies made, and then gave myself the final push to send the whole thing to my agent to see what she thought. After finishing that errand, I felt for the first time in a long time that I had nothing to do.

I was not looking forward to Thanksgiving Day, though it turned out to be much more pleasant than I had been hoping for. Rita had invited both Toby and me to spend it with her family. She had also invited Sam, and all three of her children were going to be there. That, I knew I could enjoy. And since Harriet and I had become something akin to friends, if the guest list stopped there, it would be fine. The rub was, of course, that Arthur and Alice were also expected to attend.

When I arrived, with my favorite Thanksgiving pumpkin soup (to be neatly served inside the pumpkin shell) in tow, I found a chaotic household, most of which was in a festive mood.

The exception was Harriet, who was quite upset. Arthur and Alice had cancelled at the last minute. Special friends had asked them over, they said, and had even invited Harriet. Interestingly, she had turned them down. She wanted to be with her grandchildren, but it didn't stop her from grieving over the fact that her precious son would not be here. I secretly suspected that the thought of spending the holiday with either Sam or me was too much for the poor man. Fair enough, I hadn't been thrilled about spending it with him either. I tried not to show my relief, however, unlike Brian who couldn't help it. Even Rita smiled often, for no apparent reason, when she looked on the little sea of faces in her and her mother's home.

The twins, John and Jessica, turned out to be almost as likeable as their brother, though John was slightly more reserved.

Jessica had surprised her mother and fairly shocked her grandmother by bringing along a young man she slyly introduced to me as her fiancé. It was the first the family had heard the news, and the chaos turned suddenly to absolute quiet.

"Jessica!" squealed her surprised mother. "Why didn't you tell me? Congratulations to both of you. Tom, you better be good to her. She's my little girl, you know." Rita smiled at the tall, dark-haired person who was going to become her son-in-law, and he smiled back.

"Where is your family from?" Harriet demanded.

"Grandma!" Jessica started to protest, but Harriet shushed her.

"They're from down near Syracuse," Tom answered.

"How long have they lived there, and don't they mind that you're not spending Thanksgiving with them?" How quickly I'd forgotten just how rude Harriet could be.

Tom acted as if he didn't notice. "They've lived there several hundred years, Mrs. Sloan. My mother's family and my brothers and sister and I are members of the Onandaga tribe. And no, they don't mind. We don't always make as big a deal of the holiday as other people do."

Harriet was speechless. Everyone else took advantage of this unusual state to congratulate the couple, and the festive chaos continued.

By the time the meal was truly over, I had enjoyed my interaction with this group of people, but I was ready to go home to the quiet company of my cat.

Toby had promised to have a late dessert with friends, and I took advantage of his leaving to say my goodbyes also.

Rita walked us to the door. She gave me a hug and said, "I hope you had a good time, Kat. I'm so glad you were here."

"I had a wonderful time," I assured her. "And I'm so glad I got to meet Jessica and John. It makes me miss Rowan.

I think I'll see if I can get a hold of her and Keisha and see how their Thanksgiving was."

"Be sure and tell them hi for me." She watched Toby and me walk to our cars before gently closing the door.

Toby and I talked for several minutes until the waning light and cold temperature encouraged us to move on. We agreed to have lunch on the weekend and then parted company.

Back at the house, Minette ran to the front door when she saw the Jeep pull in. I hurried us both through the door to keep out the cold. When I had things put away, I made my way to the phone to call Rowan. She and Keisha had spent the day with James and several of their friends, and I heard all the details of their huge potluck meal. They both wanted to hear about Rita and Brian and were entertained by the account of Harriet's meeting with her new grandson-in-law to be.

I missed them both dearly, but was content that Rowan would be here in less than a month. Plans had been made so that Keisha, who would be spending Christmas with her parents, would come soon after to spend another few days here before they both returned to the university.

I had laid a fire before I left so that when I was ready, all I had to do was set a match to it. I found warm pajamas and brought a comforter down from upstairs. I picked up the novel I had started earlier and pulled the rocker in front of the fireplace. Minette curled into the softness of the comforter I had laid across my lap, and I stared meditatively into the flames. It had been a good day, I told myself. And now, here I was by a cozy fire in my own house.

Then I found myself wondering how Simon had spent his day.

Chapter 15

During the next two weeks, the dreams of the circle of witches and the child named Kate made their way into my sleep more than once. They no longer frightened me—they had simply become an accepted part of me. I worked on writing Kate's story but had to put it away several times. It was an odd sort of writer's block that just wouldn't let me see the end of the tale.

I worked on a painting of Tess just for the fun of it. She was wrapped in a red cape, the color and texture matching the cape I had seen folded in Kate's lap in my dream. The painting came from the vision I had had of Tess in a field picking herbs to place in a basket she carried with her.

When Toby came by one afternoon, it occurred to me to ask him if he knew about the portraits Tess had painted of the two of them. The look on his face told me he did not. "Can I see them?" he asked after a moment.

I led him to the studio, wondering at myself for not bringing him here before this. He looked around without saying anything until I took his hand and drew him to where I kept the paintings. Tears sprang to his eyes as they rested on Tess' face. "She was so beautiful," he said, and I had to look away from his grief.

"Toby, I'm sorry," I said. "I didn't mean to make you feel bad."

"Oh, Kat, don't be sorry." He straightened his shoulders. "It's such a perfect likeness of her."

"That's what Rita and…Simon both said."

"I miss her." He touched the painting gently. "There's so much I wish could have been different. All those years… and you. But I really do think she was happy the last two years."

"You can't have any doubt of it if you look at this."

I turned him to face the portrait of himself.

"When Simon saw this, he told me that it was obvious that the artist cared very much for her subject. I agreed. It's obvious that she loved you, Toby. I'm glad you were here for her."

Toby sat on a nearby stool. "She never told me she did these," he said.

"She probably had finished them just before…before she died." A thought came to me. "Toby! I bet she did them as a surprise for you. Would you like to have them?"

He looked at both paintings and then at me. "Are you sure, Kat?"

"Absolutely. Unless…they'd cause you too much pain."

"No. I'd love to have them. But don't you want a picture of Tess?"

"I've just finished one," I told him and showed him what I had been working on.

"It's amazing," he said. "You have her ability to capture something of the actual person. This is more than just Tess' face. It's the way she stood, the way she made you feel. And you didn't even know her."

"But I feel like I do know her now. Thanks to you and Rita. And the time I've spent in this house."

He smiled at me. "Tess loved you from the distance she'd put between you. That kind of distance makes it easy to idealize someone. But I know she wouldn't have been disappointed at all if she'd gotten to meet you."

"More than anything, I'd say I was angry when I first found out about Tess," I told him. Then I smiled back. "But now, I think I wouldn't have been disappointed either if I'd gotten to meet her."

The portraits had started me thinking about the painting of the circle of women that Tess had done and I wondered, for perhaps the hundredth time, what had happened to it. The next time Rita came by I brought the subject up. "Where are the things that seem to be missing?" I asked, not expecting a real answer.

"I don't know. But the painting hasn't been on the wall for a long time. I knew that was gone, but the other paintings were there long after that. I can't tell you if they were there when Tess died or not." She closed her eyes to think, then opened them with a shrug. "You know how something is just there and you take it for granted, so you don't notice it anymore? But I do know they were there last Christmas because there was one that I always associated with Christmas—even though there was nothing Christmassy in it. Maybe it was just the way the two girls are dressed. Anyway, I remember seeing it then."

"What were the paintings that were there? Were they other artists' works or Tess'?"

Rita looked at the wall as if she could reproduce the missing artwork. "They were Tess'. She kept these Maxfield Parrishs here with them, even though his work was nothing like hers."

As I'd gotten to know more about Tess, I had been surprised that she had these reproductions. She just hadn't seemed like a person who would be into them, I suppose because they *were* so different from her work. I told that to Rita.

"I thought you would probably know who he was," she said. "I didn't until Tess told me about these paintings. They were her parents'. She said she met the artist once when she was young and liked him very much. And they're not reproductions, Kat. They're originals."

My eyebrows went up at that. "Then her things probably weren't stolen. Otherwise, why would someone take those and not the ones that are worth more money?" Neither of us knew the answer to that question. "What were Tess' paintings of?"

"There was one of her parents, one of the house and trees around it in the fall—it was gorgeous. You would have loved it. The one of the circle of witches—only, like I said, that one's been gone for a long time. And then there was my favorite." She smiled almost shyly. "It was the Christmassy one. It's of two little girls—one of them was me. She painted it when I was about seven. We had on red and green dresses which is why it reminds me of Christmas."

"Who was the other little girl?" I asked.

"I don't think it was anybody. I asked Tess when I first saw it. She said it was a friend she imagined for me. I loved that painting and asked her if I could have it. She told me she'd keep it for me, but that I could take it down any time I wanted when I was here. It was there all those years, and now it's gone."

We were interrupted by a knock at the door.

I opened it to a well-bundled Brian who took off his gloves and blew on his hands as I closed the door behind him.

"Two visitors from the same family!" I said enthusiastically. "Your mom's here, too. Come on in by the fire, and I'll get us something hot to drink."

"Thanks," he said, peering into the living room before entering. "Hi, Mom. There's been enough snow today, I thought I'd give each of your driveways a scoop on my way home."

"What a guy," I teased. "If Rowan weren't already spoken for, I'd make her marry you."

He laughed. "I don't think it would work."

"Oh, well. How about some spiced cider?"

I had a jar of the cider in the refrigerator, and it took only a moment to heat.

I came back with three steaming mugs balanced impressively in two hands to hear Rita saying, "Oh, no! How did you hear about it, Brian?"

"It's all over town. It happened this morning, so practically everybody who's stopped at the gas station asked me if I knew about it."

"What?" I asked, all ears. Was it a bug that affected anyone who stayed in a small town any length of time? I wanted to know the gossip, too.

"The library's closed until the board can figure out what to do." Rita took her cup from me absentmindedly. "Brian says someone complained about some books there, and the board wanted Simon to remove them until they could look into it. He refused so they closed the library."

"You can't be serious!" This was any book person's nightmare. Poor Simon.... "What books?"

"I don't know, except I heard they were kids' books," Brian said. "I didn't tell the worst part."

"What could be worse?" I wondered aloud.

Brian glanced cautiously at his mother. He looked like a little boy caught between glee and horror at a situation.

"It's Uncle Arthur who made the complaint. I didn't know he even went into the library, let alone read any kids' books."

"Oh, God!" Rita said disgustedly. "He doesn't do either. It was probably something Alice told him about, and he got on his stupid high horse over it. That man needs to get a real life. They both do."

I hated it when people tried to get books banned. This certainly did nothing to elevate my opinion of Arthur. "Is there a particular area of children's literature he has an issue with?"

"Nah," said Brian, wrinkling his nose. "He just plain hates kids. He probably hates all kids' books, too."

"Why in the world did he ever become a teacher if he hates kids?" I wondered.

"Best way to torture them." Brian grinned at me. "He sure tortured me when I was in school." He drained his mug and handed it to me. "I'm going to get the plowing done now. Maybe I'll see you tomorrow." He gave his mother a quick kiss and me a funny little salute before he left.

Rita looked at me. "This must be hard for Simon. What if he loses his job?"

"He won't," I said, but I wasn't so sure.

One thing I did know about Simon, he would stick by his principles. He would never agree to pull those books from his shelves. I wondered again what books they could be. There was always someone who was ready to pull *Catcher In the Rye* or *Huckleberry Finn*. I remembered the furor in several cities a few years before over a little book called *Heather Has Two Mommies*. I could well imagine Arthur jumping on the bandwagon against anything that portrayed a gay couple in a positive light. Or had he just now discovered Maurice Sendak's wonderful (but always popular with the censoring crowd) *In the Night Kitchen*? It never ceased to amaze me the number of people who were afraid that the sight of a naked little boy would corrupt children for all time. The children I knew who had read the book or had it read to them had not thought it was a big deal at all. So he had a penis. Didn't all boys?

Perhaps Arthur has a problem with his, I thought uncharitably, *and that's what this is really all about.*

I forced myself to stop right there. It was ridiculous to get all worked up until I knew the facts. There was only one way I knew of to find out those facts, and I vowed to do it.

After Rita exhausted her wrath at her brother's stupidity and reluctantly left for home, knowing her mother would side with Arthur and she'd have to deal with it, I screwed up my courage and picked up the phone. Simon's number was still at the forefront of my memory. I counted four rings before his answering machine, with Jake's voice reciting the familiar recorded message, picked up. Of course! He probably wasn't answering any calls. I froze for a minute when the message ended, wondering what to do.

Finally I stuttered into the mouthpiece, "Hi Simon. It's…it's Kat. I hope…I heard what happened about the books. Ummm…if you wouldn't mind, give me a call back." I hung up quickly, thinking how idiotic I'd sounded. And I wasn't at all certain he would call back.

But he did. A short time later, the phone rang and after my quick, "Hello?" I heard his familiar voice.

"Hello, Kat. It's Simon." As if he had to tell me. "I got your message."

There was an uncomfortable little pause before I jumped in. "Thanks for calling me back, Simon. I...I heard the board closed the library because you refused to pull books someone complained about. I just wanted to give you my support...if you'll accept it. And offer to help, if there's anything I can do."

"Thanks," he said after a moment. "I appreciate it. There's going to be a special board meeting tomorrow night. The more people there who are opposed to censorship, the better. You could certainly help that way."

"Where and what time?" I asked.

"At the library at 7:00."

"I'll be there." I wasn't about to let the conversation end yet. "Simon, what happened?"

He let out an exasperated sigh. "When I got to the library this morning, Frank Mills, the library board president, was waiting for me. He told me that Arthur Sloan had called all the board members complaining about a series of kids' books I have there as being 'morally and spiritually unfit for good Christian children.' Frank wanted me to take them out of circulation until the whole board could look them over and decide if they should be there or not. I refused to do it, so he decided to close the library."

"I'm so sorry. But this is starting to sound a bit familiar. Was it the Harry Potter books?" That would make sense. For a while they had been every intolerant fundamentalist's favorite books to hate.

"No. That's what's so unbelievable. He didn't even think to complain about those. It's a much older series of younger kids' books. Do you know the Dorrie the Witch series by Patricia Coombs?"

"You're kidding!" Patricia Coombs had written and illustrated the series about a little witch, her friends, and her mother, the Big Witch. I loved her work. "How did they even come to his attention? I can't believe Arthur's a big fan of children's books."

"I don't know. Maybe Alice was looking for something for her classroom and came across them. She comes into the library once in a while, but Arthur hardly ever does."

"That's what Rita said. She's horrified by Arthur doing this, by the way."

"I knew she would be," he said, "but thanks for telling me."

"Simon, is he doing this alone, or is there a group behind him?"

"I don't know, Kat." He sounded tired. "But even if he started the complaint himself, he'll end up with a small but loud bunch cheering him on. It could be a circus tomorrow night. And I don't know what's going to happen. Amazingly, this is the first time anyone's complained about books since I've been here. And ironically, most of the series was here before I was."

I could think of nothing else to say but the obvious. "You're doing the right thing, you know."

"Thanks. Kat...I really do appreciate that you called."

My eyes threatened to spill tears as I heard the softening of his voice. "I'll be there tomorrow night," I said quickly.

"All right. See you then. Good night."

The board meeting did look like a circus just in the sheer number of people attending. The holiday season hadn't quite started, and I was willing to bet a number of these people were here for the entertainment. The board members had set themselves up at one of the tables, and chairs had been drawn up by the first arrivals while many others sat on the floor or stood wherever there was room. I had arrived with Rita to find that Sam had gotten there before us and reserved two chairs.

Arthur and Alice were also there, sitting in the front row. Arthur did not look our way, but even if he had, I knew he wouldn't acknowledge his sister. He and Rita had already had their own run-in when, assuming their mother would want to attend, he had come to pick up Harriet. Both Rita and Arthur were surprised when Harriet announced that she had decided not to go. As Rita described the scene to me: Arthur began railing about how important this situation was, Rita lost her timidity long enough to tell him what an ass she thought he was being, and he stalked out the door. I wished I had been there.

Many of the faces in the crowd now were familiar to me. I had no idea where most of them stood on the subject. It might be painful, but this evening would also be very interesting.

Simon stood leaning against one of the children's bookshelves with his arms crossed in front of him. His demeanor was calm but serious. Jake sat with his grandparents in a chair close to his father. His cast had been removed, but he still used the crutches. They were propped against his chair.

I saw Brian slip through the door and wave in our direction just before the president of the board of trustees called the meeting to order. The room became instantly quiet.

"We have one item on the agenda tonight." Frank Mills looked at the crowd. "I know this is an emotional topic for many of you. But please, when we're ready for the public to speak, keep it civil and orderly."

I studied the other six board members present to see if I could read their faces. It was too early to tell how they felt.

Frank turned to his colleagues. "A complaint was made about specific books on the shelves at this library being inappropriate for our children. I know that Mr. Sloan has talked to each of us individually, but I've asked him to make the complaint in the form of a letter." He looked back to the front row. "Arthur, do you have the letter?"

"I certainly do, Frank. I'll read it out loud to the board." He turned so that he could take in the whole audience.

Pompous twit.

He had started the letter with a bombastic greeting to all of the "esteemed" board members. Then he got down to the nitty-gritty. "It has come to my attention that there are materials meant for children at the Newbridge Public Library that are wholly unsuitable and should be withdrawn from the collection. Specifically, I refer to a series for young children by the author Patricia Coombs that portrays witchcraft, demons, spells, and magic as everyday, normal, and even comical occurrences. One of the books even refers to a 'book of shadows' as an important part of the lives of the witches in these picture books.

"I want to make it very clear that I am not an advocate of censorship. I know that there are many people who would like to see the popular books about a young man who practices witchcraft removed from library shelves. As a Christian, I am not a fan of those books either, but I would not ask for their removal. They are for much older children who have more capabilities of understanding the difference between right and wrong and fantasy and real life. The Patricia Coombs books are aimed at little children and are filled with 'cute' pictures of things related to witchcraft. Children of the age for which these books are intended are unable to distinguish between true good and evil without help from an adult. Anyone who chooses to let their children read these kinds of books may purchase them at a bookstore. However, not all parents are that liberal, and a public library should be a place where all parents can expect to let their children browse freely through the children's section and not have to worry about inappropriate messages being taught to their young ones through seemingly harmless picture books.

"I would ask that these books be removed and that the board establish a panel of citizens, specifically parents, teachers, and members of the various churches and organizations of Newbridge, to help the librarian in his selection of future book purchases."

I was so appalled that I barely heard the closing of the letter. I looked quickly at Simon and saw that his jaw had clenched, but otherwise he remained calm. Beside me, Rita held her hands quietly in her lap, but she had balled them into fists. A murmur ran through the audience, and a very few people cheered when Arthur finished and walked slowly to the table to hand the letter to Frank Mills. He presented it with such a theatrical flourish that I was convinced he'd practiced it ahead of time.

I noted that several of the other board members looked eager to speak now, but Frank attempted to quiet everyone. "I think we should hear from our librarian first," he told the other trustees. "Simon, what can you tell us about these books?"

Simon pulled himself away from the shelf to stand straight but otherwise did not move from his spot. He looked very much as if he were subconsciously protecting the children's section.

"First of all, I would like to respectfully say that I shouldn't have to tell you about the specific content of any of the books here. I was trained and hired as a librarian, and part of my job description is to choose the books and materials for this library. It's the job of the board to decide if I'm doing that satisfactorily, but it is not the board's job to determine the actual books. I understand that not all patrons will like the same books, and that's why it's the work of a good librarian to try to have a diverse collection. I do have guidelines that help me choose what books I buy, and Patricia Coombs' books fall well within those guidelines. I also have to tell you that I have never and will never remove a book from my shelves because of censorship. I don't mean that to sound defiant, though I suppose it can't be helped. Everyone should be free to choose what they want to read from a public library, and everyone is just as free to not read what they object to.

"Having said that, I will tell you that the books Mr. Sloan objects to have won several awards and have been popular since the series was started in the late 60's. Most of the books in the series were already in this collection when I was hired, but I would have bought them if they hadn't been."

The sound of creaking could be heard as several people shifted in their seats. Simon took a breath, and it was obvious that he was not quite finished.

"There's no way to say *this* without sounding defiant either, but I have to say it. If I'm not allowed to do the job I was hired for, and by that I mean freely choose the books for this library without fear of censorship, then I would have to resign."

That set off a minor tumult, but I was close enough to the front to hear someone in Arthur's supportive little crowd mutter, "Not if you're fired first."

Though it took him some time, Frank Mills finally managed to regain control. "It shouldn't have to come to that, Simon. That's why we're here tonight to find a way to work this out. Before the board discusses the matter, is there anyone in the audience who would like to say anything?"

Was he hoping that the rest of the people were there just to be entertained and not give their opinions? That would be very optimistic and foolish of him. Several hands shot up including, I found, mine.

Frank gave a little sigh and pointed to a man sitting near Arthur and Alice. "Hank, you can be first. But everyone, keep it short and friendly."

Hank stood, and all eyes turned to him. It was clear that he relished the limelight. He spoke at length, but he really had nothing more to say than had already been said by Arthur. Several more people had their say, and it was a surprisingly mixed bag of opinions.

When it was my turn, I stood up and surveyed the room. Was it a mistake for me to speak? I was the stranger here after all. I knew that I couldn't keep quiet, though, so I pushed away the fear that I wouldn't do any good and addressed the board.

"As a writer, one of the first things I did when I arrived in Newbridge was to find the library. I'm used to all kinds and sizes of libraries, and I can tell you that this is one of the finest small libraries I've ever seen. To keep it that way, you need to fund it well, have a good librarian who knows books, and avoid bowing to any pressure to censor those books. You have the first two. Don't lose an incredibly good librarian by falling into the censor trap."

"She's one to talk—she already lost the incredibly good librarian," I heard someone near me whisper while someone else snickered. I ignored them.

"Simon was reluctant to talk about the specific books in the complaint. And I agree that he shouldn't. However, I would like to talk about them for a minute."

"Do you know the books well, Mrs. Benson?" one of the two women on the board asked me.

"Yes, I do," I answered. Before I could say more, I heard another whisper.

"No doubt, she does. Anything to do with witches in that family, eh?"

More twitters came from the same general area. This time I couldn't help myself. I paused long enough to locate the person who had spoken and stare down my nose at her.

She squirmed uncomfortably. My mission was accomplished.

"The books causing all the fuss have been around for a long time. The illustrations and stories are fun. Just the kinds of things that children love and that make them want to keep reading. The themes in the stories are all about family and friends, and a little girl who learns the same things that most kids are interested in. One of the 'subversive' stories is all about the little witch and her friends dreading school and instead learning to love it. Another of the stories involves a rummage sale and tea at the library. All pretty controversial stuff. And yes, there is a Halloween story that involves demons stealing the witches' book of shadows, which holds all the recipes for their spells. Dorrie, the little witch, saves the day and the demons lose out. Dorrie's room is always messy, and she wears wild socks, too. Pretty wicked stuff, I'd say. And my guess would be that all the fuss about removing the books will have just the opposite effect of what Mr. Sloan was hoping to accomplish. It's been my experience that whenever a book is banned, its sales go up.

"My point in telling you all this is that two people can read the same book and view it totally differently. My experience with children is that even very young ones can distinguish fantasy from fact better than some adults. All kinds of books should be available to children and not just the ones that reflect the views of any one group. And the same applies to adult books. A library is supposed to be a place of free and open access to everyone with all kinds of books in it. I personally love the Patricia Coombs books, but even if I hated them, I would have no right to have them removed from the library. No one should have that right."

As I sat down, I noticed Toby for the first time. I hadn't known he was there. He smiled at me, and my muscles relaxed slightly. Good. There were some friendly faces here.

Several more people weighed in with their opinions, and at times there was shouting and booing from proponents of both sides of the issue. Fortunately, nothing got too out of hand. No fist fights or terrible threats, though I suspected that a few former friends wouldn't be speaking to each other the next morning.

The first big surprise for me was when Donna Bartlett slowly got up to speak. I had noticed her daughter tugging on her during some of the others' speeches, but it would never have occurred to me that Donna would be brave enough to speak in a crowd. I gave her marks for courage. But if that was surprising, her words were more so.

"My...little girl asked me to say something," she began slowly. "She's having a hard time understanding what all the fuss is about, and to tell you the truth, so am I. She loves the Dorrie books, and she checks them out all the time. She wants to know if someone else can really make it so she can't check them out. I didn't know what to tell her. She asked me to say please don't take them away from her."

Donna's face was red by the time she'd finished her short speech, but I wanted to throw my arms around her and hug her.

The board president tried to end the public discussion there, but Arthur jumped to his feet again. Didn't he ever know when to quit? Later, I wished that I could have thanked him for his last little input, but he wouldn't have appreciated it.

"There is one more person here who should speak," Arthur fairly shouted. He looked to the back of the room. "None of the clergy in town have spoken, and I think they should be heard. I see Reverend Foxworth is here. Let him tell you what he thinks."

Along with everyone else, I turned to see the minister who was standing near the very back of the crowd. He was looking very uncomfortable and put his hands up and shook his head to indicate he had nothing to say. Arthur and several of his supporters refused to let it drop there and egged the reverend on until he put his hand back up. All was unnaturally quiet for a moment while he seemed to reach inside for strength. Not an unusual thing for a minister to do. But something made me sit up taller and give him a closer look.

"I have no sermon to give on the subject," he began. "Maybe I'll give that on Sunday, and you can all come hear it then." There was a polite little spate of laughter. "I want nothing but good things for children, just like everybody here. But I don't claim to always know what's good for children and don't think I, or anyone else except their parents, should dictate what they can or can't read. Or what adults can read, for that matter. I know that there are Bible stories here in the library because my wife and I have checked them out for Sunday school, and I'm really happy that they're here. But I don't see any reason to feel threatened by anything else that's here. God gave us all free will and common sense. If He decided to set us free to use them, I don't see how we should try to override that." The Reverend Foxworth looked very unhappy that he'd been forced to speak his mind, but he squared his shoulders and stood back with a quiet dignity.

What a night for surprises! *Harriet, my dear*, I thought, *I'll go to church with you this Sunday for sure*. It was likely that the minister would lose several members of his small flock of parishioners over his little sermon (despite his claim, it had been a sermon as far as I was concerned) and showing up to help fill in some of those empty pews for one Sunday was the least I could do. I was right about what I had thought about this man when he had told me he enjoyed his debates with Tess. There was more to him than first met the eye.

Arthur was furious, but he knew he had shot himself in the foot. Rita looked at his face, then at me, and smiled. He said nothing more.

The board turned to a discussion among themselves with everyone craning eagerly to hear, but the real excitement had already happened. There was a bit of tension when one board member threatened to quit if they didn't remove the books and another threatened to quit if they did.

One of the women claimed that she was not proposing censorship, but that their duty was to provide a library that was for the patrons of Newbridge and not for the ideals of anyone from some big city. No one knew quite what she was saying until she finally stated, "If the majority of people in this town object to a book, then maybe the librarian should remove it."

"What do you propose we do? Have the whole town vote on every book that Simon thinks of buying?" asked the trustee who had threatened leaving if books were removed.

His tone seemed to intimidate her, but she went on nonetheless. "Of course not, but what about the suggestion that there be a panel to help select the books from now on?"

Two of the other trustees chimed in with their opinions on that suggestion—both saying they had hired Simon to do a job and they should darn well let him do it.

One pointed out that there was a request box that Simon kept available, and anyone was welcome to write the names of books they'd like to have at the library in there. When someone else asked about another box for books that people wouldn't like to see at the library, the trustee snorted. "Don't be asinine," he said.

I had no idea what an entertaining bunch of people these board members could be. No wonder so many people had come.

It was a long night, but in the end, the board seemed to be in the same balance as the audience. The majority did not want to see the books removed, and the vote was completed to reflect that. The meeting was ended by Frank who, seeing which way the wind blew, stated that the board would continue to have confidence in the good job Simon was doing and that the library would be open at its regular time tomorrow.

Arthur, Alice, and some of their friends shuffled angrily out while other people stayed behind to talk to each other, and some wanted to talk to Simon. I was exhausted; I could just imagine how he must feel. I found myself wanting to tell Simon how glad I was that the vote had gone the way it had, but when I looked over at him I saw that he was surrounded by a small crowd. He did look tired, but he had his arm around Jake's shoulders, and his mother and father stood close by. Instead, I happily left Rita to catch a ride home with Sam, and I slipped quietly out the door.

The next day was Friday, and I felt restless the entire day. I needed to move. Cold as it was, around 3:30 in the afternoon, I slipped on my warmest jacket and boots and walked into Newbridge. It would be dark by 4:30, but the walk and cold air would do me good, and I could catch Rita before she left the post office and ride home with her.

A path had been forged through the snow beside the frozen river, and I spent some time following it. By the time my face began aching from the cold and forced me to seek the warmth of the post office building, it was very close to dark. I walked through the door, not expecting anyone to be on the other side, and collided with the person who had been about to step out. A small package had fallen out of the person's hand, and we both knelt to pick it up.

"I'm sorry...." I started to apologize and stopped. I was looking into Simon's familiar dark eyes.

We both stood up. I was aware of Rita's amused smile behind us. We seemed destined to keep her entertained at work.

Simon put his hand out as if he were afraid I would fall, and the brief touch of his fingers on my ungloved hand sent a warmth throughout my body.

"Kat," he said, and then nothing else.

I wondered if the touch had done anything to him.

My tongue became untied, and I laughed quickly. "I really am sorry, Simon. I was trying to get in out of the cold, and I wasn't looking where I was going. How are you?"

Well, that was most certainly an uninspired little speech.

Simon didn't seem to notice. "I'm fine. Now. You left last night before I could thank you for speaking up."

"There's no reason to thank me. I couldn't help myself. I'm glad things turned out all right. I want you to know that I really admired what you had to say."

"Well, like you said, I couldn't help myself. The real surprise was what Donna and the Methodist minister had to say."

I'd almost forgotten how his smile dazzled.

"I think they might have helped the most," he continued.

"Not the way Arthur was expecting when he forced poor Reverend Foxworth to speak."

We both laughed.

I was getting comfortably warm now, and it wasn't just from the electric heat of the building. Simon and I hadn't been able to be relaxed and friendly around each other for a long time, and a little seed of something (I might have called it hope) was growing in my chest. I could swear that Simon was beginning to feel the same way.

"Kat...." He put his hand toward me again, and I smiled up at him.

"Kat!" Another male voice exclaimed behind me. "I can't believe I found you here! I just stopped in to see if I could get directions to your house."

I spun around and came face to face with…James! For a minute, I was caught up in the surreal feeling that I was in one of those kids' pictures where you're supposed to guess what doesn't belong. My ex definitely did not belong in this picture!

"James, what are you doing here?" I stammered.

"Looking for you, love." He grinned like a little boy handing someone her favorite present.

Damn, damn, damn! I'd forgotten his innate, impeccably bad sense of timing. He called practically every woman he knew *love*, but Simon wouldn't know that.

I hid my consternation in proper manners. "Simon, this is James Solomon. Rowan's father. My ex-husband." Things were going from bad to worse. "James, this is Simon DeBerry." My… what? "He's the librarian here."

James, who was as outgoing as Rowan but more oblivious to what people were feeling, stuck his hand out to Simon. "Nice to meet you," he said cheerily.

Simon shook his hand politely and repeated the phrase, but he looked first slightly dazed and then as he turned his eyes back to me, I saw that the warmth that had been there only a moment ago was gone. I couldn't tell what was there now.

"I need to get going, but it was good to see you, Kat. Welcome to Newbridge, James. Maybe I'll see you around." I wasn't sure which of us the last sentence was intended for.

I watched Simon leave before I turned slowly back to James. "What *are* you doing here?" I asked again.

"Nice to see you, too, love," he said with a laugh. "I had to fly into Syracuse to give a talk at the university there, and Rowan told me it wasn't far to where you were staying. I rented a car and thought I'd just pop in and surprise you for a couple of days. You could show me around your little town."

"You certainly surprised me. You might have called first, you know." I was being petulant, I knew. There were times I was happy to see James, but this wasn't one of them.

He frowned at me. "I'm sorry," he said. "I thought you'd be happy to see someone from the West Coast, even me. I can head back to Syracuse." He looked hurt, and I was immediately sorry.

"Don't be silly. It was just such a surprise. I walked into town, so you can give me a ride now, and you won't need to ask for directions." I turned to Rita who had been desperately trying to look busy. "Rita, in case you didn't hear—" fat chance of that! "—this is Rowan's father, James. James, this is my friend and neighbor, Rita Lawrence." They nodded at each other politely. "I was going to see if I could get a ride home with you, Rita. But obviously I don't need to now. Come by tomorrow for lunch with us, okay?"

"Okay," she said, though I could see she was dying to say more. "See you about noon?"

I walked ahead of James out the door all the while wondering what I was going to do with him besides wish I could kill him for showing up at exactly the wrong time.

Chapter 16

As I sat across the kitchen table from him at dinner, I watched my ex-husband pour himself another glass of wine. I had thought James one of the handsomest men I'd known when I first met him. The years had not changed that fact. He had aged gracefully, and his dark curly hair was only slightly tinged with gray at the temples. He had a boyish energy (at times I thought of it as a spoiled little boy energy) that must have contributed to keeping him younger looking than his forty-three years.

Women had always seemed to appreciate his good looks and charm. At the time we first started dating I had been highly flattered that he was interested in me. He was a history major and, though my mother would have been happier to have us both through college before we married, she was nevertheless thrilled with my choice of a son-in-law for her. And, for a little while, I was thrilled, too.

James was a good son-in-law, a great father, but—it turned out—a less than satisfactory husband. And, if I wanted to be fair, I suppose I should concede that he found me a less than satisfactory wife, but who wants to be fair? Our ideas of what the roles of husbands and wives should be were in conflict with each other. We were young enough, and we thought we were in love enough, that we could work it out. We couldn't.

Despite the hard times we'd had together, I was still fond of him, in much the same way, I realized, I was fond of Jake. Sometimes he did remind me of a ten-year-old boy in an adult body.

He was now a history professor, like my father, and from what I'd heard, he was very popular with his students. When he would show up in Seattle, we often found time to go to lunch or dinner, and I usually enjoyed it. But now, I found myself resenting his presence here. I was sorry that I felt that way, but I couldn't help it. I should have been happy to have a visitor connected to my "other life." Instead, I felt as if he were an intruder. Ah, well. He would be here only for two days. I could be nice to him for that amount of time.

James turned the bottle to refill my glass, but I put a hand over it. "No, thanks. I'm fine."

"So, tell me," he said as he raised his glass and studied the contents, "how do you like playing country girl here in the wilds?"

"Number one, I'm not a girl. You should have learned by now not to call forty-year-old women *girls*." He smiled happily. I was rising to his bait. "And number two, I wouldn't call this the wilds. As you can plainly see, we have electricity and running water. And I'll have you know I was able to have the privy moved inside just last week." We both laughed. "Seriously, I do like it here. I had no idea I would like it as much as I do. It's certainly different than Seattle. But it's been a good place for me to work. My birth mother was an artist, too. She left a well-stocked studio."

"Rowan and Keisha told me how much they both liked this place. It's just not where I would picture you."

"Why not? I'm feeling quite at home here." I was also feeling quite defensive.

"You're used to the city and rain. Not a place without mass transit and fifty-below-zero temperatures. What do you find to do here? Play bingo on Saturday night?"

"I haven't found any bingo games yet, but I did go to a square dance at the fire hall. Does that count? And don't exaggerate: it's only ten below right now."

256

"Practically a heat wave," he said sarcastically, and I had to laugh.

"This place is very different than anything I've been used to, but I've grown to love it here. Different can be good, you know."

"And how is the library in such a little town?" he asked innocently. Too innocently.

I looked at him sharply, but he stared blandly back, waiting for my answer.

"It's surprisingly well equipped. I've been able to get a lot from it."

"And the librarian, too?" James swirled the liquid in his glass and grinned wickedly.

"Get your mind out of the gutter, you twit," I scolded him. "Simon is a very good librarian."

"Ah, ha! I did detect something happening between the two of you in our little exchange at the post office. No wonder you were snippy with me. I showed up at the wrong time, didn't I?"

"James, don't tease me about this," I said irritably. "We did go out together, but we haven't for a while now. It's a touchy subject for me, and not one I want to discuss with my ex-husband."

"I'm sorry." James turned uncharacteristically sensitive. "I really am, Kat. I hope I didn't mess things up too badly for you."

"Oh, don't worry. They were already messed up."

I rose to clear our dishes from the table. Back in character, James did not move to help me.

"Tell me about the talk you gave at the university."

By the time we had caught up on news of mutual friends, Rowan and Keisha, and his other two children, and I got to hear about his latest fiasco in the world of romance, James had yawned several times and admitted he hadn't slept much in the last two days.

"I'll put you in Rowan and Keisha's room. I don't have the others fixed for guests, but I do have clean sheets on the bed in that one. Tomorrow I'll give you a proper tour of the house and show you around town. It might be too much excitement for you, though," I teased.

"And will all that excitement take place before your friend comes for lunch?" he asked.

"Unless it snows," I said cheerfully. "In that case, we'll have to wait until my friend's son comes and plows us out. You could always go out and build a snowman if you need excitement before he gets here."

James groaned. "What's happened to the girl I used to know who liked real excitement? The one who could party all night and still meet a writing deadline the next day?"

"That *woman*," I said emphatically, "has been gone for a long time now. She's turned into someone who thinks making snow people could be very exciting." He laughed politely at what he thought was my little joke.

That's one of the reasons we're not still together, I reflected. He never knew when to take me seriously.

By the time James padded downstairs the next morning, I had long since been up and working in the studio. He poked his head through the door and looked around. "Now this looks more like you," he said after surveying the room. "What are you working on?"

"Oh, just some possible illustrations for a story," I said hastily. I had made some drawings of Kate and had no desire to talk about what I had been going through with him. "There's fresh coffee in the kitchen. Grab a cup and as soon as I finish here I'll make us some pancakes."

By the time he was back with a mug in his hand, I had set the drawings aside and was putting my pencils away. "What are these?" James asked and put a hand out to touch the open folder Tess' animal paintings were in.

Unfortunately for him, Minette was sleeping on some tan-colored cloths next to the folder and she blended in so well that he had not noticed her at all. The movement startled her, and she reached out swiftly and raked her claws across the back of his hand.

"What the bloody hell?" he shouted and sloshed coffee onto his no-doubt expensive woolen sweater. The two of them glared at each other until James began to sneeze. "You have a cat!" he said accusingly.

I tried not to laugh, but it was impossible. Rowan and I hadn't had a cat until after James left. He was allergic to them as well as disliking them. "She came with the territory. James, meet Minette."

"We've met, and she's none too friendly, is she?" He sneezed again.

"She has her moments." I scratched behind her ear, and she settled back to the cloths, purring loudly. "Did she draw blood?"

We inspected his hand, which was definitely scratched but not bleeding. "I suppose I'll live," he said, "as long as the sneezing doesn't kill me."

"I haven't heard of a case of fatal sneezing yet, but you never know." I got up from the stool I was sitting on. "The things you were asking about are paintings my birth mother did. Let's take them to the kitchen, and I'll start breakfast. You can look at them there."

"All right, but why don't you pick them up?" he asked with one eye on Minette. He sneezed again and, feeling sorry for him, I lifted the folder and led the way to the kitchen.

Breakfast was simple and quick. The weather was being cooperative—it was a gorgeous day with blue skies and the sun sparkling on the snow so that it looked like a field of diamonds from the kitchen window.

"I'll show you the attic this morning," I told James. "I suspect you'll find something to interest an historian there."

"Oh?"

"The house has been in the family since it was built sometime in the eighteenth century. And, I love telling you this, the family seems to have been matriarchal."

"You can tell this from the contents of the attic?" he asked skeptically.

"No, and you don't have to play the condescending history professor. We lay people have our sources, too." He lifted his brow in query. "Toby, someone who knew my birth mother well, said the house has been passed down to the oldest daughter in each generation."

"Ah, so perhaps this explains your strong feminist tendencies," he joked. "They're genetic."

"Oh…I like that idea."

"I knew you would. It would also explain why our daughter follows so closely in your footsteps in that area." He was pushing it now.

"You don't think that, perhaps, we're both feminists because we believe strongly in equal rights?"

"That, too, of course." He smiled. "Let's go see this matriarchal attic."

Before we could get there, however, there was a knock at the door. We had made it to the hallway, so James waited behind me as I opened the door. It took me a moment to be able to distinguish Sara Watson through her layers of coat, scarf, and hat. "Sara, is that you in there?"

"Hello, dear," she greeted me with a chuckle and pulled down her scarf. "You do have to wrap up against this cold. It's beautiful but chilly out today."

"It certainly is," I said with a shiver. "Come on in."

"Is it all right?" she asked doubtfully. "We haven't been inside in all the years Tess lived here. If it was too cold to sit on the porch, she came to us."

"Tess must have had her reasons," I said, "but I like having people here." I drew her in and shut the door. "Is everything all right? Tim isn't in more pain is he?"

"Oh, no. That last treatment you gave him helped a lot. We've been amazed that even in this cold spell his arthritis isn't too bad at all. I just wanted to drop this pie off—it's some of the blackberries I froze in August. They make fine pies in December." She peered around my shoulder curiously.

I'd forgotten, momentarily, about James. Had the gossip made the rounds already and Sara was given the task to find out the details? A cynical thought perhaps, but not at all unlikely. "James, this is Sara Watson. Sara, this is—" *Oh, plunge right in*, I told myself. "—my ex-husband, James. He had business in Syracuse, so he stopped by to visit."

"How do you do, Mr. Benson?" Sara had removed her scarf so her satisfied smile was apparent. "Are you going to be here long?"

How many details would she feel she could glean from the answer to that little question?

James was used to pouring on his charm even for old ladies. Though I'm sure the "Mr. Benson" irritated him, he didn't let on. "It's very nice to meet you, Mrs. Watson. Kat neglected to give you my full name. It's Solomon. James Solomon. She kept her maiden name when we were married." His tone invited sympathy for this little eccentricity of mine, and Sara seemed to respond to it.

I rolled my eyes at him before turning back to her. "And wasn't it convenient that I did? That way, I didn't have to change it back after we were divorced."

That shocked Sara into speechlessness. James, ever the gentleman, (or at least when it suited him) came to her rescue. "Let me take that delicious-looking pie for you, Mrs. Watson. I hope Kat lets me sample some of it before I have to leave. I'm only here for a short time. I'm very glad I got to meet you."

By the time I had shuffled her back out the door, I was afraid Sara had all the information she needed, and what we hadn't given her she would make up. It was obvious that James had charmed her. If the gossip included conjecture on our divorce, I thought I knew who would be blamed.

I turned back to James. "Well, that will fuel the gossip mill for a little while. Nice work, Mr. Benson. You had her eating out of your hand."

"It's Mr. Solomon to you, thank you." He sat on the bottom step of the stairway and looked up at me. "What did she mean about the treatment you'd given to whoever Tim is?"

I dusted a section of the railing with my fingers. "Tim is her husband. He has arthritis pretty badly, and my birth mother…Tess…used to help him by putting her hands on the parts of his body that were in pain."

"You mean faith healing, that sort of thing?"

"I don't think that's what she would have called it, but healing, yes. The thing is…I seem to have developed some of her…abilities." I knew he'd have a hard time accepting this.

"You're saying you lay your hands on people to heal them?"

"To help them, anyway."

He looked at me as if to check to see if I'd sprouted horns. "Do you actually believe that you're healing or do you do it because they think it helps?"

"I know it helps, James. Did Rowan tell you about an accident that happened while she and Keisha were here?"

"She talked about a little boy who was thrown from a horse and hurt badly. Didn't he get a broken arm or some-thing?"

"A broken leg. And…more. I helped him, and that's when I first discovered I could help."

"So basically you comfort them. I suppose that always helps."

If Rowan hadn't told him any more than that, then I wasn't about to either. It would be much easier than trying to explain what had happened and how I felt when the energy in my hands made contact with someone's pain. He'd made light of Rowan's interest in Wicca, assuming it was just an exten-sion of my feminist influence on her. I knew he wouldn't be able to accept this any better. "Yes. It does help," I said and let it go.

When Rita arrived at lunchtime, James had already forgotten about the healing question. Despite himself, he had been interested in many of the things I showed him in the at-tic. I could see the anthropologist buried within him, itching to comb through items to see if any patterns emerged. That was one of the differences between us. He looked for social patterns. I wanted to know about the individuals.

Rita arrived at the back door shortly after noon. After shedding her coat, gloves, and boots, she stooped to scratch

Minette's head as the cat appeared from the hallway. Her tail twitched menacingly in James' direction, and then she me-owed at Rita to let her out the door.

"It didn't draw blood from you when you touched it?" James asked.

"Pardon me?" Rita was confused.

"Minette." I filled her in. "She and James had a little run in this morning. He hasn't forgiven her yet."

"Well, she can be a little unfriendly," Rita offered.

"That's an understatement," James muttered.

James sat at the table while Rita and I worked at the counter. Unwilling to let him get away with watching the "women folk" do the work, I stuck a bowl in front of him filled with vegetables for a salad and instructed him to start chopping.

It was a strange meal. I watched, bemused, as James made his usual attempts to charm, but it didn't seem to be working on Rita. At first, I wondered if she was intimidated by him or feeling shy. Shy she might have been, but after some time, I realized she thought he was just silly. She was very polite, but it was obvious, to me anyway, that the old charm just wasn't working for her.

It took poor James some time to get it. He wasn't used to women not basking in his attention. The fact that his two ex-wives had long ago stopped basking didn't count. After all, that's why they were *ex* wives.

Rita must have been an enigma to him. A little mean streak I didn't know I had in me made me enjoy his failure to win this single woman over.

There was no outward hostility displayed between them. Certainly there was nothing like the dislike I felt for Arthur. It was more that they had nothing in common other than being my friend. That kept them in polite conversation, but nothing more.

I think they were both relieved when the meal was over and Rita reached for her coat. "It was nice to meet you, Rita," James said. It was said properly and politely, just no longer dripping with the effort to charm.

"You, too, James." Rita pulled on her boots. "I hope you have a safe trip back."

I stopped her before she opened the door. "Shall we go to church with your mother tomorrow?" I asked.

She looked at me in disbelief. "You want to?"

"Sure," I said. "I think Reverend Foxworth could use a couple of friendly faces just this once. I really wanted to tell him I appreciated what he said at the library board meeting the other night."

"You may be right. I can think of a few people who won't be there. But—" she glanced over my shoulder "—would James want to go?"

"He's leaving early in the morning, so I'll just see him off and meet you at your house. Shall I drive?"

She looked at me apologetically. "I don't think my mother would ride in Tess' car. I hope you don't mind. How about if I drive? I'll come pick you up here."

"That works, too. Are you sure your mother will go?"

"Because Arthur won't? I don't know. She hasn't said anything about it. She's being unusually quiet on the subject." She grinned. "We'll see tomorrow."

I reached for a coat and slipped into the boots I kept by the door and followed Rita out as far as the woodpile. I watched only for a second as she headed for the path she had trampled through the woods before the cold penetrated through my jacket. She turned and waved, and after a quick wave back, I loaded my arms with wood and carried it back inside.

James was already in the living room, absently looking through Tess' books.

I laid the wood in a box beside the fireplace.

He looked up, at the same time pulling one of the books out for closer inspection. "Chop that yourself, did you?"

"No, although I did stack it. You'd be surprised how good the physical work can feel."

He made an exaggerated frown. "Was that supposed to be a blow to my poor male ego? If so, you failed. It only very slightly bruised it. Besides, you forget how heavy history books can be. I get plenty of physical exercise hauling them around from class to class."

I knew that he also worked out at a gym regularly, but he made no mention of that.

"No bruising intended," I assured him with a laugh. "Although you have a history book in your hand now and it doesn't look all that heavy."

He regarded the book with a hint of disdain. "Some people might argue that Gimbutas' books are fiction rather than history."

"Is it so hard to accept the idea that there might have been matriarchal cultures in the past?"

"There's no proof of it," he said.

"There's a lot of evidence that suggests it. Shall we spend the afternoon debating it?" I challenged.

He gave a sigh. "No, thank you, lovely as that sounds. I've had this debate too often with Rowan and suspect I haven't heard the last of it. Flying across the country to argue it out with her mother wasn't exactly what I'd planned when I came here."

"What did you plan?" I lowered myself into the rocking chair by the hearth.

"No ulterior motives, Kat. I really just wanted to visit since I was so close. Rowan described this place in such glowing terms and said that it seemed like such a good place for you that I was curious. You really do like it here?"

"I really do. Why does that seem so impossible to you?"

He rubbed his hands together carefully before he answered. "It doesn't seem impossible that you'd find it appealing as a place to visit for a time. But that's not what I see. You've changed, Kat. You have the look of settling in."

I looked at him in amazement.

"I hadn't thought about it, but you may be right. You look horrified by the idea, James. Is it so surprising? Though I never met my mother, this house did belong to her family. *My* family."

"I don't think your feelings about a place are genetic, love, but we won't get into that argument." His tone was light, but I knew he was serious.

"Good. I won't argue it with you although I'm not sure I shouldn't. There are other things here, too. I've made some good friends in the short time I've been here."

"Like Rita?" He looked as if he wanted to say more but didn't.

"Like Rita." I watched his face. "What? Did you have a problem with Rita?"

He squirmed uncomfortably, something I wasn't used to seeing him do. "No. She seems to be a very nice woman. But...."

"But what?"

If he heard the edge to my voice, he didn't heed it.

"Isn't she a bit...provincial for you? Don't get me wrong. She is very nice. But she said herself she's never traveled far from here. Or ever went to college. And she lives with her mother! What in the world do you find to talk about with her? You don't have anything in common."

"You know, James," I began in a deceptively quiet voice, "I'm suddenly remembering one of the reasons we split up. You're a total and utter snob. There's more in life than just traveling or college. Rita could still do either of those if she wanted. Or not. But we have a great deal in common. More than you and I have. She's also intelligent, curious, and kind. And she's a wonderful teacher. She knows more than anyone I know about herbs, and she's been working to help me learn all I can. And I don't think there's a snobbish bone in her body."

"Touché," he said quietly. "I suppose I did sound a bit like a pompous ass."

"Not just a bit."

"It's just, I'm not used to the idea of you as a small town girl."

My look made him quickly amend the word.

"Sorry. Small town *woman*. I guess I didn't express it very well."

"No, you didn't." His expression was remorseful enough that I relented, a little. "I suppose I'll accept your apology."

"Thank you," he said in half mocking, half sincere relief. He put the Marija Gimbutas book back on the shelf. "For the sake of argument, I think I have to disagree on the reason for our split."

"Oh?" What trouble was he headed into now? "This should be interesting."

"Think about it, Kat. At the time I never would have agreed, but it seems clear from this side of things that we should never have married in the first place, except that we did co-produce a rather wonderful young woman."

"No argument there," I concurred. "And in case I never told you, I do think you've been a great father."

"Thanks for that. But not a great husband, right?" A pause. "Don't rush to deny it." He laughed as if he'd made a witty joke. "I did love you, Kat. But we were too young and too different. I expected things to be a certain way, and you expected them to be another. I think it was rather doomed from the start. And now, I think I've spoiled it for you as far as other relationships go."

"Of all the ego-driven ideas! You honestly think I didn't remarry because I couldn't get over you?"

"No, that's not what I was saying at all." He took a breath, knowing he was treading on treacherous ground. "I've watched you boot a couple of men who might have gotten serious about you down the road. I suspect because you were afraid they would turn out to be me." My jaw dropped. "Did you give the poor librarian the boot, too?"

"What?" I spluttered. "Of all the stupid ideas!" But was it really? "I didn't give Simon 'the boot' as you so quaintly put it. We had an argument. It was a mutual letting-go." That sounded idiotic, even to me.

"A mutual letting-go. That's an interesting way to put it. It sounds very…dispassionate." He plucked what looked like a cat hair from his sweater. "I could have sworn I saw a look that was far from dispassionate pass between you two."

"You saw that in the—oh, what was it?—thirty seconds at the most, that all three of us stood together?" I demanded sarcastically.

"I could swear I did. Was I wrong?"

I tried to say something flippant to dispel my confusion at his attempt to shed light into the psychology of my relationships. My mouth was open, but nothing came out.

"Don't be angry at me, love." James had misinterpreted my silence. "I'll keep my pop psychology theories to myself for the rest of the time I'm here. At least I'll try. This may be an unusual thing for an ex-spouse to say, but I really do want to see you happy. My other ex would never believe me if she heard me say that about her, but I hope you know that I mean it."

"James," I finally managed to say, "you never cease to amaze me."

"In a good way or a bad way?" he asked warily.

I laughed at the perplexed look on his face. "Sometimes both. I hate it when there's a possibility you might be making sense. I'm going to have to think about what you've said." I further confused him by getting up from the chair and walking to where he stood to plant a kiss on his cheek. "Let's go have that tour of Newbridge I promised, and tonight I'll take you to dinner at a nice restaurant in Watertown. It still won't be a big enough city for you, but it will do. We can talk about that 'wonderful young woman we co-produced.'"

"No more of my insights into the direction your life is taking?" he teased.

"Don't push your luck, or I'll start in on what I think you should be doing with your life."

"I won't be here that long, love."

We managed to enjoy the rest of the day and evening with no further irritations. At least, none of consequence. James approved of the restaurant that I chose, and the dinner was excellent. I had never been there before. I couldn't bring myself to take him to Tortelli's.

Chapter 17

I saw James off at 7:00 the next morning. I had resented his unexpected arrival, but by the time he left, I was glad of his visit. It hadn't been an easy one, but it had been eye opening.

I was ready when Rita came to pick me up, and I greeted Harriet as I climbed into the back seat of the car.

"I hear your husband was here to see you," was Harriet's greeting to me.

"My ex-husband, Harriet. We've been divorced for many years. He was in Syracuse on business and came to visit."

Harriet beamed her approval. "If you can stay friends, who's to say you can't get back together one day? Rita, you could follow Katrina's example. Just talking to Dan once in a while wouldn't hurt, you know."

Rita and I exchanged looks as she glanced over her shoulder to turn the car around. We were in silent agreement. It just wasn't worth it to argue a point with her mother so early in the morning. "Hmm," we said in unison and left Harriet to interpret it however she liked.

By the time church was over, I was glad I had come. There were significantly fewer bodies sitting in the pews than had been in the already small congregation the first time I was

269

there. The Reverend Foxworth must have reconciled himself to that possibility ahead of time because he let no sign of disappointment show in his face. Though he didn't mention the attempt at book censoring directly, he did speak at length in his sermon about free will and tolerance of different viewpoints.

It seemed pretty clear to me what had inspired the subjects.

He appeared happy to see me as he greeted me at the door after church. "Thank you for coming." He smiled as he shook my hand.

"I wanted to thank you for what you said the other evening," I told him. "I know it couldn't have been easy to say what you did."

"It should have been easy, but I'm afraid I'm sometimes a bit of a coward," he confided to me quietly and gave me an odd little smile. "But when it comes right down to it, you can only say what's true for yourself. No matter how much trouble that might bring you."

I gave him a big smile back. "Reverend Foxworth, you told me you enjoyed your debates with my mother. Any time you'd like to come out and debate me, you'll be welcome."

The smile traveled to his eyes. "Be careful what you say. I'm apt to take you up on that."

Harriet was clearly having a difficult time with the fact that her minister had developed such dangerously liberal leanings.

On the ride home she said to me, "It's all very well to talk about being tolerant of other viewpoints, but we all know he was talking about those books. People can have different ideas, but wickedness and evil are never all right!"

"Harriet, they're children's books that are entertaining and funny. Nobody has to read them to their children, but some people love them. Have you ever read them?"

She was aghast at the idea. "Of course not! They're about witchcraft, Katrina, and that's not entertaining or funny. Witchcraft is evil, pure and simple, and shouldn't be used as a tool for entertaining children."

I dropped it. It was still too early in the day to argue with Harriet. In fact, I wasn't sure that there was any point in the day that it was worth it.

By the time Rita dropped me off, a light snow was falling, and I felt a desire to be out in it. "Want to go for a walk with me in a little while?" I asked Rita.

"Sure," Rita replied. "Right after lunch?" Harriet looked at us both as if we were crazy but said nothing.

I made myself a sandwich and plugged the laptop in to check my e-mail. Rowan and Keisha had each sent amusing notes that kept me chuckling between bites. Rowan wondered if her father had "dropped by" yet.

Right. Thanks for the warning, I thought in her direction. I sent back quick notes to them and then scrolled through the rest of my mail.

A missive from my friend Jennifer held the happy news that a Seattle company was publishing her first book of her own text and illustrations. She was having a big party in January to celebrate and I "better plan to be there!" I was excited for her and sorry that I would miss the party.

I cleared lunch away and set about performing little odd jobs I had neglected while James was here, all the while not being able to get rid of the thought of Jennifer's party. An idea was forming in my head, and the more I thought about it, the better it seemed. Why shouldn't I go back to Seattle for a few days around that time and invite Rita to go with me? She said she wanted to travel and had never gotten to. Here was a safe way for her to start, and we could stay with Rowan and Keisha. If money was a problem for plane tickets, I was sure I could talk her into letting me help.

I bundled into warm clothes and set out on the trail. As I emerged from the little forest of snow-laden evergreens, I saw that Brian's truck was parked in the driveway. I knocked at the door, which was opened by a distracted Rita. "Hi, Kat. Come on in. I hope you don't mind, but I'm not quite ready for our walk yet."

"No problem." I stamped my boots off before stepping inside and then took them off once I had the door closed.

I unzipped my jacket as I followed her into the kitchen. Brian sat at the table and greeted me as his mother pointed to an empty chair. "Have a seat for a minute. Brian just stopped by with some news."

"Oh? What's that?" I pulled the chair out and smiled at him.

"I was just telling Mom. I've decided to move."

"Oh, yeah? To another house?"

"No." He paused while he looked at his mother. "To Seattle."

"Really? I asked, taken aback. "When?"

"After Christmas." He shifted his gaze to me. "Rowan and Keisha told me I could stay with them until I could find a place. They're going to introduce me to a group who might need a guitarist, and I'll see if I can find work as a mechanic there. I've got some money saved up." The last was said to his mother as if to reassure her that he really could take care of himself.

"Brian, that's great." I immediately wondered if Rita thought it was as great. "How long have you three been cooking this up? Rowan hasn't said a word to me."

He looked at me sheepishly. "I asked her not to. They suggested it about a month ago, and I didn't want to say anything until I was sure. But I've been thinking for a long time about wanting to go somewhere. It's just...."

"Just that you worried about your mother. Believe it or not, she can take care of herself." Rita patted his hand. "It's about time you got out and did something you wanted to. I'm really excited for you."

"Really?" he asked worriedly. "I mean, who'll plow the driveway and fix things on the house and take care of the car? And help with Grandma?"

"Brian, for heaven's sake! Why does everyone think I'm helpless? I love you dearly, but I will be able to manage."

I silently agreed with Rita that she would manage and do it very well. I also knew, as a mother myself, how hard it really was for her to let him go without letting him know it was hard.

"This is perfect!" I said brightly. They both looked at me questioningly. "I just found out a friend of mine is having a book published and wants me to go back to Seattle for her party to celebrate in January. I thought I'd fly back for a few days and was going to ask your mother if she'd like to come with me," I said to Brian. "This way, now, she'd get to see where you'll be, and it won't seem so far away." I turned to Rita. "What do you think? I'd love to help with the airfare, if you'd let me. I'd get to show you around a bit, and we'd get to spend a little extra time with our 'babies.'"

Brian rolled his eyes good-naturedly at being called a baby, but smiled broadly at us both. "What a great idea! But I could pay for your plane ticket, Mom. Will you do it?"

For a moment, Rita didn't know what to say. Her eyes widened as she said to me, "Do you know, I've never been on a plane? Can you believe that? Oh, I'd love to go, but Kat, are you sure? You're going back to see friends. I wouldn't want to be in the way."

"Rita Lawrence, don't you dare get humble," I scolded her. "How would you be in the way? We might inconvenience Rowan and Keisha a little, which I think would be a fine thing. Say you'll come."

She looked from me to her son, who nodded his head in encouragement, and then she let out a delighted laugh. "I'll do it! Arthur and Alice could either come here to stay with Mom or they could have her over there just for those few days. I told you I wanted to travel. Who knows where this might lead?"

As the three of us happily discussed plans, I looked up once thinking that I saw Harriet about to enter the kitchen. At first I thought I had been mistaken, but a moment later I heard the soft whoosh of a door closing off the living room. Either she had been listening to the conversation or had just changed her mind about joining us. Well, either she already knew the news or she'd find out soon enough.

Rita and I followed the well-plowed roadway into Newbridge on our walk. The air was cold and sharp, but neither of us minded. Rita stepped as lightly as anyone can who's wrapped head to toe in heavy winter wear. She was as animated as I'd seen her yet, and it made me glad that inviting her back for Jennifer's party coincided with Brian's leaving. It would make letting him go so much easier.

Once we were in town, we followed the river path for a ways, talking all the way. Rita scooped up a handful of snow and threw it at nothing in particular. "I can't wait to tell Sam I'm going," she said as she scooped another handful and began forming it into a ball. "I think he'll be as excited for me as I am!"

It was easy to see she was bursting with her news. "Do you want to go tell him now? We'll walk by his place. If he's there, you can stay and tell him, and I'll head on home. I bet you could twist his arm to give you a ride if you wanted."

"You wouldn't mind? What about our walk?" She was torn between her desire to talk to Sam and not wanting to be rude.

"We've already had a lovely walk. I don't mind at all. I can use the walk back to start thinking about Christmas plans. Do you realize it's only three weeks away?"

"It is, isn't it?" There was no sign of panic from her. "I've got most of the presents taken care of. Just no plans yet. I don't even know if the twins are coming home for it. They might want to when they find out that Brian's leaving."

I walked with her to Sam's house where we found him tinkering in his heated garage. He, of course, was delighted to see her. They both asked me to come into the house with them for a while, but I declined. "Thanks, but I want to get back home. Invite me another day, okay?"

As I turned a corner a few minutes later, I realized I was within a block of Simon's house. I fought an urge to stop just to talk. Some of the things James had said were still sifting through my brain, and I found myself wishing for the easy closeness Simon and I had developed before things had gone so badly awry, so that I could talk it out with him. But, I reminded myself, that closeness was gone. He probably had no desire to talk to me. I passed his street without pausing and headed home.

I spent the rest of the afternoon going through some boxes of Christmas decorations I remembered seeing in the attic. There were some lovely things, and many of them were quite old. I sorted and picked until I had rearranged enough to bring downstairs two full boxes of things I was sure I could use. By the time I had gotten the second box down, I was too lazy to go back up and shut the attic door. I decided I would do it later.

Minette had come in with me when I got home from the walk and had asked to go back out soon after. While I was eating a dinner of soup and bread and reading a book at the same time, she meowed at me and rubbed against my leg on her way to her food bowl. I petted her absently until I realized that I had not let her back in. Her secret entrance must be open again!

And then it hit me. The attic door was open. It also hit me that the time the door had been stuck open until Brian helped me fix it coincided with Minette's ability to get in and out on her own. But how would that make sense?

I left the book and dinner forgotten on the table and practically ran up the two flights of stairs. I looked around the attic, hoping paw prints or something as obvious would give her secret away, but she hadn't made it that easy for me. I decided to leave the door open. Now that I was sure that her entrance led somehow to the attic, I would catch her at it sooner or later.

That night I had yet another dream. The attic was obviously on my mind, and a different attic became the setting for a new scene.

Kate watched as her mother set up the chairs in a circle, in the room without windows at the top of the house. Father had made these chairs to be used just for the times that the circle convened. They were fine chairs, but Kate thought that they somehow came alive when they formed that sacred shape.

"Please, Mother?" she asked as she did every time the women were to meet. "Aren't I old enough to join the circle yet? I healed old Tom's cough this very morning."

She picked up the tabby sitting patiently beside her.

Her mother smiled but shook her head. "Nay, Kate. Though you are certainly growing, you are not ready yet. This is a very dangerous time. Some of the church fathers would like to hang us all, I fear, for merely doing the healing work that the Goddess put us here to do. Someday, I pray that they will see that their God and our Goddess would happily work together, but until then, we must be very cautious. You cannot join the circle until you are fully ready."

Kate pouted at that, but she really had little hope that would sway her mother. It did not. Her mother merely laughed and kissed her forehead.

"Your time will come, Kate. Meanwhile, watch by the door for me and let the women in quickly as they come. Then go find your father and ask him to take you to the shore so you may see the moon rise on the water. No doubt, he'll gallop the horse at a fine pace along the sand with you in front of him. You always like that. Just make certain you hang on tightly!"

Rose gave Kate another kiss and shooed her down the stairs.

Usually Kate did love flying across the beach on her father's horse. But this night, she did not do as she was told. When all the women were assembled, she sneaked her way back up the secret stairs to listen silently outside the door that stood barely ajar. She did not want to wait until they thought she was old enough.

And so, Kate sat and listened eagerly to the voices chant the lovely words together as the sacred ceremony was begun.

On waking from this dream, I merely opened my eyes to see if Minette was nearby. The gray light of dawn filtered through the window just enough so that I could see her sleeping at the foot of the bed. No longer disturbed by my dreams, I found it interesting that I was getting these different glimpses.

I reached for the little travel clock beside the bed. Exactly 7:00 a.m. Might as well start the day. I needed to drive to Watertown and get some shopping done, but before that I had to finish some work that an editor was waiting for.

The day was a busy one and by the time I returned from the shopping trip, it was dark and I was dragging. Minette greeted me with a demanding meow while refusing to move from her empty food bowl as I entered the kitchen to put a few groceries away. "Fine," I said wearily. "Was Tess really as much a slave to you as I've become?"

It was around 7:30, after dinner was over and I sat in the kitchen to finish the novel I'd been reading, when the telephone rang. I walked to it, holding my book in one hand and trying to quickly finish the paragraph I was on before I had to pick it up. "Hello?"

"Kat? This is Jake." His voice sounded odd, slightly panicky.

"Hi Jake. Is something wrong?"

"I don't know. I mean, I'm okay. But it's my dad. I think he's sick. Can you come over and help?"

"Calm down, Jake." I was suddenly less than calm myself. "I'll come right over. But first, tell me what's happening. Is it bad enough that we should call 911?"

"No! I mean, it's bad, but not that kind of bad. He's... he's been sick in bed all day, and he's sleeping now, but he can't get up to get anything. I need help."

My calm returned. "Does he have the flu, maybe?"

"I think so. Just, it's a bad one."

"Is it that you want company? Do you need help getting food?"

"Yeah. You could make some soup for my dad. Maybe he could eat that. When he wakes up. Will you come?"

I forgot how tired I was. "I'll be right there. Your father will be fine, okay?"

"Okay. Thank you, Kat."

"You're welcome, Sweetie. See you in a minute."

It took me very little time to get ready. I left Minette on the kitchen chair, knowing that she would find her way out if she needed. I threw on my coat and boots and grabbed a pair of gloves as I turned on the porch light and, stepping out, I locked the door behind me.

The roads were clear, and it took only a few minutes to reach Simon's house. I pulled the Jeep close to the curb and turned off the engine. Grabbing the keys and climbing out in one motion, I headed up the sidewalk just as the door was opening. I thought Jake must have been watching for me.

I expected to see him or Jasper barreling out to meet me. Instead, Simon stepped through the door, zipping a jacket and tugging on gloves before pulling the door closed behind him. I didn't understand. Where was he going when he was sick?

"Simon?"

"Kat?" he said in surprise. "What…?"

"Should you be out in this cold?"

"Why not?"

"Well, if you're sick—" But suddenly, I could see that he was not sick. Something very fishy was going on here. "Where's Jake? He called me just a few minutes ago and asked me to come over. He said you were really sick."

"He did? Are you sure?"

"Of course, I'm sure. He sounded really upset, and I got over here as quickly as I could."

Simon looked at me as if I weren't making any sense. And maybe I wasn't. I certainly didn't understand what was going on. Then Simon began to laugh.

"What is so funny?" I asked in irritation. I had been worried and came to help. I didn't see anything funny.

"I'm sorry," he said when he could finally contain himself. "I think we've been had. Come in out of the cold." He reopened the door. After I minute, I walked through. There was no Jasper and definitely no Jake. In fact, the lights were off except for a night-light that had left a soft glow through the window.

I turned back to Simon as he closed the door and turned the light switch. He removed his coat and gloves as I frowned at him. "What is going on?"

"Just hazarding a guess, I'd say Jake had something up his sleeve, and he just tried it out on us."

"Where is he?" Surely he couldn't have gone to bed this early, and I knew Simon wouldn't have gone out at night and left him. "He's not here, is he?"

"No. He and Jasper are spending the night at my parents'. I have a conference to go to in Potsdam tomorrow and since I have to leave early, he's staying there so they can get him off to school in the morning."

"Ah." Light was beginning to dawn. "You haven't been sick at all?"

"Nope. Jake may be a little on the sick side when I get a hold of him, though." His voice softened slightly. "I've been wanting to talk to you. Will you take your coat off and stay for a little while?"

"All right," I said slowly and then removed my boots and coat. I straightened to hand my coat to Simon as he held the closet door open and then it registered that he had been going somewhere. "Are you sure?" I asked him. "You were on your way out. Do you have time to talk?"

He hung my coat next to his and closed the door. "I'm sure. I was going…well, it doesn't matter. Come and sit down."

I sat and looked around the familiar room, remembering the laughter and fun I'd shared here. I also remembered the last time I'd been in this room. I'd been so angry, and so had Simon. Was it too late to go back? Apparently Jake didn't think so.

Simon echoed my thought. "Though he's in big trouble, maybe Jake is smarter than we are."

"What do you mean?" The obvious, I hoped.

Instead of answering my question, Simon simply looked at me. After a moment, he said, "Kat, you don't know how many times I've played the last time you were here over in my head. I was an idiot, but by the time I was ready to admit it, it was too late. I was angry that you thought I would talk about something you asked me not to. But I should have known—I did know—how much you were dealing with. I cared about you so much, and I was upset that you were shutting me out. I didn't want to look at the fact that I was asking more from you than you were ready for."

I hadn't been able to look anywhere but at his face. Now he broke the contact and looked away.

"I've really missed you," he said.

"You have no idea how much I've missed you," I said quietly, and his head snapped back to look at me once again. Neither of us moved. We didn't dare yet. This was still too fragile, and we were both afraid to break the thread of whatever might be left between us. "The things you said that day did hurt, Simon, but I should have known that I could trust you. I don't know how anyone found out about what happened with Jake, but I do know it wasn't you. I wanted to tell you that before tonight, but somehow I couldn't. When I saw you at the library board meeting, I wished I could talk to you, but there were so many people there."

"I know, Kat. Way back at Halloween I brought Jake out hoping to talk to you. But Rita, Sam, and Toby were there, and I guess I was too stubborn."

"You did?" I couldn't believe it. "You know, Rita told me once, we were the two most stubborn people in Newbridge. Maybe Jake *is* smarter than we are."

"At the post office the other day…I thought something was happening then…."

"So did I. And then James showed up." I made a face. "I had no idea he was coming. And before I could say anything more to you, *you* shut me out. I didn't like it. Simon, I'm sorry for shutting you out of what I was going through. It was all so strange for me, and I had to deal with it alone."

"I know that now."

"James' visit did me some good. Though I was angry at him when he suggested it, he accused me of being afraid to get close to anyone else, that I was afraid they would turn out to be like him." I drew a breath. "I don't think he was so far wrong. I think it frightened me more than a little that I cared so much about you. And I'm scared now because I still care just as much."

"God, Kat...."

In one fluid movement, Simon was up and pulling me from the chair. His arms went round me, and his lips moved through my hair. I closed my eyes until he pulled back, and I opened them to look into his face.

"I'll try not to push you into anything you're not ready for," he said solemnly, "but I hated not being able to talk to you, to touch you, or just be with you."

I tried for a light touch. "A little push might not be a bad thing," I started to say, but his lips on mine stopped the words, and my arms slid round his neck as we both pulled closer.

It was some time before coherent words started to make their way back into our speech. We finally pulled away from each other though our hands stayed clasped.

"Jake would be very pleased to know his little plan worked." The smile that I'd missed so much was back on Simon's face. "Though, of course, he'll have to be punished for it."

"Don't punish him too hard," I said.

"He won't care what the punishment is. He loves you, Kat."

"I love him, too. I'm also pretty crazy about his father."

Simon ran his fingers through my hair. "I wish I didn't have to go to this conference tomorrow. I'd rather spend the day with you, but I'm supposed to give a talk on rural libraries, ironic as that may be after what's been happening. I can't get out of it."

"Call me when you get back. In the meantime, it's at least eight hours before you have to leave."

His fingers left my hair and traced a path down my arm before he clasped my hand in his again. "So it is."

As Simon left me to lock the door and turn off lights, I watched his movements. The closet door had not shut tight, and as he pushed it to, I remembered that he had been about to leave earlier.

"Simon."

"Hmm?" He smiled that smile, and my breath caught.

"Where were you going when I got here? I hope it wasn't some place important."

"Oh, but it was," he said, taking hold of my hand again. "I was on my way to your house."

As I slowly opened my eyes early the next morning, I saw that Simon was already awake. He lay on his side with his head propped in his hand. He had been watching my sleeping face, and now he smiled. "Good morning. Did you know you're rather beautiful, even when you're unconscious?"

I grinned back at him. "Thank you. I'll have to reserve judgment on how beautiful you look until I see you actually asleep."

"Being with you isn't exactly conducive to sleeping," he teased as he played with my unruly hair.

A little wave of happiness caught me, and I closed my eyes again. "This is nice," I said in complete understatement.

Simon sighed as he turned and slipped his arm under my shoulders. "You once described my kiss as comfortable. Now this is…nice. I'm just going to have to try harder."

I laughed. "You know very well I wasn't talking about the kiss when I used the word *comfortable*. And *nice* was an inadequate, early morning word for how I'm feeling right now." I ran an exploring finger down his side. "Once again, I'd say more research is necessary to come up with the right words."

Simon caught my roving hand in his and all teasing stopped. He held my eyes with a look that was so fierce and tender that it took my breath away. After that, proper descriptive adjectives were both unnecessary and impossible.

Chapter 18

Simon and I shared a breakfast that we cooked together. As I sat across the table from him the thought passed through my mind that he definitely wasn't James. There *was* hope. He looked at me and smiled, and I forgot all about James.

"What are you thinking about?" he asked.

"How much I enjoy having breakfast with you."

"Good."

"Among other things."

"Even better."

I could get very used to this, I thought. I was still feeling nervous about the complications of a serious relationship, but it was a bit late to worry about that now. I was far happier than I'd been just a few short hours ago, and I wasn't willing to turn things back just so that I could feel safe. Being safe was highly overrated anyway, I decided, as Simon turned that lethal smile on me.

It was early when we both left, but not so early that neighbors wouldn't be starting about their day. Simon walked me to my car, but before I could open the door, he caught my hand and turned me to him. "I'll be thinking about you all day, you know. Not that I haven't been thinking about you every day for quite a while now, but there are new...aspects to reflect on today." He grinned at me. "Will you come have dinner with us tonight? I can pick you up when I get back."

"Why don't you and Jake come have dinner with me instead? I'll be home so it'll be easier for me to cook. Besides, I've missed having you and Jake and Jasper at the witch house."

"All right. We can both confront Jake, scare the pants off him, and then thank him properly."

"I've been thinking about that. We should do a little interrogating. Has it occurred to you that he might not have been alone in developing this little master plan?"

"Actually, it had occurred to me, but I wasn't going to say anything." He laughed once and then planted a light kiss on my lips.

"Has it also occurred to you," I said, "that the neighbors can see everything?"

"That doesn't bother me at all. Does it you?" he asked.

In answer, I put my arms around his neck and gave him a kiss that shook us both.

"That's what I hoped you'd say," he murmured against my hair. Then he watched as I climbed into my car and drove off in a far different mood than I had been in when I had arrived the night before.

Jasper was the first to barrel into my kitchen that night. I looked up, expecting to see Jake close behind. Instead, I had time to pet Jasper and watch Minette hiss her way out of the room before a subdued little boy walked cautiously through the door, followed closely by his father. His crutches were long gone and his injury still slowed him somewhat, but not enough to account for this slow shuffle. One might think he was afraid of something.

"Hi, Kat," he said. You could almost hear a question mark after my name. He wasn't completely subdued, though.

A smile played at his lips and kept threatening to erupt into a full-blown grin. He figured he was in trouble, but he wasn't unhappy with the results of his crime. I wanted to hug him right then, but I didn't.

"Hello, Jacob," I said.

I looked at his father, trying to keep my expression serious, but it was no use. I was just too happy seeing these faces in my house once again.

Jake watched the look that passed between Simon and me and then the grin did explode onto his face. "Dad probably wants to help you get supper," he said. "Jasper and I'll just go outside and play in the snow for a little while."

"I don't need help," I told him.

"And it's dark out there. I think you'd better stay right here." Simon put a hand on his shoulder and turned him around. "In fact, why don't you have a seat right over there."

Jake gulped and made his way, slowly, to the table. Simon touched my hand and smiled at me while Jake's back was to us, and then we followed him to the table and sat together, opposite him. Poor Jake. All we needed was the glaring light bulb to complete the scene of a police interrogation. Which of us should be the good cop and which the bad cop?

Jake put on a brave smile. "It's been a long time since we've been here. It's nice to have dinner with Kat again, isn't it, Dad?"

"Yes, it is, Jake. And I'm glad I'm well enough to enjoy it."

Jake took another swallow. "Me, too," he said sheepishly.

"In fact, your father made a rapid recover," I said. Jake turned wary eyes my way. "Imagine how surprised I was when I got to your house last night and he was already better. He was so much better, it was as if he'd never been sick at all."

Suddenly, words tumbled out of Jake's mouth. "Are you mad at me? Please don't be too mad. You just went so long being mad at each other, and I didn't want you to be anymore. I liked it when we did things together, and I just thought if you got to talk to each other, you might see you weren't really mad anymore. And see, you aren't, are you?"

We sat in amazement at his speech, and then we both began to laugh. Jake's whole body relaxed. He beamed at us.

Simon was the first to recover. He reached for my hand, and our fingers entwined. Jake watched in obvious approval. "The thing is, sport, you lied to Kat and made her very worried. I'm not very happy about that."

Jake hung his head very slightly. "I know, and I'm sorry. I really am. And you can punish me however you want to. I don't mind. But she doesn't look too worried now."

"That's slightly beside the point."

His head hung a little lower at his father's words.

"Tell me, Jake, how long did it take you and Rowan to think up this little scheme?" I asked.

Jake's head bobbed back up. "You talked to her? She told you?"

"No, you just did."

He was ready to spill everything now. "Don't be mad at her. We thought it up in our e-mails. Way back when whatever it was that happened to make you and Dad mad at each other, Rowan said we should just leave you alone and you'd work it out. But you didn't," he said accusingly. "I waited and waited and nothing happened. Last week, Rowan said it was time for us to give you a push. She said it might not work, and I'd have to be brave and expect to be punished, and I said I could do that."

"Good," Simon told his son, "because I have a brilliant punishment that will affect the other half of your little team, too. You can't use the computer for three days. At all."

"Not even e-mail?" Jake asked worriedly.

"Especially not e-mail."

Simon and I exchanged looks. "What a coincidence," I said. "I don't plan to e-mail or phone Rowan for exactly three days either."

"But she'll wonder how things turned out. I won't be able to tell her." Jake looked from his father to me.

"Exactly," we said in unison.

By the next day, it was obvious that Simon's neighbors had seen enough to spread the word. I carried the brush I was cleaning with me when I went to answer a knock at the door. I opened it to a grinning Rita. "Why didn't you just come in?" I asked her. These days, she usually knocked once and then let herself in.

"Well, I couldn't be sure you'd be alone, now could I?" Her eyes twinkled with mischief.

I pulled her through the door so I could shut out the cold. "That's true. Toby might have stopped by, or Sara and Tim, or anybody else who wanted help. But you would have seen their cars, I suspect. And that's never stopped you from coming in before."

"You know very well what I mean." She couldn't suppress a laugh. "Why didn't you tell me you and Simon got back together? I had to hear it from Linda Harris when she came to pick up a package at the post office this morning."

"And here I don't even know who Linda Harris is."

"One of Simon's neighbors."

"Oh. Well, if it helps any, you're the first person I would have told. I just haven't seen you for a couple of days. How's your mother? Sam is well, I hope?"

"Oh, no, you don't." Rita tugged my sleeve. "I'm going to sit in the living room and refuse to leave until you tell me what happened. In detail." She thought for a moment. "Well, not great detail. Some of it I can guess. Linda was up early the other morning."

I groaned. "I don't think I'll ever get used to how easily news travels in a small town. Or how fast."

"That's why it's important to tell your best friend in that town the news first," Rita informed me.

I grinned at her now. "All right, best friend. I'll remember that for the next time. Meanwhile, come on in. I'll tell you a tale of wicked children saving their respective parents from themselves." Rita gave me a look of total incomprehension. "Jake and Rowan are to blame for getting us back together."

Late in the afternoon of the third day of Jake's punishment, the phone rang. I didn't have to be a witch with psychic powers to guess who it could be. Actually, I wondered what had taken her so long.

"Hi, Mom," Rowan greeted me after I'd answered. "How are you?"

"Fine. Is everything all right with you and Keisha?"

"Oh, yeah. I just hadn't heard from you for a while and thought I'd check in. You didn't answer my e-mail."

"Didn't I?" I asked. "Was it important?"

"No, not really. How's everyone there? Rita and Sam? Brian? And...Jake? Have you seen him?" She was trying to sound very casual.

I could be just as casual. "Everyone's fine. Brian tells me he hears from you and Keisha often. I haven't had a lesson with Jake in a while. I thought you and he were e-mailing each other."

"We were. But I haven't heard from him in a few days. I just thought maybe you had."

"Oh, well. He and his father are probably busy. It's getting pretty close to Christmas, you know. Which reminds me: do you know what day you'll be here? Will you be in time for our usual Solstice celebration?" I was going to draw this out as long as possible. It served her right.

"Definitely. I wouldn't miss it. I'll be there on the twentieth. Can you pick me up?"

"Of course," I answered.

That was the end of her patience. "Okay, Mom. I can't stand it any longer. Didn't Jake call you a few nights ago?"

"Yes, he did, dear. Why do you ask?"

"Mom! Did anything happen?"

"You mean other than the fact that Jake was banned from e-mail contact with you for three days?"

"Oh? Why is that?" She tried for casual again.

"To punish both of you for your parts in the little lie that had me really worried. Simon and I thought that it would be perfect justice for Jake not to be able to touch his computer and for you to stew in anxiety for a few days." I know the smugness in my voice transmitted through the phone lines.

"Okay," she said, "punishment received and accepted. But did it do any good?"

"In what way, Rowan?"

"Mom! Actually, you don't have to answer. I can hear it in your voice. And you're much too happy about punishing me. You and Simon came to your senses, didn't you?"

I couldn't keep it up any longer. "If you want to put it that way." I laughed at her. "We've agreed to reestablish our relationship."

"What a way for *you* to put it! You at least kissed and made up, didn't you?"

"Yes, we at least did that." I steered her away from further inquiries in that direction. "Why did you do it? You knew Jake would get into at least a little trouble for it."

"Yes, but I bet he doesn't care, does he? He likes you, I like Simon, and it was obvious when I was there that you and Simon are nuts about each other. You're both just too stubborn for your own good. You needed...a little help." She paused. "And besides, you still wouldn't buy me the horse I wanted as a kid. I figured this was the only way I might get the little brother I asked for and you wouldn't provide either."

"Rowan Benson-Solomon," I intoned, "you are incorrigible!"

"Yes, I am," she agreed happily. "And aren't you glad?"

The next week found me the happiest I'd been in a long time. Simon and I managed to steal moments alone here and there—enough to keep us happy. But most of the time we spent with Jake. We played in the snow and made plans to be together for the holiday. I told them both about our traditional celebration of the Winter Solstice and Jake was intrigued. Now that he was allowed to e-mail Rowan again, they made plans together, and he informed me that they had surprises planned for that night.

Christmas Day promised to be a bit complicated, but we wanted to be together. For the five years that they had lived here, Simon and Jake had always spent the day at the DeBerry farm. The new plan was that they would go there in the morning and Rowan and I would have the morning at my house. Then we would have dinner and the rest of Christmas Day together at the witch house. I was worried that Simon's parents would be upset, but they were not. In fact, they were obviously happy for us when I accompanied Simon and Jake to the farm one afternoon to pick up a toboggan. I had been nervous about their reaction to me, but they had been very sweet.

Rita's older son, John, was coming home for the holiday, but Jessica planned to spend it with her fiancé's family. Rita told me that they usually had to spend Christmas Eve at Arthur and Alice's house for a somewhat somber version of celebrating. Then she would spend the next day cooking at home while they all assembled there. This year would be different, she decided. She would endure Christmas day as usual, and her mother would still go to Arthur's for Christmas Eve. But she and Sam, along with Brian and John, would spend the evening with Simon, Jake, Rowan, and me.

I had easily gotten Toby to agree to come also. Far from the quiet little affair I had thought this holiday would be, I was looking forward to a house full of wonderful people.

Jake informed us on the twelfth of December that he had waited long enough to get a tree. I had never put one up that early before, but why not?

The next day, we tramped through the woods surrounding the DeBerry farm and selected two perfect trees. We cut and loaded them onto the old toboggan, which Simon and

I pulled back to the farm together while Jake and Jasper ran happy circles around us.

We spent the rest of the day putting up the trees and decorating them—first at their house and then at mine. Jake didn't want to be left out of either opportunity. We put my tree in the living room, and when we were finished with the decorating, I stepped back to inspect it. It was beautiful. Along with some of the greens left from cutting branches to make it fit, the room was very festive, indeed.

It had been a long but incredibly wonderful day. We were all tired, and Jake was practically asleep on his feet by the time they left. Simon had offered to take the extra branches away, but I told him not to bother. What wouldn't fit in the fireplace, I would take out to the burn barrel the next day.

The next morning, I found Minette sitting sedately next to the tree. She looked as if the glittering evergreen was no big deal—hadn't it been there all along?

"You can't fool me, and you can't blame this on Jasper," I told her as I swept up the shards of glass that had been an ornament only the night before. "Leave the rest alone, please."

She followed me to the kitchen where I fed us both. Then I bundled up and headed out into the cold to dispose of the extra branches. It took me a couple of trips to get them from the back steps to the barrel. The tree had been bigger than it looked in the woods.

Laying the last pile down, I pulled the cover off the barrel and picked up a handful of branches. The barrel was fuller than I expected—I thought there would only be ashes in the bottom. I'd had no experience with burn barrels before. I peered in to see if I just needed to stir things a little to make room. Instead of ashes, there were several objects on top that were clearly singed but still recognizable. I dropped the branches and reached for the first item. It was a shoe. Beside it, I realized, was its partner, though it took a minute to be sure. And then my eyes began to pick out odd pieces of cloth, the handle of a hairbrush, and scorched bits of canvas and framing.

I stared into the barrel for several minutes before I finally replaced the lid with a shaking hand. I had no idea what this meant or who had placed them here and lit a match to them. But it came to me that I had undoubtedly found the remains of Tess' missing clothes and paintings.

I was stymied as to whether or not to call the police. Who could have done this? And would the police even consider it a crime?

It was unlikely in the extreme that Tess would have burned her own things just before suddenly dying. But what reason would anyone else have to do this? It could have been a prank—destroy something from the abandoned witch house. It didn't seem likely that vandals would have taken just Tess' clothes and paintings to the burn barrel but left the rest of the house neat and tidy. It may or may not be considered a crime, but it definitely was creepy.

I left the branches lying on the ground and started back to the house. I needed to think. Before I got more than a few steps, however, a movement against the snow, near the cellar door, distracted me. I turned, wondering what it was. Then, as a tail disappeared into the ground, I realized it was Minette, probably headed into her secret entrance. Despite the anxiety I felt at what I had found in the burn barrel, I decided I would follow her. I wasn't going to miss this opportunity to see where she was going.

I wished I had time to fetch a flashlight, but I realized I had matches in my pocket that I had planned to use for the branches. I quietly lifted the cellar door, trying not to disturb the cat into changing her mind. Fumbling to light a match, I finally managed it in time to see her disappear again, this time behind a huge ceramic jar set against one of the shelves.

I waited for a moment for her to reappear, but when she didn't, I blew out the match and lit another one to light my way as I looked behind the jar.

There was no cat there!

I stood mystified until the match burnt my fingers and I dropped it to the earthen floor with a squeal. I fumbled for another and got it lit so that I could find my way back up the cellar steps and out into the daylight. I went into the house for a flashlight and returned immediately to the cellar.

The flashlight illuminated the area much better, and this time I was able to see a cat-sized hole at the bottom of the wall behind the jar and next to the end of one of the shelves. I squatted down and cautiously put my free hand to the hole. I hoped there were no spiders nearby. I admired them greatly but had no wish to be bitten by one.

I felt only empty space behind the hole. As I pulled my hand back, the sleeve of my coat snagged on a jagged edge of wood and a creaking sound sent my heart up into my throat. I looked up, and at first I thought the shelf was about to topple over, but then realized that the wall where the shelf was attached had given way. I pulled my sleeve free and played the light up and down the edge of the shelf.

Surely it couldn't be…!

Well hidden by the lack of light and the shelf covering it, was a door. Where in the world could it lead?

I stood for a moment, dazed. Then, regaining my senses, I scrambled to move the ceramic jar. The door was not heavy and opened easily. Swallowing my fear of the un-known, I flashed the light into the space. It was too small an area for a room but just large enough to hold what I now saw was an old, wooden, spiral staircase. Shining the light upward I could see that the stair filled a shaft behind the chimney and wound far above my head.

I took a deep breath, went through the door, and placed a tentative foot on the first step. It creaked, but other-wise seemed sturdy enough. Clearly, Minette had been using this stair for some time, but I was far heavier than she. Had Tess used it? And where *did* it lead?

There was only one way to find out.

I stepped as lightly as I could and clung to the railing, but I needn't have worried. Though the stairs were old, they were well built and still in good condition. I wound my way slowly upward, wondering all the while where I would end up. It became apparent that the stair led to the top floor. This was how Minette had been making her way from the cellar to the attic. But I had seen no other doorway in the attic other than the one I had already been using.

I was nearing the top now and picked up the outline of a doorway in the beam of light I sent that way. The door was slightly ajar. Peering through, I was momentarily disoriented. I had fully expected to find myself stepping into a corner of the attic, but instead the light revealed several objects in a small room.

Before the objects could register in my brain, my attention was caught by the flick of Minette's tail as she slipped through a narrow opening on the opposite wall. Quickly following, I pushed the opening wider and stepped through. At first I thought that it opened directly to a wall, but when I put my hand to it, the wall moved and rippled and I realized I was standing behind several old rugs that had been hanging from a low beam in the attic. Moving forward and around the rugs, I came into the light shining through the two tiny windows of the room. Minette sat and licked one paw, and I couldn't help but think she was wondering whatever had taken me so long to find her secret. Now that I had, I wanted to explore it completely.

"Coming with me?" I invited, but Minette decided she had done her duty and turned the other way. Going back into the narrow room, I felt along the wall, hoping to find a light switch. There was none. The flashlight did reveal two hanging kerosene lanterns and one battery-powered one. I turned the switch on the battery lantern first and was more than a little surprised to find that it worked. Then, pulling the matches from my pocket, I removed the globes of the kerosene lanterns and lit them, before returning the globes over the flames. The light from these sources was sufficient to fully illuminate the windowless space. I took my first really good look around.

Against one wall was a small, old-fashioned writing desk with papers and pens covering its fold-down surface. Four plain, wooden chairs were against the wall near the desk. On a hook above one of the chairs hung a red cape. On the opposite wall hung two paintings above a narrow table with several objects on it. My breath caught when I looked more closely at the paintings. At least these two had not been destroyed along with the other burned articles. The first one was the long-lost *Dream of the Circle of Women*. I could easily see why Rita had mistaken my painting for this one. It was as if Tess and I had witnessed the exact same scene...and I suppose we had. The second was of the two young girls that Rita had described. I knew immediately which one was Rita, because the other was me. I even remembered the dress I was wearing. My mother had bought it for me for Christmas when I was seven and had taken a photograph of me wearing it. I had loved that dress and saved it long past the time that it fit.

Dragging my eyes from the paintings, I looked at the table and realized, with a start, that it was not simply a table. It was an altar. Not the stereotype of an altar meant for sacrifice, but what I'd learned from Rowan was a true witch's altar. The kind that a person placed objects upon that were loved and held sacred. On Tess' altar—for there was no mistaking that this was Tess'—were several objects that spoke of who she was and what had been important to her. There were candles of different sizes, shapes, and colors. There were things that she had obviously found outside her house: rocks, birds' eggs, a nest, and feathers. A vase filled with dried lavender. A seashell and a small china doll that looked as if it had been handled often with a great deal of love...its features were almost rubbed away. A basket with postcards from different places...possibly some of the places she and Toby had traveled to? Three small paintings. One of Toby, one of me as a child, and one of Rowan and me together that couldn't have been done very long ago. And...a figurine of a black-haired woman with a flowing red dress. These things made up my mother's altar.

And one more item. I was so overwhelmed by everything else I saw there that I almost overlooked it. At the edge of the altar was a locket. I knew this locket very well...I had seen it several times in my dreams.

I picked it up with unsteady hands and searched for the little spring I knew was there. The top popped open. Inside were two ribboned locks of hair. One brown and one black. The colors of Rose's and Kate's hair.

Without thinking, I reached into my pocket and once again drew out the matches. I lit one of the candles and stood back. Somehow, I didn't think Tess would mind. I was finally aware of how warm I had become and removed my coat. It seemed disrespectful to just lay it on a chair, so I hung it with the red cape. Then, I picked up the locket and secured it around my neck.

I stood, looking around me for some time. Had the other women in this family used the little room? Neither Rita nor Toby had known about it or surely they would have said something to me. Had it remained a secret known only to the builders and the people who had lived in this house for over two centuries? Might it have been used during the nineteenth century to hide some of those who journeyed on the underground railroad? As close as it was to the Canadian border, it didn't seem impossible.

I sank into the chair at the exquisite desk and tried to take it all in. My eyes strayed from the altar to the desk now and I saw that some of the cubbyholes held envelopes. Pulling a couple from their slots, I dropped them as if I'd been burned. The handwriting that spelled Tess' name and address was so familiar to me that it brought a wave of longing. My mother...Helen...had sent these.

And, I saw, there were more. Several held pictures taken through the years of me, first with my parents and later ones of my wedding to James and then Rowan and me.

I had thought I was finally growing used to all the strange things happening to me in the few months I had been in Newbridge, but here I was, once again, with my world turned upside-down. I gathered up the envelopes and reached to put them back where I had found them. Only then did I see what had been lying on the desk this whole time. There were several papers—all parts of what appeared to be a letter. At the top, the greeting was just one word.

A name.

My name.

Katrina.

Chapter 19

Katrina,

I don't even know where to begin, but I decided that I should put my thoughts down in a letter before I get to meet you. I don't know if I'll actually give you this letter or just use it to organize everything in my head. For that matter, I don't even know if I'll get to meet you...you might choose not to talk to me. I have to prepare myself for that possibility, but I do hope that isn't the case!

I can already tell, this is going to ramble. I'll just write it, and if I need to, I'll rewrite it later. I suppose I should start at the beginning, but I don't even know where that is. I've lived long enough that it seems to me everything is a circle. There are no nice tidy beginnings and endings. I'll try starting near your beginning and weave my way backward and forward from there.

If you are actually reading this, then we have already met and you may know some of it. But there is a great deal to tell you, and it's very complicated. Some of it you'll no doubt find hard to believe.

My family (yours, too, if you'll accept it) has never been ordinary. I'll write later of how different we are, but for now...well, as they say, first things first. I was very young when you were conceived—nineteen—and I was in college.

My family had been in Newbridge for nearly two hundred years, but we were always different. This house I grew up in has continually been passed down to the women in the family, and that alone would set us apart. I had every intention of marrying a wonderful man, Toby Underwood—who you've also already met if you are reading this—and passing the house on to our daughter. Toby should have been your father.

This next part is still difficult for me to write, even after all these years, but I must. There is no pretty way to say this. I was raped by a man I hated and still refuse to think of as your father. I will not write his name here. If you find at some point you really feel the need to know—we'll see. But I want you to know that that is not why I gave you up. When I discovered I was pregnant, I had no intention of letting that man be part of your life, but I did plan a good life for you. I hoped that Toby would understand, and we would still be married. And when he found out—bless him—he did ask me to marry him and let the baby grow up as his. But, by that time, it was too late.

I picture you standing here in front of me, and without knowing me or our family history, I am afraid of how you will take my explanations. I realize this letter will take me a very long time to write—and it will take some courage, too. In a family that was already considered odd, I have made myself into this town's strangest member of that family. I know what people say of me, and that has never bothered me. There are a few people who do not think badly of me, and I hope you get to meet them. I care what they think of me, and I find that I care a great deal of how you might think of me.

This is rambling far too much. I will stop here and take it up later.

Before I tell you the reasons I gave you up, I want to write about the parents you grew up with. I know they gave you a good life, and I was very sorry when I heard that your father died years ago and again recently when Helen died. I know you tried to find out about me after Matthew died, *and* Helen did ask me to let her tell you. I hope you won't be upset with her to find out that she kept this from you. I asked her to and, though she wasn't happy about it, she agreed.

Matthew was my history professor when I first arrived at college. He and Helen were only about ten years older than me and became interested first in my artwork. Later we became friends, and when I realized I was pregnant, Helen especially was very kind to me. When it became obvious to me that I couldn't keep you, I approached them with my idea. They wanted children very badly but, as you know, couldn't have them. I knew they would be loving parents and I could trust them to stay in contact with me over the years. I named you Katrina, and they were kind enough to keep it for you. Because of Helen, I feel that I know you and you've turned into the person I hoped my daughter would be. I hope you don't feel that I have no right to call you my daughter, and maybe I don't. But everything I've done, Katrina, was because I love you. I'm sure that will be the hardest of all for you to believe, but it is true!

It has been so hard for me not to be able to talk to you or even let you know that I exist. I couldn't help myself when I found out that Helen had died. You'll know by now that it was me who called you as one of Helen's old friends. She had written to me to tell me that she was dying, and she asked me again to let her tell you about me. I still didn't dare even then.

Hearing your voice was such an incredible experience for me! And Rowan's—she answered the phone. What a beautiful daughter you have! Helen was so proud of both of you. I was so tempted to tell you the truth then, but it would have been a terrible thing to do to you so soon after Helen's death. And to be truthful, I was too much of a coward. Toby has helped give me the courage to think of approaching you now. I was lucky enough to have him come back into my life after all this time. We're planning to finally marry, and my greatest hope is that you will have forgiven me and that you and Rowan will be at our wedding. It will be very small—the only other people I expect to be there are Toby's brother and a *wonderful woman named Rita who I love as if she were another daughter. I imagine the two of you would have been friends if things had been different and I had gotten to raise you here.*

I've been avoiding this next part long enough. For heaven's sake—this is a letter and after all, I don't have to give it to you. I'll just say this and judge later if I can really tell you. First, I'll tell you a legend about our family. At least, anyone else would call it a legend, but this story (I was told by my mother and grandmother) has been handed down from mother to daughter since it happened in the 1600's. The women in our family have always been healers. I don't mean doctors as you think of them. But they have been herbalists and women who heal with their hands. Sometimes it skips a generation—the healing ability—but most have had it. My grandmother, mother, and myself all had it that I can attest to. From what Helen has told me, it's not something that either you or Rowan has experienced. I don't know why that is. Perhaps it's part of what I brought upon us.

Besides passing down the healing ability, the women in our family have passed down certain secrets—things about ourselves that no one else would understand. I know that people here jokingly call me a witch. The real joke is that we have always considered ourselves witches in this family. Not the fairytale kind who have signature warts on the ends of their noses or that eat babies—but the real witches. The women who know how to heal, how to grow, and use plants. In the old days, they were the midwives and doctors, too.

I've been told that somewhere in the early 1600's in England, we had an ancestor named Rose Penford. Rose also was a healer and a believer in the pre-Christian pagan traditions. You can imagine how well that was received by the church leaders, and many women and a few men were hanged in England for those beliefs and abilities. Anyway, as the story goes, Rose and her circle of women healers were out among the stars, near the ocean one night, singing to their

Goddess (I'm hoping this doesn't shock you too much—Helen told me that Rowan has been interested in Wicca for some time now) when priests from the church arrived to accuse them of witchcraft and arrest them. At that time, being a female healer was proof of consorting with the devil. Rather than going back to mock trials and hanging, the women chose to drown in the sea together before the priests could get to them.

Rose had a daughter named Kate, who was young enough at the time that she wasn't with the rest of them. She and her father escaped to France, but not before she managed to put a curse on all the priests who had been involved in her mother's death. One of the things that Kate was taught but ignored is that whatever you do comes back to you three times over. Placing those curses may or may not have brought revenge, but what I have been told is that Kate had a perfectly miserable rest of her life to pay for it. Her father died soon after they made it to France. Kate later was married and had several children, but her husband and all of her children, except one daughter, died young. Kate lived to be an old woman and was a healer herself, but lived with the knowledge that the curses she placed worked against her to the point that her own flesh and blood suffered for them.

Not a very happy story, is it? It's been passed down carefully in our family, basically for two reasons. First, so that we never forget what the women in our family have gone through, and secondly (and according to my mother and grandmother—most importantly) as a reminder that we are healers and are never to do harm to anyone else, for any reason. The reason I'm telling you is so that you know our history and to help you understand what I'm going to tell you next about why I gave you up and didn't let you know about me until now.

I know that may seem like a far-fetched story to you, but I grew up with it. I learned early on that I was part of a family of witches, but there were very few people I could let know that. It was also a very basic part of my learning that I was never to wish anything harmful on someone else. All that flew out the window when I was raped. I cursed the man thoroughly while he stood over me, and I don't mean that I just swore at him. I called some very specific misfortunes down on him. I didn't regret it at the time, and still wouldn't if only I had been involved in the fallout of what I had done. But very soon after discovering I was pregnant, my parents, who I loved dearly, were both killed in a terrible car accident, and I knew that I was responsible. As much as I hated that man for what he did, I should never have cursed him. I paid dearly with the loss of my parents, but they paid even more, with their lives. I couldn't let that happen to anyone else that I loved. Not Toby, and not you. I wouldn't tell Toby what really happened—I knew that he would try to talk me out of my decisions. But I had to keep you both away from harm, so I refused to marry him and went back to New York City to stay with Helen and Matthew until you were born. Until then the death of my parents was the hardest thing I had experienced. But the day of your birth, when I got to hold you and kiss you, knowing that I was saying goodbye, was the most painful thing I've ever known. Knowing that you were safe and loved and being able to watch you grow into a beautiful, talented woman through Helen's letters and pictures was what made it bearable.

I never finished college but instead came home to live alone in this house. Oddly, though it may not make sense to you, I love this place. I've kept nearly everyone away from it, but it has been my sanctuary, despite what happened here so long ago. My art has kept me going. Matthew and Helen introduced me to some people who became interested in it while I was pregnant with you, and I've been modestly successful at selling some of my work through galleries in the city ever since then. I was thrilled to find you developing into a fine artist yourself. And a writer! And I hear that Rowan is a gifted musician. I hope I get to hear her play.

So why, after all that (I can hear you thinking) did I finally decide it was all right to contact you? I'll admit, I'm still a little frightened, but I've had a lot of years to think about it. I've had two years with Toby back in my life, and

303

they've been happy ones. I still haven't let Toby come into this house—you might call it superstition, but I see it as keeping him safe. Until I have laid all my fears to rest, I want to take no chances. He's helped convince me that I have paid at least three times over for what I did and that it's now time to let go. I realized that I could only do that by completing the circle: contacting you and giving you the chance to choose whether to accept what I have to say.

Lest you think I'm just a superstitious old woman (though that may be true, too), I want you to know that there were other things I believed I was protecting you from. I knew that besides the love they would lavish on you, Helen and Matthew would make certain that you got the opportunity for a good education, travel, and the money to pursue the things you dreamed of. Those were not necessarily things you'd get growing up here. I've always been considered odd here (though some, like Toby, didn't mind) and I knew you would grow up facing the same thing. There were also...people who I was afraid would be particularly dangerous for you to be around.

I've been three days writing this, and I see it's in danger of becoming longer than your average novel. I wonder, will it be easier talking to you directly? I'm rather nervous about that—I suppose it's my fear that you won't want to hear me out. Or that you will hear me out and just think I'm crazy.

Maybe it would be easier if I were to write a little about the people I hope you'll meet. I've already talked about Toby. We've known each other since we were very young, and by the time we were in high school, I knew how I felt about him. He's one of the few people I've told a little about our family, and that didn't scare him away! I try not to think about what could have been all the years we were apart. I'm too certain that we wouldn't have been allowed to be happy that long. In these last two years, we have traveled together and had a wonderful time. I'm looking forward to the time we have ahead of us.

Rita. Rita is a woman I've known since she was very young. She's only a couple of months older than you, and she's been a very dear friend. She wormed her way in here as a very young girl at a time when I wasn't letting anyone else near. I had horses, and she couldn't stay away from them. Her life at home wasn't always very happy and, despite myself, I grew very fond of her. There were several reasons I convinced myself that she was safe visiting here and perhaps I can tell you about them one day.

I'm tired now. I'll write more tomorrow. And before long, I'll get the courage to call you. I'm looking so forward to hearing your voice again.

Chapter 20

There was no more to the letter. Tess had never had the chance to finish it. I stared at the pages in front of me for a long time before I was aware of the tears sliding down my cheeks. They were tears for Tess, tears for Helen, and tears for me because I had lost them both.

I had more of the answers now that I had been looking for. But with them came more questions.

Who had raped Tess?

Who was this man who had fathered me accidentally by his act of violence?

My heart broke for the young Tess who had been convinced that her natural reaction of wanting to see this man punished had caused the death of her parents. In her place, I would have wanted to do more than just curse him.

She had paid heavily for what she considered her sin of wishing ill of him. She had lost people she loved. I wouldn't have been surprised if that alone had driven her a little crazy. I wished I could tell her that I didn't consider her crazy because of what she had to tell me about the women in our family. I was one of them. I was truly Tess' daughter.

Had I always had the ability within me to heal, and it had only awakened when I came home? I could understand that Tess loved this place. I had grown to love it, too, and it *was* my home.

I glanced one more time at Tess' handwriting and then left the letter on the desk. After removing my coat from the hook, I gazed at the altar, sending my thoughts to Tess.

There's nothing to forgive you for. Thank you for everything you've given me...Mother.

Then I blew out the candle. Before extinguishing the other lights, I removed the paintings from the wall. I was taking them back to a place of prominence over the fireplace.

So much had happened to my emotions in that short space of time that I had forgotten about my discovery of Tess' burned possessions. I wanted to talk of all this to Rowan but not over the telephone. Thank goodness, she would be here in less than a week.

I sat in the living room with Minette on my lap and stared into the fire I had started before going outside. Everything I had discovered in the last hour swirled round and round in my mind, and I was so lost in it that I didn't hear Rita's knock or the first time she called my name.

"Kat?" I looked up to see her standing just over the room's threshold with an ornate bottle in one hand and her gloves in the other. "You were a long way off there." She laughed. "Thinking of someone in particular? Your tree looks beautiful." She placed the bottle under it.

"Thank you," I said absently.

"You okay?" She unbuttoned her coat and took the chair nearest the fire. She had removed her boots before entering and now warmed her feet on the hearth.

There was so much to say, and yet I was at a loss as to where to begin. "Rita, I've...found some things." She followed my glance to the mantle.

"Kat! Tess' paintings! Where were they?" She got up quickly and stood where she could touch them.

"Rita...there's a room...a hidden room in this house. I found it by accident when I watched Minette go into the cellar. I found so many things this morning that it's overwhelming." She transferred her attention to me and watched as I rose from the chair, placing the cat on the floor, and came to stand next to her. "These paintings are just two of the things."

The tone of my voice must have alerted her. "What else?" she asked gently.

"First, I was going to burn some branches in the burn barrel, and when I removed the cover, I found remnants of some clothes and canvases in there. Someone had burned them."

"What? Are they Tess' clothes?"

"That's my guess. And the other paintings you talked about weren't in the room I found—just these. The pieces of canvas in the barrel must have been the other paintings." I brushed a finger across the frame of the painting of the little girls. "I'm trying to decide whether to call the police. But first, there are some other things to tell you. And...to show you."

"Of course, you should call the police! Who in the world would have stolen Tess' things and burned them?" Rita was emphatic.

"But stole them from who, if she was dead?"

She gave an impatient shrug and then said, "From you. You inherited everything of hers. Maybe it was a stupid prank. But the police should know about it."

"You're right. I will call them. But let me tell you the rest of it." I pointed to the picture I had touched. "The other little girl in this painting wasn't just an imaginary one, Rita. It's me. Tess had a snapshot my other mother sent of me in this dress, and she must have painted from that. And she loved you like a daughter. She said so in a letter that she was writing to me. She must have died before she could finish it. But she was getting ready to contact me. The letter explains some things. I want you to read it, and...I'd like you to see the room I discovered."

I believed that Tess had considered her little room sacred space and I would respect that. As far as I knew, she had shown it to no one. There were three women besides myself, however, that I felt should share in seeing it...Rowan, Keisha, and Rita.

I grabbed a flashlight and led Rita up the stairs to the attic. When I pulled the rugs enough to reveal the wall behind, I had to shine the light in order to see the barely noticeable crack that outlined the door. An old leather bridle hung from a hook in the middle. If I hadn't known the door was there, it would have been easy to overlook. The hook served as the knob to open it.

Rita stood in stunned silence as I once again lit the lanterns. What few words we did speak were said in hushed tones. After she looked over the room and the altar, I pointed to the desk. When she saw Tess' handwriting, she looked at me questioningly.

"Are you sure you want me to read this? It's yours...."

"Yes, I think you should read it, too." I nodded reassuringly and then watched while she sat and read through the pages. I saw tears sliding down her cheeks, too, before she returned the last page to the desk. She got up and walked to the altar, to stand in front of it for a time. Finally, we exchanged a look, and I put out the lights. We left the room and said nothing until we were once again in the living room.

Rita sank into a chair, but I was too restless and stood by the fireplace, close to Tess' paintings. "I had no idea," Rita said. "No idea that she went through so much. And Kat, your dreams...."

"I know. There's no denying where they've come from now." I drew a breath. "But I'm so sorry for everything that happened to her. She lost her parents, Toby, and me. And most people weren't kind to her. I don't know how she stood it."

"You can't think of it just that way, Kat. Some people weren't kind to her, but she wouldn't let most people near. And she did have things she loved. She loved this house and land, her art and healing work, knowing you were safe and happy, and in the end, time with Toby. And she was going to contact you. She died believing that was going to happen."

I could feel my eyes growing moist again, but I managed to hold the tears back. "You forgot one of the best things to happen to her, Rita. You. She loved you. I'm so glad you were close to her. And thank you for being my friend, too." The tears did spill then, and Rita stood so we could hold each other and cry.

She stayed and we talked long into the afternoon. It helped Rita as much as it did me. She had loved Tess and had no one she could really talk to about her feelings when she died. We spent little time speculating on the identity of the man who had raped Tess. He wasn't a father I would want to know. What did it matter now? I wondered aloud, briefly, if he had suffered anywhere near as much as Tess had from the curses she'd called upon him.

Eventually, we were able to get to a place where Rita could tell me again about some of the happy memories she had of Tess, and I was eager to hear them. We both saw her in a different light now, and I believe it brought Rita and me closer together. We each shared a part of Tess that no one else, except Toby, had come close to knowing.

I took Rita outside and showed her my discovery of the door hidden in the cellar and the astonishing staircase behind that door. We climbed the stair and found Minette waiting for us in the room. I swear, she appeared smug. At the very least, she looked completely at home there. She allowed us both to pet her and purred as we did.

In the living room once more, with the tree lit, I had been totally unaware of how the time had slipped by until I heard one knock and then Simon's voice as he called through the open door. Jake was going Christmas shopping with his grandparents that night, and Simon and I had planned to go to dinner. I met him in the hallway.

"I'm so sorry," I said as I took his hand. "I didn't realize what time it was. Would you mind if we stayed here instead of going out? Some things have happened today, and I'd rather just be with you here, if that's okay."

He brushed my cheek gently with the back of his hand. "No, I don't mind. What's happened Kat?"

"Rita's here. Come on into the living room, and I'll tell you." I led the way, not letting go of his hand until he needed it to shed his jacket. Then we sat on the sofa together as I told him of the day's discoveries. By the time I finished, Rita had glanced at her watch and realized she had to get home.

"My mother is going to Arthur's, and Sam is picking me up. I need to go get ready." She looked at me with concern. "Kat, you didn't call the police. You are going to, aren't you?"

"I will, Rita. But the things were burned before I got here in August, so I don't think I need to hurry now. I'll call them in the morning. Thanks for being here today."

"You're welcome. I'll check in with you tomorrow." She started toward the doorway, then turned back. "I almost forgot. I brought you a bottle of a special wassail drink Tess used to make. She gave me the recipe, and I made some today. It's really good."

"What's in it? The bottle is beautiful." I was close enough that I reached down and picked it up from under the tree.

"Oh, a little of this and a little of that." She smiled. "It has an apple base, but there are several spices, eggs, an herb or two, and of course, just enough sherry and brandy to make it all go together really well. I'll give you the recipe if you like it."

"I'm looking forward to it. Thanks. See you tomorrow."

Simon and I both said our goodbyes to her and then sat quietly as we heard the front door open and close. Finally, he reached to draw me closer, and I set the wassail bottle back on the floor before snuggling gratefully against his warmth.

"Are you really okay with all this?" he asked.

"I don't know if okay is the word," I said, "but I have more answers now, at least about what happened to make her give me up. I just wish I'd gotten to meet Tess. To tell her the things I wish I could say to her now. But I have no clue to who destroyed her things. Or why."

"That *is* very strange. You will call the police first thing tomorrow?"

"I promise, though I don't know what they'll say or what they could do."

"Just the same."

"Don't worry. It's the first thing I'll do in the morning." I pulled back so that I could look at his face. That face, I realized with sudden awareness, I had grown to love. But I couldn't tell him that, not yet. I pulled away slightly. "Simon, would you want to read the letter Tess left?"

"I would, if you're sure that you want me to."

"I do want to share it with you." I reached my hand to his again and stood up. "I'll show you where the secret doors are, too, if you like. But—I hope you don't mind—I won't take you inside the room. It's...." I groped for the right words. "It was Tess' sacred room, I think. And I'm guessing it was the same for other women in the family before her. I have a feeling no men have entered that room for a very long time. It just doesn't seem right. Oh, damn! I don't want to keep things from you. But do you understand?"

I was afraid of how he would take my words, but Simon stood beside me and placed a finger on my lips. "You didn't have to tell me about any of it, you know. Thank you for trusting me. Just show me what you feel comfortable with."

I looked at him in wonder. Where did this man come from? "That's what makes me I—" I caught myself. "That's what I like about you. Most people wouldn't understand. I've never known anyone else like you."

"I'm glad to hear that, I think." He smiled. "And ditto." With that and a kiss, he helped to dispel the somber mood I'd been holding onto.

I took him to the attic and showed him the secret entrance. Without a word from me, Simon stepped back behind the rugs before I slipped into the room and brought out the letter. He sat on one of the old trunks and read it in silence as I reread it over his shoulder. Finally, he shuffled the papers neatly back together and handed them to me. "She really was a remarkable woman, you know. And she obviously did love you very much."

"I know. And thank you for calling her remarkable, not strange. Or for not thinking I'm strange after all this, either."

"There's nothing strange about you, Kat. What's happened to you is certainly unusual. And you've handled it amazingly well." He pulled me down beside him.

"Not always," I said ruefully. "Look at what happened to us because I wasn't handling things so well."

"You were dealing with some major changes in your life. I could have handled things better, too." He put his arm around my shoulders. "But we're here now, together. And in case I haven't managed to convey it to you, I think you're rather remarkable, too."

I found a way for him to convey the message without words.

After I put the letter back where I'd first found it, Simon and I walked back down the stairs. "Kat?"

"Hmm?"

"What do you think Tess meant about people she thought it would be dangerous for you to grow up around?" We had reached the bottom of the stairway, and he held back to let me lead the way down the hall to the kitchen.

"I assume she meant the man who raped her."

"So you think he was from Newbridge?"

I looked at him, startled. "I don't know. I think I just had some vague idea it was someone where she went to college. I guess I'll never know now. She did say *people*, though. And she also said that I would have grown up with the same stigma she had of being from a strange family. Maybe that's all she meant...the danger that people would treat me differently."

We made a meal together, but I ate very little of it as we talked more of the letter and the events that led up to my finding it. Though it was dark, we bundled into our jackets, boots, and gloves after clearing the dishes, and I showed Simon the entrance hidden in the cellar and the spiral staircase behind it. Emerging from the cellar, I was struck by the beauty of the stars and the nearly full moon beginning to rise. Rather than returning immediately to the house, we walked in the moonlight and talked more, happy to be together.

When we did return, I remembered Rita's gift. I pulled it from under the tree and held it up for Simon to see. "Shall we try it?"

"Sounds like a good idea to me. Tess brought some to the library for me last year, and it was very good." He took the bottle from me.

We went to the kitchen where I began to search for fluted glasses for the wassail. I stopped in the middle of my search to tell Simon, "You know, I think Tess would be very happy that you and I met."

"I think you're right. I know I'm happy about it."

Would that smile ever stop affecting me this way? I hoped not.

I found what I was looking for and set the glasses on the counter with a musical clink. Minette strolled into the room and jumped to a stool near the counter and watched as Simon poured the golden liquid. "Sorry, this isn't for you," I told her. "It does smell delicious, though." I sniffed the glass appreciatively and was about to take a sip when a persistent knocking at the front door interrupted me. Simon's eyebrows rose in question. "Maybe Rita and Sam decided to stop back by. Go ahead, and I'll bring them back here to have a drink with us if it's them." Simon smiled at me and lifted his glass as I left the room.

Neither Rita nor Sam stood on the other side of the door when I opened it. Instead, I was surprised to see Donna Bartlett, with her arm around Kyle. "I know it's late," she said before I could utter a greeting. "But I got scared about this sting Kyle got. It's swollen up pretty bad, and nothing I put on it has taken it down. Would you look at it?" The worried look on her face and the misery on Kyle's prompted me to immediately invite them into the living room.

"Come on over by the fire, Kyle and let me see the sting." His mother helped him pull off his coat, and I saw that the whole side of his neck was swollen an angry red. I could understand why Donna was concerned, but I kept my tone light. "Well, you got something mad at you. What happened?" I began to rub my hands to warm them before placing them on his neck.

Kyle looked to his mother who nodded at him, encouraging him to speak to me. "There was a hornet's nest up in the attic. I didn't think there would be anything in it in the winter. I was going to get it down for my collection." I didn't want to know what else was in his collection. "But I poked it first and must've woken up some hornets. I got stung a few times, but most of the stings are gone now. This was the worst one."

"Is he allergic to hornet stings?" I asked his mother.

"He never has been before. And he's been stung a lot of times."

I wasn't surprised. "Sit over here, Kyle." I indicated the rocker as I pulled it closer to the fire. "I'm going to place my hands so they're barely touching your neck. If it hurts, tell me and I'll raise them." As he sat, I noted that Simon was now standing in the doorway, silently watching.

Before I even touched it, I could feel the heat coming from the swollen area. As I'd done many times now in the past weeks, I relaxed and let the energy in my hands take over. The familiar push of the pain Kyle was feeling, slowly turned to a tugging and then a pulling out and away as the energy lifted the hornet's poison from the site and surrounded it with a comforting warmth to take its place. By the time I took my hands away and smiled at him and got the second smile I remembered ever receiving from him, the red was gone and the swelling was nearly so. I was still in awe of this gift that had awakened in me. Donna was less so, no doubt because she was used to having seen it in Tess, but she was grateful.

"Thank you, Kat. I was really worried, but I knew you could help. Sara says you've made Tim feel as well as Tess used to."

"You're welcome." I tapped Kyle gently on the head. "You might want to start looking for something less organic for your collection next time."

"Huh?" He wasn't sure he understood, but he was still smiling.

"Make sure it's dead first," Simon supplied helpfully.

"Okay." Kyle turned his grin toward Simon now. I doubted he'd heed the warning next time something interesting popped up. I thought I was going to have to get used to spending time with him. He got braver now. "Tell Jake hey for me. I won't see him when school's out for vacation."

"Why don't you tell him yourself? You can come sledding with us next week if you want. Far away from hornet nests."

"That'd be cool." Donna helped him into his coat. "Thanks." Kyle's look was for both of us.

We watched them leave, and then Simon's hands traveled up my arms to begin massaging my shoulders. "It's remarkable, the gift you have. I'm certainly grateful for it."

I closed my eyes and felt the tension slip away with his touch. "You're pretty accepting, for a man," I teased him. "James couldn't accept the idea at all. He would have refused to believe it if he'd seen me work on Kyle."

Simon turned me around and looked into my eyes. "I'm not James," he said.

"No, you're not," I said happily. "And you have pretty magical hands yourself."

"I can't heal the way you do."

"Ah, but I'm feeling rather healed by your touch." I smiled lazily up at him.

"Any other spots that need healing? I'm willing to experiment."

"I'm sure we could find some."

We spent the ensuing couple of hours deep in experimentation.

After Simon left, I realized that exhaustion from the emotional discoveries of the day had caught up to me. I had just enough energy left to turn out lights before making my way up the stairs to bed. As I poked my head around the kitchen door to flip the light switch, I saw the forgotten glasses and Rita's bottle. Simon's empty glass sat beside my full one. I reached toward mine, but decided against drinking anything before going to bed. I wanted an undisturbed night of sleep. If I drank it now, I would surely have to get up to use the bathroom before morning. It wasn't worth it. I emptied the glass in the sink and put the bottle in the refrigerator. I was too lazy to wash the glasses. I could do that in the morning.

Soon, I crawled into bed and laid my head to the pillow. Sleep came quickly and easily.

Kate sat in a chair, rocking, weeping by the hearth. She was an old woman now, but she fingered the locket and crooned to it just as she had as a child.

"Mother, come back," she pleaded to the air. "I'm sorry. I wish I could take back what I've done. I still hate those men. Why did they have the right to make me lose you?"

Rose was there now, looking as she did the day she had died. She touched Kate's hand, causing her to look up in wonderment.

"You are here!" she breathed. Her face was transformed back to that of the child her mother had last seen.

"I can't come back, my love. But it's time now for you to come with me. You can't undo what's been done. But you can let go. Let go of the hate and follow me."

Rose offered her hand to help her daughter up. Indecision clouded Kate's face.

A very long time passed as she weighed what to do. But Rose was patient and in the end was rewarded with her daughter's hand slipping into her own.

Kate stood. Now she was the one eager to depart. But her mother stopped her.

"I know how you love it, Kate, but you can't take the locket where we're going. Leave it here for your daughter.

For all our daughters to come. They'll recognize the strength it offers them."

Kate obediently laid the gold locket on the chair she had just abandoned.

As the two of them left the room, there was a sound and a sudden burst of fire in the fireplace.

Stepping whole from the flames, was a woman in red with long, flowing black hair. She touched the locket once as flames leapt from her fingers.

Then she and the room vanished with a roar of sound.

I thought the sounds in my dream had woken me, and I tried to bring myself fully awake. No, there it was again. Movement. Something being shifted above me.

Tess' room! There was someone in Tess' room!

I shot a hurried glance toward the clock beside the bed. It was 3:15. I could see the moon clearly from the window. It calmed me as I looked for Minette and saw she wasn't there. It must be her above. The door into the attic was probably closed to her again.

Well, I was awake now. I might as well go let her in so we could both finish the night's sleep.

My tread on the stairs was almost silent as I hadn't taken time to put on shoes. I would only be barefoot for a short time and then would hop back into my warm bed. The final stair creaked, but that was the only sound. Reaching behind the hanging rugs, sure enough I saw I had left the door closed. I reached to pull it open. "Come on, you silly cat, and we can both get some—" Confusion stopped my tongue. "What—"

Light filled the little room. I had only seen it three times now, but the placement of every object in it had been imprinted on my mind. Now, it was in total disarray. And in the middle of it all, stood a tiny woman who did not belong here at all.

"Harriet?" I found my tongue. "What on earth are you doing up here?"

She looked at me with an eerie calmness. "Come on in, dear," she said politely.

It was only then that I saw what was in her hands. In the left hand were the crumpled pages of the letter Tess had been writing to me and in the other hand…a gun.

Chapter 21

I had virtually no experience with guns of any kind, but my guess was that the simple, long barreled weapon Harriet held was some type of hunting rifle. Whatever it was, I had no doubt of its capacity to kill. She did not point it at me, but she held it so naturally that I knew she must be experienced enough to move it quickly. Under normal circumstances, I knew that I could easily overpower her, but I was at a disadvantage at the moment. Caught in fascinated horror, I was unable to remove my eyes from the gun. Harriet noticed, and dropping Tess' letter to the floor, she indicated the gun with her free hand and said apologetically, "I'm sorry this was necessary. It's a good thing I brought it with me, though. Just in case. It's an old .22 that my father gave me years ago, but it still works just fine." She moved the kerosene lamp she had placed on a chair to the desk. "Come in and sit down, Katrina."

Her tone was so reasonable, you would have thought she was inviting me in for tea. "If you don't mind, Harriet, I'd rather not." I tried to back away, but the gun did come up then.

"I'm sorry, dear, but you don't have a choice. I used to hunt first with my father and then with my husband. I know this gun very well. I'd really like to not have to use it. It would be very messy."

Fear pumped through every part of my body, but I tried to match her calm tone. "What were you expecting to do here, Harriet?"

"What I *will* do here, Katrina. It has to be done." She didn't even blink as she waved the gun at the chair she wanted me to occupy. "I'm surprised to tell you that I'm sorry about it. I had really grown to like you and had hopes that this wouldn't be necessary. But you wouldn't just leave things alone and go back to your home where you belonged. It was too much to hope that Tess' evil hadn't passed to you. I thought maybe since you hadn't ever seen her, you might be spared. But I should have known it was in your blood."

Now I understood. This old woman was insane but in a frighteningly calm and organized way. I tried to keep the little bubble of hysteria I was experiencing from pushing its way to the surface. It would take luck and having all my wits about me to get out of this situation. I hoped to keep her talking while I weighed the possibilities of escape. It took little effort on my part—she was eager to talk. "What do you mean?"

"Don't act innocent with me, Katrina." She made a disgusted face. "Tess Whitney was an evil, evil woman who practiced witchcraft. She ruined people's lives with it, and you've stepped right into her shoes. My family suffered more than its share from her wicked ways, and you and your sinful daughter are trying to take what's left of my family from me. I can't let you do that, you see. God says, suffer not a witch to live, and you know that I have to obey God." This last was said with a chilling reverence.

"Harriet, why would you think I was trying to take your family from you?"

Her eyes widened at me. "You've seduced Rita to turn from the proper life she should be living, just like your mother did. Once *she* was gone, I knew I could get Rita to go back to the husband she should have stayed with. That is, until you showed up, a shameful divorcee yourself. And that disgraceful daughter of yours! Living with another woman! Who knows what they would do to an innocent boy like Brian out

321

there in Seattle?" She shook her head. "I can't let that happen, Katrina. I've worked too hard to keep this family together. I wasn't sorry about Tess, but I didn't want it to come to this with you. If you'd just gone back when you broke up with Simon. I thought for certain spreading those rumors would make you upset enough to make it work."

"What rumors?" My voice was hoarse.

"About your so-called healing of Simon's son. I knew you didn't want it talked about, and it was easy enough to spread it in a way that made it look as if Simon had talked. You and your mother both would have liked to fool people into thinking you were such nice, lovely healers. But if it doesn't come from God, it's not true healing. Tess made no bones about it. She never went to church. I thought when you came to services with me there was hope for you, but I see now that you were just hiding your wickedness. To be fair to you, I don't think you can help yourself. You were conceived in evil, and I think it's just pulled you in."

This woman who had seemed so frail before was frightening me more and more. She believed every word she was saying.

"How did you know what had happened with Jake's accident?"

She made a tsking sound with her tongue. "You and Rita underestimate me all the time. I know you think I'm just a crazy old woman."

I had to agree with her on that one.

"It's quite easy to eavesdrop and hide in places you're not expected when you're doing God's work."

A sound interrupted her. We were both immediately alert, but just as I was hoping to take her by surprise, she lifted the gun and never took her eyes from me. The sound came again, and I realized now that it was a pounding at the door two stories below. My heart raced with fear and hope.

"Kat? Are you here?" Rita's voice filtered up. I could hear the panic in her voice, though the distance muffled it. "Mother? Kat, my mother's missing, and I think she came here!"

Harriet showed the first fear I'd seen on her face since I'd stepped into the room, but then that unnatural calm settled over her again.

Dear God, I thought, *is she so crazy that she'd hurt her own daughter?*

I started to yell a warning to Rita, but Harriet hissed at me and cocked the gun. I said nothing, but I tried to will Rita to stay away. It was no use. We both listened in horror as Rita made her way first to my bedroom and then up the stairs to the attic. I heard the rustle of the rugs and couldn't stop myself. "Rita, no...go back!"

But it was too late. The door opened, and she stood there, barely able to comprehend the scene before her.

"My God, Mom! What are you doing?"

Harriet sighed as if she were dealing with a naughty child. "Come in, Rita, and shut the door."

"No! Give me that gun! You can't think you'd get away with hurting Kat?" Rita took a step toward her mother, but the gun stopped her.

"See, Katrina? I told you, you both underestimate me." She looked sadly at her second child. "I do what I have to do, Rita. Come sit with your friend. I was hoping to save you. That's what this has been all about. But it's clear now that God means you to share Katrina's fate. You always wanted to be a witch, too, didn't you dear? I'm not angry with you. I'm really very sad. But now you'll have to burn like the other witch should have. At least I managed to burn some of her things. Brian will be very sad, too, but maybe I can still save him."

Rita moved carefully to the chair beside me, but her gaze, wide with disbelief, never left her mother's face. "Mom, please. Just let us both go, and everything will be all right. I promise."

Harriet laughed gently. "Of course, it won't, dear. I can't let you go now. I should have burned the whole place when I had the chance, but I wanted that picture of you as a little girl that that horrible woman painted and the locket she used to wear when we were young. I know she placed her power over you in them somehow, and I wanted them so I could get you back before I burned everything else. I've looked for them all this time—all through this house until Katrina came. I snuck over here behind you today and when I overheard the two of you talking about this room I was so happy because I was sure they must be here. But I still didn't find them. I finally see now that I wasn't meant to save you. But I do want you to know that it's very painful for me to have to do this."

Well, wasn't that comforting?

"Tell me how you came to know all this, Mom." Rita's voice was surprisingly soothing.

Oh, good for you, I sent the thought out to her. *Keep her talking, and together we might be able to catch her off guard.* Hope stirred in my chest.

Harriet looked at us with what might have appeared to be compassion in a sane person. The gun never wavered, but she did seem to come to some sort of decision. "All right, I'll tell you all of it. Then you'll understand that I'm doing what I have to. For your sakes, too. I have hope that God will take your souls."

Not yet, if I can help it, you crazy old woman! I willed the thought not to show on my face.

"I never liked Tess Whitney, even when we were kids!" A little of the old feisty Harriet showed through with that declaration, but she reined herself in, and the frightening calm settled back around her. "But I didn't know how really evil she was until she started casting spells over my poor Henry."

"What kind of spells did she cast over Dad?"

I was fighting an urge to ignore the gun and take the woman by the shoulders and shake her. Rita was using a much more sensible approach and speaking to her gently. I was amazed at her strength in the moment and set about trying to match it.

"He was a happily married man, and we had a wonderful little boy, but she couldn't stand that. She had Toby Underwood panting after her and who knows what she was doing when she went off to New York City! But she kept throwing herself at Henry, though she tried to make it look like she wouldn't have anything to do with him. But I knew! It got to the point that poor Henry drank to get away from it. Everything would have worked out if she had just stayed away. But not that one! She came home, supposedly for a visit with her parents. They were gone for the weekend, and it was clear to me, after, what her real purpose was. Having her back here again drove Henry to drinking harder than usual that weekend, and I woke up to find him gone." Harriet paused, and I grew aware of the sick feeling in my stomach.

"I knew she must have made one of her spells, so I came here and saw what she did to him. It wasn't Henry's fault—he didn't even remember after that it happened—that's how evil she was. And then she screamed at him and cursed him! Can you believe that? She seduced him to do filthy things to her, and then she had the nerve to curse him. I'm sorry to tell you this about your own mother, Katrina, but you need to know why you're the way you are. I know you've had relations with Simon, and you've encouraged Rita to do the same with Sam Taylor. And you both with husbands already!"

Neither of us pointed out to her that we were divorced from those husbands. That obviously didn't make any difference to this woman.

"I won't dwell on the sordid details." I was thankful to be spared that, at least. "But because of that woman, our lives became a living hell. I had just found out a few days before that I was pregnant with you, Rita. Henry didn't even know yet. After that, he never...we...well, she made it so you were the last child we would ever be able to have. And later I found out she was pregnant, too! And she wasn't content enough with all that. You were a very willful little girl, Rita, and I tried my best with you, but she stole you, too. Do you see what I've been through at that woman's hands?"

All I could see was that Harriet was a very disturbed individual. But if part of what she was saying was true, then it had been her husband who had raped Tess. I would never call him my father, but I knew now why Tess was afraid to let me grow up in this town. Had she known even then that there was something dangerous about Harriet? Or had Harriet snapped after all the years of excusing "poor Henry" and laying the blame on Tess? What had made her break now?

"Harriet," I said with as reasonable a tone as I could muster, "Tess is gone. There's no more threat to you. There's been no real harm done here tonight. Just let us go, and I could still go back to Seattle. Rita's loved you and taken care of you all this time."

"That's right, Mom," Rita jumped in. "You and I could go home, and Arthur can come over if that would make you feel better."

Harriet rolled her eyes. "I'm not crazy, you know." I could beg to differ, but I kept my mouth firmly shut. "I know what you'd really do. You'd both have me locked away somewhere. My own daughter, even! Arthur would never do such a thing to me. He's always known how hard I've tried to protect my family from evil." She looked at Rita with sad eyes and then turned those eyes to me.

"If only you'd drunk what Rita brought to you today, we wouldn't have to be doing this now. But obviously you didn't."

Panic rose in me anew. "What are you talking about?" *Oh, please! Don't let it be what it sounded like.*

"It seemed appropriate, dear, to give you something you loved. I crushed up one of your herbs you're so into. I even prayed to God to make it as painless as possible for you. I told you, I like you, despite what you are."

There was no way I could remain calm now. "What herb, Harriet?" I demanded. "What did you put into that drink?"

"Something beautiful," she said soothingly. "Both times I've used something beautiful. Not one of those horrible things like deadly nightshade. I would never let Rita have anything like that in our garden."

"What?" I shouted again.

"You don't have to be rude," she said petulantly. "I put foxglove in it. It's such a pretty plant—that tall stalk of purple bellflowers. I had some all dried in my room. It seemed appropriate for you."

Simon! Oh, God, Simon! my mind screamed.

I had to get out of here and get to him! I hadn't touched my glass, but he had finished his!

"Harriet, please! You have to let me at least call 911! Simon drank it! Even you have to see he has nothing to do with this."

"Oh, I'm afraid not, dear. Unlike Henry, he chose to have a relationship with a witch. And when you marry, it should only be once. That's the way God intended it. He should have stayed faithful to his poor dead wife. I stayed faithful to Henry. No, I didn't mean for him to drink it, but he'll just have to live with the consequences." She looked confused for a minute and then smiled at her unintended joke. "Well, I guess he won't live with them, will he?"

"Mother, he has a little boy!"

I think it finally dawned on Rita how far lost in insanity her mother was.

"Stop this now!"

Harriet's calm began to crack and anger showed through. "Don't talk to me in that tone of voice, Rita Sloan! You're the most defiant little girl I've ever known. Why couldn't you behave like your brother? He never ran off to this witch house and humiliated me, like you're always doing. Well, it all stops here! I thought when I killed Tess that would be the end of it, but her wickedness just lived on in you two."

I was aware of the tears sliding down Rita's cheeks. I was less aware of my own. "You killed Tess?"

"It was surprisingly easy." Her mood switched again. She seemed quite pleased with herself now. "Rita gave me both opportunities, although I admit this second one hasn't been so successful. She's always bringing some kind of food or drink over to this house. She made a special soup and brought it and a basket of flowers over to Tess for May Day. Tess was always celebrating some immoral pagan holiday. I just cooked up some lovely lily of the valley bulbs to put in Tess' soup along with a little water that the flowers had been sitting in. I could have used one of her horrible herbs, you know. But I wouldn't stoop to her level."

"Why, Mom?"

"Why what, Rita? Oh, you mean why did I kill her? It's perfectly obvious. Because she was evil. And then after all that time of hurting other people, she was back sleeping with Toby Underwood. The woman had no shame. Did you know she'd talked him into marrying her?"

In frustration, I clutched at the front of my nightshirt and felt the locket tucked inside. I had forgotten to take it off. Harriet was afraid there was some kind of power infused within it. Could I use that fear somehow? As I pulled it out carefully, I saw at the edge of my vision that Minette had slipped quietly through the door. A tiny spark of fear for her registered somewhere within my brain, but it got filed with all the other fears floating around in there just now. Then all my fears dissolved into one as things happened very quickly.

"Katrina, what have you got there?" Harriet demanded. But I believe she already knew. A gasp escaped her as she saw what I held. "I should have known," she hissed. "I tried to be kind to you, but I should have known you would try to use witchcraft yourself! God will punish you!" She lunged at the locket with one hand, just as Minette jumped to the desk. She hissed and clawed in Harriet's direction, which caused Harriet to spin and cry out in fear. "That cat should have died with its owner, and now it will!" she screamed and aimed the gun at her. Minette leaped from the desk, upsetting the lantern, which crashed to the floor at Harriet's feet and set alight the papers strewn there.

"No!" I heard myself scream as I moved to wrench the gun from Harriet's hands, but I was too late. The sound the gun made was softer than I would have expected, but it was just as deadly. Minette disappeared through the doorway, but not quickly enough. I saw, with horror, that there was blood on the floor and then turned when I heard Harriet scream again.

Harriet had dropped the gun to the floor. I rushed to pick it up but stopped as I realized what had made her let go of it. The fire was already spreading and had caught her polyester dress in a blaze. Rita was desperately struggling to push her mother to the floor to smother the fire, but Harriet was just as desperately resisting. "Kat! Help me!" Rita's words brought me to action, and we both worked to get close enough to smother the flames.

Harriet barely seemed to notice the fire burning her skin, so intent was she on keeping us away from her. "Don't touch me!" she cried.

In her movement across the room, she had set afire some of the things she had broken and scattered from the altar. I tried stamping some of it out at the same time I was trying to stop her, but the fire had spread too far already. We had to stop her and get out of here!

I was dimly aware of the smell of burnt flesh and the sight of Harriet's hair being licked by fire. I brushed by the red cape hanging from its peg and grabbed it off the wall. Rita saw what I was doing and caught a corner of the cloth. Together we threw it around Harriet and managed, finally, to pin her to the floor as we wrapped the cape around her to smother the fire consuming her.

She lay still but moaned in pain. Rita pulled the cloth away and I was shocked at what I saw. Harriet's face was no longer recognizable and the rest of her body was badly burned. I had no time to dwell on it, though.

"We need to get out of here, fast!" I said. Rita nodded. Without another word, we picked up her mother as gently but quickly as possible and fled. I managed to turn enough to pull the door shut with one hand as we passed through. I think I had some vague hope of containing the fire.

When we got to the second floor, I made Rita stop. "Can you carry her the rest of the way outside by yourself?" The words rushed out of my mouth.

"Yes." She took the weight of her mother's body from me. "What are you going to do?"

"I'll get some blankets and call 911. Get her to the porch, and we'll try to keep the cold away from her. I'll be right there. Go, Rita!"

I ran as fast as I could to carry out what I had said I would do. All the while my mind kept repeating the mantra: *Please let me get to Simon in time!* I refused to acknowledge the despair that threatened to overwhelm me and tell me that it could already be too late. I hadn't even told him that I loved him. I wanted the chance to do that!

The 911 call took only seconds, but of course, it felt as if it took forever. The dispatcher assured me the fire trucks and ambulance would be here right away.

As soon as I could disconnect, I fumbled to dial Simon's number. It rang three, times, then four.

Pick it up, Simon or Jake, please!

Seven, then eight. Why was no one answering? I wasn't thinking rationally or I would have called 911 again to send an ambulance to Simon's house. Instead, I rushed outside thinking I would throw the blankets to Rita and leave her to wait for the rescue workers. I had to get to Simon!

With tears streaming, I shouted my intentions to Rita as I grabbed the boots I had left by the door. I didn't take the time to get a coat.

"Hurry!" was all she said.

I heard the first vehicle rush into the driveway but didn't look up as I struggled to open the Jeep door. It was locked! I fumbled with the keys, barely aware of the screeching halt of the other vehicle and the door opening and slamming shut.

"Kat!" I paid no attention to my name being called. I had to get there! "Kat! Stop!" Strong hands seized my shoulders, and I was turned around to find myself against Simon's solid body.

"Simon! You're alive! You have to get to a hospital right away!" I grabbed his arm, but he pulled me back.

"Wait," he said. "Tell me what's happened." We heard the first sirens scream through the night air just as a flame shot out the roof of the house.

"It's Harriet," I cried impatiently. "She killed Tess, and she tried to kill Rita and me. She put poison in the drink Rita brought over. I didn't drink any, but you did. We have to get you to the hospital!"

"It's all right, love. Really, it's all right!" How could he say that? He could die! "Kat, listen to me. I didn't drink it."

I finally stopped struggling and looked at his face. I watched his mouth move, but it took a moment before I understood what he was saying. I shook my head to clear it. "What?"

"I didn't get a chance to drink any. Just as I was about to, Minette jumped up on the counter and made me spill it. I cleaned it up and then went to watch you work with Kyle. I forgot all about it."

Life flooded back into my body. I threw my arms around him and held tightly for a few seconds. He did the same. "That's three lives that cat has saved tonight. The poor thing." Tears flooded my eyes. "Oh, Simon. Harriet shot Minette! She ran off, but she could be still in the house and she's hurt...or worse."

A roar made us both look upward as new flames shot through the roof. Simon looked sadly back at my face. "I'm so sorry, Kat. But you know you can't go back in there. She might have gotten out ahead of you and she's hiding out somewhere."

He was right. There was nothing I could do for her, except hope. I looked to the porch. "I've got to go help Rita, Simon."

He followed and grabbed one of the quilts to put around me as I rushed to Rita's side. She was holding her mother carefully in her arms. "Rita," I said as I began rubbing my hands together. "Let me help her."

She put her hand over mine. "No, Kat."

I was surprised at how quickly the hurt spread through me. "You don't believe I can help her?"

"I know you can," she said softly. "But think of what it would be like for her. You could heal some of her body, but you could never heal her mind. She killed Tess! She'd spend what life she had left in an institution. The only thing she's said since I got her out here is to ask me not to let you touch her. I'm so sorry, Kat, but I agree with her. We need to let her

331

go. Let me have a little time alone with her, okay?" Tears slid silently down her cheeks, but her resolve was strong.

It was almost a physical ache within me, not putting my hands to someone in pain, but I dropped them to my sides. I had to stand up and walk away. Simon followed me but at first didn't touch me.

Finally, I stopped walking and turned to look at his face in the moonlight. "What are you doing here? How did you know to come this time of night?" It had finally dawned on me how strange it was.

"Anyone else wouldn't believe me," he said, "but you might. I woke up a little bit ago because I heard you call my name. Twice. Your voice sounded frantic. And it wasn't a dream. I couldn't just go back to sleep. I called your number, but there was no answer, I had to come see if you were all right."

"You left Jake alone?" I asked worriedly.

"No, he's bundled up in quilts in the back seat with Jasper. He never even woke up when I grabbed him and rushed out the door."

I looked at him for a long moment. "I love you, Simon." Why had that been so hard to say?

"I know," he said to me. "I was just afraid you'd never realize it."

"No!" I shook his shoulders before sliding my arms around his neck. "You're supposed to say, I love you, too, Kat.'"

"I love you, too, Kat." His arms came around me then. "I have since the day you walked into the library and let me annoy you. And I always will."

The fire truck and ambulance arrived together with a police car close behind. We went back to the porch to stand beside Rita and watched as the same paramedics who had helped Jake worked to do what they could for Harriet. They moved us all quickly away from the house so the fire fighters could do their job.

My tears began to flow again as I saw some of the men tear through the roof and turn the hoses on the flames.

"Don't worry, love," Simon said as tears stood in his own eyes. "We'll rebuild it if we have to."

I squeezed his hand. I loved this house. Tess' house and now mine. But it could burn a thousand times, and I wouldn't care as long as the people I loved were safe. And most of all, right now, I was grateful that Simon was alive.

Harriet's stretcher was being lifted into the back of the ambulance, and I reached out my hand to Rita. "Do you want me to ride there with you?" I asked her.

She was the calm one now. Not in the same way Harriet had displayed calm. Rita's came from a new strength. As we had listened to Harriet's rantings in the secret room, I'd been afraid of what it might do to Rita. I needn't have worried. She was far stronger than any of us had given her credit for.

She actually smiled at me now, though it was colored by sadness. She took my hand in hers. "You stay here for a while and take care of whatever you need to. Look for Minette. I hope she's alive. When you're ready, have Simon drive you to the hospital. I would like you to be there with me then." She let go of my hand, but instead of turning away yet, she put her hand gently to my cheek. "I'm sorry for all the awful things that've been done. But do you realize, we're sisters?"

"And Tess knew it," I told her. "She loved us both. I'm sorry about everything, too, but I can't be sorry about having you as my sister." She hugged me and climbed into the ambulance beside her mother.

"Would you do me a favor?" she called down as the doors started to close.

"Anything."

"Call Sam and tell him what's happened."

"Of course. And Brian…and Arthur?"

"I'll call them from the hospital."

The doors closed, and they pulled away. The sirens blared once more.

Chapter 22

The local sheriff was a man that both Simon and Rita knew well. As the ambulance left the driveway, he introduced himself to me as Allen Smith. "I'm sorry, Mrs. Benson, but I need to ask you some questions."

How could the "Mrs. Benson" irritate me at a time like this?

"Ms. Benson, or Kat, please," I said irritably and then was immediately sorry. Simon put his arm around me once again.

"Ms. Benson," the sheriff said with no other hint that he'd noticed my reaction, "what happened?"

I hesitated for only a second. "Harriet's been getting confused lately and coming over here. She was more confused than ever tonight, and I woke up to find her in the house."

"Where?"

"In the attic."

His eyebrows shot up. "Any idea what she was doing up there?"

"Like I said, she was confused." I brushed a dirt-stained hand across my forehead. "Rita woke up and found her gone. She guessed she might be over here and came to find her."

"So she's done this before?"

"Not late at night like this. But other times, yes." I wasn't lying, precisely. I was just leaving certain things out.

"How did the fire start? Did Harriet do it?"

I wondered how much he was guessing about what had happened. "My cat scared her, and they both tipped over a kerosene lantern. The fire spread very quickly."

"And that's how Harriet got burned?"

"Yes. She was very confused by then, and when her clothes caught fire it took Rita and me some time before we could stop her from running around and get it put out. I grabbed blankets and called 911 while Rita got her outside."

"Simon, you were here?"

Simon held me tighter. "No. I woke up knowing something was wrong and came over just now."

Amazingly, Sheriff Smith accepted that without further questions. He looked at me with sympathy and... something else. "Thank you. I'll want to talk to both you and Rita again. Will you be going to the hospital?"

I nodded. "Very shortly."

"All right. I'll find you there."

Simon watched him walk away, and when the sheriff was out of earshot, he turned to me. "What else happened, Kat?"

I told him, in halting sentences, trying to get a handle on my disbelief of the events of the last hour. "I couldn't tell him the whole thing, Simon. Not yet. Not until I talk to Rita."

A shout from one of the firemen caused me to look toward the house. The hoses were being trained on the windows in the attic. All that history! Everything that had been accumulating in the last two hundred years would be destroyed in such a short time. And Tess' sacred space. It had already been defiled. Now it would be gone, except what I held in my memory. And then I remembered everything that was in the house that belonged to the present. My work and Tess'. There was nothing I could do to save it now, but I couldn't stand here and watch it all go either.

"Let's check on Jake." My voice was choked as I turned away. "And then I want to see if I can find Minette.

You're right. She might have gotten away." I knew it was most likely that she was in the house somewhere, and she was probably beyond help anyway. But I wouldn't accept that yet. I had to do something.

We were astonished to find Jake still sound asleep, wrapped in his arctic-strength sleeping bag and quilts. Jasper whined as Simon opened the door, but otherwise stayed close to Jake. Simon then pulled a flashlight from his glove compartment, and we began our search.

We found her curled into a corner of the barn. When I called her name, she didn't move, and I was afraid this was where she had come to die. But when I touched her back, she raised her head and hissed, and I was never so glad to hear the sound of a grouchy cat in my life. I raised my hand to her head, and the hissing stopped. Her breathing was a bit labored, and one hind leg was covered in blood.

"All right, your highness," I said to her. "I'm not going to lose you. You'll have to let me lift you into my lap so I can work on you."

She uttered a pitiful meow when I picked her up but otherwise offered no resistance. Simon shone the light so that I could see what I was doing as I carried her to the straw bale and sat on it. Smoothing her fur gently, I prayed to the lady in red or whoever was out there, to make my gift work for animals as well as people. Then I positioned my hands over the wound and let the energy do what it would.

By the time I was finished, Minette was much improved and regaining a little of her old disposition. To her dismay, I hugged her close and felt her fur growing wet. That was enough! I wasn't going to cry anymore this night. I also wasn't going to leave her here. I carried her to the car, and we delivered her, along with Jake and Jasper, to the DeBerry farm.

By this time, it was after 5:00 a.m. It wasn't hard to wake Simon's parents. Jake, too, had finally awakened. Simon gave all three of them a brief explanation of what was happening and appropriate places were found for the two animals and the still sleepy boy.

I called Sam from there. When I told him why I was calling, he came immediately awake and said he would see me at the hospital.

I was impatient now to get there myself, but Simon pointed out that I was still in my nightshirt. All my clothes were in the burning house! Gratefully, I accepted Ruth's offer of some jeans and a sweater. We weren't exactly the same size, but I was beyond caring.

Rita was just emerging from Harriet's hospital room when we arrived. Sam was with her, and she was clearly exhausted. "How is she, Rita?"

She shook her head. "Alive, Kat, but just barely." She tried to stifle a yawn but couldn't manage it. "I called Arthur. He and Alice are on their way. And Brian should be here soon." She studied my face. "Did you find Minette?"

"Yes. She'll be all right." Relief for that at least showed on her face. "Rita, you and I have to talk for a minute."

"Sam and I will go get you some coffee." Simon had read my thoughts. "We'll be back in a minute."

I watched them go and then sat with Rita on a bench in the hallway. "Sheriff Smith asked me what happened."

"What did you tell him?" She brushed hair from her face. "There are a number of crimes my mother committed, Kat. You weren't going to keep that from him, were you?"

"I never thought I'd be making a decision like this. Rita, what good would it do? I told him the truth, so far as it goes. I said Harriet had grown more confused, and when you found her gone, you came over because she's been ending up at my house. I said I found her in the attic, Minette startled her, and they both tipped over the lantern. Simon knows what really happened, but no one else."

"Are you trying to protect me?" Though her smile was sad, it was genuine. "I'm tougher than you think, you know. I think we should tell Allen everything, but I also think he'll keep it quiet. My mother's no longer a threat to anyone. And there are other people who need to know. Toby for one. Arthur for another."

"Are you sure?"

"I am. I'm so sorry, Kat. I knew Mom hated Tess, but it never crossed my mind that Tess died of anything but natural causes. And she used me as her delivery person to poison her! It's too horrible to think about."

I shook her arm. "Tess' death had nothing to do with you. Your mother's been a very sick woman, but no one saw it."

"And my father...." She grimaced. "*Our* father...though I know you'll never want to think of him that way. He wasn't all bad, Kat. He could be so kind when he wasn't drinking. My family has done an awful lot of harm to yours. Tess would have kept you if it weren't for my parents."

I tried to lighten the mood. "You're part of my family, remember. I always wanted a sister, and here I have the very one I would have chosen. Besides, I grew up with parents I loved, and it wouldn't have worked very well for you and me to grow up together, you know."

"Why not?"

"We would have gotten into way too much trouble. I just know that between us we would have come up with that spell to change Arthur into a toad."

Right on cue, the grating voice of Rita's brother sounded down the hall. My brother, too, if you wanted to be technically correct. The thought was too repugnant.

"Rita, what happened? Where is she? You wouldn't give me any details on the phone!" He stopped short when he saw that I was on the bench beside her. "What are you doing here? Rita says my mother was at your house. What did you do to her?"

"Arthur, try for once not to be a complete ass. Kat and I have both been through a lot tonight, and I'm not about to put up with your nonsense."

Was this the same Rita?

Simon and Sam were headed toward us armed with coffee cups, and I saw Sam speed up to stand protectively beside Rita. I didn't think she was going to need anyone's protection, however.

"Mom is very badly burned, and if you want to see her before it's too late, I suggest you go in there right now."

"I will," he said acidly. "But when I come back out, I want some explanations."

I expected Alice to follow her husband mutely, but instead she turned to Rita. "I'm so sorry about your mother. He does love her, Rita. Try to put up with whatever the grief does to him."

"I've put up with enough, Alice. But thank you for saying that." Rita took the cup that Sam held toward her and drank gratefully.

The rest of that long morning and part of the day are mostly a blur to me now. Brian arrived soon after his aunt and uncle. I recall Arthur being unpleasant again, but Rita shocked him into losing his bluster. She told him exactly what had happened and everything Harriet had told us. Though he tried to insultingly suggest it was mostly our imaginations run wild, she fixed him with a look that told him she wasn't going to tolerate any more from him. It surprised him into uncharacteristic silence.

Sheriff Smith arrived soon after and asked to talk to Rita and me together. Arthur and Alice went back into Harriet's room while Simon and Sam waited on the bench we vacated.

The sheriff led the two of us to a quiet waiting room and shut the door. "All right," he said gently, "tell me what *really* happened."

And so we did.

"Rumors will fly in Newbridge." He sighed. "They always do. But the official report will read just as Ms. Benson reported it to me. I hear Harriet isn't expected to live. I'm sorry, Rita. But that means there's no one to press charges on for murder now, and we really have no proof that Tess Whitney *was* murdered. As for the rest, well, the fire sounds like an accident started by a confused old woman. Did I sum it up about right? Ms. Benson, is that the way you see it?"

"Yes, sheriff. It is."

"Thank you, Allen." Rita stood up. "Is it all right if I get back to my mother now?"

"Sure. I have everything I need." He touched her arm. "Rita, I really am sorry. I have good memories of earlier days with your mother and father."

She gave him a tired smile. "Thank you. So do I."

Rita stopped me outside the door to the waiting room. "Kat, do you want…would you come into Mom's room for a few minutes?" Did I want to? Did I want to be in the same room again with the woman who had killed my mother? Who had tried to kill me and destroy everything around me? I remembered the other Harriet. The one who had been so happy that I agreed to go to church with her and had delighted in telling me of the history of her town. The one whose life, and finally her sanity, had been destroyed by the same senseless act that had devastated my mother's life and, ironically, had created mine. Not trusting myself to speak, I merely nodded.

Arthur looked up as I entered. I knew he would have liked to send me right back the way I had come in, but Alice placed her hand gently on his shoulder and he said nothing. Harriet was barely recognizable as the meddling little woman I'd come to know. She was not conscious, and I hoped that she was no longer in pain. Despite all the pain she'd inflicted and had still intended to inflict, I couldn't wish it back on her.

Harriet, I'm sorry, I found myself thinking. *I wish things would have been different. I'd like to hate you but I can't. Look what hate did for you. I hope you find peace now."* I looked into her ravaged face. *I can't be sorry that you failed in your last attempt to destroy everything connected to Tess, but I am sorry for what your hate did to her and to you. Goodbye.*

I hugged Brian, then bent to kiss Rita on the cheek. She took her eyes from her mother's face to look at me. "Go with Simon and get some rest," she whispered to me.

"What about you? You need to rest, too."

"I will soon. Don't worry about me, Kat. I'll be all right."

"I know." I squeezed her shoulder and left the room.

Simon and I were walking to his car when it really hit me...I had no place to go. The house I had come to think of as home was destroyed. I stopped walking. "Simon, where will I go?"

He tucked a lock of hair behind my ear. "I was hoping you'd come home with me. This isn't the way I really wanted to bring it up, but I was sort of hoping to make it a permanent arrangement. It would make me happy, Jake and Jasper would be happy, and we'd try our best to make you happy." I could feel him tense slightly as he waited for my answer.

"Are we talking about *permanent* permanent?"

He tensed even more but nodded.

I took his hand and began walking again. "I think we could come to some kind of arrangement. You're stuck now, though. If you take me in permanently, you have my cat to contend with, too."

He relaxed and let out a laugh. "If my dog agrees, I think I can handle it. The rats might have a harder time, but I think I can persuade them."

"Good." I yawned. "We'd appreciate that."

Harriet died later that morning, peacefully, without ever having regained consciousness. Rita stayed at the hospital long enough to make all the arrangements necessary—Arthur was not ready to do so. Brian helped his mother, and then Sam brought her home. We all got what rest we could, but it was not easy to sleep despite the exhaustion. Late in the afternoon, I woke to find that Simon had retrieved Jake, Jasper, and Minette. The latter two were having a difficult time adjusting to each other, but Jasper was definitely having the easier time of it. Jake took the dog out into the yard for a time out, and Minette curled up in a chair as soon as he left. She would adjust to whatever life would bring, I decided. And so would I.

The phone rang. After a very brief conversation, Simon handed the phone to me.

"Hi, Kat. It's me, Rita. Did you get enough rest for a bit?"

"Yes," I answered. "Have you gotten any yet?"

"I'm fine." There was something odd in her voice. "I couldn't help myself. I walked over to your place. I think you should get over there. I'll meet you in a few minutes."

"Why, Rita? What is it?" What more could possibly be wrong?

"Get Simon to drive you. See you there."

"Rita?" She had hung up.

As we turned into the driveway, I braced myself. I hadn't wanted to come back so soon and see how much I'd lost. I had to face it, but not yet. The first thing that I saw was all the cars and trucks. What in the world...? And then I looked toward the house. As soon as Simon stopped the car, I jumped out. The house was still standing. The roof was open and scorched in several spots but there were several people busy securing tarps over the areas to keep out the snow. Other people were hauling debris that had fallen to the ground and piling it in the back of the trucks. I looked around me. Several people greeted me. Some I knew by sight. Others I had met when they had come to ask if I could help them in the same way Tess had. Brian, Toby, and even Reverend Foxworth were there. Others, I didn't know at all. Rita reached me at the same time Donna and Kyle did.

"What's going on?" I asked. It was obvious, but I was so overwhelmed I didn't know what else to say.

"Half the town is here to help clean up," Rita said. "And the other half is busy bringing food to my house."

"I can't believe this." I looked around me.

"Why not?" Donna asked. "It's just what neighbors do for each other."

My neighbors worked until near dark before climbing into their cars and trucks and heading back to their own homes. I knew that in this small town, people would talk and speculate and make up stories, but I learned that they also genuinely wanted to help and didn't hesitate when someone was in need. It would take some major adjustments, but I now knew I could learn to love living among these people. I made certain to tell each one how grateful I was.

I recognized at least two of the firemen who had worked to put the fire out. They came to tell me what they knew. The house was much less damaged than I had feared. The top floor was gutted—the accumulation of two hundred years of family history simply gone. The second floor had received heavy water damage, but the fire had barely reached it. The bottom floor was virtually untouched and everything there seemed to be in good condition except for the smell of smoke that hung in the air. But it wasn't gone! The studio was just as I had left it the night before—Tess' art and my work exactly where it had been. The decorations on the tree in the living room glinted in the faint light filtering through the windows from the setting sun. There was no electricity, and there would be no celebration here this year, but next year, I vowed, I would invite everyone in the town to a party in this house.

Simon helped me to put together the things I needed to take back to his home. I could easily wash the smell of smoke from my clothes, and I hoped rewrapping presents would make them as good as new. I took a few art supplies and the painting of Rita and me as children. I had one more gift to attend to. I would paint a copy of the picture and give the original to Rita. It had always been hers, anyway.

After everyone else had left, Simon and I carried everything I was taking to our cars and then stood together to survey the scene.

"It could have been much worse," I said. "This I think I can deal with."

"You really love this place, don't you?" Simon put an arm around my shoulder.

"I do, Simon. How attached are you to your house?"

"I don't own it, so not very. Shall we get your house repaired as soon as possible and move the whole menagerie out here after we're married?" It was the first time he'd said the actual word, and I was quite pleased to find it didn't make me hyperventilate. In fact, despite all the horrible things that had happened in the last day, it made me quite happy.

"That sounds like a good plan. I'd like to add one thing to the menagerie. Actually, two things."

"Oh?" Simon asked, one eyebrow arched.

"Two horses. We have to have two because I don't want anyone or anything here to be lonely ever again. I think that would be agreeable to both Jake and Rowan, don't you?"

"You sure you don't need a third one for Keisha?" Simon teased.

"They can take turns, ride together, or borrow one from your parents. Any other questions?"

"Just one," he said casually. "How soon can I get you to marry me?"

I opened the door to the Jeep. "What are you doing tomorrow?"

We didn't marry the next day. We were too busy rearranging everything from holiday plans to life plans. As soon as Rowan and Keisha heard of what had happened, they made new arrangements for both of them to come to Newbridge within the next couple of days. Jake was beside himself, both from the news about his father and me and our plans to move to the witch house and from the fact that Rowan and Keisha would soon be here. Simon's tiny house would be crowded with all of us staying in it, but no one seemed to mind.

Minette, even, was growing slightly less intolerant of Jasper. She amused herself by swatting at him from time to time and terrorizing the rats whenever she could slip into Jake's room to peer at them through their cage.

I went to Toby's house the next day and told him the truth of Tess' death and what she had kept to herself all those long years. I knew it would be hard for him, and it was, but I got him to promise to still spend Christmas with us. I had a feeling that he wouldn't stay in Newbridge for long. There were just too many sad memories for him here. I hoped that he would stay in touch with me wherever he went.

Rita's twins came home as soon as they heard. She made arrangements for a service for Harriet at the church on the twentieth but left the details up to Arthur. It seemed to help him cope, though not necessarily make him more pleasant. It appeared that practically everyone in Newbridge was at the funeral. I thought that Harriet would have been very pleased with the turnout.

That evening, Rowan and Keisha flew into Syracuse. Brian picked them up and brought them to Simon's house. Rita was with us when they arrived, and we all sat together and talked. It was obvious all evening that Brian had something on his mind, and he finally spilled it. He wondered if he should wait on his move to Seattle because of all that had happened.

"Of course not!" his mother said emphatically. "I want things to start getting back to normal or better as soon as possible. And besides, I've been looking forward to that trip to Seattle with Kat. You wouldn't take that away from me, would you?"

"Well, not if you put it that way." Brian grinned.

"Hey, cool! Do we get to go to Seattle, too, Dad?" Jake wanted to know.

"Not this time, sport." His face fell.

"Why not?" I asked.

Rowan echoed me. "Yeah, why not? You're letting us stay at your place even though it's not giant like the witch house. Our apartment's small, but we'd have the whole family

345

there!" She laughed. "Mom, aunt, cousin, step-father, and baby brother!"

"*Baby* brother?" Jake was indignant.

"How about pre-adolescent brother? Is that better?" Keisha offered.

"Sure, I guess." He brightened. "But we can go, right, Dad?"

Simon smiled at me and then Jake. "Well, I guess we don't have a choice since it's a family affair."

Simon and I had one more piece of news for everyone that night. Christmas, we told them, was going to be really different this year. Since everyone was already assembled in one place, (making it easier and cheaper, I pointed out) we wanted Rita's family, along with Sam and Toby to spend the day with us at the DeBerry farm. That evening we'd have a simple wedding with the people we most wanted to be there. And, we told them, we expected Rowan, Keisha, Brian, and Jake to provide the music. There was little hint of sadness left the rest of that evening.

The next day I received an e-mail from my agent. The package I had sent her of my story and Tess' pictures was in the hands of a publisher who was very excited about it. Would I meet with them right after the holidays?

Well, Tess, I thought, *I wish we could have had more of them, but it looks like our one collaboration is a success.*

There was one last thing I had to do before truly getting on with the future. Late in the afternoon of the Winter Solstice, well before the evening festivities were planned, I gathered up Minette and told Rowan and Keisha to get ready. Rita had agreed to meet us there.

Jake saw us pulling on coats and boots. "Where're you going?"

"Out to my house for a little bit, Jake. We won't be long," I told him.

"Can I go?"

His father stepped in before I had to tell him no. "No, sport. You and I are staying here."

"We'll all be out there together before too long, sweetie," I said. "With horses and everything." He cheered up at the prospect. "But there's just something we have to do there right now."

"What?" he wanted to know.

"Say some goodbyes, Jake, so we can make the house ready for our new life there."

Simon put his hands on his son's shoulders and smiled at me over his head. I was looking forward to a lifetime of seeing that smile.

I had brought some candles with me and decided we should be in the living room. I wished this could have happened in Tess' room in front of her altar, but the fact that it was no longer there was part of why we were doing this. It was time to release the unhappiness that had lived here for so long and start the healing. And, too, I wanted to acknowledge my dreams and say goodbye to Kate and Rose. I found solace in a fantasy of seeing them and Tess together, with all the anger, fear, and hatred for what had been done to each of them gone. Though it was Harriet who had said, *It all ends now,* I meant it to really be so. We would have our own little ritual, we four women, to help the living and the dead find peace.

Rita had not yet arrived, and I left Rowan and Keisha inside to set up our tiny sacred space while I went outside to walk around the house one more time. Though some of the herbs had been trampled, both when the fire was being fought and when so many came to help after, the damage didn't appear to be too awful. Plants would grow back. The rosemary bush seemed to be completely intact, and as I looked it over, a flash of color in the snow at its base caught my eye. I hurried over and stooped to pick up whatever the object was. I knew what it was just before I touched it, and my hand hovered above it for a few seconds. Then I snatched it up and held it in front of me. It was the figurine of the lady in red that had stood on Tess' altar. The bottom of her gown was slightly singed, but otherwise she was in the same shape she'd been when I had last seen her.

I was lost in thought and didn't hear Rita approach. "What have you got, Kat?"

I held it up to her. "Do you believe this? It's almost spooky. And I keep getting this silly thought that it was sent from Tess. Isn't that ridiculous?"

She was silent for a moment. "I wouldn't be the one to call it ridiculous. I haven't told you yet, why I was here that night—the night my mother—did what she did." She was very serious.

"What's there to tell? You woke up and found your mother gone."

She fixed her eyes on mine. "I didn't just wake up. I had a dream. Tess came to me and said you were in trouble and needed my help. She wanted me to get to you right away. Then I woke up and got into my clothes to go check on you. The dream was that strong. I stopped to peek into my mother's room before leaving, and that's when I found her gone."

So many things that had previously been outside my experience had happened to me in these last few months that I accepted Rita's revelation easily and gratefully. "I guess she thought sisters should look out for each other," I said and smiled. "Let's go light some candles and thank her properly."

The candles were lit, and the lady in red presided over them as I removed the locket from round my neck and placed it on the temporary altar. Minette sat quietly nearby and watched the proceedings. The little ceremony was short and simple. We each said something aloud—about Tess, Rose, Kate, and even Harriet; about the house, love, and forgiveness. But it wasn't what we said that was important…it was what we felt. And at that moment, I felt peace and contentment settle over the witch house.

I gazed at the figurine and thought about why the red dress seemed so beautiful to me. Red is the color of life. I looked around me and realized that I was back where the dreams had begun, but this time it was starting with a new life, not death.

And once again, it was starting with a circle of women.

More Spiritual Suspense from Spilled Candy Books

Access:
A Spiritual Suspense Novel
(Book 1 of the Lorelei Files)
By Lorna Tedder

ISBN 1-892718-12-X
Trade paperback, 464 pages
$19.95 retail

> **An exciting tale that makes readers believe in the authenticity of various New Age elements.** *—Book Browser*

An abandoned baby brings back paralyzing memories for a tough-as-nails negotiator for the Department of Defense. Tired of being everyone else's pillar of strength, L. Madison Steele longs for the luxury of being weak —just once— but too many people depend on her. Framed for espionage and murder, Madison must reach deep into her soul if she is to recover stolen biological warfare secrets and ultimately save the world.

Lieutenant Jon Colter, son of a psychic hypnotherapist and a militia leader, knows a terrifying secret: that far too many people—from the Iraqi government to international terrorists to backyard militia groups to the kid down the street—have access to biological weapons and reason to use them. Reluctant to accept his own psychic gifts, Jon makes it his mission in life to protect Madison Steele. Only Jon has seen the cracks in her veneer. Only Jon has heard her weeping in her sleep. Only Jon shares with her an ancient past and a dangerous future.

> **Fun read ... fast-paced and interesting ... enough of the mystical thrown in among the technological jargon to satisfy the spiritual side as well as the intellectual.**
> *—The Crow's Calling*

> **If you're a fan of *"Alias," "La Femme Nikita,"* and *"The X-Files,"* you'll love this thriller!"**
>   —Vicki Hinze,
>   bestselling author of *Lady Liberty* and *Lady Justice*

A Duet of Witchy Romantic Suspense

Witch Moon Rising
By Maggie Shayne
And
Witch Moon Waning
By Lorna Tedder

ISBN 1-892718-33-2
Trade paperback, 160 pages
$13.95 retail

In *Witch Moon Rising*, internationally bestselling author **Maggie Shayne** delves into the ethics of Wicca: should a pagan school teacher defy her administrators, neighbors, and a student's father to teach a lonely student the truth? Will the peace of mind she can give this student spell disaster for the teacher's career, friends, and even her life? Maggie Shayne weaves a wonderful tale of faith, love, and suspense.

In *Witch Moon Waning*, a young witch falls in love with a college student, who neither understands nor accepts her religion. More than anything, Lydia wishes her lover could understand her faith, and eventually she performs a full moon ritual to make him understand. As they say, Be careful what you wish for....

> **...A beautiful story filled with mystical magic, love, and hope.**
> **...a lesson on everyday values in the Wiccan lifestyle. This is**
> **one great story that you would never want to miss.**
> **—The Healing Alternative**

Witch Moon Waning, a powerful prequel to *Access,* tells the story of Jon's parents and the destiny foretold at his birth. *Witch Moon Waning* is a complete, short novel, packaged with bestselling Maggie Shayne's *Witch Moon Rising.*

> **...A magical ride of suspense, wonder, and amazement. I**
> **highly recommend this great book; it has everything**
> **needed in a novel, one that you will read over and over**
> **again just for pure enjoyment. —Candle Crafters**

𝓡iveting 𝓢uspense and 𝓛ightning-𝓕ast 𝓐ction

Flying By Night:
A Coven of the Jeweled Dragon Novel
By Lorna Tedder

ISBN 1-892718-44-8
Trade paperback, 275 pages
$16.95 retail

> A suspenseful, alternative tale, and strongly recommended to fans of the genre as being a unique and very different kind of mystery.
> —*Midwest Book Review*

"The last time I saw my two husbands alive, they were standing naked before the Altar of the Goddess."

So begins a harrowing tale of suspense, mystery, and spirituality. Kestrel Firehawk is framed for the murders of her lovers and forced to flee for her life on Beltane Eve.

Almost as dangerous as a cold-blooded killer is Dylan MacCool, the burned-out detective on Kestrel's trail. His pursuit of answers will bring him to his knees--and take him to a destiny he never knew existed.

Praise for *Flying By Night*

Marvelously well written...a tale that keeps one on the edge of their seat, and is virtually impossible to put down.
>   —*Paranormal Romance Reviews*

A wonderful mystical witchy read that will thrill Goddess-worshippers everywhere.
>   —Rosemary Edghill, *Bell, Book, and Murder* (Bast mystery series)

More twists and turns than Celtic knot work—and just as carefully crafted.
—Evelyn Vaughn, *Waiting on the Wolf Moon*

A gripping story of romance, magick, and adventure.
— Gail Wood, *Sisters of the Dark Moon: 13 Rituals of the Dark Goddess*

Sizzles with power, pulses with heart, and glows with the unmistakable light of pure spirit...nothing less than a gift from the Goddess! —Maggie Shayne, *New York Times* bestselling author

An Imaginative Fairytale for All Ages

Pelzmantel:
A Medieval Tale
By K. A. Laity

ISBN 1-892718-46-4
Trade paperback, 216 pages
$16.95 retail

When her mother dies in childbirth, the young Princess Hallgerd finds sanctuary with her family's caregiver—a centuries-old Irish witch, Carae Mna, known to her charges simply as "Nanna."

In this retelling of the Grimm Brothers' tale "Allerleirau," Hallgerd grows up in exile under the witch's tutelage while the realm stagnates in the hands of her grieving father, who has come to be under the control of Thomas, a mage from Nanna's homeland.

The story is told from Nanna's point of view, allowing her to weave many other tales into the telling of Hallgerd adventures. The narrative is infused with actual stories from medieval Ireland and Scandinavia as well as inventions nonetheless firmly rounded in the author's thorough knowledge of the time period.

Medieval magick plays a major role, from genuine herbal cures to complex prognostications about the dangers facing the young royal. The focus throughout the novel remains on women's experiences in the medieval world, revealing the complexity and richness of this less well-known sphere.

> An engaging read from a writer who, as a Ph.D. candidate in Medieval studies and a Pagan herself, knows her stuff.
> —*The Beltane Papers*

> Laity's fast-paced book is a pleasure to read, and it will truly entertain those from age 12 to 112.
> — *New World Finn* magazine

Spiritual Teachings Disguised as Fiction

The Temple of the Twelve:
Novice of Colors
By Esmerelda Little Flame

ISBN 1-892718-32-4
Trade paperback, 284 pages
$17.95 retail

"This book had a powerful transformative effect in me spiritually," says Freya Aswynn, the acclaimed author of *Northern Mysteries & Magick* and one of the foremost authorities on runes. "I think it is in the same league as *The Celestine Prophecy.*

"The twelve chapters form Path Workings easy to visualize due to the vivid imagery used by the author. In using colors as Deities of Initiation, the author transcends all differences between the various paths of Pagan spirituality and unifies them all. I don't need Runes to predict that Esmerelda Little Flame has a great future as a spiritual writer. This book contains deep Mystery Teachings so desperately needed in the New Aeon. I will never look upon colors in the same way."

[Esmerelda Little Flame's] prose is music to the mind...a whimsical tapestry of warmth and delight.
  —Silver Ravenwolf,
    bestselling pagan author of *To Ride A Silver Broomstick*

What Readers Say:

I can count on one hand the number of books that have drawn me in so totally that I couldn't force myself to put them down till the end, and *The Temple of the Twelve* has been added to this list. My 13-year-old daughter is always asking me to help her learn my ways and beliefs, and I will definitely be giving her this book to read. It not only provokes thought, but it will be a wonderful tool to provoke conversation between us and aid both of us on our paths. —**Timbermoon**

As a parent of five and an active member in the Pagan community, I plan to take these lessons to heart and try my best to pass the lessons of the colors on to our future in projects and meditations. A complete book of inspiration! This book is an excellent learning and teaching tool.
                —**Hawthorn Circle**

Read It Free,
Read It Now

A Reverence for Trees:
A Love Story
By Lorna Tedder

Ebook Format only (pdf)

Free at SpilledCandy.com
and from some of your favorite online
metaphysical vendors, communities, and circles.

Lorna Tedder's short read was originally published by Berkley Publishing Company in 2002 in the *Words of the Witches* anthology and is the first of Spilled Candy's Re-Published Treasures series.

> **... The truest account of a sacred marriage in a very long time.**
> — *Sage Woman* **magazine**

For more metaphysical fiction as well as non-fiction guides, visit us online at www.spilledcandy.com. Our website features articles, tips, pictures, artwork, interviews, and lots of freebies.

Some of Spilled Candy's current and upcoming books include:

Gift of the Dreamtime: Awakening to the Divinity of Trauma
        by S. Kelley Harrell
Embracing the Goddess: One Catholic's Path to Enlightenment
        by Talitha Dragonfly

Pagan Homeschooling by Kristin Madden
Hidden Passages: Tales to Honor the Crones
        by Vila Spiderhawk
Once Upon a Beltane Eve by Selene Silverwind
If Mermaids Could Dance by Lady Lilith
Coven of the August Moon by Agona Darkeagle
The Astral Grail by D. Jason Cooper
Ring of Fire by Marline Haleff
The Earth Child's Handbook
        by Brigid (Smallwood) Ashwood
Pagan Parenting (revised) by Kristin Madden
Field of Jonquils by Selene Silverwind
A Witch's Diary by Lady Lilith

Printed in the United States
20316LVS00004B/73-78